I0601239

Also by Mark Teppo

The Potemkin Mosaic
Rudolph! He Is the Reason for the Season
Lightbreaker
Heartland
The Doom That Came to the Coffee Shop
In the Mansion of Madness
Beyond the Walls of Sanity
Longspur

THE FOREWORLD SAGA

The Mongoliad (co-authored with Erik Bear, Greg Bear,
Joseph Brassey, Nicole Galland, Cooper
Moo, & Neal Stephenson)
Katabasis (co-authored with Joseph Brassey,
Cooper Moo, & Angus Trim)

The Lion in Chains (co-authored with Angus Trim)
Cimarronin (co-authored with Ellis Amdur,
Charles C. Mann, & Neal Stephenson)

Sinner
Dreamer
Seer
The Beast of Calatrava

SOLITAIRE

STONEBROOK & THE JUDGE #1

MARK TEPPO

51325 Books

This book was printed in the United States of America. It is a product of Firebird Creative (Clackamas, OR).

I'll get the horses . . .

Book Design by Mark Teppo
Copy Edit by Shannon Page

First **51325 Books** edition: April 2018.

http://www.markteppo.com

This one is for
Rich

SOLITAIRE

1872
MISSOURI

1

To DESCRIBE THE THREE MEN STANDING ON MILKING STOOLS as "sullen" would be to overlook the heavy ropes knotted around their necks. The ropes went over a thick limb of the old oak tree, and the other end of each rope was tied to the saddle of a horse. The oak tree was more than thirty feet tall, and it had been here longer than the tiny scrap of a town struggling to flourish near the narrow trickle of a rocky creek that lay to the west. The residents of the town—named, inexplicably, Burlap's Rest—numbered less than one hundred, and most of them, young and old, were gathered around the old oak and the three men waiting for their sentences to be carried out. Their mood, were one to describe them as plainly as the three *doomed* men, was dour.

An old man, whiskers growing everywhere on his face, neck and head, had sifted through the remnants of his aged memory and informed Elm the last time there had been a hanging in Burlap's Rest had been before the War. *Back when we's mor' civilized*, he had said. Sliding his words together, and punctuating his proclamation with a squirt of black tobacco juice.

The Judge was making a speech. He always pontificated before delivering his judicial opinion. He knew his role in this sullen and dour ceremony was to provide the good people of Burlap's Rest—of any town, really, that asked him to perform his God-appointed duty—with an explanation which would work to salve their communal conscience. *A rationale*, as he said to them. *A divine reasoning, as elucidated through the laws of man that held this great nation together.* He was the harbinger of justice—he gave them permission to stand witness to death, and he gave them absolution as well. *Our society remains constant and continuous because we elect to hold fast to certain laws.*

Elm had heard this speech—or variations of it—many times, and he could, if pressed and under the influence of a glass or three of locally-brewed spirits, recite it from memory. He could even mimic the Judge's delivery: bringing the thunder when the words demanded it; showing them open arms as he begged their forgiveness for the declaration he was about to utter; and letting his voice soften and falter as he spoke of the terrible atrocities committed by the men who stood accused.

It was—to speak bluntly—the sort of patter one might hear from a traveling salesman or from the pulpit of a wilderness preacher who used fear to manage his flock. Even the silky-tongued words used by refined ladies in those velvet-walled establishments along the waterfront in New Orleans were of the same ilk. Which isn't to say that such speech didn't have its place and purpose, or that it wasn't the sort of well-spun oratory that mesmerized simple folk far away from the more civilized centers of society. It most certainly did have power in the right place, but for Elm, it had become part of what he privately thought of as the Willard Vernon Wallace Road Show.

And, if Judge Wallace was the golden-throated liar who summoned folks from near and far to hear his tall tales and to see his spectacles, then what did that make him? It was a question that wasn't as easy to answer.

Elm stood at the back of the crowd, leaning against a post of the ragged fence surrounding the graveyard behind the town's church. He was a wiry man, narrow in the shoulder and hip, but not like those who spent their days indoors and away from physical exertion. He was slight because he had been born bare of foot and fleet of spirit. His mother claimed he could climb before he could walk, and his father—well, there had been very little sight of him in Elm's life—but it may have been from his father that he had his penchant for exploration and curiosity. He climbed everything that presented a challenge: rocks, trees, trellises, and columns. His eyes were blue in some light, green in other, but always quick and intelligent, and he kept his hair short and his cheeks and chin free of scruff and beard. His hands were restless, much to many a lady's delight, and he could drop a bird out of a tree at eight hundred paces with his rifle.

The latter skill had been tested time and again during the War, the conflict that had—according to Burlap's Rest's most-bewhiskered elder—separated *civil* from *uncivil*. Elmore Stonebrook—once a volunteer member of Company C of the 1st United States Sharpshooters—had been party to some of that separation.

But that was ten years past, and now Elm was simply the traveling companion of the Right Honorable Judge Willard Vernon Wallace, and there wasn't much call for his rifle.

His knife and his pistol, though? Another matter entirely. Traveling with the Judge was fraught with its peculiarities and peccadilloes. One of which was bound to come to the fore shortly after the Judge finished his sermonizing.

"As a duly recognized advocate of the people whose magnificent efforts with their hands and hearts have built this sprawling union of states, I—Willard Vernon Wallace, *iudex vulgivagus populo*—having heard the testimony of the upstanding and passionate citizenry of this hale settlement, do pass judgment on these miscreants who have, with foul intention and blasphemy, appropriated property to which they have no compelling right or contract."

The Judge had placed himself so that the great oak tree was behind him, and as he raised his left arm to deliver his summary judgment, he knew his pose would be seen by the assembled crowd as mirroring the tall tree behind him, down to his extended arm being a symbolic representation of the hanging branch over which the ropes had been thrown.

Quod est inferius est sicut quod est superiu, he was fond of quoting. *That which is below is like that which is above.*

The second principle of alchemy, as conceived by Hermes Trismegistus in a time when the world was still raw and wild. Though, in the Judge's learned opinion, the world was still quite raw.

"Ralph Bonner," the Judge intoned, pointing at the first man on the left. "Douglas Bonner," he continued, pointing at the next man, and then—"Henry Greer"—his finger indicated the last of the three. "You have been accused of unlawful seizure of property, theft of property, and the willful disregard for the safety and security of the innocent citizens of Burlap's Rest. Testimony has been heard in regard to these accusations, and it is the decision of this tribunal that—for these crimes—you shall be sentenced to a swift and merciful death by hanging."

The Judge dipped his head and touched his fist lightly against his brow. "*Deus misereatur nobis*," he said after a moment of solemn reflection. *God have mercy on us all.* And then he raised his head and lowered his hand. He opened his fist, stretching his fingers into a stiff line. He drew his flattened hand across his neck, like a knife, and the men standing beside the horses smacked each animal on the rump, spooking them into motion.

The old oak's branch creaked and groaned under the squirming weight of the three condemned men. The ropes pulled taut as the horses strained, and the Judge kicked the milking stools away from the spasming feet of the hanging men. Ralph Bonner, the youngest of the trio, was the most spirited in his final moments. His face reddened as his weight pulled against the rope, and his eyes bulged. Spit flew from his lips as he tried to form words. He bounced several times, and as his face darkened to an ugly shade of purple, he flung a leg at the Judge, trying to inflict injury on the man who had sentenced him to die.

The Judge stared up at the dying man, and his dark eyes showed no sadness and no empathy for the young man's suffering.

Then, with a sickening snap, something broke in Bonner's neck, and he went limp.

In the audience, someone started weeping. A breeze rustled the leaves of the oak, and high overhead, the sun drifted behind a cloud, as if it wanted no part of the proceedings.

The Judge walked down the line of swaying bodies, looking intently at the swollen face of each man. Looking for some sign that life still persisted, and if not life, then the presence of true and final death.

"*Et eorum animos ad Deum,*" the Judge pronounced when he was finished with his examination. *Their souls to God.*

He waved a hand at the men near the horses. As the horses were brought under control, the ropes slithered across the branch and the bodies gently sank to the ground.

The crowd nervously milled about. The horrible truth of what had happened was starting to sink in, and the Judge could already tell that some of them were having second thoughts. There was no way they could undo what they had done. Even though the Judge had been the instrument of their justice, they had given testimony and they had stood as witnesses to the delivery of that justice. Tears would be shed, and doubt would creep into the minds of some. While a few might sleep soundly, there was still a stain on their souls. They were all marked in some way.

The Judge dug his watch out of a pocket in his waistcoat and looked at the time. Three hours until sundown. *Time enough yet*, he thought.

He put his watch away and indicated the dead men. "These bodies will need to be burned," he said.

Collectively, the townspeople froze, as if they had all been caught by a vicious winter wind and transformed into icy statues. "Wha-what?" someone stuttered.

"Burned," the Judge said again. "You should cut off their heads first, though. Just to be sure."

"Are you—have you lost your mind?" The stutterer broke from the rank of shocked townsfolk. He was round of face and body, and he wore a black coat and a white collar. "These men were Christians. For all their transgressions. They still deserve decent burial."

The Judge looked the town preacher over, his tongue poking at the inside of his mouth. "They're dead, and if you want them to stay dead, you'll burn the bodies," he said.

"We will do no such blasphemy," the preacher snarled.

The crowd was starting to split into two camps: those who had had more than enough of territorial justice and wanted to be gone from the field near the church where the hanging tree stood, and those who were reacting to the Judge's proclamation with outrage similar to the preacher's. The Judge didn't blame them. Such a reaction was a way of coping with the enormity of their decision. A proper Christian burial would ease their guilt, would it not? They had acted justly and respectfully, in the end. God would forgive them. But decapitation and burning? That was an unforgivable transgression. They might be living on the frontier, but they were not savages. They were God-fearing folk, and if they did right by God, God would do right by them.

The Judge looked past the muttering crowd. His man—Elm— leaned against the fence post near the graveyard. He met the Judge's gaze and shrugged, as if to say, *Get on with it, old man.*

The Judge slipped his fingers into the other front pocket of his waistcoat and drew out three coins. He held them up for the crowd to see. The coins were gold, and each had the face of a sanguine woman on one side and an eagle and thirteen stars on the reverse.

"I have three double eagles," the Judge said. "And I will offer them as a wager."

"A what?" the preacher sputtered.

"Bury these men," the Judge said, indicating the corpse next to him. "And I'll place one of each of these coins on the graves. If these coins are still there, undisturbed, when the morning sun crawls over those hills, then I will apologize for my disturbing and ill-spoken commentary on the interment of these Christian men. And you may keep these coins as a tithe to your parish."

The preacher frowned and looked to the men standing near him for guidance. He saw no help in their equally confused expressions, and he turned back to the Judge. "I don't understand," he said. "What would disturb these coins?"

There was grumbling from the crowd, and the Judge heard a voice call from the back: "Someone might steal them."

The Judge directed the crowd's attention at Elm. "My man will stand watch," he said. "And you can provide as many guards as you like for your own peace of mind."

The preacher looked at Elm, who stared laconically back at him. There was more muttering among the crowd, and when the preacher returned his attention to the Judge, a cunning light had bloomed in the round man's eyes. "And if the coins are moved?" he asked. "What then?"

"Then you'll burn these fucking bodies like I asked you to, and hope to God there aren't any more," the Judge said.

2

DURING THE WAR, ELM HAD FOUGHT WITH THE UNION. HE had been at the Siege of Vicksburg, where his company of sharpshooters had harried the Confederate soldiers for more than a month during that hot summer of 1863. The Confederate Army—outgunned, outmanned, and out of supplies—valiantly attempted to withstand General Grant's particular persistence, but it was all for naught. There were no reinforcements coming to save Lt. General Pemberton and his men. There were no hidden caches of supplies that would alleviate the hunger and sickness bedeviling the men trapped within Vicksburg. And with the Union sharpshooters putting a round into any grey-capped head foolish enough to pop up, morale was in danger of expiring as well.

The sharpshooters of Company C of the 1st United States Sharpshooters worked in squads of three: one spotting, one shooting, and one resting. They kept their distance and chose their targets with deadly precision. By the third week of the siege, they had ceased to be men and had become ghosts. Angels of Death. God's Finger.

But, most of the time, they sat and watched. And waited.

It was important to have a steady hand, but it was also important to know patience.

As the sun dipped below the eastern horizon and the valley filled with shadows, Elm made himself comfortable at the base of the old oak. The Bonner brothers and their cousin, Henry Greer, had been placed in makeshift coffins that had been hastily knocked together by local carpenters, and the pine boxes were laid next to one another near the entrance to the town's tiny graveyard. No graves had been dug, as the final disposition of the bodies had not occurred to the townsfolk of Burlap's Rest. No one had given the matter much thought to prior to the hanging of the three men.

It hadn't mattered to the Judge. Once the lids had been nailed shut on the coffins, he had placed one of the twenty-dollar coins on each box. After speaking briefly with the preacher, the Judge wandered over to the oak. *He'll leave some men who will be asleep before the moon comes up,* he had said to Elm.

And you? Elm asked.

I'm going to enumerate the ways in which a modicum of civilization can help a man forget what he had done, the Judge replied.

It's never enough, Elm said.

The Judge stared at him. *Should I send up a bottle?* he asked.

Elm nodded toward the group of concerned citizens who roamed—like nervous cattle—along the edge of the graveyard fence. *You think that's a smart idea?*

The Judge snorted. *For you,* he said. *Not for them.*

It might interfere with my aim, Elm said.

I doubt that, the Judge said.

Are they coming back . . . ?

I hope not, the Judge said. Which was the Judge's way of saying *Yes* when he'd prefer not to answer at all.

And so, Elm sat beneath the oak tree and kept an eye on the four men who stayed behind when the crowd finally dispersed. He watched them shuffle about, whispering among themselves as they stared at the coffins and the three gold coins.

Elm waited. He was a patient man.

A year—no, it was closer to two years ago now—he had wandered into a town that lay beside a sprawling lake. Named after an Indian chief. Choctaw, maybe. Tishomongo, perhaps. Something like that. He had been drifting south, idly following the course of the Tennessee River when he cared to track where he was. He had his horse and his rifle, and his purse was half full. He was neither indolent nor indifferent; he was merely invisible: a state he preferred to cultivate following the War. In Tishomongo, he had wandered into a nameless saloon where he had found a card game.

And the Judge.

His first impression of the Judge was that the man was as vain as a peacock he had once seen wandering freely about Silverglen—the estate where he and his mother had lived. The bird would strut back and forth along the long porch that wrapped itself around the main house of the sprawling estate, and whenever someone approached, it would spin about and spread its tail feathers into a broad fan. He had remarked on the beautiful display of shimmering greens and blues, and the young lady of the house had told him how the peacock spreads its feathers to appear larger than it really is. *Those markings?* Miss Rebecca had pointed at the long feathers. *Those are eyes, are they not? In a moment, this scrawny bird can transform itself into a multi-headed monster.*

That's ridiculous, he had snorted. *They're just feathers.* When he went to approach the bird, it whirled on him, shaking its wide fan and hissing angrily.

Feathers or not, he hadn't approached any closer.

There were five men at the table that afternoon, and after purchasing a bottle of whisky from the barkeep, Elm wandered over to the table and inquired if he might join. The Judge—leaning back his chair, puffing his chest out—peered at the bottle in Elm's hand. *You buying your way in with that?* he asked.

I guess I am, Elm said, and he put the bottle down on the table.

They made room for him, and he fumbled enough change out of his purse to get himself into trouble.

And it hadn't taken long.

He played loosely for awhile, waiting for the weariness of the saddle to leave him. On his right was a grubby-faced cowboy with a mustache made uneven by the bulge of chewing tobacco in his cheek. Sitting across from him was his partner, a hatchet-faced man with no sense of humor. The man sitting on Elm's left was either a local dandy who dreamed of being recognized as someone important or a down-on-his-luck riverboat gambler who had crawled into this town to drink himself to death.

Across from Elm was the Judge. He wore black—like a priest or a villain—though he had the air of neither. His face was gnarled like an old pine tree that had withstood years of cold winter storms, but there was humor in his eyes and in the way his lips moved. His hands were large, and he wore a silver ring on the pinkie of his left hand.

The last player was a man with whiskers that went all the way down to this chin and then curled up and out, creating the impression that his head floated atop his body. The man's belly strained against his belt, and he had a tendency to count and recount his money, as if some of it might vanish if he didn't touch it with round-fingered regularity.

When the bet passed to him, the other players grew restless. The cowboys eyed the Judge and Elm, the Judge rolled a gold coin across his knuckles, and the dandy kept licking his lips and staring at the shiny coin as it flipped across the knobby landscape of the Judge's hands.

Finally, the fat man tossed in a dime, and the bet passed to the Judge, who flipped the coin off his knuckles. He held it lightly between his thumb and finger as he made eye contact with the dandy sitting to his right.

You in or out? the Judge asked.

The coin was a double eagle—a twenty-dollar gold coin. It was, Elm assessed, more than the dandy had in the pile of money scattered before him.

The dandy licked his lips again, a tremor showing in his hands as he played with the edge of his cards.

The Judge smiled wolfishly and flipped the coin into the pile of money at the center of the table. *I'll see your bet and raise*, he said to the fat man, though his eyes never left the dandy.

The two cowboys stared at one another, and the mustachioed one had momentarily forgotten about the wad of tobacco in his cheek. Hatchet Face sat very still. Elm didn't like the way the pair seemed to be talking with their eyes.

The dandy laughed, and Dirty Mustache twitched. For a second, Elm thought he was going to swallow the plug in his cheek, but he recovered and spat noisily into a brass spittoon on the table near his cards.

The dandy apologized for his outburst, delicately holding a lace-edged handkerchief up to his lips. He dropped it on the table as he leaned forward and shoved his entire stake into the pot. *I think I can match that,* he said. When he dragged his handkerchief off the table, Elm saw his fingers do something beneath the lacy fabric. Had he switched a card?

Hatchet Face hadn't noticed. He was too busy staring at his partner. Something passed between them. A twitch in the corner of an eye from Hatchet Face. A tiny shrug from Dirty Mustache.

The Judge was looking at Elm, the wolfish smile still on his lips.

I'm in, Hatchet Face said. With his left hand, he shoved his stack of coins toward the middle of the table. His right hand drifted off the table.

And that was enough for Elm.

We're all in, he said. He flipped his cards over and tossed them onto the table. In the brief moment while the other players were watching his cards slide across the wooden surface, Elm drew his pistol and stuck the barrel into Dirty Mustache's ear. *Everyone*, he said. *Turn your cards over and put your hands on the table. Where I can see them.*

Hatchet Face started to rise out of his chair, and Elm calmly cocked back the hammer on his pistol.

Everyone froze. Dirty Mustache's eyes were wide, and his mouth gaped open. The fat man was breathing noisily through his nose. Hatchet Face shot out of his chair. The dandy held his handkerchief to his lips. The Judge rolled his tongue around the inside of his mouth.

You sure you're pointing your gun at the right guy? he asked. He nodded toward Hatchet Face, who was giving Elm a death stare. *He's going to shoot you if you shoot his partner.*

Elm raised his left hand from his lap where he had palmed the tiny Derringer he kept tucked in the sleeve of his heavy coat. He pointed the small gun at Hatchet Face.

Hatchet Face's eyes crossed slightly as he focused on the gun in Elm's hand. *That?* he laughed. *I've had flea bites worse than that.*

It's not the size of the flea you should worry about, Elm said, lowering his aim. *It's where it bites that matters.*

Hatchet Face glowered for another moment, but he sat back down in his chair. His right hand was still cocked back by his side.

Elm pushed the barrel of his pistol a little deeper in Dirty Mustache's ear. *I can't see your friend's hands,* he said.

And the world stood still. A frozen moment that Elm could recall with perfect clarity even now. Each player at the table was caught on the cusp of what came next. What were they all thinking? How many of them were afraid of dying? Would he shoot both Dirty Mustache and Hatchet Face before Hatchet Face pulled his own gun? Had Hatchet Face ever shot a man before? Would he aim for Elm's head or his chest? Would any of the other men at the table produce a weapon and start shooting too?

Elm was calm. He knew these questions would sort themselves out, eventually. He could wait. He was God's Finger, after all . . .

Elm was stirred from his reverie by a commotion among the men left to watch over the coffins. One of the men was shaking the others awake, his voice urgent and tight.

The sky had gone black, and the moon hadn't yet come out of hiding. The church was a white shadow off to the right, and the pair of lanterns the men had with them made long shadows.

As Elm watched, the four men—now roused and fully frightened by the antics of the one watcher—cautiously crept along the graveyard fence. The weak glow of the lanterns finally illuminated the long shapes of the wooden coffins. Three of the men laughed and jostled the fearful fourth, harassing him for being so skittish. The watcher protested vainly, insisting that he had heard something.

One of the men hitched himself over the fence and approached the coffins. He waved the lantern over each box, and Elm saw a glint of light from the gold coin resting on the top of each coffin. "They're still here," the man said. He laughed noisily, and then rapped his knuckles heartily against the first box. "Yep. Still here," he repeated after he did the same on the second.

And when he knocked on the third box, something inside knocked back.

3

BY THE TIME ELM REACHED THE GRAVEYARD, THE FOUR MEN were in high hysterics. Guns had been drawn. One of them was swearing, a second was praying, and the other two were loudly arguing whether to run or open the coffins. "It's a God-damned joke," the surliest of the four said, pointing a finger at Elm. "They're having a laugh."

"Do I look like I'm laughing?" Elm asked.

One of the men raised his lantern to better see Elm's face—checking to be sure, no doubt—but his examination was cut short by a violent thumping from one of the coffins. The man squeaked like a rat and nearly dropped his lantern. The other men whirled on the coffins and pointed their guns at the wooden boxes.

"What's doing that?" the one who had been swearing whispered. "Is it rats?"

"Rats don't make noises like that," the third man hissed back.

"Maybe they ain't dead," the squeaker squeaked.

"Their necks was busted," the surly one said. "They smelled dead when we loaded them in the coffins."

"Then what's making that noise?"

"I don't know!" Surly waggled his gun at the coffin, and then turned and waggled his gun in Elm's direction. "What's making that noise?"

"You don't want to know," Elm said patiently. He took one step to his left, putting himself out of harm's way from the man's shaking gun. "Just leave them be."

The coffin rattled again. Whatever was inside was definitely trying to get out. The lid on the next box over rattled as well.

"They're still alive," the squeaker protested again. "We've put them in coffins, and they're still alive. What kind of Christian behavior is that?"

"They're not alive," Elm said. His hand drifted to his gun.

The third box rattled once, and then all three coffins went still. The graveyard was silent. In the distance, Elm heard an owl hoot. One of the four men started to whimper.

"This is bullshit," Surly said. He stared at the nearest box, and his tongue nervously wet his lips. "Let's just burn 'em," he said. "Right now."

"We can't do that," the squeaker protested.

"They deserve a Christian burial," the third man said, agreeing with the squeaker.

Surly gestured with his pistol. "You open it," he snapped.

"Me?" the squeaker squeaked.

"Yeah, you, Delmar. Or Grover there. I don't care which of you. Someone needs to open one of them boxes."

Delmar—the squeaker—shook his head. "I'm not going near 'em," he said.

Surly looked at Grover, who shook his head too. "It was your idea, Jeremiah," he said.

Jeremiah waved his gun at the last man. "Lew."

Lew drew in a sharp breath. "Me?"

"Yeah, you. Go open one of those damn boxes."

Elm shook his head. "That is a very bad idea."

Jeremiah whirled on Elm. "You don't want us opening these boxes," he snapped. "You're trying to cheat us out of those double eagles."

Elm glanced over at the gold coins on the top of the coffins. "I'm really not," he said patiently.

A low moan interrupted further discussion. To Elm, who was familiar with the sounds made by dying men on the field of battle, it sounded like the ragged cry of a man with a hole in his gut he could not plug. A man who had been lying in the mud and muck for hours, waiting for the end, but knowing it wouldn't come fast enough.

The other men—several of whom had been small children when the first wagons had rolled across the hills to the east and Randolph William Burlap had declared this spot was as far as he was willing to go—had never listened to a man weeping and dying, and so, to them, the sound was not unlike the lowing of a lost heifer, who had been separated in the night from the rest of the herd.

"Did you hear that?" Lew asked.

Grover and Delmar nodded, their eyes big and wide.

"Oh, for the love of Christ," Jeremiah exploded. He shoved his gun back into his belt and snatched one of the lanterns from Grover. "I'm going to open the coffin."

Elm drew his gun and pointed it at Jeremiah. His aim, unlike Jeremiah's, was straight and true. "I wouldn't do that," Elm said. The tone of his voice brought Jeremiah up short, and the man slowly looked over his shoulder at Elm.

"Are you going to shoot me?" he asked.

Elm nodded. "If you touch that box, I will."

Jeremiah licked his heavy lips. "You will not," he countered.

Elm cocked back the hammer on his pistol. "I'm not in the mood to be tested," he said. "Step away from the box."

The top of the nearest coffin exploded outward, chunks of pine flying into the night sky. Something leaped out of the box, something wreathed in malevolent darkness. It collided with Jeremiah, and wrapped its arms and legs around the shrieking man. Jeremiah dropped his lantern and danced about, like he was a puppet whose strings were tangled.

The other three men fired their pistols wildly, and Jeremiah's dance turned into a jerking parody, like he was doing the Fox Trot all by himself. His eyes were glazed with shock, and his mouth yawed open like that of a dead fish. The thing—all arms and legs and a head that would not remain upright—clawed at Jeremiah. The three men kept firing, and Jeremiah danced up against the ruined coffin and fell over it, leaving a smear of blood along the side of the pine box.

Jeremiah continued to scream and thrash. Even though he had been shot several times by his companions—mortally so, in fact—he fought back against the monster clinging to him. As if, on the cusp of death, he knew his soul was in danger.

Elm fired once, and Jeremiah's cries were immediately silenced, as if a knife had severed the thin thread connecting his soul to this realm. And now, the only sounds were the noises of cloth being torn and a wet, pulpy thwack that each of the men slowly realized was the sound of flesh being torn from a body.

Elm went over the fence and picked up the lantern Jeremiah had dropped. He threw it at the thing crouched atop Jeremiah's still-warm and quivering body, and the glass shattered. A sheet of fire billowed, and for a brief instant, the men saw the face of the thing that had come out of the box. It had been Henry Greer once, but its eyes were dead and its mouth was red.

It screamed at the flames and tried to get away, but Elm shot it in the face and it collapsed on top of Jeremiah's corpse.

"The other lantern," Elm said. "Throw it on the coffins too."

The other coffins were vibrating and shaking, as the reanimated bodies of Ralph and Douglas Bonner were trying to break free of their pine prisons. Delmar's arm shook as he flung his lantern, and it sailed high over the coffins and landed on the ground beyond. The glass broke and the oil caught fire, but the spreading stain of flame did not reach the coffins.

Delmar whimpered and raised his hands defensively as the other two men glared at him.

Elm shook his head and walked over to the burning bodies and remaining coffins. His face showed no emotion in the light of the fires, and he calmly put two bullets in each of the coffins.

The fire spread to the first coffin, the fresh pine sizzling and popping as the flames heated the wood.

Elm calmly reloaded his pistol.

Eventually, the Judge opened the door of the rented room. His white hair was in disarray, and his undershirt was untucked from his trousers. He wasn't wearing his boots, and one of his suspenders was off. He had a mean glint in his eye, but whatever diatribe he had mentally prepared to unload on the unsuspecting idiot who had interrupted his reverie died in his throat when he saw Elm standing outside the room.

Elm glanced past the looming figure of the Judge and nodded lightly at the young woman kneeling on the bed. She was wearing a lacy shift that had been pushed up to expose her pale and tender ass—her "*derrière*" as Miss Rebecca had corrected him once upon a time—and a heavy leather-bound book lay open across her lower back.

"Aristotle," the Judge said, noting Elm's gaze. "*The Nichomachean Ethics.*"

"Of course," Elm replied, and what flickered in his eyes was neither doubt nor disrespect.

"A good life is one based in regular habits and routines, compounded by the manifestation of virtues—"

Elm raised his hand and tossed something to the Judge. The gold coin glinted in the weak light, and the Judge reacted quickly, catching the double eagle. Elm tossed him a second one, and the Judge caught it as well.

"And the third?" the Judge asked.

Elm revealed his empty hand and shook his head. "A contribution to local causes," he said.

The Judge sucked on a tooth and rattled the two double eagles in his hand. "Did they rise?" he asked.

"They did," Elm said. "Just like you said they would."

"And . . . ?"

"And that preacher fellow has reached a certain fallacious conclusion as to cause and effect. If he isn't explaining his thinking to a mob already, it's only because he's still trying to figure out the best chapter and verse to quote to them."

The Judge's tongue worked against his teeth again. "Job," he said finally. "Chapter thirty. Verse twenty-six. *Expectabam bona, et venerunt mihi mala—*"

"I think he'll go with Psalms," Elm interrupted. "'Break thou the arm of the wicked and the evil man; seek out his wickedness till thou find none.'"

The Judge nodded. "That will certainly play better with the mob," he said.

Looking past the Judge, Elm raised a hand and touched a finger to the edge of his forehead. "Miss," he said politely. "My apologies for disturbing your education."

He returned his attention to the Judge. "I'll ready the horses."

4

FOUR DAYS LATER, AS ELM WAS GNAWING ON A GRISTLY PIECE of meat in a public house in Bitter, word of what had happened in Burlap's Rest caught up with him. Two men came in and wandered up to the long bar. They asked the bartender a few questions, and the man pointed in Elm's direction.

Elm kept chewing on the meat. As tough as this piece of meat was, it was better than the mystery stew the Judge cooked more often than not when they were camping rough.

The men wore heavy work clothes and walked with the side to side motion of men who spent their waking hours in the saddle. They were tall and lean, faces burned by wind and sun, and their hats had been shaped more by weather than by hand. Neither wore a gun belt, which suggested they weren't going to interrupt his meal. As tough as it was.

Elm leaned back in his chair and wiped his fingers clean on the ragged piece of cloth he had been using for a napkin.

The one on his left spoke first. "The barkeep says you've come from the north."

"You've been to Burlap's Rest," the other man said breathlessly.

Elm swallowed the piece of meat he had been working on, and washed it down with a mouthful of warm beer. "I may have," he said.

"Story going 'round about a hanging there," the first man said. "A couple of cattle rustlers."

"I suppose that is what happens when cattle rustlers get caught," Elm said.

The two men looked at each other, and it was the one on the right who continued. "Word is those men didn't stay dead. Even though they were hung until there was no life left in them and then buried—"

"They weren't buried, Benjee," the one on the left interrupted.

"They were too," Benjee said. "Right behind the church."

"That's consecrated ground. They couldn't be buried there."

"That's the way I heard it, Purnell. You weren't there, were you? No? So, let me tell the damn story, okay?"

Elm swallowed another mouthful of beer as the two men argued. "This sounds like quite a fantastic story," he said when they had finished. "And you boys don't strike me as the type to believe in fairy tales."

Benjee—the one on the right—narrowed his eyes, while his companion, Purnell, nodded. "I believe what I see with my own eyes," he said.

"It's a wise approach," Elm said.

"You were there?" Benjee asked.

"I was."

"And these men? They came back, didn't they?"

"They did."

"And then what happened?" Benjee asked. "Was it like in one of those books?"

Elm raised his eyebrows. "I'm not sure which book you are referring to," he said.

"You know the ones," Benjee said. "They got 'em at the store down the street. Don't cost much." He nudged Purnell. "Who's that writer? The one who tells them fancy stories?"

"Vance," Purnell said. "Meriweather Vance."

Benjee snapped his fingers. "That's him. Like that explorer fella."

Elm waited patiently for the two men to finish their discussion of popular reading material.

"Was it like one of them books by Vance?" Benjee asked, trying to find common ground that was familiar to all three of them.

Elm shrugged. "I have to admit a lack of familiarity with the man's oeuvre," he said.

"His what?" Purnell wrinkled his nose.

Elm sighed and toyed with the handle on his mug of beer. "What did you two want?" he asked. "Perhaps we can get to that, and then I could finish my meal."

"Oh, yes, of course," Benjee said. He glared at his companion, as if the awkward moment was all Purnell's fault. And Purnell glared back in a way that suggested their relationship was based on a long-standing disagreement about fundamental principles. Elm hoped he would not get dragged into an extended revisitation of the history of this disagreement.

"Our employer would like to invite you out to Thrush to hear a proposition," Benjee said. "You and your friend."

Elm looked around. "Which friend are you referring to?"

"Judge Wallace," Purnell said. "Tell him Aloysius Gunter Van Horn's daughter is asking to see him."

Elm nodded. "I'll be sure to pass along the request."

The two men nodded in return, and for a second, Benjee seemed like he was about to say something, but a nervous shiver shut his mouth, and he followed his friend out the door. Elm watched them go and then let his gaze wander around the room. No one appeared to be curious as to the nature of the conversation that had just happened. Even the barkeep was busy polishing glasses.

"Daughter, huh?" Elm said quietly to himself.

He knew little about the Judge, other than the man had once been a highly respected jurist in Baton Rouge prior to the War Between the States. At the end of the War, when Texas and Louisiana were put under military rule as part of the Reconstruction, the Judge stepped down from his position and become an itinerant jurist.

There were, at that time, only nine circuit court judges recognized by the United States Government. Each presided over a portion of the country, and part of their job was to provide judicial assistance in cases worthy of the federal government's attention. In some parts of the frontier, a local judge would roam across several counties, providing services as necessary, but, to Elm's knowledge, there were no officially recognized jurists who roamed across state and territory lines.

Then again, there was also no precedent for the manner of cases the Judge tended to preside over, either . . .

After finishing his meal, Elm wandered down the main street of Bitter. Compared to Bishop's Rest, Bitter was a well-established town. It had two hotels, a handful of saloons, something that passed for a museum—no doubt the history of the town's name could be learned there—and a number of sundry shops that looked to carry a broad assortment of goods. Elm finally found the Judge in a tiny barber shop between the office of a shipping company and an apothecary's shop.

The barber had finished trimming the Judge's impressive shock of grey hair, and was stropping a straight razor along a leather belt. The Judge lay half-reclined in the barber's chair, a towel wrapped around his throat. He cracked a eye open as the tiny bell mounted over the door tinkled to announce Elm's arrival.

"This young man is your next customer," the Judge informed the barber.

Elm took off his hat and held it in his hands. "I'm fine," he said.

"Nonsense," the Judge snorted. "Look at the tangled mane of yours. You look half-feral."

"I don't mind half," Elm said.

The barber looked up from his efforts and appraised Elm's appearance with a professional eye. He raised an eyebrow in response to Elm's statement.

"I mind," the Judge said.

Elm ignored him. "We've been asked to pay a visit to a local ranch," he said. "A place called Thrush."

The Judge popped his lips. "Thrush," he said, trying the word out. He raised his eyes, looking for the barber. "Curious name for an estate. Is it a bird sanctuary?" he asked.

The barber shook his head. "Cattle ranch. Owned by the Van Horn family."

"Van Horn?" The Judge frowned slightly as if the name rang a bell somewhere in the capacious palace of his memory.

"Aloysius Gunter Van Horn," Elm suggested.

The barber nodded gently. "God rest his soul," he said. "Miss Van Horn runs the ranch now." He unwound the cloth and proceeded to apply a generous swath of foam to the Judge's pink neck.

"Miss?" the Judge asked.

"His daughter," Elm clarified.

"Well, I'll be . . . " A shadow passed across the Judge's features, and he waved a hand to dismiss his thoughts, nearly clouting the barber in the face as he did so. "When you are done scraping the scales off my neck, good man, you will tame my friend's unruly contention of a crown."

"I really don't need a haircut," Elm said.

"We're calling on a lady," the Judge said.

"I'm not looking to make an impression."

"The world remarks on you whether you care for it or not, son," the Judge said.

Elm stared at the Judge for a moment. "'Hear, ye children, the instructions of the father, and attend to know,'" he said dryly.

The Judge laughed and slapped his knee, a sudden motion that caused the barber to step back, pulling his straight razor away from the Judge's soapy neck.

"Proverbs," the Judge chortled. "'Take fast hold of instruction; keep her, for she is thy life.'" He waggled a finger at Elm. "You should know better than to quote Scripture at a man of God." As the barber cautiously approached the Judge's neck again, the Judge levered a stern eye at Elm. "Now sit down and get a haircut. I won't be bringing a wild animal into a lady's house."

Elm sat down on the bench near the door, resting his hat on his knees. "I'm happy to stay with the horses," he said.

The barber laid a firm hand on the Judge's forehead and held the older man still. His hand was steady and his motion was true, and the razor neatly lifted soap and whiskers from the Judge's throat.

Elm smiled pleasantly at the Judge, who was forced to remain silent as the barber shaved his neck.

Miraculously, the Judge's silence continued as they rode west from Bitter, following the muddy trickle of a creek. The young man at the livery stable had said once the road crossed the river, it would split near a stand of crooked poplars. They would want to take the right-hand fork of the road, and follow it over a hill and into the next valley where they would find Thrush, the cattle ranch named after a species of small bird—a number of which the Judge pointed out during the ride. As their horses ambled along the road, Elm found his thoughts going back to Silverglen, Mr. Rothacher's estate in Ohio, and Miss Rebecca, the daughter of Mr. Rothacher's recently deceased sister. She was an ethereal presence about the main house, a tiny flame that had drawn him like a moth, and he seized every opportunity to approach the broad building with its ivory columns and tall windows. Fetching wood for the kitchen. Trimming the hedges along the walk. Washing the stone steps and porch. Hauling the chamber pots out to the pit behind the servants' quarters. Finally, he saw her up close, and she was even more magical and beautiful than the image his fevered imagination had painted in his mind.

She saw him too, and for the rest of that summer and into the fall, they circled each other, drawing ever closer. Until the Confederates had fired on Fort Sumter, and everything was knocked askew.

Five years later, when he returned to Silverglen, he found the estate abandoned and in disrepair. A few of the old servants still squatted in the rotting bedrooms of the main house, but none of them recognized him. Wild pigs rooted through the remnants of the gardens that had once painted the fields with wild sprays of color. A pack of children flocked after him like baby chickens as he walked the grounds, and the tallest one had a broken peacock feather woven into her hair . . .

Their horses crested a rise, and the Judge made a noise in his throat that brought Elm back to the present. The road dipped and ambled down into a valley that spread out below them. A line of pine and poplar ran along the northern verge of the valley which ran for some distance to the west. A herd of cattle were strung out across a few acres of scrub, and Elm estimated the number was more than a hundred head. Clustered at the eastern end of the valley, just another mile or so down the road, were a collection of buildings: a ranch house, a barn, a bunk house, and a long warehouse. A corral near the stable held a few horses, and Elm spotted a few people passing back and forth between the buildings. Just another day at a working ranch.

As their horses followed the road, a small shape left the front porch of the main house and darted up the road to meet them. It was a short-haired black dog with a white spot on one of its ears, and when it came within a dozen yards or so, it stopped and started barking. The Judge halted his horse and leaned on the horn of his saddle, staring down at the dog. Elm brought his horse up next to the Judge's and stopped as well.

"He is very intent upon his duties," the Judge noted. The dog made more noise than one would expect from an animal his size.

Elm nodded. He patted his horse's neck, feeling the animal shift beneath him.

Eventually, the dog realized the two riders were not going to be put off, and he sank to his haunches, letting his tongue loll.

"It's noisy work, isn't it?" the Judge said to the dog.

The dog yipped once, and the Judge chuckled. "Run off and tell your master that we've arrived," he said, lifting his arm and making a shooing motion. The dog didn't move, and the Judge clicked his tongue, nudging his horse forward. The dog, wary of the horse, let loose with a final bark, and then dashed back the way it had come.

The Judge chuckled again and let his horse pick its way along the road.

The dog started barking again when it reached the house, and its noise drew the attention of the ranch hands. By the time Elm and the Judge reached the flat ground in front of the main house, a half dozen men in work clothes had gathered on the porch. Elm scanned the faces for the pair who had come into town, spotting Purnell and Benjee at the back of the group. The assembly of men stared at the Judge and Elm, who stared back, and that impasse seemed like the course of action for the remainder of the day. The dog, bored by the lack of conversation, lay down on the porch.

Finally, a man and a woman came around the side of the house.

She was dressed in denim pants and a work coat like the ranch hands, and from a distance, it would have been easy to mistake her for a man, but up close, there was no mistaking the generous curve of her breasts and the sensual curve of her lips. Her cheeks were red and her eyes were bright, and Elm turned his attention to the grizzled man beside her before he was caught staring at the dark-haired beauty. The old man had a face like a turtle and a shock of facial hair like the waddle on a moose. He walked stiffly, but he was still spry enough to keep up with the woman, who strode in an easy ground-covering stride.

There was no doubt she was in charge.

She stopped a few paces from their horses and tilted her head back to look up at the Judge. Her hair was long and dark, plaited into a braid that hung down her back. The Judge quickly removed his hat, and coughed noisily for Elm to do the same. Embarrassed to not have done so already, Elm snatched his hat off his head, and his motion drew her attention.

The woman stared at him, and he held her gaze without aggressively staring back. The corner of her mouth quirked slightly, and she tilted her head a bit as she returned her attention to the Judge.

"Well, you old son of a bitch," she said. "I guess I shouldn't be surprised that you aren't dead."

5

AFTER HER PRONOUNCEMENT, THE WOMAN INDICATED THE PAIR should follow her inside. Elm slipped down from his horse and handed the reins over to one of the hands, and he followed the Judge up the steps and through the front door of the ranch house. The woman took off her hat and placed it on a table near the door, and then walked into a sitting room on the left. The three of them—Elm, the old man who had been shadowing the woman, and the Judge—stood awkwardly in the hall. The Judge finally handed his hat to the old man, and went on in to the sitting room. Somewhat apologetically, Elm did the same.

The room contained a tall bookcase, a side table with several crystal decanters and a set of short tumblers, a pair of low-backed chairs with dark seats, and a long backless divan. There was a small fireplace in the corner and an iron grate stood in front of the dusty ashes. The Judge poured a measure of spirits into three glasses, and he handed one each to Elm and the woman. "To not being dead," the Judge said, raising his glass.

Given what they had seen in Burlap's Rest, the toast was a bit odd, but Elm was accustomed to the Judge's peculiarities and he raised his glass and took a polite sip. It didn't burn his throat, and he marveled at how smooth it was. It'd been awhile since he'd had anything that was properly aged.

The Judge smacked his lips, clearly pleased to be drinking something other than the "caustic piss"—as he liked to refer to it—that was offered in the shanty saloons and dusty public houses they had stopped in during the last few weeks.

The woman gave the Judge a hard stare, and the muscles at the base of her throat worked as she considered her words. "Most of my family no longer qualifies for such remembrance," she said.

The Judge looked down at his glass and deep lines creased his forehead in an unusual display of consternation. It was rare for the older man to be at a loss for words, and Elm came to his rescue. As curious as he was about the history between these two, he wasn't sure he was eager to learn it in this manner. He gulped the remainder of the whisky in his glass and then cleared his throat. "This is mighty fine whisky, and I would enjoy taking this bottle out to the porch where I might spend the afternoon, sipping it slowly, while the two of you have whatever conversation you need to have." He gestured toward the bottle in question.

The woman put back her head and laughed, and the motion cleared whatever had been caught in her throat. She held out her hand to Elm. "I should join you," she said. "We can let him stew in his guilt awhile."

He accepted her hand, finding it warm and firm. "I fear he stews very little," he said. "I am Elmore Stonebrook, and it is a pleasure to meet you."

"Indeed," she replied. She removed her hand from his and took a sip from her glass, eyeing the Judge over the rim as she did.

The Judge had wandered over to the broad window that looked out on the porch and was ignoring both of them.

A fleeting smile touched the corner of the woman's mouth, but it was quickly dismissed by the hard light in her eyes. "I am Isadora Van Horn, and this ranch has been in my family for three generations. I run it now, and I will do so until the land is no longer mine—a time which may come sooner than any of us suspect, unless certain matters can be resolved."

"And what matters might those be?" the Judge asked, his attention still on the world outside the room.

Isadora shook her head slightly, as if to say that she would answer his question soon enough. "Recently, I heard talk among my men about an unusual occurrence up north. A hanging that didn't end the lives of the men whose necks were in the nooses. A nightmarish tale, on all accounts, and the sort of tale these men tell when they are attempting to spook one another. Normally, I would have ignored such nonsense, but when I inquired about the source of this story, I was surprised to learn it was not entirely without credence. And so, I asked my men to learn more, and, if possible, invite the individuals who were party to this hanging to visit us here at Thrush." Her eyes flashed as she looked at the Judge. "I was not prepared to see an old *family* friend."

The way she stressed the word *family* suggested there was some lingering animosity in the relationship between the Judge and the Van Horns.

The Judge cleared his throat, started to speak, and then decided against saying what was on his mind. He raised his glass instead, draining the contents, and then he looked toward the side table, his gaze sliding past Elm and Isadora.

"You're not going to say anything, are you?" Isadora asked.

He looked at her finally, though he wouldn't hold her gaze. He rubbed a thick finger against the rim of his glass. "It's been a long time," he said. "I stayed—"

"You ran away, you mean."

Some of his formidable fury flashed in his eyes. "Now, wait a minute—" he started.

"You fled Baton Rouge like a cowardly cur," Isadora snapped. "Leaving my mother behind. Leaving my father to flounder."

"There were extenuating circumstances—"

"You broke her heart!"

"I left so that I wouldn't do that."

"That is what men always say, but as they have no hearts of their own, how could they possibly know the damage they do?"

"Now, look, Isadora—"

"Miss Van Horn, sir," she said sternly. "We are not as familiar as you would like to pretend."

"—Miss Van Horn," the Judge amended. "I cared—" He stopped and fiddled with his glass.

Elm cleared his throat. "Well, I really should have taken that bottle and left when I had the chance," he said.

In a flash, the anger brewing on Isadora's face vanished and she laughed again. "Both charming and diplomatic," she said, raising her glass to Elm. "God knows what he has done to deserve you."

"It's certainly not the pay," Elm said.

Before the Judge could comment, the door opened behind Elm and the old man entered. He was carrying a tray with a jug of water, a plate of freshly cut bread, churned butter, and a jar of dark preserves. He maneuvered around Elm and put the tray on the side table. After fussing with the items for a moment or two, he nodded at Isadora and withdrew.

Elm took advantage of the interruption and went to the side table, where he discovered the bread was still warm. He slathered both butter and preserves across two pieces, and he offered one of them to Isadora. She demurred, and he shrugged as if it was of no consequence to him and bit into one of the pieces.

The Judge looked at him, an eyebrow raised, and Elm waved his other hand toward the table. "Butter your own," he said around a mouthful of bread. "I'm busy being charming and diplomatic."

"I'm beginning to like you, Mr. Stonebrook," Isadora said.

"Please, Miss Van Horn," Elm said after he swallowed. "Elm is fine."

She inclined her head. "Elm it is, and you needn't be so formal with me, either."

The Judge approached the side table and the food, and as his back was to Isadora, only Elm saw him roll his eyes toward the ceiling.

Isadora sat on the divan, resting her glass lightly on her knees. "My candid language aside," she said, "what is your relationship with this old philanderer?"

Elm took another bite and chewed it slowly as he considered his response. "He made a wager once upon a time," he said. "I'm waiting to collect."

"And what sort of wager was it?" she asked.

Elm swallowed. "Ah, let's call it a philosophical one."

"And is it?"

"That's a matter of interpretation," he admitted.

She turned her attention to the Judge. "Interpretation is indeed a slippery word with this snake."

The Judge made an effort to look pained by her words, though Elm suspected it wasn't too much of an effort. The old man was attending to his bread, but it was clear to both Elm and Isadora that he was not ignoring either of them.

"Well, to be perfectly frank with you, Miss Van Horn—" Elm started.

"Isadora."

"—Miss Isadora, in this instance, he's not the slippery one."

She raised an eyebrow. "Really? Well, now my surprise is replaced with something else. Something almost like . . . curiosity."

She stared at the old man as he leaned against the side table, nibbling at the corner of a piece of bread. "He does have that way about him, doesn't he?" Some of the critical tone had left her voice, and for an instant, her face softened. Elm felt a stab of something in his chest—what was it? Jealousy? Sorrow? Longing?—as he recalled the last night he had seen Miss Rebecca at Silverglen.

Elm brushed aside the long ache surfacing in his chest. "Perhaps we should talk about why you wanted to see us, Miss Isadora," he said.

"Yes," she said briskly. "Perhaps we should get to that." She ran a hand along her knees, collecting her thoughts. "I am in

the middle of a range war," she said. "And I am going to lose."
She stood up and wandered back to the window. After taking
a sip from her glass, she spoke again. "Let me tell you a little
about the history of this land, to give you some perspective on
the individuals involved. Missouri became a state in 1821, and
because there were other states around it already, the state only
had to designate two of its borders—in the west and north. Do
you know the history of these boundaries?"

"I do not," Elm admitted.

"They are the Osage Boundary and the Sullivan Line. There
has been some dispute over the years about the Sullivan Line,
even after Missouri was admitted into the Union, including
a dispute with the Iowa Territory that nearly came to open
conflict. Once Iowa become a state, the issue over the location
of the border was settled, once and for all, and those who
had been homesteading in these disputed areas were granted
amnesty against any action that might seek to take these lands
from them.

"My grandfather was one of those men, as were three others.
Elder Montelbaum, Knock Fellhauser, and an Irishman named
Darbie O'Halloran. They all worked in concert with one another,
planning their crop rotations in a way that, regardless of the
weather—which they had discovered was terribly mercurial—
could not cause one of them to have a failed season.

"This worked well for many years," she continued, "until Elder
Montelbaum died. After that, Darbie O'Halloran lost interest in
farming. The land wasn't bountiful enough to match his aspirations, and so he bought a hundred head of cattle after a season's
harvest. The following winter was hard, but the spring was
better, and by the following summer, he had nearly one hundred
and fifty head. Two years later, he had nearly five hundred, and
he didn't have enough land for them to readily range across. He
needed more land, and so he made Joshua Montelbaum—the
old man's son—an offer, and Joshua took it.

"My father suffered in the wake of my mother's death"—she threw a hard look at the Judge—"and when my grandfather asked him to come home and help with the farm, he sold his business and house in Baton Rouge and moved us—my sister and I—back to Bitter. Norwood, my uncle, came home too, and for a few years, the farm thrived under the stewardship of two generations of Van Horn men. When Knock Fellhauser passed, his widow sold my grandfather their land. She did not like the O'Halloran clan, and her generosity nearly doubled the size of our land. But there were too many hard winters and too many meager springs. The land resisted our efforts to grow crops, and after my grandfather passed, my father and Norwood realized they had no choice but to switch to cattle as well if they hoped to keep this land in the family.

"And so they did, and it has been a never-ending battle with the O'Hallorans since then. We are in constant competition with that family: for feed, for customers, for help. There have been many times when I believed this land to be cursed by God. So many have died. In both families. My grandmother. Bart O'Halloran—Darbie's son—lost his wife during a winter that took many cattle. Two of his sons died the following spring. A year ago, a virulent fever swept through this house, taking my father and two of the staff. Shortly thereafter, my husband . . . "

"Your husband?" Elm asked as she trailed off.

She offered him a faint smile. "We were only married five months when he passed. Formally, I am Theodore Mulbridge's widow, but once my father died and I took over running the range, the hands found it awkward to refer to me as Theodore's widow. To them, I was the Van Horn name.

"Anyway, Bart O'Halloran wants all of the land from the creek to the border of Iowa, and I have resisted all of his efforts to obtain the family land. He has tried to buy me out. He tried to turn the town against me. He even offered to marry me. None of it has worked, and so he decided to wait me out. His herd is larger. His influence is greater. He buys more supplies than he needs, and I must send men farther north to get supplies, which costs me more in time and money. It is a war of attrition, one that might take me several lifetimes to win, though I have, in the last year, persevered such that I have managed to make enough to pay back some of the loans this farm has been saddled with."

"I don't understand," Elm said. "You said you were going to lose this battle. Yet, it seems like that isn't the case . . ."

"So I thought," she said. "But in the last few months, I have been losing cattle."

"Rustlers?"

She shook her head. "The animals have been savagely mutilated."

"Are there wolves in these hills? Mountain lions?"

"The wounds are too large for mountain lions, and if it is wolves, they are larger than any wolf ever seen in this region."

"Have you sent out hunting parties?"

"We have, and, to date, they have killed six wolves and three mountain lions."

"But the killings haven't stopped."

"They have not." She took a deep breath and let it out. "And I have heard that O'Halloran's herd is not subject to the same terror."

The Judge made a noise in his chest. "You think O'Halloran is behind the attacks on your herd?" he asked.

She looked at him, and Elm saw a bloom of light in her eyes that belied the strength radiating throughout her body. "God help me, I do," she said. "But I do not know how he manages such a feat."

6

Boots pounded on the porch, and a moment later, one of the hands burst into the sitting room. "Miss Van Horn, there's trouble," he announced in a rush. "Out past Tempter Creek."

"What sort of trouble?" Isadora asked.

"Rudy took a team out this morning to round up strays, and Deke just got back with a pair of heifers who're in sad shape. He says there's more of them out there, past the creek." The man paused, trying to catch his breath. "Gunshots, ma'am. They're far off, but we just heard 'em."

"Damn that man," Isadora said. She came away from the window like an enraged tiger, and her man took a step back even though he knew she wasn't going to lash out at him. "He's gone too far this time," she snapped. "I'm not going to let this pass un—"

"What are you going to do?" the Judge asked. His voice was quiet, but there was a tenor to it that cut to the quick.

"I'm going to respond in kind," she replied.

The Judge shook his head. "You can't do that."

"I'm not some little girl to be summarily dismissed," she snarled. "I'm in charge of this ranch. I am responsible for these men."

"I'm not suggesting you aren't," the Judge said. "But you can't go off half-cocked."

She glared at him, and it was clear in her gaze that she didn't understand how he could be so daft. "Does my uncle know?" she asked her man.

"Yes, Miss Van Horn," he replied, nodding vigorously.

"Ride with me," she said to the Judge. "Let me show you what this bastard is trying to do."

The Judge narrowed his eyes. "If this O'Halloran is responsible—and I'm just positing that possibility for the sake of our conversation here—do you think you're actually going to find him out there in the woods?"

"He wants my land, and since he can't get it by legal means, he's going to run me off."

"And what is his plan for accomplishing this feat?"

Isadora waved the Judge's question aside with a short stroke of her hand. "This is pointless talk," she said. "My men are in trouble."

Elm spoke up. "Aye, and what happens when you ride out there? Are you going to save them yourself or are you going to be putting yourself in harm's way?"

"Or while you are out chasing phantoms in the woods, perhaps another party is going to come here and put everything to the torch," the Judge said. "Which would, in fact, be a more effective and swift resolution to his conflict with you."

Isadora rocked on her heels slightly as she considered both options. "What am I supposed to do?" she asked. "My men are in danger. I can't not go to their aid."

"Someone should," the Judge said. He offered her a smile that was both kind and cold, and she shivered slightly at the sight of it. "But it shouldn't be you."

"Who then?"

"Stay here," the Judge said. "And I will stay with you. We can sit on the porch with a couple of glasses of this fine whisky. We'll have shotguns near at hand, like perfectly polite rural folk do. Elm will ride out with your uncle."

Isadora turned her attention to Elm. "And if they shoot at you?"

"Fortunately, I have some practice at shooting back," Elm said.

The party—Isadora's uncle Norwood, Elm, and a quartet of rough riders—went south to the edge of the forest, and then cut west, following the ragged line of the pasture fence. The fence dropped away as the forest thickened. Cattle were lazy, and they would roam where they could find food and water, and there was little of either among the trees. In the summer, when the sun baked the ground, the cattle would seek the shade beneath the trees, and the hands would have to keep a close eye on stragglers. But for now, the gentle slope of the hill was enough to keep the cattle in the valley.

They rode along a narrow track that was only wide enough for one rider, and the riders leaned over their saddles to keep from being plucked off their horses by overhanging branches. As they neared the top of the hill, gunshots echoed through the trees, and Norwood slapped his horse to make it run faster. The other hands followed suit, and Elm fell behind. His horse was blowing hard, and it wasn't accustomed to such a race along a rocky and uneven path. It would be a disaster if it tripped on a tree root or stepped wrong on loose rocks.

The woods parted, and Elm rode into a broad meadow; the sudden glare of the sun made him blink. A thin track of muddy water flowed off to his right, and there were several downed cattle near the creek. Norwood and his men had stopped riding. When Elm counted horses, he realized there was an additional animal without a rider.

The horse was grazing nonchalantly near the water, and it looked up as Norwood's horse approached. It didn't flinch as Norwood leaned over and grabbed its dangling reins.

"That's Rudy's horse," one of the other cowboys said as Elm joined the group.

"And where is Rudy?" Elm asked. He scanned the meadow for sign of the missing man.

"There's blood here," Norwood said, pointing at a dark stain on the horse's saddle and blanket.

"How many men went with Rudy?" Elm asked. "And one of them came back. What was his name?"

"Deke," a cowboy provided.

"Where are the other horses?" Elm asked.

A cowboy nudged his horse toward the downed cattle. "They've been shot," he said.

"Damn them," Norwood swore.

The cowboy near the creek gave a shout as he urged his horse through the shallow water. Elm followed, and he saw what had caught the man's attention. There was a body slumped near a fallen tree upstream a little ways.

The cowboy reached the body first, and he jumped down from his horse to inspect the fallen man. "It's Rudy," the cowboy announced as he lifted the man's head. "He's still alive."

Norwood grabbed a satchel as he slid off his horse. He splashed through the creek, racing to the wounded man. Elm got off his horse and splashed through the creek. He crouched next to Rudy and started his examination.

Rudy's eyelids fluttered and he twitched as Norwood poked at him. There was a lot of blood on his coat and pants, and when Norwood pulled at his shirt, he let out a loud groan.

Blood pulsed from a hole in Rudy's abdomen and Elm shook his head at the sight. Even if Norwood was a brilliant battle-field surgeon, there wasn't anything he could do to save Rudy. Elm had seen too many wounds like that. Belly shots went foul quickly, even if there was no bullet to take out. Rudy might last a day or two, but his final hours would be spent in feverish agony.

A rifle sounded in the distance, and for a moment, they all froze. Listening for an answering shot. None came, and Elm thought he heard the faint sound of raucous laughter—the sort of braying noise men make when they are inflicting torment on defenseless creatures.

Elm slid off his horse. "There's another man out there," he said. He grabbed the oilskin-wrapped parcel and the satchel of cartridges from his gear. "I'll bring him back."

Without waiting for a response from Norwood and the other riders, he jogged along the creek, following it for a hundred yards or so before he drifted into the trees. He moved quickly and quietly, threading his way through the sparse forest. He listened for sounds that would help him locate the missing cowboy and the men who were shooting at him.

He heard them before he saw them, and he slowed down, looking for a good vantage point. He spotted a moss-covered trunk of a fallen tree, the stump like a blunt thumb sticking up at the sky, and he knelt behind the stump, peering under the gnarled trunk of the dead tree. He had a broad field of view, and he soon spotted movement.

Elm put the oilskin bundle down, and without looking, undid the rawhide ties that kept the rifle wrapped. The Sharps rifle had been given to him by Company C's quartermaster shortly before the failed Union effort to take Fort Darling, replacing the old black powder musket he had been carrying since he had mustered with the rest of the young, untrained men. The Sharps had been through rain and mud and fire with him, and the walnut stock was smooth and polished. The barrel was not polished because a glint of sunlight off the metal would give away his position, and on more than one occasion, he had seen his targets first because they had not taken such precautions. The rifle carried no bayonet because Company C prided itself on never being that close to the enemy.

He took a moment to inspect the gun, and satisfied that the oilskin wrap had protected it, he laid the barrel across his left forearm, and dropped the breech with the lever. He fumbled with the strap on his satchel and got it open.

During the War, the rifle had used paper cartridges, but after the War, he had had the gun modified to take the new metal cartridges—the .50-70s. He grabbed a cartridge from the satchel and slipped it into the rifle. He closed the breech, but before he cocked the hammer back, he peered through the gap under the fallen tree. There, he thought, past those two oak trees.

The two trees leaned toward one another, forming a V-shape, and a man crouched behind the rightmost oak. He wore a coat but no hat, and he had a pistol in his hand. His face was shiny with sweat, and blood matted the side of his head. He peered furtively out from behind the tree, his eyes nervously scanning the forest.

He was hiding, and not from Elm.

A rifle sounded, and the man behind the tree flinched as wood splintered several inches above his head. He stuck his hand out and fired his pistol blindly.

Elm slowly crept to his left, peering around the other side of the moss-covered stump. The man behind the tree was the missing cowboy from the ranch, and he was being hunted by others. O'Halloran's men, if Miss Van Horn—Isadora—was correct. Elm lay still, like a lizard sunning itself on a rock, like a snake waiting for prey. Only his eyes moved, flicking back and forth as he scanned for the men with the rifles.

When a rifle fired again, he caught sight of a puff of white smoke about sixty yards away. He waited, listening for any sound that would tell him if the man was changing position. "Run, little mouse," someone yelled. "Run!"

He glanced back to his right, and caught a flash of motion as the ranch hand leapt from his hiding place. He was injured, because his gait was not fleet of foot, but more of a bouncing hobble. The man jerked and staggered for a few yards, and then tripped over a root and went down.

Elm heard two distinct voices as the riflemen laughed at the ranch hand's predicament. The ranch hand struggled to get up, whimpering as he put weight on his injured leg. He fired his pistol again, aiming at nothing. The man was in the grips of an all-consuming fear.

The riflemen were toying with the cowboy, like predators do with bloodied prey. Elm had watched coyotes play with field mice. A coyote would bite a mouse hard enough to bring blood and break a leg, and when the terrified mouse would try to crawl away, the coyote would pick it up and throw it. Then it would pounce again, snaring the mouse between its paws. The game would continue until the mouse died of fright or blood loss.

Elm brought his rifle forward until its stock rested against his shoulder.

Men weren't mice. They did not deserve to be the subject of such a sadistic game. Even during the War, he never shot a man who wasn't shooting back. While he had little desire to argue the nuances of the differences between the Confederacy and the Union, he knew well the reasons why men fought and died. During the War, life had been simple: follow orders; shoot at those who are shooting at you. Without the structure and discipline provided by the company of men who he fought with, he would have fallen to a life that would have been much shorter and nastier. A man made brutish by his lack of opportunities.

He had been given a choice, and he had taken it. Every man had a choice, and the effects of that choice were known only to God prior to that fateful moment. But afterward? Every man deserved what they got.

He rested the barrel of the Sharps rifle on a rounded hump of moss and peered down the sights. His breathing slowed as he squinted carefully, watching for some sign of movement in the trees. The men were going to move on the wounded cowboy. He cocked back the hammer on the rifle, and then lightly pulled the back trigger on the two-trigger assembly to set the rifle.

A flash of red caught his attention, and he shifted the barrel of the rifle to the left. He drew in a slow breath, held it for a second, and slipped his finger around the front trigger. When he saw movement again, he touched the trigger with a light caress.

The Sharps rifle sounded, and it made a much deeper noise than the report from the smaller rifles the men were using. About sixty yards away, a man was knocked back from the bush he had been hiding behind. His arms were flung wide, and there was a shocked expression on his face.

Choices, he thought, as his hands unconsciously lowered the breech on the rifle and removed the spent cartridge. *They made theirs, and I have made mine.*

He remembered the first time he had fired his rifle, during the Union march toward Yorktown. Most of the men in Company C had never fired their rifles at a target that might fire back, and they were apprehensive about being able to aim carefully enough while under duress. But it hadn't taken long for those jitters to vanish. By the end of the first reconnaissance ahead of the main army, all of the sharpshooters had killed at least one Confederate soldier. All of them were men who had now firmly chosen a side in the conflict between North and South.

While the remaining rifleman shouted at his companion, Elm risked a glance to his right. The ranch hand was standing dumbly in the open. He didn't understand what had just happened. *Move, you idiot*, Elm thought fiercely, *don't waste the opportunity you've just been given.*

That was all the time Elm spared for the cowboy. He had the other rifleman to deal with.

Blood had been spilt. There would be a war between the Van Horns and the O'Hallorans. He hadn't started it. He didn't want to be a party to finishing it. But he was in it now, and he was going to deal with it the way he always had. The way Company C always dealt with the enemy.

He slipped a second cartridge into his rifle and closed the breech.

Behind him, a twig snapped. Elm turned his head and caught sight of a man sneaking up behind him. He barely had a chance to register the presence of a knife before the man lunged at him.

7

ELM ROLLED TO HIS LEFT, WHIPPING HIS RIFLE AROUND. He pulled the trigger and the gun went off, spitting out a cloud of white smoke. He knew he wasn't going to hit his target, but the noise and smoke might give him a slim chance to avoid whoever was coming at him.

The noise of the Sharps rifle momentarily stunned Elm's attacker, but he recovered quickly and thrust his long-bladed knife at Elm. Elm brought his rifle up and got the barrel under the man's outstretched hand. The blade went past Elm's head and thunked into the stump behind him. The man's momentum carried him into Elm, and Elm grunted from the impact.

The man grinned, a feral display of bad teeth, and his breath stank of whisky. His face was long and his nose was canted to the left. A thin scar ran along the base of his hair, arcing down the side of his head.

"Long gun ain't much good in a knife fight," the man laughed. He jerked the knife free of the stump, and before he could swipe the blade down, Elm surged forward. He shoved the man back with his shoulder and the rifle. They rolled away from the stump, and the man swung the knife wildly. Elm jerked his head back and felt a tiny breeze as the blade swept past his face.

The man stopped his backward motion and fell into a lazy crouch. He held his knife ready before him.

Elm rolled off his hip and got his feet under him. He held his rifle out, the stock wedged against his side. He had no bayonet, but the long barrel would keep some distance between them.

"You gonna poke me with that?" the man asked, gesturing at the rifle with his knife.

Elm's response was to work the lever and drop the breech of the rifle. Without taking his eyes off the grinning man, he plucked the spent cartridge out of the rifle and let it fall from his fingers.

The man's eyes narrowed, and his grip on the knife tightened.

Elm felt across the ground near him, and his fingers touched the softness of the oilskin wrap. He tried to remember the location of the satchel of cartridges. It had been in easy reach when he had been lying down, which meant it lay—where was it? He let his fingers drift across the ground.

The man ran his thick tongue along his lower lip. His eyes watched Elm's movements, and his breathing was quick and shallow. He was alert to what Elm was doing, but he didn't seem particularly concerned.

Elm's fingers bumped against the rough leather of the cartridge satchel.

A pistol sounded behind Elm, and both he and the knife-wielder started from the sudden noise. By the time a rifle shot rang out in response, the moment of surprise had passed, and both men were in motion; Elm tugged at the satchel, digging for another cartridge; the knife-wielder sprang forward, leading with the knife.

Elm leaned forward, pushing the barrel of his gun. The man had to adjust his attack or he was going to risk running into the end of Elm's gun. Elm's fingers fumbled for a cartridge. He almost had it.

The man grabbed the barrel of Elm's gun and yanked it down. As he did, he flicked the end of his knife up and over, and the glitter of sunlight reflecting off the blade caught Elm's eye. He flinched, and when he tried to muscle the gun between them, the man brought the knife down in a vicious arc. The blade slicked through the thick fabric of Elm's coat. A life of fire opened across his chest, and he gasped sharply.

His left hand closed tightly, an automatic reaction to the sudden pain, and he felt something hard against his palm.

The man turned his wrist and brought the knife back up, and Elm fell back, levering the gun up. The barrel caught under the knife-wielder's arm, and spoiled his attack. The knife scraped noisily off the metal of the lever, and Elm let go of the rifle for a second and threw a punch at the man. There wasn't much force behind his blow, and it probably hurt his hand more than it hurt his assailant, but it surprised the knife-wielder. Elm dropped his hand to the butt of his rifle and shoved the weapon down, hoping that the knife was still caught underneath. The man's arm went down and his torso leaned in, and Elm snapped his head forward, catching the man square in the face.

They separated. There was blood on the knife-wielder's lips, and Elm felt blood running down his chest from the knife cut. His breath was hot in his throat, and old snakes he had thought long buried were crawling out of dark holes deep in his belly. An old ache for violence. For doing what was necessary for survival.

They had switched positions, and now it was the knife wielder who crouched beside the log. Elm got his feet under him, and braced his rifle against his knee. The breech was still open.

The knife wielder glanced down and looked at Elm's satchel of cartridges. He nudged it with his other hand, and then smiled—a mouth full of crooked teeth. "It's just a stick," he said, waving the tip of his knife at the rifle in Elm's hand. "Mine is sharper."

Elm held up his left hand, his fingers still clenched in a fist. "Mine hits harder," he said. He opened his hand and thrust the cartridge he was carrying into his rifle. In a smooth motion, he brought up the rifle as he closed the breech. The knife-wielder opened his mouth, a yell rising in his throat.

But Elm wasn't aiming at him. He was aiming at the man standing in the open, beyond the stump. It was the other rifleman, who had approached while the two men were fighting. The rifleman was aiming his weapon in their direction, waiting for a clear shot at Elm.

Elm pulled both triggers on the Sharps rifle, and it boomed loudly. The other rifle answered, a puff of smoke rising from it, and then the rifleman was knocked down by the force of the bullet from the Sharps rifle.

The rifleman's aim was good, though, and Elm grunted as something struck him in the shoulder. There was a ragged hole in the sleeve of his coat, and he smelled smoke and blood. Before he could do more than realize he had been hit, the knife-wielder attacked again.

Elm tried to get his arm to move, but it wasn't working right. Unable to shift the rifle quickly enough, he threw it at his attacker instead, freeing his hands. The knife-wielder knocked his rifle aside with a snarl, and lunged at Elm. Elm clumsily blocked the attack with his lazy arm, bringing him close to the other man. He made a rough grab with his left hand and got his fingers around the man's wrist.

They struggled with the knife. The man was stronger than he looked, and he forced Elm to take several steps back. Elm's boot heel snagged on a root, and he hesitated for a second, trying to find his balance. The man surged against him, twisting his wrist and bringing the knife up. Elm had no choice but to fall back, and the man fell with him. Elm turned his body as he stumbled, and he landed on his side with the man on top of him. The knife missed his chest, but it went through the lapel of his coat and stuck in the ground.

He was pinned! Like a butterfly mounted for display in a naturalist's curiosity cabinet.

As he struggled to pull away from the knife, his assailant hit him twice in the face. The world spun, and Elm tasted blood in his mouth. He flailed wildly, trying to grab the man's hands or coat, but the man got off him.

The man retreated out of reach and leaned over, his hands on his knees. He watched Elm struggle, huffing and puffing, and as Elm reached for the handle of the knife, he darted forward and went to kick Elm in the ribs. Elm saw it coming and gave up on the knife, dropping his arms and shoulders in an effort to protect himself.

The man tried to kick him again, and then danced away when Elm tried to grab his boot. "Naughty, naughty," he cackled. He hocked up a glob of saliva and blood and launched it at Elm.

Elm squirmed on the ground, trying to reach his own knife, which was in a leather sheath at the small of his back. It was positioned for a right-hand draw; he couldn't twist his left arm enough to reach the thin handle.

The man watched him struggle, manic glee written across his face. "Whatcha lookin' for?" he asked. He raised his fists, grinning as he thought about how he was going to pummel Elm. He noticed the blood on the knuckles of his right hand, and the light in his eyes got brighter. He lifted the hand to his mouth, and his tongue darted out. Tasting the blood.

"I'm gonna—"

That was as far as he got before he was interrupted by the loud sound of a hammer being cocked back on a pistol. The man froze, and when nothing happened, he slowly looked to his right.

The cowboy from Van Horn's ranch was standing a few yards away. He was in sorrier shape than Elm, but he had a gun in his hand. It was cocked and pointed at the knife-wielder. The cowboy's face was white with tension and his hand only trembled a little bit.

The knife-wielder went cross-eyed as he focused on the tip of the pistol. "You think you've got—"

The cowboy pulled the trigger, and the hammer came down. The knife-wielder flinched. And then blinked.

The gun didn't fire.

Tears streamed down the cowboy's face, and his hand trembled even more. He didn't know what to do.

The gun was empty.

The knife-wielder threw back his head and laughed. "I looked that bitch in the eye," he crowed. "Death was right there, and she don't want me. She likes the way I do her work for her." He grinned at the shaking cowboy. "And when I'm done with this one down here, I'm going to gut you goo—"

Elm yanked the knife out of the ground. He rolled over and brought the blade down, jamming it through the top of the knife-wielder's boot.

The man's words turned into a wordless howl of pain.

Elm crawled to his rifle, and using it as a brace, he levered himself to his feet. Holding the weapon loosely in his hands, he looked over at the furious knife-wielder. The man's face was red, and the muscles in his neck tensed and jumped as he twitched. Every motion made the knife cut him more.

Elm looked over at the shaking cowboy. "You got any more bullets for that gun?" he asked.

The cowboy shook his head, the gun dangling from his hand.

Elm looked around for his satchel of cartridges. He spotted them near the moss-covered stump. Without looking down at what his hands were doing, he dropped the breech on his rifle and plucked out the spent cartridge. "I have more bullets," he said. "You want to try it again?"

With an agonized yell, the man reached down and pulled the knife out of his boot. His face was streaked with sweat and his lips were wet with spit. Elm readied himself for another attack, but the knife-wielder turned and fled instead, howling and crying with each step.

By the time Elm got to his satchel and loaded another cartridge into his rifle, the knife-wielder was gone.

The rifleman who had taken a shot at Elm and the cowboy was sitting on the ground, holding his stomach and rocking back and forth. A low and steady whine issued from his lips. Eventually, the man realized Elm was standing nearby, and his head came up sluggishly. His eyes were clouded with pain. He remembered the rifle he had been carrying, and he cast about for it, and it took him a few moments to realize that it was in Elm's hands.

When the man's attention came back to Elm, Elm worked the lever on the rifle, ejecting the spent cartridge and loading another.

The rifleman's lips moved, but no words came out.

"Were you the one who shot that cowboy in the gut?" Elm asked.

The rifleman managed to find his voice. "Wha—wha—what?" he croaked.

Elm cocked back the hammer on the rifle. "Down by the creek," he said. "Along with those cows. You kill them too?"

Tears streaked through the dirt and blood on the rifleman's face. "It wasn't me," he whined.

"Who, then?" Elm asked.

"T-t-t-tommy," the man stuttered.

"Tommy O'Halloran," the cowboy said. He had come up behind Elm. His face was pale, and he swayed a bit as he tried to stand steady.

"He the one who ran off?" Elm asked.

The cowboy nodded.

Elm looked down at the rifleman. "Tommy left you here to die," he said.

"No, no, no," the rifleman moaned.

Elm looked up at the sky. The sun was bright and warm on his face. In the distance, he heard crows cawing.

He had read that ancient Vikings believed winged women in shining armor would carry them off the battlefield when they died. They would be taken to a place called Valhalla where they could eat and drink and tell stories of their valor for all eternity. Elm couldn't imagine drinking and reminiscing with all the men who had died by his hand. Why would anyone want to relive that horror again and again?

He had never seen any winged angels on the battlefield. The only thing with wings were the crows, and their raucous cries sounded like the laughter of the damned.

"*Deus misereatur tu*," Elm said softly to the dying rifleman. *God have mercy on you.*

He pulled the trigger.

Et animam tuam ad Deus, he thought after the echo of the rifle's report had fled. *And your soul to God.*

The crows remained. As they always did.

8

ELM JERKED UPRIGHT IN THE METAL WASHTUB WHEN SOMEONE knocked on the door of the narrow room, and tepid water sloshed out of the tub. He had dozed off, and he struggled to reconcile his current location—and state of undress—with recent memories of the fight in the woods.

"Mr. Stonebrook?" Isadora knocked lightly on the door again.

"Yes?" He ran a hand over his face, rinsing off an imagined layer of grit and sleep. His face and chest were sore from his injuries.

"Are you finished?" Isadora asked. "I'd like to talk."

A lantern on a nearby bench offered the only illumination, and Elm glanced about for some manner of towel or robe. His clothes were strewn on the floor between the tub and the door, and his boots were in the corner, laying on their side. "Just a moment," he called out. "I'll be . . ."

There was no towel or robe. Short of putting his dirty and bloody clothes back on, he had no way to cover himself. The water in the tub was murky—most likely from the blood and dirt that had come off his body—and the cut on his chest was an angry red line. The wound in his arm was a mere scratch in comparison—the bullet from the rifle had gone through his coat and creased the flesh off his bicep.

The latch clacked, and the door swung open. Isadora stepped into the room, and he thrashed in the tub for a second, trying to figure out a way to cover himself. She closed the door behind her and leaned against it. There was a light smile on her face as she waited for him to settle down.

"I have some towels and clothes," she said, indicating the bundle in her arms. "I hope they are sufficient." She nodded toward the bench beside the tub. "May I?"

Elm nodded as he drew up his knees and scooted his rear along the bottom of the tub. He let his hands rest on his body. Hopefully that would be enough to make him decent.

Isadora didn't even glance at him as she put the bundle on the floor within easy reach of the tub. She had traded in the demin jacket and pants she had been wearing earlier for a simple cotton dress with narrow sleeves and an open collar. Her hair was still in a braid, but some strands were now loose about her forehead. Her shoulders slumped as she sat on the bench, the strain of the day showing its weight on her, but there was a merry light in her eyes as she looked at him.

"I've seen my share of naked men, Mr. Stonebrook," she said. "I am familiar with the male anatomy."

"Such familiarity leads to other familiarity is my understanding," Elm said, and his comment brought a slight flush to Isadora's cheeks. "And you should call me Elm," he said, pretending as if he hadn't noticed the change in her demeanor.

"Yes, that's right. Elm. We are already familiar," she said, and it was Elm's turn to blush. Her hands brushed at her dress, and Elm was not unaware of the shape of her breasts beneath the cotton fabric.

"We lost two heifers and a steer," she said. "And Rudy, too." She sighed and her hands twisted in her lap. "You killed two of them in the woods."

"I did," Elm admitted.

"It's not a fair trade," she said.

"For you or them?"

A hard laugh slipped out of her mouth before she could stop it. "He finally went too far," she said quietly. "And now that blood has been shed, more will follow."

"It usually does," Elm said.

She looked at him. "You fought in the War, didn't you?" she asked.

"I did."

"Pete says you shot one of them in cold blood. Says you spoke some strange words before you did. He said it sounded like preacher talk."

Elm nodded. "Yes, ma'am, I suppose it was."

"Why?"

He looked at her, not quite understanding the question. "If a horse were to break a leg, would you not put it out of its misery?"

"A man is not a horse."

Elm shrugged. "Suffering is suffering. It doesn't matter if it is in a man or an animal. We should treat it with the same decency."

"He could have survived."

"Norwood thought the same about Rudy when we first found him," he said, and she blinked at the tone of his voice.

"So it was vengeance?"

"No, ma'am. Vengeance never solves anything."

She blew out a lungful of air. "I doubt Bart O'Halloran will be of the same opinion."

Elm dragged his hand through the water in the tub. He didn't say anything. He knew what she was thinking, and it was better if he let her work through all the same thoughts he already had.

"His men were on my land," she said. "They shot at my herd. They shot my man."

"They did," he said.

"Two heifers. One steer. One man. One *good* man."

"That is my accounting too."

"I sent men out to bring those dead cows back. I want them here when the sheriff comes. I want him to know that I was protecting my property. My land."

"As is your right," Elm said.

She brought her gaze back to him. "Things are going to get worse," she said.

"A worsening," he said.

She wrinkled her nose. "A what?"

"You said matters were going to get worse," he said. "Hence: a worsening."

"Is that . . . I don't think that is even a word," she said.

He moved his hands through the water. "It might be. It should be, don't you think?"

"I think you are more well read than you let on, Elm."

"Because I think worsening is a word?"

"No, I saw the way you looked at the bookcase in the sitting room earlier today. That was my schoolhouse. That was all the learning I ever got. But you, you merely glanced at the books. Not dismissively—like you didn't care—but more like you had passing curiosity at them, but no more. As if you were already familiar with all of them."

"I was distracted."

"Were you now?" she asked. She leaned toward him. Her shoulders were no longer slumped with exhaustion.

"Yes, ma'am," he said. He looked at her, and she looked back. His hands moved idly in the water, no longer attempting to cover himself.

Without breaking eye contact, she slid off the bench and knelt beside the tub. "What is this?" she asked, pointing at the tattoo on the left side of his chest. "Some sort of native sign?"

"No," he said. "It's not."

"Is it a brand? I think I've seen something like it on a cow's back end before."

"I doubt you have," he said, admiring the way the light from the lantern lit up her eyes.

"Are you going to tell me what it is?"

"No," he said.

She stared at him, searching his eyes for a hint of the secrets she was sure were hidden within him. She didn't find what she was looking for, and her gaze dropped to the wound on his chest. "We should dress this," she said. She brushed a finger lightly along his chest, making him shiver. "And that one too." She let her finger trail up his arm to his shoulder. "And there's some dirt here still," she said as her finger traced across his collarbone and up to his jaw.

"My hands are wet," he said. "I might need some help."

"I didn't want to presume, but I thought you might," she said. She leaned back, reaching for the pile of clothing. Her dress was caught under her knees, and the motion stretched the fabric tight along her body. He admired her shape, outlined by the cloth, and when she turned back with a long strip of cloth in her hands, he quickly dropped his eyes so as to not be caught staring.

Isadora motioned for him to sit up, and when he did so, she went to wrap the cloth around his chest. Her face was close to his chest as she reached around his body, and he noticed she smelled like lilacs.

"Sit back," she said when she finished wrapping his chest. "Let me look at your face."

He slid back on his rump until his spine was pressed against the side of the tub, and he raised his face toward the ceiling.

She wet another piece of cloth in the water and rubbed it gently across his cheek. She was daubing at him like she was blotting water from a china vase, and he gently grabbed her wrist and moved her hand more firmly against his face. "I won't break," he said.

Her eyes examined his face. "No, I don't suppose you will," she said, her voice not much more than a throaty whisper. When she applied the cloth again, her efforts were much more robust, and he set his mouth in a hard line against the pain that flared in his cheek.

He squirmed a bit in the tub, but that was more in reaction to sensations he was feeling in other parts of his body. Sensations that said he didn't mind her touch. Not in the slightest.

How long has it been? The thought presented itself in his head, and he rudely pushed it aside.

"That's much better," she said when she finished. "I don't think we'll need to put a dressing on it. We certainly don't need to . . ." She made a motion of wrapping cloth around an object.

"That would be awkward," he said.

She nodded, a shy smile curling her lips. "We wouldn't want anything to be awkward, would we?"

He was painfully aware of how close she was: her body pressed against the tub, her hand holding the dirty cloth over the water. "No, we wouldn't," he said. His throat was suddenly dry.

She dipped the cloth in the tub and squished it back and forth. Her teeth worried her lower lip as she squeezed excess water out of the cloth. The water made ripples in the now-cold water of the tub. "Can you swim?" she asked. Her eyes were bright with a light that was both inquisitive and haunted.

"Pardon?"

"Do you know how to swim?" she asked again.

Elm furrowed his brow. "No," he said. "I don't."

She carefully spread the cloth out on the surface of the water. When she let go, the cloth floated for a second and then it started to sink. They both watched as it settled on a portion of Elm's anatomy. "Swimming keeps you from sinking," she explained, a mischievous smile touching her lips.

"And I thank you for that observation," Elm said. His groin was now covered by the cloth, which only served to highlight the erect shape down there.

She leaned over the edge of the tub and gave him a quick kiss on the cheek, right where she had burnished his face clean. "Thank you," she said.

And then, as if suddenly embarrassed by her actions, Isadora rushed out of the room, leaving Elm much cleaner but slightly puzzled at what had just happened.

After drying himself off and dressing in the borrowed clothes, Elm went downstairs to the large kitchen at the back of the ranch house. There, a slight woman with grey hair offered him a plate of warm biscuits and hash. He nodded at her and sat down at the sturdy table. He had a solid appetite, and he dug into the food with gusto, pausing only briefly when the old woman put a mug of steaming coffee on the table near his hand. "Thank you," he mumbled around a mouthful of food.

"You are welcome, Mr. Stonebrook," the woman said.

"Elm," he said. "Call me 'Elm.'"

She inclined her head. "I'm Mrs. Walphin," she said. "Norwood is my husband," she explained.

"Miss Isadora said she came out here with her father after her mother passed," Elm said. "She and her sister. They were all alone in this house until you arrived, weren't they?"

Mrs. Walphin frowned. "Girls shouldn't grow up alone."

"What about you and Norwood—Mr. Walphin? Do you have any kids?"

"No," she said. Her gaze softened and she looked out the windows.

"What about Miss Isadora's sister?" Elm asked, changing the subject. "She isn't here any more, is she?"

"No, she lives in St. Louis now. Married a broker. Has three children."

"You ever see them?"

Mrs. Walphin tapped her fingers against the table. "Eat up," she said. "No sense in letting it get cold."

"Yes, ma'am," Elm said, and he tucked back into the food. While he was curious to know more about the Van Horn family, now was not the time to ask rude questions. While it was unusual for a woman to be running a ranch—especially when someone like Norwood was still around—it wasn't impossible, and Miss Isadora clearly had the respect of the hands. The War had changed many things about the states—both North and South—and not just because the slaves had been freed. Many didn't care for the elevation of women to roles traditionally reserved for men, but Elm had seen time and again that a woman was just as capable as a man in riding a horse, shooting a gun, and running a business. This sort of emancipation was sure nearly as threatening as the freedom of the slaves to many in the South, but to Elm, it all seemed like a natural progression—the right person finding their way into the right job. Much like having the right tool. Or the right gun.

The door at the back of the kitchen opened, and the Judge's tall frame squeezed into the kitchen. He doffed his hat and gave Mrs. Walphin a broad smile. "Perhaps I might trouble you for a cup of coffee."

"You might," she replied. She got a cup down from the cupboard as he sat down at the table with Elm. She filled the cup from the pot on the stove and put it in front of him.

He made a production of sipping the coffee and commenting on how hot and fresh it was.

Mrs. Walphin wiped her hands on her apron and nodded toward the pot on the stove. "There's more when that cup is gone," she said. She nodded at Elm, offering him a kind smile, and then she bustled out of the kitchen, leaving them to sit and sip.

Elm alternated between large swallows of coffee and forkfuls of food, and the Judge watched him eat.

"Did you have a nice bath?" the Judge asked after awhile. "Good and relaxing?"

"I did," Elm said. "And it was."

"Get all the dirt out from under your nails?"

"And off my soul," Elm said. "Though it took a little scrubbing."

"I would hope so," the Judge said. He took a sip from his cup. "You made a mess of things out there," he said.

Elm paused, his fork poised over his plate. He frowned at the Judge, wondering if the other man was being particularly obtuse or just his usual ornery self.

"It was good of you to let them tear you up a bit, though," the Judge said. "It'll make it easier to convince local law enforcement you acted honorably and in your own defense."

"Well, those were the thoughts rolling around my head while the guy with the knife tried to gut me," Elm drawled. He moved the last few bites around on his plate with his fork.

"Tommy O'Halloran," the Judge said.

"That's what I hear."

"It's a good thing you didn't kill him."

"Well, not for a lack—" Elm started.

The Judge shook his head. "Don't say it."

Elm grunted and shoveled up the last two bites.

The Judge blew out his cheeks and sipped from his cup again.

"You want to tell me about what happened in Baton Rouge?" Elm asked.

"No," the Judge said.

"I could ask her."

"You could," the Judge admitted.

"Might be better if you told me."

"It won't."

"She's going to cast you in a poor light."

"And she should."

"It might influence my opinion of you."

The Judge looked closely at Elm. "I doubt that," he said.

Elm gave him a fierce grin. "I don't know why you are pretending to be so bent out of shape," he said. "We're going to help her."

The Judge raised an eyebrow. "We are?"

Elm indicated the kitchen with his fork. "We wouldn't be lolling around here, sipping coffee and passing the time, if we weren't staying."

"Maybe I like the coffee."

Elm tapped the Judge's cup with his fork. "It's fine coffee, but it ain't whisky," he said.

"No, it isn't," the Judge replied. He glanced at the dregs in his cup, his beard twitching as he frowned. "Don't hurt her," he said.

"No," Elm said. "I'm not like you in that regard."

The Judge blinked in surprise and sat back in his chair. He stared at Elm for a moment, his fingers forcefully turning the cup in his hands. "Well," he said, finally, his voice cold and steady. "I'm glad we got that sorted out."

He pushed his chair back and stood up. He adjusted his vest and ran his hands through his beard. "Sheriff will be here later," he said gruffly. "It's best if you stay out of sight."

"I know," Elm said.

"This matter is going to get a lot worse."

"I know," Elm said. "A worsening."

"A what? A *worsening*?"

"Yeah," Elm said, looking up at the judge. "Matters get *worse*. The situation has *worsened*. Hence, a—"

"A *worsening*." The Judge shook his head. "What in all the—? Lad, there are times when I cannot fathom the education you received."

"It's all right," Elm said. "I cannot always fathom the world in quite the same way you do either."

The Judge rubbed several of his fingers together. "A *worsening*," he said quietly. "We have the same assessment of the situation, at least."

"Aye," Elm said. "We do."

9

BITTER'S SHERIFF WAS A BROAD-SHOULDERED MAN WITH A HEAVY gut and a big hat. He looked uncomfortable on his horse, and his horse looked less than thrilled to have had to carry the man so far out of town. Two other men accompanied the sheriff, and both had silver stars pinned on their jackets as well. Deputies. One was a young man with a pale dusting of hair on his cheeks and a perpetually bewildered look in his eyes; the other deputy slouched in his saddle—*such is the role model he has before him,* the Judge thought. The only thing about him that showed any life was the way his mouth worked on a thin piece of wood.

The dog had alerted the ranch to the approach of the law, and the Judge, Isadora, and Norwood met them out in front of the main house. A handful of cowboys lingered nearby. Rudy had been well liked by the men, and they wanted to know what was to be done about avenging their fellow ranch hand.

"Afternoon, Miss Van Horn," the sheriff said as he brought his horse to a stop. The Judge got a look at the man's sidearm. His holster was strapped to his thigh with a rawhide strand run through the bottom of the leather shape. The handle of his pistol was cherrywood, and polished to a fine shine. A dandy's gun, the Judge thought. The sort of ornamental nonsense meant to impress the locals who had elected this man. The Judge was willing to bet a gold eagle the sheriff hadn't fired his pistol at anything more threatening than an empty bottle.

"Sheriff Taggert," Isadora replied. "What brings you out to my ranch so late in the day?"

"I understand there's been some trouble."

She glanced at the two deputies, taking her time, before she returned her attention to the sheriff. "I've lost a few head," she said. "And one of my men."

The sheriff wrinkled his nose, which made his broad mustache twitch. He glared at the Judge, pretending to take note of the man for the first time. "Do I know you, sir?" the sheriff asked.

The Judge shook his head. "While I would be delighted to hear that my reputation has preceded me, I suspect that is not the case."

The deputy with the toothpick stirred, struck by a passing quirk of curiosity, and he raised his eyes and examined the Judge.

"Let's just consider me an old friend of the family," the Judge added.

That was not what the deputy wanted to hear, and his attention wandered away. The sheriff waited a little longer for the Judge to provide more information, and then he frowned when he realized he wasn't going to get anything more. "Why don't you tell me what happened," he said to Isadora.

"Why don't you tell me what prompted you to pay me a visit," Isadora countered.

The sheriff shifted in his saddle. "Now, Mrs. Mulbridge . . ." he started. "Let's not take that tone . . ."

Isadora gave the Judge a look he knew well—if not from her, then from every woman who had ever suffered such conde-scension from a man. He lifted his shoulders, as if to offer an apology for his sex's brutish behavior, but he knew such a gesture was far from atoning for such nonsense.

"Sheriff Taggert, you are on my land," Isadora said. "As I have yet to invite you and your men to come down from your horses and partake of my hospitality, perhaps you might reconsider your tone, sir."

"Now, look, Mrs—"

"That is 'Miss Van Horn' to you," she corrected him.

He flushed and sat up straighter in his saddle. "Young woman, you are a widow, and it is proper to address—"

"I will not be defined by the lack of a man in my life," she snapped. "I am the sole owner and operator of this ranch, and you will afford me the respect such a position entitles me to, sir."

Sheriff Taggert flushed further. In an effort to distance himself from his embarrassment, he removed his hat and slapped the dust from its brim. The wide-eyed deputy's eyes got wider, and the lazy deputy continued to gnaw on his toothpick with well-practiced indifference. *They are not unlike a pair of cattle,* the Judge decided, and immediately realized he was being unfair to all bovines everywhere.

"Missus—Miss Van Horn," the sheriff said. "Some men have been killed today. And it's my job as the duly elected—"

"Who told you about these men?" Isadora interrupted.

"I don't see the importance of such details," the sheriff said. "Crimes have been committed, and—"

"She has the right to know her accuser." It was the Judge's turn to interrupt.

The sheriff looked down at him. "Does she now?"

"She does," the Judge said. "Guaranteed by the Constitution of these United States as well as the statutes of the fine state of Missouri. All of which are quite explicit in their rendering."

The sheriff narrowed his eyes at the Judge. "Explicit," he said.

"Written out in plain language that a layman can understand," the Judge said.

"I know what the word means," the sheriff said petulantly.

"I assumed so," the Judge said. He pointed at the wide-eyed deputy. "I was just clarifying for that young man there, who appears rather overwhelmed by the verbosity of our discourse."

"Verbosity?" The sheriff looked at Isadora, his mustache bristling with annoyance.

She shrugged. "He's just getting started."

The sheriff jammed his hat back on his head. "Miss Van Horn. You will show me these men who have been killed—"

"No," she said.

"What?" The sheriff looked around in disbelief. "I'm the sheriff. I am the law. And—"

"And you're Bart O'Halloran's lap dog," Isadora said.

The sheriff sputtered for a few seconds before he managed to form words. "Look here, young lady. That is an outrageous accusation. I am the law. How dare you speak to me like that."

"I've lost three head of cattle and a man of mine has been murdered," Isadora said. "Why have you not shown any interest in those crimes? Is it because Bart O'Halloran forget to mention those details when he sent you scurrying to harass me?"

"Mr. O'Halloran is an upstanding member of this community. His contributions to the welfare of the people—"

"Do you see what I have to put up with?" Isadora said to the Judge.

"Corruption at the highest level," the Judge noted, shaking his head. "It happens all too often in communities that fail to properly police their own. I'm sure you can find someone in the Governor's office who will listen to your story."

"St. Louis?" She raised an eyebrow. "That's quite a ride."

"I can go this very afternoon," the Judge offered.

She looked at the sheriff. "No, it can wait until morning," she said. "That'll give everyone a chance to calm down."

The sheriff looked like he had swallowed a bony piece of fish, and it was stuck in his throat.

"Good afternoon, Sheriff Taggert," she said. She offered him a cold smile. "Now, get off my land."

She turned and walked back to the house. The hands who had been standing nearby looked at one another, unsure of whether they were supposed to stick around or if all the excitement was over. Eventually, they decided they could leave too, and they dispersed, leaving the Judge alone with the sheriff and his deputies.

The Judge ran his tongue along the inside of his lower lip. "That didn't go like you thought it would, did it?" he said.

The sheriff's face was red and his breathing was fast and shallow. The Judge was worried that the man might pass out, and he snuck a glance at the pair of deputies. Neither was in any position to break the man's fall should he lose his senses.

It would be a shame if such a thing happened, the Judge thought. "You be sure to tell Mr. O'Halloran the part where she sent you scurrying off with your tail between your legs," he said.

"I am not scurrying," the sheriff exploded. He shook a finger at the Judge, and his fury was evident in how the motion made his whole body quiver.

"No, you are correct. I misspoke." The Judge inclined his head a fraction. "It will be your horse that scurries. You'll be flogging it dearly."

"I—I am the sheriff of this town. I am the law."

"You've said that several times now, as if I am supposed to be cowed, but I'll have you know that I've been practicing law since before you dropped out of your mother and hit your head on the floor, so you're going to have to work a little harder to impress me."

"She . . . she impugned me," the sheriff hissed, jabbing a finger toward the house.

"She asked you a simple question, and you never answered it," the Judge said. "You brought such cogent analysis of your character upon yourself."

"Those men . . . those men who were shot—"

"You mean, Rudy—her foreman?" The Judge shook his head. "The man was gut shot, I hear. Left to die. What a terrible way to spend your last few hours on this earth. Who would do that to a man?"

The sheriff frowned. "No, I meant—"

"Oh, you're talking about the two men who Tommy O'Halloran abandoned in the woods?"

"What?"

"Mr. O'Halloran didn't tell you?"

"No, I—Tommy? That's not what I—"

"Now I'm not one to tell you—no, wait, I am—but you should really get your facts straight before you go out lawing," the Judge said. "Those stars are awfully shiny and all, but they aren't worth a jug of horse piss if you aren't acting lawfully. Which any lawyer in this hick town will tell you, if you can find one. Or you could ask the opinion of a duly recognized circuit court judge of the United States." He smiled at the sheriff. "How fortunate for you that you are in the presence of such an august personage."

The sheriff jerked the reins of his horse, and the beast snorted at the sudden pull at its bridle. With a wordless shout, the sheriff whacked his mount on the rump with his hand, and the horse jumped forward. The Judge stepped back, giving the animal ample room, and he smiled and waved at the deputies as they quickly pulled their mounts around. They rode after the sheriff, who was kicking his horse into a gallop.

"*Sapientiam atque doctrinam stulti descpiciunt,*" the Judge said, quoting Proverbs. Fools were always wary of wisdom and instruction, much to their eternal dismay.

The barn contained stalls for a dozen horses, a wide loft, and a narrow room for tack and smithy tools. Elm stood inside the high doors, and inhaled the smell of dry hay, horse shit, polish, and charred bone. Much had changed across the states in the wake of the War, as both sides struggled to come to terms with what they had lost: the death of so many sons, the death of Lincoln, the freeing of the slaves, the utter devastation of many cities and communities. Many read President Grant's re-election as a sign that some normalcy was returning to the country. Grant was a familiar face, and while some might not like his face, there was comfort, nonetheless, in such familiarity.

Not unlike the smell of a barn, which was always the same and always comforting.

Elm's horse was out in the paddock behind the barn, and even though the beast had been fed and watered, it still nosed at the ground along the fence, looking for fresh grass. The Judge's horse was cropping along the far fence.

After finishing his meal, Elm had wandered out the back door of the kitchen and across the yard to the barn. He assumed his saddle and tack were stored there, and he figured he might as well check to be sure. The barn would also be a good place for him to remain out of sight while the sheriff visited.

There was a black mare in the nearest stall, and she approached the gate as he wandered over. She was a beautiful horse, and he suspected she belonged to Isadora. For a moment, he imagined horse and rider, black mane and black hair streaming in the wild, and then he pushed the image aside.

He wandered farther into the barn and spotted Purnell and another man in the tack room. The two men broke off their conversation as Elm approached. "I was looking for my gear," Elm explained.

"It's all there," Purnell said. He nodded toward the wall beyond him, and Elm saw his saddle and bags piled atop one another. Propped next to the saddle was the long shape of his oilskin-wrapped rifle.

"I'm obliged for your care," he said. He stuck out his hand to the man he didn't know. "Elmore Stonebrook," he said.

"Freddie Varrett," the young man said. He was wearing a coat a size too big for him, and his mustache looked like it needed a few more years before it was more than a scattering of dirt over his upper lip. His grip was solid, though.

"And you're Purnell, right?" Elm offered his hand to the other man. "We met in town."

"We did," Purnell said.

"Nice to meet both of you. You can call me Elm."

Everyone said each other's name, completing the slightly awkward round of introductions, and then they lapsed into a more awkward silence.

"So, what do you do here, Freddie?" Elm asked.

"I, uh, ride the herd, mostly."

"You like that?" Elm asked.

"Ah, yeah, sure. I like it well enough."

"That's good. What about you, Purnell?"

"What about me?"

"You like what you do for Miss Isa—Miss Van Horn?"

Purnell narrowed his eyes. "Sure," he said.

"What about your friend? What was his name? Benjee. What about Benjee?"

"What about him?"

"What's he do around here?"

"Miss Van Horn isn't looking to take on new hands right now," Purnell said.

"Oh, you think I'm looking for a job?" Elm was surprised by Purnell's statement, though it explained the other man's taciturn reaction to his questions.

Purnell and Freddie looked at one another, and it was Freddie who broke first. He looked down at the floor and scuffed the dirt with the tip of his boot. "Naw, we just figured . . . what you did for Pete—" His gaze darted toward the long shape of Elm's rifle.

"The Judge and I are just passing through," Elm said. He looked at Purnell. "We came and heard Miss Van Horn's proposition—like you asked us to. That's it."

Purnell frowned. "There's going to be a reckoning," he said. "For what you done."

"I fear that is likely to be the case."

"It's gonna come down on us," Purnell said. "Whether you are here or not."

"I guess we should stick around then," Elm said. He waved a hand toward the ceiling of the barn. "Is there a place where I can bunk down. Upstairs?" He didn't mention the bunk house. There was space there, but he didn't want to exacerbate the situation with the men by taking over any space that had been Rudy's.

Freddie let out a brief snort. "You're staying at the main house," he said.

"Am I?" Elm leaned forward and dropped his voice down to a conspiratorial whisper. "In, like a real bed?"

Freddie snorted again, and Purnell's hard stare softened slightly as the ghost of a smile licked at the corner of his mouth.

"I can stuff some rags into a sack for a pillow and leave it up in the loft for you," Freddie said. "In case you can't, you know, get comfortable or something."

"That's a mighty kind gesture. I might take you up on that." Elm waved a hand at the stalls. "There's something about this smell that's so comforting and—"

"No, it isn't," Purnell said. "It's smells like horse shit in here."

They all laughed, finally finding some common ground, and then Freddie broached the subject he and Purnell had been discussing when Elm had wandered into the barn. "Is that it?" he asked, pointing at the wrapped rifle. "Is that the gun that . . ." He mimed aiming and firing a rifle.

"It is," Elm said.

"Did you blow that man out of his boots?"

Elm shook his head. "Your boots are on pretty good. That's not what happens."

"Oh, I see." Freddie fidgeted, a puzzled expression on his face. Elm realized he was young enough that he hadn't been part of the War, and from the look on his face, he felt like he had missed an an important part of becoming a man. The realization was like a knot, tightening in his gut, and he shuffled his feet a bit to loosen the feeling. "Look," he said. "It's a terrible thing. Killing a man. It's nothing worth celebrating."

Purnell looked at Freddie, who flushed, embarrassed to have been caught, and the silence that followed between the three of them was old and familiar to Elm. He had felt it time and again since the War. He wasn't much for idle conversation, much of which came around to discussion of one's past and experiences, and when folks learned of what he had done during the War, they were either horrified or fascinated. And the conversations that followed were never to his—or their—liking.

Elm had never quite mastered the art of the polite lie. Not like the Judge.

"I'll just take my stuff up to the house," Elm said, and both Purnell and Freddie nodded, eager to escape the dour air that was filling the tack room.

Elm gathered up his saddlebags and left the barn.

10

THE FOLLOWING MORNING, ELM TOOK HIS BREAKFAST ON THE back porch. Mrs. Walphin had given him two still-steaming biscuits and a cup of hot coffee, and he watched the slow shift of colors along the horizon as he ate. A few stars twinkled overhead—mischievous lights that refused to go out as the night lost its grip on the sky.

He had slept poorly. Not because the mattress had been uncomfortable, but because his dreams had been marred by things moving in darkness—like the presence of an alligator beneath the surface of a bayou. He could feel them lurking, but they were not inclined to reveal themselves. They would, in time; for now, they were content to whisper and creep about.

It was always like this, though he had expected the haunts to come more quickly after the incident in Burlap's Rest. It was as if these monsters—dispatched from the physical world—still echoed in a phantasmal state that his dreaming mind was overly receptive to. They would fade—they always did—but for the time being, they were ghosts who tried to haunt him.

He had mentioned this curious ephemera to the Judge once, and had been surprised to learn that the Judge felt no such affliction following an encounter with the supernatural. The Judge snored loudly, his slumber untainted by darkness, leaving Elm to stare up at the stars and wait for the night-scouring fire of dawn.

You are too open to the horrors, Orchilí had told him. *You cannot unsee what you have seen, and they know it. They want your soul, and they can find their way in through your eyes.*

The Romani woman had taught him about wards and guards, and she would idly trace occult patterns on his skin when they were naked in her wagon. Circles drawn around his scars; esoteric lettering that would make him shiver, even though he did not understand the words she was writing. After she was gone, he had visited a tattoo artist in Barcelona and had had the man ink one of the circles she had taught him. Both as a way to protect his heart and to remember her.

A current of warm air swirled along Elm as the back door opened. The Judge hove into view, and he offered Elm another biscuit. "She's going into town today," the Judge said. "Right after breakfast."

"By herself?"

The Judge shook his head. "A couple of men are going with her. I'm going to stay here. In case O'Halloran or his men do something stupid."

"More stupid than yesterday?"

A wry grin tugged at the corner of the Judge's mouth. "*Beatus homo*," he said. "*Qui invent sapientiam . . .*"

Elm snorted. "I think they may have missed that sermon," he said. *Blessed is the man who finds wisdom*, he thought, translating the Latin in his head. It sounded like something from Proverbs, and if he gave the Judge half a chance, the older man would rattle on for an hour or more, depending on his mood . . .

"You want me to go with her?" Elm asked.

"Of course."

Elm nodded. "And if Tommy O'Halloran shows up in town?"

The Judge looked out at the barn where Purnell and Benjee were hitching one of the horse to a wagon. "Don't draw first," he said.

"That's what you always say."

"It's a good policy. It's kept you out of trouble so far."

Elm eyed the men and the horse. "You have a loose understanding of that word."

The Judge grunted. "The West is undergoing a transformation, son. Towns like Bitter aren't going to remain little specks on the map for long. Not with the railroads laying track every which way. When this town starts to grow, Bart O'Halloran wants to be growing with it. While he may be inclined to let his lads go a-raiding, it won't do to have word get back to St. Louis that he is indiscriminately killing local folk. The marshals are going to come sniffing around, drawn to the scent of something rotten." He knocked his boot heel against the edge of the porch. "There's no money in running a rotten town," he said.

"No, I don't suppose there is."

"Of course, that presupposes that Bart O'Halloran is a smart man."

"*Beatus homo*," Elm said.

"Well, I wouldn't go that far," the Judge replied. "Keep her safe. Don't let her men get dragged into something stupid. That sheriff isn't going to help you, either."

"This sounds better and better all the time."

The Judge gnawed on the inside of his cheek for a moment. "There's all manner of rational reasons not to go," he said.

"But she's going anyway."

The Judge let out a long sigh. "They go every week for supplies. If she doesn't go, O'Halloran will know she's afraid."

"She can't have him thinking that now, can she?"

The Judge shook his head. "Damn fool woman," he muttered.

Elm put his hand up to his mouth as if he were going to finish his biscuit, but mostly he was trying to hide a smile that had slipped past his guard. The memory of her finger tracing its way up his arm was a bright thought that banished the last of the nighttime darkness from his mind.

The horse drawing the wagon ambled along the road at its own pace. Purnell and Benjee sat side by side on the wagon seat, and another man brought up the rear on a horse of his own. Elm and Isadora rode in front of the wagon, and as soon as they crossed the muddy creek, Isadora nudged her horse to a trot.

Isadora wore a fringed jacket over her denims, and her hair was loose beneath her hat. As she let her horse find its own pace, the wind lifted her hat off her head, and had it not been for the thin strap hanging from the brim, she would have lost it. It bounced on her back, and the bright sunlight made her black hair shine like polished stone. She looked over her shoulder as her horse pulled ahead. When she said something, the wind caught her words and all he heard was the merry sound of her voice.

He urged his horse to run after the spirited black mare.

Isadora leaned forward as if to whisper something in her mare's ears, and the beast broke into a full gallop. Elm was about to goad his horse to run faster, but he relented. They were caught in a revelry, free to run and be wild. What was it that Baudelaire had said about the mystery of a misty sky? He tried to recall the lines. Something about how the sky could be as seductive as a beautiful woman. Watching Isadora ride, he felt as if he understood what the poet had been trying to say.

But when the horse and rider disappeared over a rise, he shook off the melancholic weight of his wool-gathering and urged his horse to catch up with Isadora.

Her horse had gone off the path and was trotting and snorting in an open meadow, jerking its head against Isadora's efforts to remind the beast who was in charge. As Elm's brown gelding approached, the black mare calmed down and Isadora was able to coax her back to the path.

"She can be very frisky," Isadora said. She rubbed the mare's neck affectionately. "She doesn't get to run as much as she would like."

"She runs well," Elm said.

Isadora's cheeks were pink, and her eyes were bright. Elm thought the horse was not the only one who had enjoyed the run.

"Theo and I met here a number of times," she said. She pointed out a pair of white-streaked boulders that marked the verge of the field. "Father would let me go to town for supplies, but he always sent me with a different hand. He said it was to make sure I got to know them all a little because, one day, he'd be gone and the ranch would be mine. When that happened, it would be better if the men trusted me." She brushed her wild hair away from her face. "But I think he didn't want any of them to know me too well."

Elm thought of Miss Rebeca and how she spent more and more time finding excuses to visit the tiny schoolroom where his mother had taught him and the other children. Eventually, Mr. Rothacher had spoken to his ward about her familiarity with the dirty children who were a perpetual nuisance on the estate. Miss Rebecca hadn't said anything to him about it, but his mother heard about the conversation from one of the other servants who worked in the big house's kitchen. "Yes," Elm said. "I can fathom the concern which he must have held about such knowledge."

"Theo made a deal with the hands. He would pay them a day's wage to wait here for us, and then he would trade places with them and go the rest of the way into town with me. We would spend the day together, and then he would hand me back over."

"Theo? Was this your husband?"

Isadora nodded, her gaze distant and unfocused.

"What happened to him?"

"He drowned." She gave Elm a sad smile. "He didn't know how to swim."

Elm thought of the narrow creek they had crossed on the way to Thrush. He didn't see how it could be deep or swift enough to warrant danger. There was more to the story, but as she didn't seem inclined to offer any more details, he didn't press her.

He had his own secrets too, after all.

"Did Judge Wallace charge you with keeping me safe today?" she asked.

"Yes."

"You didn't bring your rifle," Isadora pointed out.

"It'll draw too much attention."

"Ah, well, we wouldn't want that now, would we?" There was an impish glint in her eye and he wasn't quite sure what she was referring to.

Behind them, the wagon bumped over the rise, and when Elm glanced back at it, she urged her horse away from him. "Try a little harder to catch me this time," she called back as her horse snorted and started to run.

When they reached Bitter, Isadora left Elm and Purnell with the horses at the livery stable. She went ahead with Benjee and the wagon. When the horses were all taken care of, Elm followed Purnell down the street to the dry goods store. The wagon was out front, and the laconic horse attached to it was nibbling contentedly at the greenery along the base of the wooden walk.

Elm ducked into the store, looked about, and felt his heart skip a beat when he didn't spot Isadora. "Where is she?" he asked Benjee, who was standing near a barrel of apples. The other hand was talking with a man wearing an apron. They were consulting a list the ranch hand had brought with him.

"She went to the bank," Benjee said.

"And you let her go alone?"

Elm didn't wait to hear Benjee's answer. He stormed out of the store, and scanned the street for any sign of the willful ranch owner. He spotted her beyond the public house where Purnell and Benjee had found him the other day. He hustled after her, and as he passed the barber shop, he tipped his head at the white-coated man leaning against the doorframe of his shop.

He didn't recognize anyone else on the street, and he reached the wooden porch of the bank shortly after she disappeared through the tall doors. His boots clattered against the steps, and he hurried inside, where he came to a sudden halt.

The vestibule of the bank was a narrow chamber with a counter at one end. Iron bars prevented anyone from leaping over the counter, and the teller was a thin man with a stiff mustache and long fingers. To the left was a heavy door with a sign that said 'Mgr.' Two customers were queued in front of Isadora, and the bank teller was counting change back to a third—a woman wearing a checkered shawl.

"Here you are." He sidled up next to her.

Her face was hard and furious.

"What happened?"

Before she could reply, a portly man in a waistcoat appeared behind the bank teller. The man adjusted his spectacles, peering out at the customers in the lobby, and his face creased into a nervous smile when he spotted Isadora and Elm. "Mrs. Mulbridge," he said loudly, much to the surprise of the teller whose ear he was shouting into. "Such a pleasant surprise to see you this afternoon."

The portly man bustled out of sight, and a moment later, the door to their left swung open. The portly man waved a hand at them. "Come in. Come in," he said.

Elm followed Isadora, and the man swung the door shut behind them. He led them to an office in the back, and as they stood awkwardly in the center of the room, he bustled past Elm to a sideboard where there was a crystal decanter and a tray of glassware. He poured an ample measure of whisky into two of the glasses and offered them to his guests. Elm accepted a glass out of politeness, but he made no move to drink. It was too early in the day for him, but Isadora did not share his reservations. She downed the contents of her glass in one big gulp, and then held the glass out for more.

The bank manager hesitated a moment before pouring her a slightly smaller measure.

"What brings you to the First Regional Bank of Bitter today, Mrs. Mulbridge?" he asked.

"I was just at Murphy's store, and he said my line of credit was no longer good."

"Oh," the bank manager said. He fumbled with the decanter for a moment, his eyes straying to a glass, but then he thought better of it and left the whisky alone. He scurried around his desk and sat down.

"I'm sure you can explain this to me, Mr. Phineas," Isadora said. There was even more fire in her voice than there had been a moment before, and not all of it stemmed from the whisky.

"Well, I don't know the details off-hand," Phineas started.

"Murphy seemed to be very clear on the details."

"Yes, well . . ."

"I am current on my loan payments, Mr. Phineas."

"Yes, yes . . ." His head bobbed up and down as he fished a ring of small keys out of the pocket of his waistcoat. He found the right key for the locked drawer in his desk, and he drew out a heavy ledger and dropped it on the desk. "Yes, let's see . . . right here . . ."

Isadora looked at Elm, and the fire in her eyes was even more clear there than it was in her voice. He understood the bank manager's apprehension.

"Yes, here it is." Phineas's finger stopped moving. "Your father, Aloysius Gunter Van Horn—"

"I know my father's name," Isadora snapped.

Phineas swallowed heavily. He fidgeted in his chair, and his gaze strayed to the decanter. Rethinking his decision to not pour himself a glass. "Mr. Van Horn applied for a loan of twenty thousand dollars," he continued. "He used the ranch as collateral." His finger moved down the page. "He made payments until . . ."

"I know of this loan," Isadora said. "We have continued to make payments on it after his death."

"Yes, yes." Phineas's finger kept tapping. It moved down again, resting on a different line of tiny numbers. "But the interest . . ."

"What about the interest?"

"You haven't been keeping up on the loan's interest. As a result, the bank can't—in good faith—extend you any further credit until such time that you are . . . ah . . . *truly* current with the loan."

Her mouth firmed into a tight line. "How much?"

Mr. Phineas squinted up at the ceiling, as his fingers drummed on the ledger page. "Seven hundred and forty-eight dollars," he said, once he finished some mental calculations.

The color left Isadora's cheeks. "And when is that money due?"

"It's been due for quite some time, my dear."

"When is it due?" she shouted.

He started, his fingers scrambling across the open ledger. "Mrs. Mulbridge, there is no need to shout like that. I am sitting right here."

She started toward him, but Elm laid a hand on her arm and stopped her. She was shaking with rage. "When. Is. It. Due?" she repeated, spacing out each word as if it was being chiseled in stone.

"You can pay it anytime," Mr. Phineas said. He cleared his throat and toyed with his glasses. "Though, by the end of the month, the bank will have to . . . "

"What?"

"It's not my policy," he said, his voice starting to whine. "I am merely an agent of—"

"What will the bank do?" she snarled.

Elm tightened his grip as he felt her start forward again. She struggled for a moment and then took a deep breath. When Elm eased his pressure, she pulled her arm free of his grip. She levered a stiff finger at the bank manager. "You are a—a—" She didn't finish. She made a fist as she took another deep breath, and when she spoke again, the fire in her voice had been replaced with something colder and—to Elm—even more dangerous. "Seven hundred and fifty dollars. By the end of the month. You shall have it."

Isadora whirled and stormed out of the office, letting the door slam against the wall as she left. Mr. Phineas, emboldened by her departure, called after her. "And another four hundred and sixty dollars. For the next installment of the loan."

He gulped noticeably when she came back. His hands gripped the edge of his desk and his face paled as he braced himself for another outburst.

With visible effort, Isadora gave him a pleasant smile. "Mr. Phineas, I do not wish to discuss finances with you any more. But you need to unlock the outer door of this prison so that we may leave. If you do not . . ."

"Oh, yes. Yes, of course." He heaved himself out of his chair and nearly tripped over his own feet as he rushed out of the office to unlock the door to the lobby.

Isadora looked at Elm, and he saw the barely contained fury in her eyes. He shook his head at the unspoken question she was asking him.

"Why not?" she asked after they had found their way to the nearby public house.

"Violence never solves anything," Elm said.

"Surely, it does."

Elm shook his head again. He offered her an understanding smile as he reached for the glass of beer on the table. The bartender had poured two glasses at Elm's request and he had brought them to the table near the door where he had convinced Isadora to sit. She squirmed in her chair, still furious from the conversation with the bank manager. He knew her anger would pass—more quickly, in fact, if they sat and had a drink. Keep her safe, the Judge had said. Stay out of trouble. Having a drink in an empty saloon would satisfy both those requirements.

"Why aren't there any male whores?" Isadora asked suddenly.

"Excuse me?" Elm followed her gaze and looked over at the piano player who was hunched over his dusty instrument at the back of the room. The man was practicing the same song, over and over, and he wasn't getting any better at it.

She sighed. "What am I supposed to do for company when I get . . . what is it? What excuse do men use?"

"Lonely," Elm supplied.

"Yes, that's it. What am I supposed to do when I get lonely?"

"Women don't get lonely," Elm said. "Not when they have houses to keep and children to raise."

She snorted. "Don't be like that." She put her glass down on the table. "You are an educated man, Elm Stonebrook. Tell me something I haven't heard before about my station in life. Yes, I should be home, cooking and cleaning. I know that. And you have no idea how lonely such an existence can be when you are nothing more than a dull-witted creature who keeps the food hot and the bed warm."

Elm thought for a moment. On one hand, Isadora wanted to be distracted from her financial straits; all she wanted from him was some lively conversation. On the other, there was an urgent honesty to her question. What could he tell her? He recalled a poem Orchilí had loved. "'*Tu contains dans ton oil le couchant et l'aurora*,'" he quoted.

Isadora gave him a blank stare.

"It's French poetry," he said.

"But what does it mean in English? I suppose that sort of nonsense works on big city ladies who are easily impressed by a man with a clever tongue, but—"

"'Your eye holds both the evening and the dawn,'" Elm translated.

Isadora cocked her head to the side.

Elm thought of the rest of the poem, and realizing portions were not quite in keeping with the present mood, decided to skip to the end. "'I don't care if you are angel, devil or spirit,'" he said. "'As long as your velvet eyes and perfumed head and magical moments, o queen, make this world less dreadful and mean, and this time less like being dead.'"

"Oh." She cleared her throat. "I see."

"Or something like that," Elm said. "It's been awhile since I've read 'Hymn to Beauty.'"

"A hymn? Who wrote it?"

"Charles Baudelaire. It's from a book of poetry called *Les Fleurs du Mal*. It was banned for being obscene."

"Banned? How do you ban poetry?"

"The books themselves," Elm said. "The books can't be printed."

"But you've read them. How did you manage to do that if there aren't any books?"

"Not all of them were destroyed. The ban only prevented the publisher from making more."

"And you've read these poems enough to memorize them? Does that mean you are banned too?"

"I . . . don't know, really," he said. "I never thought about it like that, I guess."

"Will they arrest you if you go to France?"

"I suppose they might." He laughed. "If they ask me to recite poetry before I get off the ship."

"Is that why you left France?"

Elm shook his head. "No, I didn't . . . how did you know I've been to France?"

"Where else would you learn French poetry?"

He inclined his head. "That is an astute observation," he said.

She picked up her glass and sipped from it. "Did you recite poetry to her too?" She asked the question casually, and it caught him off-guard. He nearly choked on his beer.

"I'll take that as a 'yes,'" she noted when he was done coughing.

"Your questions pierce me quite vexingly, Miss Van Horn," he managed.

"Hmm," she mused. "Maybe when we get back to the ranch, you could do this again."

"Do what? Try to drink and breathe at the same time?"

She shook her head. "I'd like to hear some more of this French poetry." Her eyes flashed. "And then, perhaps this day won't be a total disappointment."

11

THE JUDGE WALKED THE WIDTH OF THE CLEARING, AND THEN walked along the trees in a counter-clockwise direction. *Widdershins*, he thought, a turning away from the sun. It was a term he had learned from Elm when they had been investigating a barn haunting in Ohio. Supposedly walking in such a path was bad luck, but he wanted to see the meadow in a different light. If he stepped along this path, could he see any darkness that refused to be driven away by the sun?

Two weeks ago, the ranch hands had stumbled upon a lost steer, which had been killed and gutted in a ferocious manner. The cow's throat had been torn to shreds, and its stomach had been ripped open. Whatever had killed the steer had done so out of sport, rather than a need for food. Even now, a swath of the grasses were still stained red where the steer had struggled in its death throes.

A damn waste, Norwood had told the Judge. *By the time we found it, the scavengers had already feasted on it.*

It wasn't the first, the Judge had learned. There had been six others, killed in a similarly ruthless manner.

Norwood said he could take the Judge to each of the sites where the cattle had been slaughtered, but as the Judge finished his circuit of the field, he wondered if seeing the other locations was worth the trouble. This site was the freshest, and he didn't see anything. Time, the weather, and other animals would have ruined any clues he might have found.

It was like visiting the battlegrounds where the Union and Confederacy had fought, those fallow fields where sons and brothers had fought and died. Nothing remained of those battles but fields of sallow grasses and unkempt hillocks. Occasionally there would be a pall in the air—a vague unease that chilled the bones and made one wish they were in a saloon, drinking bitter beer and warming their feet by a fire.

"Did you burn the corpses?" the Judge asked as he returned to his horse.

"Aye. Nothing else to be done," Norwood said.

"You did the right thing."

"Nothing right about it. The steer that died here could look some of the men in the eye. It would have taken a dozen horses to drag its corpse back down to the valley. Whatever killed this cow did so on its own. There were bite marks all over its neck. Claw marks on its flank. Deep wounds that a man could put his finger all the way in."

"I didn't know wolves got that big in this territory."

Norwood shook his head. "They don't. And anyway, we've gone hunting every few days for the past month. If there is a wolf anywhere between here and Iowa, it's more clever than we are."

The Judge squinted at the tree line. He had seen marks on the trunks of several oaks—jagged cuts in the bark like the sort left by a bear, but high enough on the tree trunk that the bear must have been standing upright. Not impossible for a bear—once, he had seen a brown bear stand taller than a man—but this wasn't bear country. "Well, it isn't a wolf or a bear, what is it?" he asked.

Norwood chewed on the corner of his mustache.

The Judge hauled himself into his saddle and regarded the other man. "The sun is shining, and we are in the middle of an open field. There are no shadows here, my dear man. Whatever bogeyman you've invented can't hurt us here."

"It isn't my idea, you understand. It's just talk, among the men. They're not schooled like you and I. They are more prone to believe such stories . . ."

"What kind of stories?"

"Some of them—that fellow, Benjee, for instance, and some of the other younger ones—have been talking about Burlap's Rest. About a hanging that took place there nearly a week back."

"What have they been saying?"

"They said three men were hung. That night, those three men came back from the dead. Tore up the town pretty good before they were put down again. And burned, this time."

"There was no tumult in that town," the Judge said. "Just the death of a fool who didn't listen."

"Listen to what?"

The Judge sighed. "I was there. So was my man, Elm. I pronounced justice on those three men. I watched them swing from their ropes. And I told them—I told them square—if they didn't dispose of those bodies properly, then, yes, they were going to come back. They were shamblers. Whatever evil they had let into their souls wasn't done with them, and it animated their corpses. Filled them with an unnatural hunger. They have a taste for flesh—these revenants—and the only way to stop them is fire."

"You've seen them before . . ."

"I never wished to be an expert on such deviltry, but it would appear such intelligence may be my station in life."

"Miss Isadora—though she may pretend otherwise—believes your intelligence may be our salvation."

The Judge rubbed the side of his face. "I had not thought her to be as superstitious as some of her men appear to be."

Norwood waggled a finger at the Judge. "It is just you and I out here, sir. There is no need for such pretense with me."

A smile flitted across the Judge's face. "No?"

"I have heard many stories about you. Few of them good. You left a mark on this family."

"Such was not my intent," the Judge said.

"After you left Baton Rouge, Grace wasn't the same. When she fell sick, she wasted away. It was as if she didn't have the will to fight her illness. Aloysius once told me that his love wasn't enough to sustain her. She pined for someone else."

A deep furrow creased the Judge's forehead, and his lips tightened into a hard line.

"It was hard for all of them. The girls didn't understand why their mother left them. Isadora, especially. She loved you. You were always so kind to her. You made her mother laugh. And then, within the space of a year, both she and you were not there any longer. Six months later, her father brought her here. Everything she knew and loved was gone."

"If I had stayed, I would have . . ."

"Hurt them?" Norwood shook his head. "How much more could you have hurt them by staying?"

The Judge made a face and looked away from Norwood. "Such speculation brings no relief to anyone. The past informs us. We cannot let it snare us."

"You used to tell her stories about fairies and trolls and wild spirits in the woods," Norwood said. "She adored you. She believed you. What sort of woman do you think this girl grew up to be?"

"An intelligent one, I hope. One who knew such stories were merely stories."

"You're right about the first part, but the latter . . . ?"

The Judge sighed and stroked his horse's neck. "You speak as if there is a weight on my soul that I might hope to remove."

Norwood leaned toward the Judge. "Whatever is in your soul is between you and God, sir, but yes, if you feel a burden toward this family, I hope you will seek to ease it."

"Mr. Walphin, your efforts to manipulate me are undignified."

"I don't care if my efforts are dignified or not," Norwood said. "You owe this family. If the past is a snare, then by God, you should stick your head right in it."

Elm found the Judge sprawled in a rocking chair on the front porch of the house. The Judge's head was tipped back, and his mouth was slack. A leather-bound book lay forgotten in his lap. As Elm stepped up to the porch, the dog, who had been lying next to the Judge's chair, raised his head and thumped his tail against the wooden porch. Elm scratched the dog behind the ears and then sat down in the other rocking chair. He pulled off his boots, dropping each one as he did, and the noise startled the Judge out of his nap.

The older man blinked and leaned forward in the rocking chair. His tongue ran around his mouth, and he wiped his hand across his beard. "What day is it?" he said, his voice rough with sleep.

"Same day as it was this morning," Elm replied.

The Judge smacked his lips as he fumbled for his pocket watch. "Should be supper time soon," he said.

"You look like you've had a busy day."

The Judge caught the book as it slid out of his lap, and he tucked it away between his thigh and the arm of the chair. "I've been cogitating," he said.

"Is that what you were doing?"

"Thinking is a critical aspect of discovery, my boy. Any solution to a perplexing problem can only be achieved by the application of a strong and disciplined mind."

"And what did you discover while you were sitting here with your mouth open?"

"My mouth was not open."

"It was. I considered tossing a rock in when we rode past earlier." Elm pointed at the ground in front of the porch. "From over there, in fact."

"You would have done no such thing."

"I would have," Elm said. "If Miss Isadora had dared me to do so."

The Judge narrowed his eyes. "You too?" he grumbled.

"Me too, what?" Elm asked. "Did I miss an important revelation between you and the other men?"

The Judge waved a hand. "Never you mind that," he said. "Tell me about your visit to the town."

Elm gave the Judge a brief summary of their visit to Bitter, highlighting their visit to the bank and the discovery of how accounting was done in this part of Missouri.

"And how is accounting done in this part of Missouri?"

"Egregiously."

The Jude pursed his lips. "How unfortunate."

"You owe me fifteen dollars," Elm said. "As they were unable to procure credit, someone had to pay for the supplies."

The Judge nodded distantly as if he was not concerned about the money. "And the rest?" he asked.

"Over twelve hundred dollars. Due at the end of the month."

"End of the month, huh? And what does that cover?"

"Unpaid interest and next month's principal on the loan her father took out on this property."

"So that is how O'Halloran is going to take her land, is it?"

Elm nodded. "He owns the town. You are right about that. The sheriff. The bank. I suspect the trouble at the store wasn't because of her credit, but because O'Halloran is already leaning on the proprietor to cut her off."

The Judge scratched along his belly. "The end of the month will be here in less than two weeks," he said.

The black dog got to its feet and stretched. It shook itself, all the way from its nose down to its tail, and then, having been exercised, it padded over to Elm's chair and flopped down next to it. Elm put his hand down and scratched the dog behind the ears again.

"I saw one of the places where the steers were slaughtered," the Judge said. "Not much to see: trampled grass, old blood stains, some claw marks on trees."

"What kind of marks?"

"Big and deep." The Judge raised his hand above his head. "About this high off the ground."

Elm raised his eyebrows. "Bear?"

"Big damn bear."

"And no sign of it anywhere?"

The Judge shook his head. "No scat. No den. Whatever is killing these cattle isn't eating them, and if it was a bear—especially one that size—it would be feasting on its kills."

"Well, if it isn't a bear, what is it?"

"*Non sunt multiplicanda entia sine necessitate*," the Judge said.

Elm made a face and looked down at the dog. "He always does this," he explained. "It's *novacula occami*—Occam's Razor—and it means you shouldn't complicate a theory beyond the essential possibilities."

"If it isn't a natural creature that is killing the cattle, then it must be unnatural," the Judge said.

Elm sighed. "I really dislike it when we get to this part of the conversation."

The dog lifted its head and barked once.

"He doesn't like it either," Elm translated for the Judge.

"You are more informed of creatures such as these than I," the Judge said. He plucked the book out from where he had tucked it and tossed it to Elm.

It was covered in dark leather, and it was unmarked on the cover and spine. Leather straps woven into the cover kept the book closed. The leather was old and supple, and Elm undid the straps, letting the book fall open in his lap. There was an ornate drawing of a serpent with tiny wings on the page, and on the recto page, lines of neatly inscribed Latin were written. Fascinated, Elm turned the heavy pages, looking at a parade of strange beasts. "Where did you get this?" he asked. His mouth was suddenly dry.

The Judge cackled. "I was keeping secrets long before you were born, boy."

"This is a bestiary," Elm said. "I have heard of such compendiums, but I have never seen one. How long have you had it?"

"Awhile," the Judge said. "I got it from that bookseller in Springfield."

"When? When we visited Lincoln's grave?"

"You visited. I had seen it already."

Elm shook his head at the Judge's comment. He showed the Judge a picture of a skeletal figure. Half of the man's face was a decaying mess, and the rags he wore only partially covered the squirming putrescence of his rotting body. "A revenant," Elm said. "We have seen creatures like this."

"Indeed," the Judge said.

Elm turned a few more pages and then stopped. "A wolf who walks on two legs," he said, showing the Judge the picture which had caught his eye.

"Aye," the Judge said. "And there is the simplest solution to our problem."

12

As the sun dipped toward the horizon, Elm walked along the northern edge of the pasture, following the fence of crossed posts and long rails. He carried his rifle in the crook of his left arm, and his satchel of cartridges was shoved through his belt. The herd spread across the field to his left like a brown stain. Benjee and Freddie walked a few paces behind him, and he paid little attention to their chatter as he scanned the treeline for signs that men or beasts—or beasts that walked like men—were stalking the herd.

During the afternoon, after they had conceived the plan for this evening, he had recalled an earlier encounter with a revenant—a *shambler*, as the Judge called them. He had been traveling with the Judge for a short time—less than a month, as he remembered. Keeping company with the gregarious man had come about more from happenstance than any other reason, and they had stopped for the evening in a small town not far from Vincennes, Indiana, somewhere along the serpentine course of the Wabash River. The Judge had been asked to preside over the jury of a farmer who had been accused of killing another man in a gambling house dispute. There had been a dozen witnesses, and hearing testimony took only an hour before the Judge grew bored and pronounced his judgment upon the man.

Their impressions vindicated by the law, the townspeople hung the man that same evening. Elm had not been involved in any part of the action against the farmer, but after the deed was done and the townsfolk had brought the dead man down, he had joined the Judge as the townsfolk dumped the body in a pine coffin.

And that was when the Judge had said that Latin phrase. *Occam's Razor*, he explained to Elm. *All things have a simple explanation, even if it eludes our comprehension.*

And what eludes us here? Elm had asked.

Wait and see, the Judge had said.

During the night, Elm—and much of the town as well—were woken by terrified screams. When a torch-lit mob gathered in the square, they found the coffin broken and empty. A trail led them to a house of the dead farmer, where they found the shambler, feasting on a horrifically mutilated corpse.

The farmer's widow had let her dead husband back into the house, and the monster had attacked her, having no human sense left in it. All that remained was an unholy hunger.

Kill it again, the Judge said, *and burn the body this time.*

The revenant hissed and snarled at the mob, like a wild beast intent on protecting its bloody prize. While the townspeople noisily and fearfully debated how to dispatch the monster, Elm had calmly walked to the door of the house and shot it twice. No one was brave enough to drag the body out of the house, and so after a hasty conference, the townspeople decided to burn the entire farmhouse down.

You knew this monster would rise, Elm said to the Judge after the crowd had lost their passion for watching the fire and dispersed.

And you knew how to put it down. Neither of us is as simple as we seemed.

And what is the simple explanation of this monster? According to this Occam fellow?

God has forgotten us.

That's not an explanation.

No? Then I put the same question to you, sir, the Judge said. *Tell me how such a monster exists. Explain to me how the dead do not stay dead. Elucidate for me the source of this unnatural mystery.*

Elm could not, any more than he could strike that word—*unnatural*—from his mind. He had seen much since the War, during his travels abroad, and every time he encountered the unnatural, Elm felt he knew less about everything—about the sky, the trees, men, and beasts—than he did the day before. *Everything has a simple explanation,* the Judge said, but such explanations were not always possible, as far as Elm considered. The monsters depicted in the Judge's book were the stuff of folktales and children's fables. Winged serpents. Giant worms. Trolls. Devilish mischief-makers. The dead who were not dead. Cursed men who transformed into savage beasts. They were not real creatures.

Except . . .

The simplest explanation was that they, in fact, did exist. And so where did they fit in the grand design of the universe? Had God forgotten them, or were these monsters rude manifestations of the Devil's influence? If the latter were true, was the Judge—and he, too, to some degree—doing God's work? Were they crusaders in a holy war against Evil?

The same was said of men who traveled from their homes to the Holy Land during the Crusades, but history recorded that most of those crusades failed to truly protect Christendom. Occasionally, one of the Union generals would call upon God as he exhorted the blue-clothed men to charge into battle against their grey-clad enemies. *Show them that we have God on our side!*

And yet, on the battlefield, God had been indifferent to the color of a man's uniform.

The fence made a sharp left turn and marched across the pasture. Elm stopped, having reached the farthest corner of Thrush's land. He crouched and examined the crossed poles and wooden rails before him. The fence was there to keep the cattle from wandering too far. It was not sturdy enough to stop the herd should they spook and stampede. A man could duck under the rail just as easily as a horse could be encouraged to leap over it.

Benjee and Freddie joined him, and Elm walked over and kicked a post as if to verify how deep the wooden stake was driven into the ground. "Sturdy," he pronounced.

"That fence is older than you, Freddie," Benjee said.

"No, it isn't," Freddie retorted. "There hasn't been cattle out here more'n ten years. This was all farmland before that."

"Still need a fence," Benjee said. "Got to keep the deer out."

"Ain't worth shit against rabbits, though," Freddie said.

"Where did all the deer go?" Elm asked, interrupting their conversation.

Benjee shrugged. "North," he said, though from his tone, Elm thought he wasn't sure.

"Those slaughtered cows. Were they stragglers?"

"What do you mean?" Freddie asked.

"How close to the herd did this wolf come? Did it creep past the fence and threaten the herd? Spook a few of them into running, and then hunt them down?"

"They stick close, mostly," Benjee said. "But that fence isn't as sturdy as it looks in a few spots. Some cow will lean against it and it falls over. Eventually, a couple will wander out through the gap. Rudy would send me 'n Purnell out to round them up."

"So you found some of the dead cows?"

"Yeah, I found a couple." Benjee fidgeted. Elm's questions were making him uneasy. He was thinking about things he had seen—sights he wanted to forget.

"And you never saw anything?" Elm asked.

"I saw things no man should have to see. The way those cows were butchered . . ."

"But no sign of what had done it?"

Benjee shivered, touched by a specter of an ill thought he prayed would never come any closer. "No, sir."

"What about you, Freddie?" Elm asked. "You ever see anything?"

Freddie shook his head. "No, sir. I ain't seen nothing."

The rail across the pasture had been straight once, but it had been broken and repaired enough that it wiggled out of true. Would the beast leap the fence like a deer, or would it knock over a section like Benjee said the cows did? There was some sense to the tactic of harrying the herd to cull a few head. Elm could not imagine what sort of monster would stand firm before a stampede of frightened cattle. But why did it chase them into the woods? Why didn't it hunt them down here in the pasture?

Elm had ridden through the forest the other day, and he had seen elm, willow, and pine. There were cottonwoods too, a lazy line running along the base of the hill. There was probably other species too. The woods of Missouri were still relatively untouched by men and ax, and what trails through these forested areas had been cut by wild deer. Cattle were still fairly new to this region.

Elm peered at the trees closest to the corner of the pasture where they stood. There was a stand of birch, standing tall and resolute, and in the middle were a pair of oak trees that leaned against one another. He didn't know why one of the two had grown at an angle, but it gave him an idea.

He turned and looked in the other direction, gauging the distance between the trees and the herd. The cattle were farther away than he liked, but he had worked with greater distances. Besides, he liked the trees better than the open field.

He pointed at the leaning oak. "I'm going to climb up there," he said. "You two should go back to the house."

"Why?" Benjee asked.

"Because I'm going to sit up there all night," Elm said. "I'm going to watch the herd."

"You're going to wait for that creature to come back, aren't you?" Freddie asked.

"I am," Elm said.

"What if it can climb trees?" Benjee asked.

"I'm going to hope that it cannot," Elm said.

After dinner, Isadora and the Judge retired to the sitting room, where she poured a generous measure of whisky for both of them. The Judge took his glass and stood by the window, while Isadora picked out a book from the shelf and sat down on the divan. She read quietly for awhile, sipping occasionally from her glass, and the Judge stared out into the night surrounding the house.

The two cowboys had returned, and the Judge knew Elm had found a place from which he could watch and wait. Isadora had been against the plan when the Judge and Elm had informed her of it shortly after dinner, and while the Judge didn't entirely agree with Elm's decision either, he had had to admit he had no better idea.

Until there is a better idea, we will go with this one, Elm had said, and that had been the end of that discussion.

He had spent the afternoon looking through the bestiary, and like Elm, the wolf that walked on two legs—the *lycanthrope*—was the simplest solution to the mystery facing Thrush. The man who had sold him the book had said it was a copy of a medieval manuscript—a compendium of fantastic creatures that were nothing more than imaginary monsters culled from nighttime horror stories and folktales. There was text that accompanied each picture, but most of the descriptions were enigmatic and hyperbolic. They were not instruction on how to slay such beasts.

The Judge wondered if such a book actually existed, and a chill walked its way up his spine as he considered how such a collection would be assembled. *How much horror would one have to witness?* he thought. And would the weight of such experience drive a man mad?

Isadora lowered her book and looked over at the Judge. "He knows French poetry," she said.

"Pardon me?"

"Your man. He quoted French poetry to me today."

"Did he?"

"I had hoped to hear more tonight," she said. She glanced down at her book. "'Cloud and eclipses stain both moon and sun,'" she read. "'And loathsome canker lives in sweetest bud.'"

The Judge turned his attention away from the window. "That isn't French poetry," he said.

"It's Shakespeare," she said. "It's the closest thing I have." She gestured at the shelves. "You used to read some of those books to me."

"That I did," the Judge admitted.

"I spent many years being angry with you," she said. "I thought I would hate you forever, but . . . " She shook her head. "I just forgot about you. You were part of a life that was no longer mine, and as the years passed, it became more and more like a fairy tale—like one of those stories you used to read to me. And one day, I realized I had forgotten your face. You had faded like so many other things from my childhood. Like the memory of my mother, too. I still love her, but she's just an ache in my heart. A longing for something that I haven't had for a long time. But you? There is nothing left. No ache. No anger. Just . . . nothing."

"Then I suppose I did the right thing in leaving," the Judge said quietly.

Isadora shook her head. "'All men make faults, and even I in this,'" she read. "'Authoring thy trespass with compare, Myself corrupting, salving thy amiss, Excusing thy sins more than thy sins are.'"

"I don't want forgiveness," the Judge said.

She closed the book and returned it to the bookcase. "I'm not inclined to offer it," she said. "But this land is all that remains of my family. If you ever had any affection for us—if you loved her—"

"That's why I am still here," the Judge interrupted her.

She stopped and stared at him. "And your man?"

"He's not beholden to me."

"Elm, then. What of him?"

"You should ask him yourself."

A smile tugged at her lips. "I might. I will."

"Good." The Judge turned back to the window and sipped from his glass. "Whatever is bedeviling your herd is not your only problem," he said. "Elm and I may be of assistance in that regard, but there is little we can do about the bank. Not in a scant fortnight . . . "

"Unless there was another way to quickly acquire a supply of funds."

The Judge raised an eyebrow. "How quickly?"

"Overnight, perhaps."

He turned from the window and regarded her. "You aren't suggesting something illegal, are you?"

She shrugged. "I am not overly concerned about the legality of any action undertaken to save this farm."

"Taking the law into your own hands is a dangerous path," the Judge warned.

"Oh, I'm not suggesting that I do any law-breaking," Isadora said. "Merely that such actions would not be looked upon with disdain, were they to be successful."

The Judge laughed and raised his glass. "Oh, when you put it that way . . ."

The herd was moving, and some of the cows were lowing. Their nervous noises roused Elm from the torpor that had seeped into his frame. He had found a perch between the two oaks where several thick branches crossed, and with the aid of a thick leather strap, he was not in any danger of falling. He was, however, stiff, and he needed to pee.

The moon hung low in the dark sky, swollen and nearly full. Its light dressed the cattle in silver cloaks, and he peered intently at them, trying to spot the cause of their unease. A faint breeze blew from his right, but he didn't smell anything that suggested the presence of another—man or beast.

His fingers were cold and stiff, too.

Beneath him, the brush rustled. A branch snapped, and the sound was a like a rifle shot in the night.

Elm held his breath, trying to hear anything over the loud pounding of his heart.

A long groan rose from the herd—a single heifer voicing alarm.

He wanted to shush the beast. *It's already here*, he thought. *I don't need your help, you dumb cow.*

He leaned to his left, the leather strap digging into his side. It made it hard to breathe, but he wanted to look below him. He searched for some sign, but there was nothing but a scattered play of silver and shadow beneath him.

A low growl rose up from the ground, and the sound made the hairs on his neck stand up. He had heard such a noise before. During the second or third winter of the War, he and another sharpshooter from Company C had been on watch for enemy movement along the Union army's flank, and a wolf had stumbled upon their position. It had stared at them, and there had been nothing but hunger in its yellow eyes. But before it could attack, Elm's companion let loose with a blood-curdling yell. He had charged the wolf, shouting and waving his arms, and the sight had spooked the wolf so completely that it had turned tail and run. Both men laughed themselves hoarse afterward, expelling their fear through hilarious pantomime.

But he never forgot the sound the wolf had made as it had confronted them. A predatory growl that communicated a vision of fang and claw and blood. It was a sound that was clear to any species: *I am violence and death.*

His rifle lay across his lap, and when he moved it, the barrel scraped against bark. The sound was faint, but in the silence of the wood, he might as well been shouting.

Brush shivered beneath him, and something massive slammed against the trunk of one of the oak trees. The branch beneath him jumped, and he started to slide. The leather strap dug into his belly, and he gasped. Instinctively, he tried to grab onto something, and only as he opened his hand, did he realize his mistake.

His rifle slipped from his lap. It banged off a branch on the way down, and then vanished into the brush.

He cursed silently, blaming his stiff fingers for not reacting quickly enough.

In the pasture, the herd started to move as more cows began lowing in alarm. A storm of hooves was brewing.

He wrapped one hand around the leather strap and fumbled for his pistol with his other as something large and monstrous chuffed and snorted below. When it slammed into the tree again, he was ready, and the shuddering motion of the tree failed to dislodge him.

He spotted a swirl of light as leaves moved, and he brought his pistol to bear.

He didn't fire. Even though his heart was hammering in his chest, he waited.

He was patient.

The brush exploded as something large and dark leaped at the tree. Claws scrabbled at the bark of the oak, and at first, Elm thought the hissing whine was coming from the tree as it cried out, but then he realized the sound was issuing from his throat.

He could see it now. It was trying to climb the tree!

He closed his eyes—more to preserve his nighttime vision than to look way from the lupine shape of the monster's head—and pulled the trigger. His pistol barked, and he saw the flash even through his eyelids. The beast yelped, and the tree shook.

He opened his eyes, struggling to make sense of the shadows—*damn the flash of the pistol!*—and he wildly fired his gun again, reacting more to a sense of movement than any real target.

He gasped for breath, his chest heaving. His pistol remained steady, searching for a target, but he couldn't see anything. The shadows were too deep. But he remained vigilant, one hand wrapped in the strap, half-leaning out of the tree. Straining to hear any sound that might give away the location of the beast below.

It was down there still. He knew it. He could feel it in the base of his skull and in the tightness of his knuckles.

In the distance, the storm increased—a rolling thunder of hooves.

His breathing slowed. The shadows lessened. Sweat dripped down the side of his face. And still he waited.

He hadn't killed it.

Then, from deeper in the forest, came a long and lingering howl.

Elm pulled himself back into place on the branch. He lowered his pistol to his lap and slowly pried his fingers from their grip around the strap.

The beast had fled, like that wolf he had faced during the War. But unlike that animal, this one was not done with him.

"Aaaoooooo," Elm breathed, softly echoing the beast's howl. There had been pain and outrage in that cry, bestial as it was. It was a challenge being voiced. A promise of bloodshed to come.

13

"Didja see it?"

"Was it a wolf?"

"How big was it?"

"Didja see its teeth?"

The questions poured out of the men packed in the kitchen. Elm sat at the table, his hands wrapped around a mug of hot water. He replied to the constant barrage of questions in a methodical manner, giving the men brief tidbits which only drove them into a greater frenzy.

"Enough." Isadora's voice broke through the babble, and the questions dribbled to a stop. "You heard him. He saw something. He fired his gun at it. It ran off. There's nothing more he can say right now, and I will not have us turning this night into a babble of nonsense. There is work to be done. Dave: take some men and go calm the herd. Purnell and Benjee: check around the buildings. Take your rifles. The rest of you go back to the bunkhouse."

The men hesitated, and when she slapped her hand against the wooden table, they tried to leave the kitchen all at once. Finally, the cavalcade of limbs and the cacophony of voices eased, and the kitchen was empty but for Elm, Isadora, the Judge, and Norwood. The Judge had been standing near the cupboards, and when he caught Elm's eye, he hefted the whisky decanter in his hands.

Elm downed the rest of the water in his mug and held out the empty cup. The Judge filled it halfway, and then went about getting more cups and filling them.

Isadora sat down across from Elm. "What was it?" she asked.

"It's a wolf," Elm said after downing a large swig from his cup. "It is the largest I've ever seen."

The Judge paused in his pouring, and he quirked an eyebrow at Elm, who ignored him.

"It knew I was in the tree," Elm continued. "I fired my revolver twice. I may have hit it once."

"It's wounded," Isadora said hopefully. She looked at the Judge. "I can have the men ready a hunting party, and we can—"

Elm shook his head. "We should wait," he said.

"Why?" Isadora demanded.

"It's dark, which will make it nigh impossible to track," Elm said patiently. "And the horses won't like it. If they smell it, they will be hard to manage."

He didn't say anything about the men who would be riding in the party. How were they going to react if the beast turned on them? His fingers tightened around the cup. He knew it would. It wouldn't run. It would fight back.

"We have to go after it," Isadora insisted. "This may be our only chance."

"It'll be back," Elm said.

The Judge drained his cup and poured himself another measure. His hand shook slightly as he put the decanter down. "Aye," he said softly.

Isadora looked back and forth between Elm and the Judge. "What are you two not telling me?"

The Judge sipped his whisky and looked at Elm.

"It'll be back," Elm said.

"And what happens when it does come back?" Isadora wanted to know.

"We'll be waiting for it."

"How many more of my herd are going to die? What if it decides to attack the horses or the men?"

"We'll be ready," Elm said.

This talk wasn't satisfying Isadora and she looked at Norwood. "What do you think?"

Her uncle raised his shoulders up to his ears. "I don't like this, Miss Van Horn. Elm said that beast knew he was in the tree. We've never seen any sign of it when we were out looking. It's smart. It knows how to hide and how to hunt."

"Which is why we wait for it to come to us," the Judge said, warming to Elm's line of thought.

"Why would it come to us?" Isadora asked.

"Because it has been challenged," Elm said. "And because it wants something."

"What does it want?"

Elm looked at her, and she flushed under his scrutiny.

The Judge cleared his throat, gathering everyone's attention. He hefted the decanter of whisky. "I suggest we all get some rest. Tomorrow will arrive soon enough and the day will not be long enough for our needs. We have other matters to resolve, as well."

Norwood nodded. "Oh, yes. I, uh, I talked with Mrs. Walphin, and she—without my knowing—took up a collection."

"She did what?" Isadora demanded.

"Two hundred and eighty-four dollars," Norwood said. "Plus another hundred dollars she'd been saving for, well, it doesn't matter now. 'Won't do me no good to save up if I don't have a place to sleep at night, will it?' she said to me."

"Norwood . . ."

He shrugged off her look. "I agree with the missus," he said. "This is our home too. We'll contribute as we see fit, and that'll be the end of that."

Isadora nodded and looked away, her eyes bright.

"The Judge owes me fifteen dollars," Elm said. "And I have thirty more."

The Judge frowned when Elm looked at him. He tapped his fingers against the table. "That leaves quite a bit," he said. "I

don't have enough to make up the difference. Not without—"
He grimaced and shook his head. "And even if I did, what
happens next month?"

The question hung in the kitchen, weighing on them all.
Finally, Norwood shrugged and wiped at his nose. "That's a
problem for next month," he said. "When we get there."

"If we get there," the Judge corrected him.

Norwood stared at him. "*When*," he reiterated. The Judge
didn't argue, and Norwood stood, looming over them. "*When*,"
he said again, and then he left the kitchen.

The Judge sighed. "The optimists are never there at the end,"
he said. "They are always the first to get eaten."

"Says the pessimist," Elm replied.

Isadora stared at a spot on the wall next to the Judge's head.
"You're right, though," she said. "There's ten thousand dollars
left on the loan. Even if we manage to pay the bank at the end
of the month, I can't pay them next month. I won't have enough
money to pay the men, either. The season is nearly over. I don't
know how we're going to make it through the winter. It will be
spring before we can drive any of these cattle to St. Louis. I used
to be able to sell a handful here and there to local butchers, but
now, with O'Halloran . . ."

"You need ten thousand dollars. Maybe more," the Judge said.

"I do."

The Judge looked at Elm. "Earlier this evening, she suggested
we take a more laissez-faire approach to the law."

"And by 'we,' you mean 'me,'" Elm said.

The Judge shrugged. "I am a man of the law. Ignoring these
noble statutes tarnishes my reputation and diminishes my
standing among the local communities."

Elm sighed. "I'm not going to rob a bank."

"I didn't say anything about robbing a bank," the Judge said.
"Besides, such actions are beneath men of sterling character
and earnest morality."

"You are getting so tangled in that tongue of yours, I do not know the language you are speaking."

"Plain English, boy," the Judge said, banging his hand on the table. "It's not that complicated."

"It is when you say it."

Isadora put her hands on the table and gave Elm a stern look. "Are you going to sit here all night and argue with this scoundrel?" she asked, and he wasn't sure if she was serious or not. "Must I go alone? What happens when I lose my temper with Mr. Phineas?"

The Judge laughed at Elm's expression. "Good night. I'll leave you two to sort this out." He left the room, and Elm was sorry to see the decanter of whisky go with him.

Isadora smiled as she watched his gaze linger after the Judge. "I know where there is another bottle."

"I'm not sure that will help our clarity of thinking."

"No," she said. "But it might help with other things."

The Judge repaired to the narrow guest room at the top of the stairs. He set the decanter of whisky down on a small table in the corner of the room, and then proceeded to take off his jacket and boots. He fetched a wooden case from his saddlebags, along with the bestiary, and a piece of blank paper he had been saving between two pages of the heavy volume of Aristotle's treatise on ethics. He arranged everything neatly on the table and then took a swig of whisky directly from the decanter. Retrieving the lit lantern from a hook by the door, he placed it at the back of the table. He sat down, had another sip, and opened the bestiary to the entry for the lycanthrope.

The text was in Latin, which posed him no trouble, and he read it several times, sipping from the decanter as he did. When he was satisfied he had discerned all the secrets hiding in the text—and there were only a few—he set the book aside and opened the wooden box. Inside was a quill with a sandalwood handle and a pot of ink. He shook the pot and placed it on the corner of the blank page.

Dipping the quill in the ink, he wrote out a translation of the Latin, adding his own literary flourishes and leaving out a few details. When he finished, he added a brief note at the bottom of the page, and then signed the document with his majestic scrawl. He blew on the page until he was convinced it was dry, then folded it into thirds and wrote a name on the back.

He cleaned the quill, re-stoppered the bottle of ink, and then turned the chair around so that he could put his feet up on the bed. With the lantern light shining over his shoulder, he stared up at the corner of the ceiling where the light didn't quite reach and let his mind wander. Sleep would come, eventually, but he had some thinking to do in the meantime.

The beast would come. Elm was right in that regard, and when it did, they needed to be ready.

Elm had demurred any further talk of robbing banks or French poetry or other things, as Isadora had so obliquely mentioned, and he had bid her good night and gone up to his room. He didn't bring lantern or candle up with him, and he undressed in the dark. His room was near the front eaves, and the outside wall sloped at an angle; when he stood upright, he risked banging his head against the ceiling. The bed was a plain mattress on the floor—no fancy bed in the big house, after all—and he slipped under the pair of heavy blankets. Moonlight streamed in from a tiny window, and after awhile, his eyes adjusted to the dimness in the room.

When she came in later, he was able to see the rounded slope of her breast as she shucked off her long nightgown. He noticed the pale hollow of her throat, and how her dark hair fell unbound across her back. Without a word, she lifted his blankets and crawled into the bed beside him. Her hands were cold, and he gasped slightly as her fingers slid across his belly and hip. He turned toward her, putting an arm around her and pulling her close. Her feet were chilly too.

Her mouth found his, and she crushed her body against his chest. Her breath was hot, and her tongue teased his lower lip. He kissed her hungrily, and she responded, pushing her hip against him. Her cold hands wandered down, and he made a noise in his throat at her touch. She giggled, and her teeth ground against his lower lip. He grabbed her hips, and she sighed and leaned against him, her breasts rubbing against his chest. He felt her nipples harden, and he responded in kind.

She pushed him onto his back and straddled him. Her mouth quivered as he positioned her and slid himself inside her. As they began to move together, he stopped noticing how cold her hands and feet were.

And in a little while, everything was warm.

Bart O'Halloran was a hard man who could have been carved from granite. His shoulders were square and the top of his head was flat like a piece of shale. The whiskers descending the slope of his jaw were neatly curled and trimmed, and the shape of his mouth would never be described as kind or forgiving.

He stood on the porch of his sprawling estate—Bart O'Halloran was not a man who would sit when he could stand—and he stared out at the night. He held a cigar tightly in his fist, and at precise intervals, he would raise it to his unkind mouth and suck heavily. Tobacco crackled in a fierce panic, and the tip of the cigar burned an angry red.

Behind the house, dogs started to bark. The sort of noise made by hunting dogs who had caught the scent of something more violent and bloodthirsty than themselves.

A shape moved in the darkness beyond the glow from the many lanterns, and as Bart O'Halloran stood, glaring and smoking, the shape twisted and flexed. Shrinking. Contorting.

The dogs barked more furiously for a moment, and then stopped as one.

The only sound was a whimpering gasp, as if from a man who had found himself squeezed into a tight embrace and then suddenly released. The sound did not come from Bart O'Halloran. He would not know how to make such a sound.

A bowed shape staggered into the lantern light. It was a naked man, and his hair was matted with sweat and blood. His mouth was filled with a feral set of teeth. He crept up to Bart O'Halloran and cringed.

"He shot me," Tommy O'Halloran whined. "It hurts."

"Go clean yourself up," Bart O'Halloran said.

And after his son crawled past him and into the house, Bart O'Halloran remained on the porch, glaring at the night. As if he was waiting for God or the Devil to challenge him. Knowing that neither would, because they knew what sort of man he was.

14

THE JUDGE LEFT HIS HORSE AT THE LIVERY STABLE, AND WALKED up Bitter's single street to the sheriff's office. The sky was high and blue, and the gentle wind blowing up the street carried with it a hint of rain—but not, he thought, before mid-afternoon. The Judge wore his black suit—his only suit, frankly—and he had laundered his white shirt that morning before departing Thrush. Under his coat, he wore his gun belt, and he walked with a hiccup in his step, unused to the weight on his right hip and the pressure of the holster against his thigh. He had grown accustomed to Elm's company, and he had fallen out of the habit of wearing his sidearm—a habit, which he acknowledged now as he walked, that he should not have abandoned so readily.

He whistled a jaunty tune as he walked. Where had he heard that song? St. Louis. At that bawdy house with the blue curtains. *Yes, that piano player had spent some time in Chicago,* he thought, *where he had learned the latest songs.* He had been quite good. As had the ladies, and it was recollection of their attention that brought to mind the jaunty tune, in fact.

It would not be unreasonable to say the Judge was in town to make mischief, though he would quibble and say his intent was merely to settle matters in a quick and judicious manner. Semantics were important, he believed, as was frank speech. It was imperative to communicate plainly and clearly—both in prose and in voice. Many conflicts could be avoided if the active parties simply talked to one another.

The Judge doffed his hat as he entered the sheriff's office.

There was a wooden desk, several chairs, and then a metal cage in the back that was partitioned into two distinct cells. The Judge noted that both were empty, and he wondered how often that was not the case in this town. What with the power Bart O'Halloran undoubtedly held.

The sheriff sat behind the desk, and one of the deputies—the one who had been working the toothpick in his mouth the last time the Judge had seen him—was sweeping the floor.

"Ah, 'tis a pleasant morning, my good men," the Judge said. "I would ask a favor of you, Sheriff Taggert."

The sheriff was finishing a breakfast of biscuits and gravy in a metal tin, washing the food down with coffee from a battered mug. "Good morning," he said, once his mouth was empty. "I—I remember you. A *friend* of the family. Out at Thrush."

"I was," the Judge said. "And still am, in fact."

"I don't recall your name," the sheriff said.

"Of course you do not, for I—in a manner both ill-inclined and uncouth—had not shared it with you."

The deputy leaned on his broom, in no rush to complete his work.

The sheriff cleared his throat. "So," he started. "Mister . . ."

"Judge," the Judge corrected him. "Willard Vernon Wallace. *Iudex vulgivagus populo.*"

The sheriff scratched his nose, and the deputy stared at him with the sullen glare of the uneducated who feel as if they were the butt of a joke.

"Judge of the common folk," the Judge explained.

"Well, Mr. Wallace—"

"Judge, please."

The sheriff paused for a second before continuing. "Judge Wallace. What can we do for you today?"

"I need a letter delivered," the Judge said. He produced the piece of paper he had written on the night before and laid it on the edge of the sheriff's desk.

The sheriff read the name written on the document. "Bart O'Halloran."

"Yes," the Judge said. "I'd like that delivered to Mr. O'Halloran. Within the hour."

The sheriff pursed his lips—perhaps to hold back a smirk—and looked at his deputy. The younger man shrugged. "Well, perhaps you should take that down to the mercantile. They typically deal with parcels and letters for residents of this town. We're more in the . . . law enforcement business."

"Oh, I'm well aware of the nature of your business, Sheriff Taggert," the Judge said. "Which is why I didn't think it would be much trouble for you to run this message to your master."

The sheriff stiffened in his chair, and his lips firmed into a thin line. He adjusted his vest, tugging at the base so that the silver star pinned to his chest caught the light. "I'm gonna assume there has been some misunderstanding here," he drawled.

"Oh, it is certainly within the realm of possibility that I have made a gross exaggeration, and I am eager to hear your explanation as to how I came to the wrong conclusion," the Judge said. He crossed his hands, holding his hat loosely in his hands.

Taggert looked at his deputy again, whose jaw moved rhythmically, unconsciously chewing on a phantom piece of wood. Seeing nothing to help him there, the sheriff sighed and leaned back in his chair. "Rupert, do we have any pressing business this morning?"

The deputy stopped chewing. "No, sir," he said sullenly.

"Are you about done with that sweeping?"

"I was gonna—"

The sheriff made a small noise in his throat and the deputy changed his mind. "—Yes sir," he finished. "I'm about done."

"Why don't you help our guest out, and run this letter over to Bart O'Halloran's place."

"I could do that." Rupert leaned the broom against the wall and came over to the desk. He picked up the piece of paper and started to open it.

"Ah, hold on a moment there," the Judge said, stopping him. "Your name is not on the letter, young man. I would appreciate you not taking an illicit—and potentially illegal—gander at the words I have written expressly for Bart O'Halloran and Bart O'Halloran alone."

"It's just—" Rupert started, but he stopped when he caught the sheriff's glare. "Yes, sir," he said—more to the sheriff than the Judge. "I'll run this right over."

"Excellent." The Judge clapped his hands lightly. "Your assistance is duly appreciated."

The Judge smiled and waited until Rupert had left, and then he turned his attention to the sheriff again. "In an hour or so after Deputy Rupert there delivers that letter, Mr. O'Halloran will come into town and he will be looking for me. You should tell him that I will be down at the hotel, passing the time at the card table." The Judge put his hat back on his head. "And Sheriff? I hope you recall your—what did you say?—your law enforcement duties, when you remind Mr. O'Halloran, along with the men who will be riding with him, that while I am armed, I have not acted in any manner whatsoever that could be construed as aggressive or dangerous or otherwise contrary to the peaceful comportment of a simple bit of business on this fine day. It would be a shame if a conversation between two men ended in a gun battle."

"I'll . . . I'll be sure to remind him," the sheriff said.

"Most promising." The Judge tipped his hat and left the sheriff's office. The song he had been whistling before came back to him again as he continued on up the street.

It is a fine day, he thought as he walked, and it has gotten off to a fine start.

The next part was going to be a little trickier, though he was confident it would all come together as he had planned. Bart O'Halloran was sure to be a prideful man, and pride made a man easy to manipulate.

There were only three men in the card room at the hotel, and they were seated at a table near the center of the room. They were hunched in their chairs like somnambulant birds, and as the Judge strode toward the table, the skinny one with a shock of blond hair started to deal a new hand.

The Judge put his hand in the pocket of his waistcoat and felt the muscles of his stomach clench. Just in time, he thought, and when he exhaled, he reached into that other place for a double eagle. He tossed the coin onto the table where it made that solid thunk that only gold can. "Deal me in," the Judge said as he dragged over a chair to the table. He fervently wished for a glass of whisky to chase away the metallic aftertaste that always hung in the back of his throat after he did that trick, and he chided himself for not stopping at the bar before coming over to the table.

"The ante is only—" a sallow-faced weasel of a man started, but the Judge interrupted him with a wave of a hand.

"Call it my ante and first bet," the Judge said. "I don't want to disrupt the magic of this moment." He grinned to himself, knowing full well they had no idea what he was talking about. "Please, let the play continue. I'm feeling lucky."

The blond-haired dealer looked at Weasel Face and the other player—a whiskered ranch hand who was ill-mannered enough to leave his hat on. Both men shrugged and put their antes in. The dealer nodded and he dealt the Judge in as he counted out five cards for each player.

The Judge glanced at his cards and saw low cards and no matching suits. *Ah, well*, he thought, *maybe I can bluff this one out.*

Two hours later, when door of the card room slammed open, the Judge had not yet won his double eagle back yet, though he had a strong suspicion why the cards were not falling in his favor.

Weasel Face was facing the door, and he stiffened in his chair as he spotted the men barreling into the card room. The Judge glanced over his shoulder and counted six men, all lean and rangy and dressed not unlike the men from the Van Horn ranch. The seventh man to enter the room was tall with a dark hat and spurs that jangled as he strode across the wooden floor to their table.

"Which one of you is Wallace?" he asked. He wore a well-trimmed beard that made his jaw more defined than it was, and an ugly curl played on his lips.

The Judge glanced at his cards again—a pair of threes was all he had—and he raised the bet a dime before he looked up at the leader of the posse. "Come now, young man. Use the apparatus given to you by God, and look upon us with some intelligence. Ask yourself which of these fine gentlemen seated before you appears most capable of handwriting a note like the one that sent you scurrying hence."

The man in the dark hat put his thumbs on his gun belt. The way his coat fell suggested he was wearing a gun on his left hip—the hip closest to the Judge.

"You must be Wallace," he said to the Judge.

The Judge gave him no recognition for being correct, and he motioned to the other players—were they playing cards or pretending to be jackdaws? The whiskered cowboy shook his head, his gaze stealing up at the man standing by the table, and he tossed his cards down. Weasel Face looked like he was going to piss himself, if the Judge had any capacity to read a man's mood from the way his eyes jiggled; he folded as well. The blond-haired fellow, who was the only one at the table—other than the Judge—with any acumen for the game, frowned at his cards, but made no move to give in.

"My father wants to see you," the man in the hat said.

"I'm right here," the Judge said.

"You'll come with us."

"I will do no such thing."

The young man flexed his jaw and flared his nostrils. His fingers fidgeted on his gun belt. None of which made the Judge any more inclined to leave the game.

"Are you going to bet or not?" he groused at the blond-haired man.

"I am giving some thought as to the continuation of my health," the blond-haired man said, his gaze lingering on the outraged O'Halloran.

"Nonsense," the Judge snorted. "Gambling calms the spirit and sharpens the mind." He gestured around the table. "You have the opportunity to meet interesting people, hear stories of far-away places, and learn the nuances of the human spirit. This gentleman, for instance"—he indicated the whiskered man to his left—"is disinclined to take risks and rarely bets unless he has a high degree of confidence that his hand will win."

"Mr. Wallace—"

"That's Judge Wallace," the Judge interrupted, raising a finger.

"My father is a very important man—"

"And I am not?"

The O'Halloran progeny flushed.

"Run along, boy," the Judge said, making a shooing motion with his hand. "Remind your father that sending a boy to do a man's work reflects poorly on the man. If your father does not wish to palaver with me face-to-face, then I will assume he is as much a coward as he is a boor, and I will conduct my business accordingly."

The young man swept his coat back, revealing the familiar shape of a revolver on his left hip. His right hand dipped toward the butt of the gun.

"Richard O'Halloran!"

The sheriff stood at the door of the card room. His coat was pushed back behind his gun too, and his hand rested on the polished butt of his gun.

Richard O'Halloran turned his head slowly and looked at the sheriff. His right hand remained where it was, and his long finger tapped the curved shape protruding from the holster.

"I cannot see your hand," the sheriff said. "You will move it so that I can see it."

O'Halloran's finger slowed its motion.

"Now," the sheriff barked.

O'Halloran raised his hand suddenly, and showed the sheriff his palm.

The sheriff turned his fierce gaze to the other men standing near Richard, and several of them gave him looks that said they were not cowed by his badge, but they were careful to keep their hands in plain sight. The sheriff walked stiffly over to Richard O'Halloran and stuck his hat in the young man's face. "It is my understanding that this gentleman petitioned your father for a meeting," he said. "And given the tolerant manner of his speech with you, I would suspect his request was polite and courteous. Now, as long as I am sheriff in this town, I will expect such civility to be returned to our guests."

O'Halloran let out a short bark of laughter, and the sheriff blinked. But he didn't pull his gun, nor did anyone else in the room.

O'Halloran stepped back from the sheriff, and he pointed his long finger at the Judge. "I'll be seeing you," he said. He touched the rim of his hand and nodded to the sheriff. "Sheriff," he said. "I'll be telling my father about this conversation."

"Do that, boy," the sheriff said.

O'Halloran's lip curled at the sheriff's pejorative tone, and he stalked off, spurs a-ringing.

When he was gone, the sheriff let out a loud whoosh of air, and he dropped his hand from his gun. He turned toward the table. "You, sir, are going to make my day troublesome," he said to the Judge.

"I'm just playing some cards," the Judge said. "You should join us."

The sheriff took off his hat and ran his hand through his brown hair. "I might be inclined to do that," he said. "I suspect I should stick around for awhile."

"Though, I should warn you that this game is rigged," the Judge said.

The sheriff frowned. "Rigged?"

The Judge looked at the blond-haired man. "How do you feel about cheating?" he asked. His question was directed at the sheriff, but his gaze was on the man sitting next to him.

The other players and the sheriff all looked at the blond-haired man. "I don't much care for cheating," the sheriff said.

"I fold," the blond-haired man said. He tossed his cards on the table. There were two sixes and an ace in his hand.

The Judge shrugged and leaned forward to collect the coins scattered on the table. "I do believe we can make some room for you, sheriff," he said.

"Wait a moment," the blond-haired man said. "What did you have?"

The Judge shook his head. "You weren't interesting in paying for the privilege of seeing my cards."

Weasel Face had been dealing, and he had gathered up the rest of the cards already. He looked at the Judge's cards, but he made no move to grab them.

"Turn them over," the blond-haired man said.

"I will do no such thing," the Judge said.

"You just accused me of cheating."

"Did I?"

"Turn them over."

"Are we not civilized men?" the Judge asked. "Can we not play cards without resorting to harsh demands?

"Turn the cards over," the sheriff growled.

The Judge relented his cards, and Weasel Face turned them over. Everyone stared, trying to figure out what the Judge had been hiding.

"You had a pair of threes," the whiskered cowboy said thickly.

The blond-haired man's eyes were wide and his face was turning scarlet. "You were bluffing," he said in a strangled voice.

"I never bluff," the Judge scoffed.

The sheriff laughed, and he nudged the dealer with his hand. "Make some room, sir," he said.

The dealer shuffled his chair to the side, and the sheriff brought over another chair and sat between the dealer and the blond-haired man. He smiled at the nervous faces around the table. "Let me make sure I understand this," he said. "He's not bluffing"—he pointed at the Judge, and then he indicated the man to his right—"and he's not cheating. What about you two?"

Weasel Face said something under his breath that the Judge couldn't quite hear, and the cowboy merely shrugged and stared at his hands.

Now, the Judge thought as Weasel Face dealt the next hand, *maybe I can get my double eagle back.*

The blond-haired man left the game an hour later, when the sheriff caught him dealing off the bottom of the deck. The Judge had learned to distrust the promise offered by the hands dealt by this man, and so he wasn't as offended when the truth came to light. Play continued after the expulsion of the cheater, and by mid-afternoon, the Judge had retrieved his double eagle and had won an additional five dollars.

When Weasel Face went broke, that was sign to the other players that the game had run its course. The whiskered cowboy excused himself from the table—eager to spend his meager winnings on whisky—and that left the Judge and the sheriff.

The Judge tossed the double eagle over to the sheriff's side of the table. The sheriff looked at the coin, his mouth moving around something distasteful. "What's this?"

"I believe you are down a few dollars," the Judge said.

"How I fared in this game is none of your business."

The Judge shrugged. "Perhaps not. Give it to the orphans, then."

"There aren't any orphans in Bitter," the sheriff said.

"The day isn't over yet," the Judge said ominously.

"What was in that letter you wrote to Bart O'Halloran?"

"I merely asked him to meet and discuss a business proposition."

"What sort of proposition?"

The Judge inclined his head and looked at the sheriff. The sheriff shook his head and looked around the card room. "She doesn't know what she is doing," the sheriff said. "That ranch will never be profitable. Bart O'Halloran made her a generous offer a year ago. Did she tell you that? She ran him off her land. What sort of woman does that to a man who comes to her with his hat in his hand?"

"Marriage?" The Judge laughed. "Is that what he offered her?"

The sheriff frowned. "He's a proud man. He's done a lot for this community. It's not right for him to be rebuffed like that. It was a generous offer."

"It was a foolish offer," the Judge said. "He clearly did not know Miss Van Horn."

The sheriff leaned forward. "And you? Do you think she will throw herself on you?"

"I have no such illusions as to Miss Van Horn. She is a wildcat, and I prefer my female companionship to be much more demure and delicate."

The sheriff nudged the gold coin with his thumb. "Keep your money. I sat down with full awareness of the possibilities incurred by my actions. I do not require patronage." He pushed his chair back from the table and stood. Adjusting his hat, he looked down at the Judge. "If you were to seek my opinion, I would say that Bart O'Halloran is not inclined to take your meeting."

"I believe your opinion may be sound, sir," the Judge said.

"Good day, Judge Wallace. Please do not take this unkindly, but I hope to never see you again."

The Judge smiled. "You are not the first man to hold such hope, Sheriff."

The sheriff stuck his tongue in the corner of his mouth. "Maybe I'll have better luck in that regard than I do with cards."

"Maybe," the Judge admitted, but the look in his eye said that he wouldn't take that bet.

15

Elm lay on his belly and watched the seven men and their horses mill about. They were waiting behind a stand of trees less than a mile from Bitter. He was on the ridge farther south, and he had been there since the morning, when he and the Judge had parted company not far from that very stand of trees.

You're a damn fool for poking the bear, he had said to the Judge.

We don't know he's a bear.

Said the blind man staggering around the woods, with honey smeared on his hands.

What harm can come from a little poke?

Elm hadn't dignified that question with a reply, and since the Judge had gone on to town, there had been little activity along the road. A single rider—one of the deputies, Elm assessed after peering through his spyglass—had ridden out of town and then back again. Shortly thereafter, the seven men had passed. They had gone into town, stayed for about an hour, and then come out again. But they hadn't kept riding. They had stopped at the trees.

Elm had inspected them with his glass. There was a familiarity about the one who looked like the leader of the band—not quite as lean as the man he had fought in the woods, but the same feral face. Another one of O'Halloran's sons, no doubt. The rest looked like hired help, but he judged them more handy with whip and stick than plow or basket.

The wind was a steady mistral from the east, and Elm adjusted the long scope on his rifle accordingly.

He had had time to think about his nocturnal visitor, and such thoughts had provided pleasant distraction during the long hours of waiting. They hadn't spoken during their tryst, as if doing so would have broken the dream they were sharing. Elm had closed his eyes when their motion together had become more urgent, and all their communication was done through touch—finger, hip, and mouth. Afterward, she had lain supine on him, her hand stroking his chest. The dream tightened around them, and when he had woken from a light doze, she was gone—almost as if she had never been there. But she had. He could still smell her and feel the memory of her presence on his skin.

When the Judge announced he was going to town, Elm had quickly agreed to accompany him. Not out of shame for what had happened the night before, but more because he still wanted to savor the intimacy of their private dream. He wasn't ready to see her and be forced to acknowledge—one way or another—what had happened.

There had been an urgency in her touch. An eagerness to fill some emptiness within her. And he had met her touch firmly with his own. He knew that same emptiness. *What am I supposed to do when I get lonely?* she had asked him when they had been sitting in the public house. He had looked at her and let her read his answer in his eyes. He had quoted Baudelaire, knowing full well what he was doing and saying. *We all suffer from loneliness,* he had said. He thought about the woman he had seen in the Judge's room in Burlap's Rest.

And in the wake of her visit, he had slept without dreaming. And he wondered if the presence of a woman such as Isadora in his life—*we all need some company, now and again*—could drive off the shadows, once and for all.

The men behind the trees stirred into action, and Elm squinted toward Bitter. There was a single horse and rider, picking their way along the trail. Dark smudges against the green landscape.

He picked up his glass and peered through it. He couldn't make out too many details, but he was sure it was the Judge. He swung the glass down and looked over the band of men again. *Rifles and pistols*, he noted, pausing on each figure to assess how well armed they were.

The O'Halloran and another man ambled out to the trail and waited for the Judge to reach them. The other men remained hiding behind the trees. They were not on their horses, which were clustered in a bunch next to the trees. Elm finally spotted a picket line. The horses were all restrained. The men were not ready to give pursuit should it be necessary.

Elm lightly touched the six cartridges he had laid out on a strip of leather. His Sharps rifle was already loaded. Elm lifted a handful of dirt and let it slip through his fingers, gauging the strength of the wind in the way the sand trickled to the ground. It hadn't changed.

The Judge spotted the two men, and he let his horse slow to a stop several yards away. Elm couldn't hear what was being said, but he didn't like the way the two men held themselves as they confronted the Judge. They were agitated. Angry.

It was too soon for the Judge to have aggravated them, which meant they had been in that state as they waited for him. Elm knew that men who cultivated the fire of rage in their bellies would stoke it hard, believing they would need its fury soon.

He reached for his rifle and slid it forward until the stock rested against his shoulder. He rested the barrel on a flat rock over which he had placed a cloth. The gun was steady, and he peered down through the pair of sights. Watching. Waiting.

Don't do it, old man, he thought. *This cub is not worth it.*

The wind brought him a brief snatch of conversation. Heated words, coming from the O'Halloran boy. Not the Judge. The Judge looked calm and steady.

Which only made Elm's heart beat faster.

The five men behind the trees were nervous too. Two of them

had rifles, and one of them was pointing his weapon at the Judge. Elm fought the urge to shift his aim. He didn't think the man had a clear shot at the Judge, but he wasn't sure. And if he was wrong . . .

Don't pull first, the Judge had told him. Never start the fight, but be ready to finish it.

Elm took up the slack on the trigger. He tried to watch the pair on horseback and the man with the rifle at the same time, but he couldn't focus on both. Finally, cursing the Judge and the man's foolhardy nature, he shifted his aim to the man with the rifle. His finger tightened further.

The two horsemen moved, and Elm nearly jerked the trigger. They were backing off, making room for the Judge on the trail. Elm exhaled noisily, and let his finger up a hair.

The Judge kneed his horse forward, and it ambled along the track, passing between the two men. Words were exchanged between the Judge and O'Halloran, and Elm tightened his finger again as O'Halloran reacted to the Judge's laughter. *The fool had mocked O'Halloran's son*, he thought. *Now he's done it.* O'Halloran's horse danced sideways, and two of the five men started forward.

And then the Judge was beyond the pair. He raised a hand and waved over his shoulder as he rode on. He didn't look back, and Elm held steady, his rifle pointed at the men on horseback.

The Judge kept riding. The men behind the trees milled about. And finally, the two riders drifted together, their horses moving without direction.

Elm moved his finger away from the trigger. He rested his forehead against the side of the rifle and listened to the pounding of his heart.

He hadn't pulled first, but it had been close.

The Judge's horse cropped at the grass in the meadow, and the Judge leaned against a large stone that was part of a rocky scree. He had a knife and a piece of cheese in his hand, and his hat sat loosely on his head.

Elm dismounted and let his horse join the Judge's in an idle forage. The Judge offered him a strip of cheese as he walked over.

"I've had an interesting day," the Judge said as he cut another strip from the block.

"I saw part of it," Elm said. "'Interesting' isn't the word I'd use."

"You and I disagree about vocabulary quite often," the Judge pointed out.

"It is keeping with our disparate views of the world through which we move."

"What word would you have used?"

"'Fraught.'"

"Fraught?"

Elm nodded as he nibbled at the piece of hard cheese.

The Judge made a dismissive noise with his lips. "I wasn't in any danger."

"Not from the pair on the trail," Elm said. "The five guys hiding in the trees were another matter."

"Ah, so that is where they were." He smiled at nothing in particular. "That was one of the O'Halloran's boys. Richard, but I have taken to calling him something less regal in my head. Richard was a King of England. Dickie Boy is just a thug."

"I saw him."

"I do not care for such arrogance—untested and unwanted—in the youth of today. They have done nothing of value. They are a blight."

Elm shook his head. "They have not been properly tempered," he agreed.

"I looked at the bank," the Judge said, changing the subject, "and I do not think the fine banking establishment in Bitter has ten thousand dollars in its vault."

Elm coughed heartily, clearing his throat, and then spat the offending piece out before it could get wedged wrong. "You can't be serious."

"I most certainly am," the Judge said. "That bank might have five thousand dollars."

"No, I mean, serious about robbing it."

"I would not be robbing it," the Judge reminded him. "Regardless, I think it is a fool's errand. There isn't enough money there. We—you—would have to embark upon a spree of robbing banks, all the way to the Mississippi River." The Judge shook his head. "That sounds like a lot of work."

"Perilous work," Elm said.

"Fraught with danger," the Judge added, and Elm nodded in agreement.

"We should come up with a different plan then," the Judge said. He reached into the pocket of his coat and produced a metal flask. He took a sip before offering it to Elm. It contained whisky, and Elm coughed as the harsh spirits burned his nose.

"Terrible stuff they have in Bitter," the Judge said. He took the flask back and drank again. "I must ask Miss Van Horn where she procures her spirits."

"You were speaking of another plan," Elm said. He wiped away a tear caught in the corner of his eye. "A better plan."

"Yes, a better plan," the Judge said. "And, fortunately, while I was putting together a little seed money for our venture, I lucked upon the perfect opportunity. One of the fine gentlemen who ably contributed to our cause told me about a fine lady we must meet. *Salacious Sally.*"

"Who?"

"It is a riverboat, my boy. It wanders up and down the mighty Mississippi, catering to the whims of gentlemen of wealth and taste. Its circuit is from Fort Madison all the way down to St. Louis. Girls. Gambling. Spirits. This lady has it all."

"Does she now?"

"Aye," the Judge continued. "And the gentleman I met told me there was a tournament aboard this boat—one luring gamblers from New York and Chicago. A very large purse is at stake."

"How much?"

"Enough to solve Miss Van Horn's financial difficulties."

"And the cursed beast? How will this *Sally* solve that difficulty?"

"Oh, gambling will be of no assistance there. We will have to resort to a more mundane method there. We must make a trap for the shape-shifter."

"And how do you propose to do that?"

The Judge smiled and tipped back his flask. His throat worked and he gasped as the whisky burned. "You need bait to make an successful trap," he said.

"And what bait are we going to use?" Elm asked.

The Judge smiled. "Me, of course."

Elm squinted at him. "I thought you said gambling would be of no use for dealing with the monster."

"We're not gambling."

"Are you sure?"

The Judge was in the process of raising the flask again, and his hand paused momentarily before he drank. "Of course," he said.

"You're bluffing."

"I don't bluff," the Judge snorted.

Elm looked across the field and watched a crow lazily ride a current of wind. "I know when you're lying," he reminded the Judge.

"Well, don't tell the others. No reason to alarm them unnecessarily."

16

After dinner, they held council at the dining room table. Using cups, saucers, and table linens, Elm constructed a functional map of the ranch and pastures. "It is my belief that the beast will come tonight," the Judge said when Elm was finished arranging the map. "And I will be its target." He waved off the question that rose in Isadora's throat. "Never mind why. Let us concern ourselves more with how best to prepare for the creature's assault. And how to kill it."

He tapped the tea pot designated as the main house. "All those who are not critical to this enterprise will be upstairs in Miss Van Horn's bedroom. The door will be locked and barricaded from the inside. You will, under no circumstances, come out of this room until one or more of the men have given you sign that the danger is passed." He gave Isadora a stern look. "There will be no discussion in this regard."

Isadora looked at Elm, and he spread his hands to say that he would not side with her. While he wasn't convinced that the beast would come for the Judge, it mattered little in light of their plan. They had to keep Isadora safe.

"The men will drive the herd to the near pasture," the Judge continued. "If the beast wishes to get at the cattle, we cannot stop it, and so we will not waste men guarding what can't be guarded. However, if we restrict the movement of the herd, we increase its size and number, which may give the beast pause. It has not—so far—indulged in mindless slaughter. It hunts. It kills. It vanishes. That is its nature."

The Judge pointed at a pair of cups and saucers. "All the horses will be stabled in the barn and the barn doors will be shut. Six to eight men will be inside the barn with the horses. They will be armed with shotguns and torches. They will wait for sign of the beast, whereupon they will emerge and engage the monster."

His finger drifted to the other cups. "The rest of the men will be in the bunkhouse, armed with rifles and torches. Two men will wait in the kitchen; Elm will be on the roof, with his rifle."

"Where do you want me?" Norwood asked.

"I think you should be in the barn, with the men there. They will follow your lead."

Norwood looked pleased to have been given such authority, and Elm felt a momentary spasm in his gut. How many times had he seen men thrill to receive command, only to never see them again after the next battle?

"What do we tell the men about this . . . about this monster?" Isadora asked. Before dinner, Elm had shown her the Judge's bestiary. They had retired to the sitting room for privacy, where she had looked at the picture of the wolf that walked on two legs. *And these?* she had asked, after looking at the other pages in the old book.

I don't know, Elm said. *I hope to never find out.*

The Judge shrugged. "We tell them that it is a large wolf, for that is what it will be. We don't need to tell them how large."

She looked across the table at Elm and he met her gaze. *What if all the stories from our childhood are true?* she had asked. *What fools are we to have thought them nothing more than idle fancies?*

It is better to know we are fools than to be foolish in our ignorance, he said.

They had been sitting on the divan, their thighs almost touching. Her black hair lay across her shoulders, and he wanted to brush a stray lock of it back from her neck.

"How certain are we that it will come tonight?" Norwood asked, snapping Elm back to the present.

"Because tonight is the full moon," the Judge said. "And this beast is strongest on this night."

Elm looked at Isadora again, and his thoughts were filled with memories of moonlight streaming through the tiny window in his room. And the pale shape of her naked breast in that mysterious light. She caught his gaze, easily reading his thoughts. She flushed and looked away, raising a hand to cover her mouth, but not before Elm saw a hint of a smile curling her lip.

The night was crisp and clear, and the moon moved slowly across the heavens, as if it were unused to the weight of its full belly. Occasionally, a cow would low, but the call was always gentle and inquisitive in tone. There was no sense of alarm in any bovine voice. Elm lay on the roof of the big house, wrapped in his heavy coat to keep the chill from settling into his bones, and his gaze wandered across the immense canopy of stars. He saw a handful of shooting stars, and he passed the time identifying as many of the old constellations as he could. Bostán, Orchilí's youngest cousin, had memorized all of them—as he was wont to remind Elm—and the boy always enjoyed teasing Elm about how much better he was at remembering them than Elm.

Elm hadn't minded. He liked the boy, and when the nights were like this and Orchilí was away, he would sit out with Bostán and play the naming game.

When the moon reached the peak of its path, flooding the valley with its silver light, Elm gave up on the stars and crept to the edge of the roof and looked out over the yard behind the big house. The windows of the bunkhouse were lit with orange, and a similar light flickered in the high windows of the stable. The herd was a slow eddy of black on black off to his left. The horses in the corral behind the stable were silent.

Everything was still, including the wind.

The heavy coat was too hot all of a sudden. Spots on his back itched. He felt restless. He let his gaze roam across the landscape one more time, searching for something out of place. But nothing moved.

Shaking his head, he inched along the roof until he reached the short ladder that he had cleared earlier. He clambered down to the balcony off the master bedroom and crept to the door where he tapped lightly on the glass.

"Something's not right," he said when Isadora unlocked the door and peered out at him. He squeezed into the bedroom before she could say anything. He nodded at Mrs. Walphin, who sat at a small table where she and Isadora had been playing cards and drinking wine. With Isadora's help, he moved the heavy dresser away from the bedroom door, and he admonished her to lock it behind him as he went downstairs.

Halfway down, he stopped suddenly, and Isadora bumped into him. He turned, and she opened her mouth to say something, but he put his hand over her mouth and shook his head. He would have a talk with her later about leaving the safety of the bedroom, but at the moment, the prickling alarm that was crawling up his back was more important.

He continued down to the kitchen, surprising the two cowboys who were sprawled in chairs at the kitchen table. "Something's not right," he said to them as he went to the back door.

The Judge sat on the porch, a shotgun in his lap and a lantern at his side.

"Something's not right," he said to the Judge, who started slightly when Elm spoke, and Elm realized the old man had been asleep.

"You damn fool," he swore.

"What?" the Judge snapped. "There's nothing out here."

"How would you know?" Elm asked. "You were asleep."

"I was not," the Judge bristled. When Elm growled at him, he relented. "I may have been resting my eyes, but the dog—"

Elm stalked to the edge of the porch and scanned the yard. "Where is the dog?" he asked.

"Right beside . . ." When the Judge looked and saw no sign of the dog, his voice faltered.

"Get back in the house," Elm snapped at Isadora. He clenched his right hand, and noticed that it was empty. Where was his rifle?

He looked up, realizing he had left it on the roof.

Out past the barn, the dog barked.

The sound was followed by a loud thud from the barn itself, followed by cries of alarm from the horses. They heard the thudding noise of hooves against wood and the frantic shouting of men. There was another thud, and the barn shuddered as if had been rattled by a storm, though there was no wind. The voices—man and horse screaming indiscriminately—became more strident. Elm noticed the bay door of the loft was open— hadn't they closed that earlier?—and through the door, he saw a flickering light. "Fire," he breathed.

He leaped off the porch. "The barn is on fire," he shouted over his shoulder as he raced across the yard.

Gun shots sounded inside the barn, and when Elm reached the door, he smelled the hot and dry stench of burning hay. Thin tendrils of smoke curled out from beneath the door as he grabbed the handle and pulled.

The door refused to budge.

More guns fired. The horses were kicking the walls of their stalls. The glow from the loft door brightened, and he heard the crackling noise of fire as it eagerly devoured the dry hay.

Elm yanked on the handle again, with no more success. Something slammed into the door on the inside, and he heard a terrified voice screaming about fire and blood.

And about the monster locked in there with them.

The door flew open without warning, and Elm was knocked back. He landed heavily, the air driven out of his body, and he struggled to breathe as a flood of hot air, fire, and terrified horses exploded out of the barn. He curled up, covered his face with his arms. Trying to make himself as small as possible so the panicked horses wouldn't trample him. A hoof caught him in the small of the back, and he winced at the blow. Another horse stepped on his hair, and he was thankful the hoof hadn't landed an inch closer. In another moment, the thunderous flight of horses were gone, and he could lower his arms.

The inside of the building was a flaming abattoir. Bodies of men and horses were scattered throughout the burning barn, and the wet blood sizzled in the heat. The air was hot and hazy, and he blinked heavily as his eyes stung from heat and ash. Something eclipsed the fire; something large and black, with shining eyes and bloody teeth.

The wolf stalked out of the barn, its fur steaming and smoking. There was blood on its muzzle and chest. Elm stared, unable to move. It was . . . so much larger than than he had imagined. It was . . .

"Hah! Fell beast!" the Judge shouted. "Attend to your doom."

The wolf, who had been nosing at Elm's boot, raised its head and snarled. Elm saw a ragged line of teeth, a feral grimace filled with—

The Judge's shotgun boomed, and the wolf flinched. A hail of birdshot, iron, and God knew what else peppered the beast. The Judge had insisted on repacking several shells for the shotgun, though Elm had not understood the Judge's insistence. Birdshot was meant to scatter tiny pellets across a wide swath of ground. The pellets would kill game birds, but they wouldn't do more than break the skin and draw blood on a larger creature. What good would come from angering the wolf?

The Judge fired the other barrel of the shotgun, and Elm felt the sting of pellets as they tore through his pants and boots.

The wolf howled. It was bleeding from a dozen or more wounds, and steam rose from its bloody hide.

The Judge dropped the shotgun and drew his revolver. In a display of martial prowess that surprised Elm, the Judge fanned the hammer, quickly emptying the weapon of all of its ammunition.

In a flash, the wolf was gone, a shivering howl fading in its wake.

"This time, we hunt it down," the Judge said, a grim smile on his face.

17

THEY RAN THROUGH THE WOODS—ELM IN THE LEAD; THE JUDGE, Benjee, and Purnell following. The light of the moon cascaded through the trees, dappling the forest floor in a silver-hued splendor. Elm had his rifle slung across his back, and he kept his eyes on the path ahead. The others carried lanterns and torches, and he didn't want his night-sight to be ruined by the orange fire.

There were broken branches along the course the monster took, and the wolf's blood was spatters of oily darkness on the ground. Even injured, the beast was fast, and Elm worried they would not be able to catch up to it.

They ran north from Thrush, and after crossing a narrow stream that was probably the same stream where they had found the cows a few days earlier, the trail turned west. It followed a ridge of packed sand along the base of a hill, and near a section of the hill where the slope had given way in a jumble of rocks, Elm lost the trail. He was still searching for it when the rest of the hunting party caught up with him. The Judge trailed the pair of cowboys, gasping and wheezing as he staggered up.

"We should have brought the horses," he gasped, leaning against one of the stones. His chest heaved as he struggled to breathe.

There had been no time. Isadora and the rest of the men had been frantically trying to douse the fire in the barn—hoping to get to the men and horses who were still trapped inside. The horses that had fled were scattered across the ranch. It would have taken hours to find mounts, calm them, and get them saddled. In that time, the beast would have run so far, they would have had no chance of catching it. As it was, unless Elm could find a clue as to which direction the beast had gone, they might already be too late.

Elm ranged back and forth along the rock fall, trying to spot some sign of the creature. Frustrated, he grabbed Benjee's torch and used its flickering light to illuminate the darker shadows among the boulders. There was no gap big enough for it to crawl through. There was no sign in the dirt near the rocks. It hadn't kept going west. It wasn't hiding. Where was it?

And then his frantic search revealed a gleam of drying blood. He stopped and raised the torch, peering up the rocky wall.

The beast had climbed the landslide.

"Where did it go?" the Judge asked.

"Up," Elm said. He waved the torch, making the shadows on the rocks dance. "We can't follow it. Not unless we are goats."

"We are not goats," the Judge wheezed.

"We have to go around," Elm said, and he didn't try to hide his frustration. He kept Benjee's torch as he ran along the base of the rocky jumble. The Judge and the two men trailed after him.

The landslide wasn't wide, but the ground past it was hard and little grew on it. Elm tried to hug the ground and move like a goat as he scrambled up the slope, and he only slipped a few times. His breathing eased when the slope eased and he moved quickly along the flat ground, searching for sign of the beast's passage. He found blood spatter soon enough, and he waited for the other men to catch up before he started off again.

"That's O'Halloran's land over this hill," Purnell said.

Elm looked at the Judge, who met his glance with a steely gaze. "Then we go onto O'Halloran's land," he said.

Elm nodded, and they started off again. The trail was easier to follow. The blood spatters were larger and more frequent. Scaling the rock wall had tired the beast, and it was still hurting.

The ground continued to slope upward, and the rocks became more numerous. Eventually Elm slowed to a cautious walk. There were many places for an ambush, and he knew the torches were both a boon and a bane. Their light allowed the men to move more readily across the uneven ground, but he also knew the light revealed the position. If the wolf wanted to surprise them, it would have plenty of time to plan its attack.

As he neared the top of the hill, a long howl filled the night sky. The sound turned his legs to stone and made his heart shudder to a stop.

As the howl faded, Benjee whispered to Purnell, "Did you hear that?"

Purnell started to respond, but Elm shushed both of them with a wave of his hand.

It was close. Very, very close.

He held his breath, listening intently, and heard something move up ahead. He inched forward, moving cautiously around a boulder. A shelf of stone formed an arc along the crest of the hill, and a deep swell of darkness lay beneath the overhang. He had no idea how far back the space went, but he knew the beast was hiding there.

"It was so big," Benjee whispered. "And its eyes. Did you see its eyes? I've never seen anything as big as that."

"No one has, you jackass," Purnell hissed.

"It was bigger than Smoke, and she's fifteen hands tall."

"She's not that tall," Purnell argued back.

"Stop it, you two," Elm hissed. He gestured that they should stop arguing and join him. They edged closer, their faces pale and pinched. "There," Elm said, pointing. "It's right there."

Purnell raised his lantern. "I don't see nothing."

"It's hiding in those shadows," Benjee whispered. "Like it did in the barn. It's waiting for us."

"I'm not going in there," Purnell said.

"Me neither."

Elm gave Benjee back his torch and patted the nervous man on the shoulder. "Stay here," he said. "Keep watch."

"It ain't coming out, is it?" Purnell whimpered at the same time that Benjee squeaked. "We're not going in there!"

Elm ignored them both as he wandered down the hill to meet the Judge, who was huffing loudly as he climbed. "It's up there," he said. "Up in some rocks."

The Judge squinted up at Purnell and Benjee who were still whispering intently. "God in Heaven," the Judge asked, sucking in air between each word. "How did we end up with those two?"

"You'll have to ask God," Elm said. He nodded at the shotgun the Judge was carrying. "What did you load that with?"

"Silver," the Judge said. "Bits of wood from a cross."

"And you didn't think to tell me?"

The Judge's mustache twitched. "I thought you knew," he said. "It was right there in the book."

"You only shared the book that one time," Elm reminded him. "I didn't memorize what was written there."

The Judge lifted his shoulders. "Ah, well, there wasn't time to do more than a few shells anyway. But it worked, didn't it?"

"Aye, the beast is hurt," Elm acknowledged. "But we should have stopped it before it got into the barn." He shook his head. "It must have climbed the wall somehow. I don't—"

The Judge hefted the shotgun. "It doesn't matter. We'll stop it now. That is the best we can do for those who died."

A low moan issued from the shallow cave. It wasn't quite a howl, but it was louder than an involuntary whine. Benjee yelped, and he and Purnell came tripping down from the boulder where they had been hiding.

"Did you hear that?" Benjee whispered.

Purnell slapped him on the shoulder. "We all heard it, you moron."

Elm shoved his way past the two men and climbed to where he had a clear view of the overhang. He saw nothing, and he motioned to the others to follow him. Drawing his pistol, he moved slowly toward the dark spot under the rock.

Claws scrabbled on rock, and he froze. His heart beat hard and fast, as if it were trying to break out of his chest and run away. He had a sudden vision of the beast charging out of the darkness—much like it had charged him earlier—and he found himself rooted to the spot.

Claws scraped against rock again, followed by an agonized whine. The noise made Elm gasp lightly, and the panic holding him prisoner vanished.

"That's . . . that wasn't a wolf," Benjee hissed behind him. "That sounded like—"

Purnell hissed at him to shut up. Elm breathed shallowly, staring hard at the darkness, trying to see what was hidden beneath that rock. Was it a wolf or was it a man?

"Fuck all this stealthy nonsense," the Judge grumbled as he strode past Elm. He raised the shotgun and pulled the first trigger. The noise of the blast was magnified by the rock, and it echoed back on them. Like thunder sounding overhead. Birdshot ricocheted around them too, and Elm instinctively ducked.

The shadows shifted, and the Judge adjusted his aim. His finger was tight on the second trigger, but he didn't pull.

Something . . . something much smaller than they expected staggered out of the darkness. Its pale arms were raised, and its eyes were wide and feral. Its mouth was caked with blood.

Elm stared in horror at the bloody and naked man. He recognized him, and the shock of such recognition cut deeper than he had anticipated. "Tommy—" he started.

The Judge pulled the second trigger, and the blast of shot and silver blew Tommy O'Halloran off his feet.

The Judge discarded the empty shotgun and drew his pistol.

Shaking off his shock, Elm hurried after the Judge. He stumbled to a halt at the sight of the naked body lying on the ground near the rocks. Tommy's body was covered with numerous wounds that oozed blood. The second blast from the Judge's shotgun had ravaged Tommy's chest.

But he wasn't dead. Tommy's throat worked as he tried to form words, but when he opened his mouth, all that came out was a gush of blood and a weak whistle of air.

Before Elm could stop him, the Judge drew his pistol and fired twice. Both bullets made Tommy twitch; and then he shivered once more as the life left him. He jaw gaped and his eyes became fixed and dull.

Benjee and Purnell came up beside the Judge and Elm.

"That's Tommy O'Halloran," Purnell said, somewhat unnecessarily.

"His father is not going to like this," Benjee said.

"No, he certainly won't," the Judge said. His shoulders sagged as he holstered his pistol. "But I warned him."

They all stared at the body for a minute, each lost in their own thoughts—replaying what they had seen, trying to forget what lay before them—and then the Judge blew out a noisy breath of air. "All right, let's get some wood," he said.

"Wood?" Benjee squeaked.

"We have to burn the body," Elm said.

The Judge nodded. "It's the only way to be sure."

It took awhile, but they managed to gather enough wood for a makeshift pyre. Purnell and Benjee wouldn't touch the body, and so the Judge and Elm each took hold of one of Tommy's arms and hauled the corpse atop the pile of wood. Elm used Benjee's torch to light the wood, but it didn't catch quickly, so the Judge took the lantern from Purnell and threw it on the stack. The glass shattered and the oil caught, and soon thereafter, the pyre was burning nicely.

The men watched the firelight dance on the rock walls. Benjee made a face as the body began to sizzle, and the stink of burning flesh drove them all farther away. The Judge caught Elm's eye and nodded toward the top of the hill close to where they were standing. They went to the top and looked down at the valley beyond. Moonlight made a distant river sparkle like a snake covered in shining scales, and closer to the hill, there was a cluster of orange lights that Elm realized marked a ranch property.

"O'Halloran's ranch," the Judge said, nodding toward the lights. "How many head of cattle do you think he has?"

"A couple thousand is my understanding," Elm said.

"He needs the Van Horn land, and he's not going to stop trying to get it."

"Even if we help Isadora pay off the loan?"

The Judge narrowed his eyes. "The loan is no longer the issue here," he said. "Not after what we just did."

"Should we have done something else?" Elm asked. He was curious to hear the Judge's answer. His effort to forestall the Judge from shooting Tommy had been futile, and now it seemed as if the Judge was having second thoughts.

The Judge shook his head. "That was justice," he said, his voice calm and cold. "Pure and simple. That boy was wrong, and he deserved no trial by peers or sentencing by courts. We did what was right. We did what had to be done."

"Bart O'Halloran will say we murdered his boy, and he won't be wrong," Elm said.

The Judge snorted and shook his head. "He asked her to marry him," he said after a moment. "Did you know that?"

"Who?"

"Bart O'Halloran."

"No. Who did he ask?"

"Who do you think?"

"Isadora?"

The Judge stared at him. "You are daft sometimes, boy."

A flush rose in Elm's cheeks, and he turned his gaze toward the valley. "What did she say?"

"She told him where he could shove his proposition, is my guess."

"Good," Elm heard himself say, and he wondered why he cared. But as quickly as that query formed in his head, he dismissed it. He knew why, and that thought made his blood hot.

"Would have prevented all this, though," the Judge said.

"But what about her?" Elm asked.

"What about her?"

"He doesn't love her."

The Judge cocked his head to the side, and he eyed Elm, assessing the vehemence of Elm's response. "Bart O'Halloran loves power and money," he said eventually. "That is all he cares about."

Elm stared down at the lights in the valley. His blood pounded in his ears. "You want to take those things from him."

"Aye," the Judge said. "I do. *We* have to."

Elm nodded slowly, an idea forming in his mind. "*We* might have to break the law," he said carefully.

"We might," the Judge replied after a moment.

"We might offend God," Elm added, wondering if he could do the thing he had in mind. If he should do it. *You cannot unsee what you have seen*, Orchilí had cautioned him.

"I can live with that," the Judge said.

18

It was two days' ride to Keokuk, on the Mississippi River, where they would find the steamboat and the tournament, but before they could leave Thrush, there was work to be done. Six men and four horses had died in the barn fire, and among the dead were Isadora's uncle, Norwood, and the young hand, Freddie. The other men Elm did not know, but they had been well-liked by the rest of the ranch hands. Their loss cast a pall over the survivors, who went through the motions of their daily tasks with shadows filling their eyes.

Elm and the Judge took over for Mrs. Walphin in the kitchen, giving her time to grieve. They knew how to cook, being men of the trail, but managing to feed a dozen men was another task entirely. As they finished preparing and cleaning up after one meal, it seemed like they had to start the next, and after a few days, Elm marveled at how anything else got done beyond keeping the staff fed.

He and Isadora saw little of each other and spoke less. The loss of her uncle haunted her, and news of the monster's death had been received brusquely—nothing more than a clipped affirmation of the deed. He had tried to reach out to her once, but she had stared at his hand like she had no idea what it was, and when he offered to read poetry, she had shaken her head and left the room.

In the evenings, he and the Judge sat on the porch and watched the night lay blankets of deep shadows over the burned husk of the barn. Elm avoided sleep, but when it surprised him and dragged him under, he would fight his way back to consciousness as soon as he realized what happened. The shadows were there, cackling and screaming at him, and when he woke, drenched in a cold sweat, he realized their cries were harsh mockeries of the screams he had heard from the barn.

The last time he had fought sleep so assiduously had been after Antietam, because when he closed his eyes, he was flung back to the mud and smoke of the battlefield. Forced to watch the unnecessary death of every man and boy—both Confederate and Union—and he could never look away.

He was not the only survivor of that bloody battle who believed they had been cursed. The ghosts of the dead held them tight, demanding to be recounted and remembered by those who were more fortunate. A handful of men in Elm's regiment killed themselves in the weeks following, unable to bear the burden levied on them by the dead.

In time, Elm experienced worse things than the battle at Antietam and those ghosts lost their grip on him. And perhaps that is what caused him so much panic at night. What had happened to him that he could no longer grieve at the unnecessary death of innocent men?

A week after the attack, he and the Judge and Isadora departed for Keokuk. They had tried to argue that she had no place with them, but she cut them short with a simple declaration—"This is my ranch; these were my men"—and they had relented. Mrs. Walphin emerged from her room, dry-eyed and dressed in black, and her presence in the kitchen—oddly enough—gave strength and courage to the rest of the men.

Additionally, her biscuits were moist and flaky, unlike Elm's, which were not unlike clumps of dried dirt.

They had six hundred dollars between the three of them. It was the Judge's understanding that they needed a thousand dollars to buy their way into the tournament. If they couldn't raise that money in Keokuk before they got on the boat, then the deaths at Thrush would have been for naught.

They reached Keokuk after nightfall, and before they found lodging, the Judge insisted on looking upon the *Salacious Sally*. She was a long, white steamboat with fancy letters painted across the wooden shell covering her paddle wheel. According to a pair of sailors they spoke to on the dock, they had arrived just in time. The *Sally* was scheduled to leave on the morrow—mid-morning—which was going to come too quickly for their liking. While Elm and Isadora made arrangements with a livery for the horses, the Judge went looking for lodging, and all he could find were drafty rooms in a ramshackle building several blocks away.

They each had their own rooms, and Elm paced about his for an hour or so, refusing to lie down on the lumpy mattress. His restlessness did not abate, and eventually, he put on his boots and wandered down the hall to the Judge's door. There was no response to his knock, and so, with some trepidation and a bit of a thrill moving up his spine, he moved on to Isadora's room. She came to the door when he knocked, and stared at him without saying anything.

"May I come in?" he asked, and she turned away. She did not shut the door, and so he went in. He stood awkwardly by the door as she wandered over to the single chair and sat down, her hands loosely clasped in her lap.

"I, uh, I see you have a view," Elm said, indicating the room's single window. "All I can see out my window is the building next door. There's a window there too, but no one came into the other room. So, it's just . . . it's just a window." He had thought that speaking to her would calm his heart, but the reverse was happening. He was struggling to breathe. There was no air in the room. He wanted to open that window and stick his head out.

"Has he gone out?" she asked, and Elm knew she meant the Judge.

"Yes, ma'am, he has," he said, and when he realized how distant and formal he sounded, he panicked and babbled on. "We need more money, and he must have gone out to fetch it. Yes, that is where he must be. He does this sort of thing, you know. Making decisions without consulting anyone else."

"He is very sure of himself."

"He is."

"Do you think he has any doubts about what he has done?" She was looking at him now, and Elm swallowed heavily.

"He does not," he said. "You have heard him speak of the law. He believes it is his calling. Even when . . ." He faltered.

"Even when he is killing," Isadora finished for him.

Elm frowned. "I suppose so," he said.

"And you?" she asked. "Do you share his righteous fervor?"

Elm shook his head. "I see their faces too often," he said softly. "I hear them crying out."

"I do too," she said. "Part of me wants to scream back. Wants to yell and curse at them, and tell them to leave me alone. Another part of me craves their presence. I want to be reminded over and over again of how I failed them. How they died because of my pride."

"That isn't what happened," Elm started, but she wasn't finished.

"I can't embrace that pain," she said. "I saw what it did to my father. Dear God, Elm, I love my father's memory, but the death of my mother devoured him. Bit by bit, over the years. I do not want to wither like that."

"You don't deserve such a fate," Elm said.

"But how do I avoid it? How do I live with the guilt and the shame?"

He walked across the room and wrapped his arms around her. She stiffened at first, but then something broke in her and she buried her head against his belly. He stroked her hair with care and affection. "You make amends," he said. "You do what is right for others. You tip the balance as best you can for those who are still with us."

Her arms tightened. "Is that why he left my mother?"

"Yes," Elm said, even though he knew he had no right to speak for the Judge in this regard.

"And now? Is that what drives him now?"

Elm shook his head, even though she wasn't looking at his face. He ran his fingers through her hair. "The Judge wants to knock the scales over, once and for all time."

She shivered slightly and her arms tightened. "And you? Who are you protecting? Him or everyone else?"

"Let's not speak any more of that," he said, avoiding her question. Avoiding the thought of what he had done under the aegis of "protection." "Not tonight," he added.

She held him a while longer, and when she spoke again, her voice was so quiet, he had to bend over to hear her words. "This is but a dream," Isadora said. "Isn't that what Shakespeare said? Everything that has happened since you two showed up at my ranch has been nothing but a dream. I could wake at any moment—I know this—and if I did, the barn would still be there. The horses would be out in the paddock. My uncle would be yelling at the men about keeping the cows from wandering. It would be like any other fall afternoon."

She shivered gently. "But I stay in this dream. This . . . terrible dream where the barn is gone, Rudy is gone, my uncle is gone—all dead because of a monster that could only exist in a nightmare such as this—and I have not mourned the death of any of those dear to me because I'm about to take a steamboat ride up the Mississippi River. My two champions are going to win me ten thousand dollars. This money is the key to my freedom, and it is all I want in the world. At least, it is all dream me wants. Money and freedom."

Elm nuzzled his face against her head. "And what about the you that isn't dreaming? What does that woman want?"

She leaned back so she could look up at him. He offered her a crooked smile, and she leaped to her feet, her hands snaking around his neck. Her mouth sought his, and he responded in kind.

Elm undressed her and she lay on her bed, hugging her arms to her breasts. Tiny shivers coursed through her body as she watched him undress. Her eyes were hooded and mysterious, but he knew there was a great gulf of yawning emptiness hiding behind her gaze. When he climbed onto the bed, she surged against him, wrapping her arms around him with a startling hunger. He threw the heavy blanket over them and lowered himself onto her. Her mouth found his again, her teeth gnawing at his lip. Her hand slapped at his hip, clasping him tight to her, and when he snaked his arms around her, she let out an involuntary sigh that turned into a choking sob.

He held her as her body shook. Gently, he kissed her neck and shoulder, bringing warmth to her cold body. Her hands curled into fists and beat against his back and buttocks. She writhed under him as she felt his growing hardness, and when she opened her legs and let him press against her, she bit his ear hard enough to draw blood.

She wasn't quite ready to take him, and she groaned deep in her chest as he slid into her. Her hands clawed at his back when he sought to draw away from her, and her hips bucked against him with an urgent frenzy. She threw her head back against the mattress as her body responded to him, and he rocked his hips back and forth. "Yes," she moaned into his ear, and she kept repeating the word over and over. Eventually, the word slurred into a sibilant sigh, and the world went with it, sliding away into darkness.

He fell into it, knowing he was not alone. Knowing that this darkness was peace, and he knew not when he might feel it again.

Eventually, the Judge found a worthwhile card game. The room was filled with cigar smoke and the stink of too many desperate men. There were three tables, eight players to a table, and as many men hovered nearby like eager vultures, ready to climb over the corpse of a broken man. Brandishing a handful of double eagles, the Judge bulled his way into a spot at the table in the corner, and he quickly lost two of them before he could catch the rhythm of the players.

The players were a rough bunch, prone to swearing and accusations of cheating and malingering over the cards. The Judge felt right at home, and after a few hands (and a few whiskies), he was roaring with salty curses that made the other players roar with laughter. The men whose mothers he'd accused of fornicating with goats and whose sexual prowess he likened to that of a three-legged blind dog trying to fuck a hedgehog were less amused and their play became more agitated, which was the point of such talk, after all, because their ire made it easier for the Judge to take their money.

A few hours later, the Judge reckoned he was up nearly two hundred dollars, which was not a bad bit of work. He had busted two of the players, and when the other two bowed out, he smiled wildly at the new players who sat down. Their pockets were deep and full, he knew, and there was room yet in his.

The deal passed to him, and he shuffled the cards adroitly. "We shall play as if God is watching us, gentlemen," he said, which elicited barks of laughter and snorts of derision from the crowd. As he started to deal the cards, the crowd parted to make room for a tall man in a dark hat.

The sight of the newcomer unnerved the Judge for a split second, and his hand trembled as he threw a card to the man on his left. The card sailed into the man's lap.

"Oops," Richard O'Halloran said. "Did I make you miss?"

19

"O'HALLORAN IS HERE?"

The Judge shrugged laconically, as if Isadora had asked about the price of butter at the market. "Dickie Boy is, at least. We should assume his father is, too." He crammed a half-buttered biscuit into his mouth.

"Why?" she asked, looking back and forth between the Judge and Elm, searching their faces for some insight into what she had missed.

The Judge mumbled something about money around the food in his mouth.

"Why would O'Halloran need money?"

Elm devoted his attention to the hot biscuits and hash on the plate in front of him.

Surprisingly, the food in the restaurant next to their hotel was much better than the lodgings. Not that Elm had much to complain about his room, as he had not spent more than an hour or two there since they had checked in.

The Judge slurped noisily at his coffee and then smacked his lips before responding to Isadora's question. "I suspect that the bank will not give him your ranch outright," he said. "For all his influence, he will still need to acquire the outstanding loan. They'll be willing to take a loss, but they'll expect him to pay the bulk of it." He shrugged. "Maybe Bart O'Halloran isn't as flush as he wants everyone to believe."

Elm thought there might be another reason, but didn't say anything out loud.

Isadora caught Elm's glance at the Judge and she looked back and forth at the two of them. "What have you two done?"

"You'll have to be more specific, my dear," the Judge said, mopping the gravy on his plate with a biscuit. He smiled wolfishly at her. "We've done a lot of things. Sometimes we have done things independently of one another. Maybe I should be asking you this question, hmm?"

Isadora blushed slightly and ran her hand across the back of her neck.

"What happened at the card game?" Elm asked, pulling the conversation away from any discussion of what he and Isadora might be doing out of sight of the Judge.

"Dickie Boy wanted to play cards," the Judge said.

"And?"

"And he's not very good." The Judge tapped the table with a long finger. "He gets impatient."

"Did you take his money?"

The Judge pursed his lips and shook his head. "He didn't have much on him. Besides, he had a message to deliver."

"A message?" Isadora asked.

"His father wanted to inform me that he was going to break us. And when he's done taking everything you have, he's going to burn it all down." The Judge picked up his mug and waved it back and forth. "And Dickie Boy will probably piss on the ashes of your family homestead. That sort of nonsense."

"I'd rather die before giving O'Halloran anything," Isadora hissed.

"Why make it easy for him?" the Judge asked. He smiled at her expression, and her face lost some of its anger.

"He's going to be on the boat, isn't he?" Elm asked, suddenly understanding O'Halloran's presence in Keokuk.

The Judge nodded, his eyes on Isadora. "I guess we'll just have to take his money too," he said. "Won't that be poetic?"

"What about his son, Richard? And his other son, Tommy."

The Judge frowned at his mug, as if he was disappointed by the lack of coffee in it, and Elm focused on chewing his food. They had agreed to not tell Isadora who they had killed on the bluff, and they had sworn Purnell and Benjee to secrecy, though Elm suspected both men wouldn't be able to keep their mouths shut long. As long as he and the Judge kept Isadora away from the ranch, they could keep her in the dark as to the demise of Tommy O'Halloran. Eventually, such a secret would not matter . . .

"I wouldn't worry about those boys," the Judge said distantly. "Things have a way of sorting themselves out."

Isadora glanced at Elm, who shrugged. "He means me," he said.

She fidgeted with the collar of her blouse for a moment, and it was clear to Elm that something was on her mind. "That monster which . . ." she started finally. "Where did it come from? How did O'Halloran have sway over it?" She leaned forward and lowered her voice. "And if it was as your bestiary said it was, who was it?"

"We burned the body," the Judge said, and he held her gaze as she stared at him. Daring her to ask him again. Letting her know he wasn't going to tell her.

"Was that the only one?" she asked.

The Judge blinked in surprise. He opened his mouth to reply and then shut it again. Elm paused, a last spoonful of congealing gravy halfway to his lips.

"Let's hope so," the Judge said finally, but his tone wasn't very convincing.

The Judge added his late-night winnings to their purse, which made them only a hundred dollars short of the tournament buy-in. The Judge had an idea how to solve that problem, but before the boat left, he wanted to take Isadora shopping for a new dress or two. *To help sell the characters we are going to play*, he explained.

But the cost of such attire will diminish our stake, Isadora had pointed out.

I wouldn't worry about that, the Judge had said. He winked at Elm as he escorted Isadora out of the dining room, and Elm got the hint. No, the Judge wasn't going to worry about the last bit of cash they needed. That concern fell to Elm. After they departed for the millinery, he wandered along the docks for a little while, thinking about how he might acquire some funds in less than a few hours.

The Romani knew many ways to steal, swindle, con, and otherwise lift money from naive bystanders. But such work required a team of pickpockets, performers, and confidence men. It was rare to work alone, and even the scams that could be accomplished by a single person usually only netted a purse or two. It would take him many hours to get a hundred dollars, much less twice that amount. Also he needed someplace more populous than Keokuk. He needed crowded streets and a bustling market or two, and words such as 'sprawling' and 'bustling' would never to be used to describe the streets of Keokuk.

An old handbill, peeling away from the brick wall of a mercantile, caught his eye. The letters and drawing were faded from weeks of sunlight, but it was still legible. At the center was a picture of a bear riding a bicycle, with another bear astride its shoulders. The second bear was juggling a dozen balls.

MILTON'S MENAGERIE.
THE GREATEST COLLECTION
OF OUTRAGEOUS ODDITIES &
SURPRISING STRANGENESS
IN ALL THE AMERICAS.

The handbill advertised a traveling circus, one complete with trapeze artists, bears that could perform great acts of dexterity, talking snakes, conjoined children, and bearded ladies. Near the bottom of the sign was a secondary advertisement for a Western show that include stunt riding, tricks with ropes, and an "amazing display of sharpshooting and martial prowess the likes of which had never been seen."

It was this last phrase that reminded Elm of a trick he had seen once. A confidence game that could be done solitaire . . .

The *Salacious Sally* floated luxuriously in the Mississippi, ready to take on passengers as soon as her crew brought over the gangplank. Isadora and the Judge joined the lengthy queue of eager passengers shortly before noon. The Judge, red-faced and sweating, was burdened with a large trunk, and he kept picking it up and putting it down as the line shuffled forward. Isadora ignored his continual stream of invective about the pace of the line. She kept scanning the crowd for Elm.

"He'll be here," the Judge said for the fifth or sixth time.

"I don't understand why he isn't here already," she said. "Why did he leave the hotel without us?"

"I am not his keeper," the Judge said, trying to look innocent.

A broad-shouldered man with a jovial glint in his blue eyes was standing behind them in the line. He wore a straw hat and a brown suit that was a touch too snug for his ample belly. He smiled at Isadora every time she turned around, clearly enjoying the excuse to make eye contact with her. After the sixth—or was it the seventh time?—she looked for Elm, he cleared his throat and doffed his straw hat. "It is astonishing that a lady as beautiful as yourself could be so perplexed," he said. "What man, in right possession of his eyes and spirit, would abandon such a heavenly creature as yourself?"

Isadora eyed the loquacious gentleman with a glance she usually reserved for the dim-witted dandy who dared approach her on the streets of Bitter, but the man was immune to the coldness of her gaze. "Meriweather Vance," he said, holding out his hand.

He was equally undeterred by her indifference to his gesture, and with some reluctance, she finally relented and offered hers. He swept it up to his lips and made to kiss the back of her hand, though he kept a decorous distance from her actual flesh. "I'm enchanted," he said.

"I'm her uncle," the Judge said, appearing at her shoulder. "Willard Vernon Wallace." He seemed disappointed when Vance didn't offer to kiss his hand. "And the man we're waiting for works for me, which means his eyes and spirits are only beholden to the gold in my purse."

"Oh, does he now?" Vance licked his lips as he put his hat back on his head. "Marvelous. Such marvelous news. I assume that you are queuing for the same destination as I, and that we shall have ample opportunity to see one another as we float in the embrace of the mighty Mississippi."

"We are," the Judge said. "Though I am hoping there will be more gambling than embracing on this trip."

"Ah, well, it is good for a man to enumerate his priorities," Vance said, his gaze lingering on Isadora. "And you, dear lady?"

"Oh, bird watching," she offered. "Maybe some catfish spearing. And throwing boorish men overboard when they get too annoying."

"Delightful," Vance crowed. "This might be the most exciting tour yet."

"You've ridden on the *Sally* before?" the Judge asked.

"I have," Vance said. "This crowd is always filled with most fascinating of characters." He touched his chest lightly and gave Isadora his full attention. "I'm a writer," he said. "Maybe you've heard of me . . . "

She gave him the benefit of a half-second of thought before shaking her head. Unwilling to watch him pout, she scanned the crowd once again for sign of Elm. *Where was he?*

"No matter," Vance said, waving away her lack of awareness of his notoriety. "It is certainly not my place to malign the quality of your literary education, my dear; not when there are always opportunities to procure copies of my books at numerous stalls and finer establishments in St. Louis. I would be delighted to escort you to one of these emporiums and personally inscribe a copy for your library."

"Well, enough about your literary aspirations," the Judge said. "Let's talk about gambling. All this nonsense about watching people like they're at some circus aside, can we assume you are not indifferent to the illicit thrill of games of chance?"

"How illicit?" Vance asked, his eyes narrowing.

"I'll wager you one hundred dollars—right here and now—that my man makes this boat."

"Oh, come now, Mr. Wallace, do I look like a buffoon to you? For all I know, you two are a pair of consummate shysters. She has been urgently looking for this man of yours, but I would not know him from Adam. It is entirely possible that is he lingering but a few paces back in the line, waiting for some signal from you so that he can rush up, thereby allowing you to win this wager."

The Judge stroked his beard. "You are not a fool, Mr. Vance. I see that. But you may be missing an opportunity here to increase the size of your purse before you even step foot on the boat,"— he glanced behind him—"which we are going to stumble onto very shortly."

"And that is exactly what I expected you to say," Vance said, his eyes dancing with glee. "You're making me feel as if I am missing an incredible opportunity—an opportunity that doesn't exist, mind you, but you are still attempting to seduce my more foolish nature."

"Of course I am, my most perceptive fellow," the Judge said. "I expect you to see through all my efforts at guile. You'll either take this wager or not. Why would I attempt to coerce you into a course of action which you are already considering?"

"I am most certainly not! This is a fool's wager."

The Judge shrugged. "I can find someone else to take the wager," he said. "I'm sure I won't have to wander far to find a fool."

Isadora stared at the Judge, wondering if he was bluffing or not. Was this his idea as to how he was going to raise the final amount they needed for the tournament? Had he and Elm performed some similar stunt in the past, where Elm wandered off on some errand and then came racing back just in the nick of time? Were they as practiced as that? She couldn't be sure; there was something about the Judge's mien that suggested he was implementing ideas as soon as they hatched in his brain— *Good God! Had he learned nothing in all the years since he had left Baton Rouge?*

"I'll sweeten the wager," she said, instinctively making a decision.

The Judge raised an eyebrow.

"Do tell, dear lady. I'm as attentive as a hound for a chop," Vance said.

"Take the Judge's wager," she said. "If you lose, you may sit next to me at dinner tonight."

The Judge raised the other eyebrow. Vance's eyebrows were up as well. "And if I win?" he asked.

She smiled at him. "You'll have won a hundred dollars," she said. "Don't be greedy."

Vance flushed, and the Judge threw back his head and laughed.

"Do we have a wager?" she asked, looking back and forth between the two men.

"Oh, we do," Vance said. "We most certainly do."

Waiting at the gangplank were a pair of white-coated stewards and a sandy-haired man in a pale suit. "Good afternoon," he said cheerfully as they approached. "Ah, Mr. Vance," he continued when he spotted the writer behind Isadora and the Judge. "So nice to see you again." He indicated the gangplank. "Please come aboard. Joseph here will see you to your cabin."

"In a moment, Mr. Chester," Vance said. He nodded at Isadora and the Judge. "I am enjoying a momentary dalliance with my new friends here."

"Oh, excellent. We appreciate the arrival of new friends." Mr. Chester gave them a broad smile. "Are you here to play some cards . . . ?"

"We are," the Judge said. "Wallace. Willard Vernon Wallace. This is my niece, Isadora."

Beside her, Isadora heard Mr. Vance repeat her name several times under his breath.

Mr. Chester shook the Judge's hand and clasped Isadora's briefly. "Is this the entirety of your luggage?" he asked, indicating the trunk at the Judge's feet.

"Perhaps," the Judge said. "We're waiting on my man with the rest."

"Ah, yes," Vance said. "Indeed, we are waiting."

Mr. Chester's brow furrowed as he realized there was some conversation to which he was not entirely privy, but he was too accomplished a host to let such confusion put him off his patter. He waved them toward the gangplank. "Come aboard; come aboard," he said. "You can explain all of this to me shortly. There are others behind you still, and we must depart shortly."

Isadora looked behind her once more, scanning the crowd for Elm. There was no sign of him, and her heart beat faster when she realized just how short the line was. Elm had less than fifteen minutes before the steamboat sounded its bell and departed for St. Louis.

Where was he?

Elm was lost. He hadn't gone that far from the docks, but somewhere along the way he had gotten turned around, and he had wasted a lot of time heading in the wrong direction before he had realized his error. His hip ached and the heavy pockets of his jacket slapped against his side as he jogged. None of the buildings looked familiar, and he chided himself yet again for not planning a better route back to the boat.

He reached an intersection and paused, chest heaving. He had been running for awhile, and he was fairly certain he had lost most of the crowd who were pursuing him. Though, there were bound to be a few hold-outs, and he didn't want to stop too long. He looked right, and saw rows of buildings crowding a street that curved to the right. He looked left, and let out a sigh of relief. In the not too far distance, he saw the river.

With a quick glance over his shoulder, he started toward the river, glad to have finally found a landmark.

When he reached the docks, he looked about for the Salacious Sally, and he was grateful to spot the white shape of the steamboat still at the docks. Though, the plumes of black smoke rising from its twin stacks suggested the boiler was well stoked. There was a small crowd on the pier in front of the boat, and he saw lots of people already on board.

He was almost out of time . . .

He heard shouts behind him, and he didn't bother looking back. His pursuers had spotted him again.

His hip complained as he ran; he knew his gait was a loping shuffle. He wasn't fast, and there was a chance the men chasing him would catch him before he reached the boat. He gritted his teeth, and did his best to push past the pain.

The steamboat's bell sounded three times—signal that the boat was departing—and the crowd on the pier started to disperse. The boat's gangplank was being drawn away from the wooden pier. Black smoke belched fiercely from the stacks, and the water beneath the boat started to foam from the thrashing paddles.

He ran faster. Someone shouted and waved at him from the prow of the boat, and there was a momentary confusion of bodies. The gangplank hung, half-extended, as the boat slowly backed away from the pier.

Elm dodged a pair of onlookers, and heard muffled curses and the sound of bodies colliding behind him. He didn't look back. He didn't want to know how close the men chasing him were. He focused on the wooden plank sticking out from the boat. He could make that jump.

He put on a burst of speed and leaped from the edge of the wharf. His arms pinwheeled, and for a moment, he didn't think he was going to make it, and then his feet hit the board. It bowed with his weight, and he scrambled forward, clawing at the wooden slats across the board. Running like a squirrel along a tree branch, he went up the gangplank and dropped onto the deck of the steamboat.

He was surrounded by a bunch of well-dressed individuals, which was quite a change from the rough sort he had been surrounded by less than an hour before. He spotted Isadora, and then the Judge.

Isadora's eyes widened at the sight of the bruises and dried blood on Elm's face. "What happened to you?" she gasped.

"A horse," Elm said as soon as he could draw breath. He looked back at the dock, and a tight smile danced across his face as he spotted the crowd who were shouting and gesticulating angrily. None of them dared to make the same jump he had, and that opportunity vanished as a pair of deck hands drew the gangplank all the way onto the boat.

The Judge turned to a rotund man wearing a straw hat who was standing beside him. "My man has arrived," he said, clapping the man on the shoulder. "I win our wager."

"Indeed," the man in the straw hat said. "And what an arrival it was." He reached into his suit coat and withdrew a leather wallet, from which he extracted a handful of bills. He gave them to the Judge, who folded them quickly and made them disappear.

Another man, dressed in pale suit and with an air of being in charge, dismissed some of the crowd with a flicker of his hands. "Is he with you?" the man asked, looking at the Judge.

"He is," the Judge said.

The man glanced at the wharf and the outraged gang. "Will there be any more?"

Elm shook his head.

"And luggage . . . ?"

Elm let his hand rest against his bulging pockets. "I must have left it at the hotel," he said. "I was in a bit of a hurry."

The man in the straw hat laughed. "You three are delightful," he said. He winked at Isadora. "I'll see you at dinner tonight, my dear. I am so looking forward to it." With a wave of his fingers, he wandered off.

Isadora came over to Elm, and her expression was full of concern. "I was asking about your face," she said, referring to the bruises.

"Oh, that." Elm touched his cheek. "That was the guy on the horse."

"What horse? What guy?"

Elm waved a hand toward the receding pier. "I lost him, back there somewhere."

The Judge approached the wooden railing that surrounded the open prow of the boat. He squinted at the men on the dock. "Did you take advantage of some of the locals?" he asked.

"Perhaps," Elm admitted. He patted one of his pockets and the Judge's eyes lit up at the sound of metal clanking against metal. "I found the roughest pub I could find. I walked in and wagered that I could beat any man—in any physical contest of his choosing."

"What?" Isadora's eyes widened. "That's crazy."

Elm nodded. "That's what they thought, especially after I lost the first few matches." He gave her a broad smile. "But then I dared them to come at me again—but only if they doubled their bet."

The Judge laughed and slapped a hand against the railing. "How many of them did you beat?"

"Four," Elm said. "And then I gave one some of his money back and thanked him for throwing the fight—the biggest guy, of course. I didn't need him coming at me again. And while everyone was wondering who was working who, I ran with the rest of the winnings." He touched his cheek lightly. "The guy on the horse was particularly peeved."

"I don't believe this," Isadora said. "You two are the greatest rogues I have ever known." Her tone was sharp, but there was a glint of mad humor in her eyes. "No wonder you're constantly on the run."

The Judge looked hurt by her comment, but after he smoothed his beard, he regained his regal composure. "We have enough funds to enter the tournament," he said. "Plus whatever Elm here managed to acquire."

"Which is enough that we didn't need that wager you made with Vance," Isadora said.

"True," the Judge acknowledged. "But it wasn't my idea to sweeten the pot."

Isadora glared at the Judge for a moment and then she whirled and stomped off.

"Did I miss something?" Elm asked, somewhat befuddled by her behavior.

"No more so than usual with women," the Judge said. He rubbed his hands together. "How much did you get?"

20

THE JUDGE INSISTED THEY WASTE NO TIME IN SECURING THEIR place in the tournament, and without waiting for Elm, he darted up the broad staircase that led up to the main deck from the boiler deck. With a groan, Elm followed, and they made their way past the passenger rooms to the grand salong at the back of the boat.

There were doors to the salon on either side of the boat, and inside there were gambling tables as well as a long bar along the the inner wall. Heavy carpet covered the floor, and the walls were covered with a dizzying number of landscape paintings. The tables were already filled with noisy players, and beyond, there were billiard tables, a roulette wheel, and a couple of faro tables. Broad windows looked out at the stern of the boat, and in the corner of the room there was an iron staircase spiraling up to the deck above.

Next to the stairwell was a broad desk, behind which sat a small man with a thin mustache and a receding hairline. Standing nearby were two men, dressed in black. They wore frock coats, pushed back so that everyone could see the heavy revolvers hung at their hips.

The Judge nodded at the pair and then took off his hat. "Good afternoon," he said to the man behind the table. "I am curious about a tournament being held. Could you tell me how—"

"One thousand dollars," the small man said humorlessly. He tapped a finger on the table, indicating the only way their conversation was going to continue.

"I do admire a man who gets right to the point," the Judge said as he reached into his coat for his battered wallet. It bulged unnaturally, and Elm could almost hear the leather sigh as the Judge extricated a thick sheaf of bills.

The man behind the table counted the money with brisk efficiency, and there was a momentary pause when the funds came up short. The Judge grunted and dug into the pockets of his pants for the money he had won from Vance. The accountant took several bills from the wad and handed the rest back to the Judge.

The Judge laughed and showed the bills to Elm. "Wasn't as short as I thought," he said.

The accountant opened the long drawer in the desk and slid the Judge's money into a bin that was already overly full with bills. He grabbed a narrow box from the drawer—Elm noted there were only three more—and put it on the desk. The accountant opened the box and showed them the contents.

There was a row of round chips, nestled in a velvet-lined tray, along with a silver medallion. "Here are your chips," the accountant said. "This medallion is what allows you to sit at the table. You may purchase more chips if you need them. Play commences in an hour, and there is a break for dinner."

"After dinner?" the Judge asked.

The accountant shrugged. "As long as there are four or more players, you can play all night. The tournament ends when we dock at St. Louis, four days from now. There will be other announcements as the number of players decreases."

"Sounds pretty straightforward," the Judge said.

"Cheating and accusations of cheating will be dealt with swiftly and summarily."

"Of course."

"Forfeiture of your medallion or failure to sit at a table during at least two sessions during a day will disqualify you from the final round in the tournament."

"Naturally."

"Mrs. Peabody will take your name and enter you on the roster." The accountant closed the box and indicated the iron stairwell to his right. "Go right on up, gentlemen. Good luck."

"Thank you," the Judge said. He picked up the box and smiled once more at the two enforcers. "Let's go meet Mrs. Peabody," he said to Elm.

The room upstairs was smaller than the grand salon, a more intimate affair for more upscale patrons. At the back of the room was a wooden bar and coiled in front of it were a trio of divans, wrapped around each other. There were three large tables, two of them already filled with gamblers.

As Elm eyed the players, an elegant woman in a dark blue gown with a shapely crinolette and layers of lace swished up to meet them. "Good afternoon, my dears. Welcome to the inner salon. I am your host, Mrs. Peabody, and yes, I see by that box in your hand that you have stumbled into the right place."

The Judge was inspecting the players too, and he tore his attention away from the tables to smile at their host. "Mrs. Peabody, I am delighted to have stumbled—as you say—though I must insist that I would only ever stumble at the sight of such a gorgeous creature such as yourself. Otherwise, I am as surefooted as an ox."

"But so much more charming," she said with a smile. She offered her hand, which the Judge was quick to take.

"Naturally," he said. "I do not speak with my feet. I use my lips and my tongue for such fair, and I am told that I am quite nimble in that regard."

"My heart trips at such possibilities. And your hands? Are you as dextrous with your fingers as you are with your tongue?"

"Ah, while I am here to dazzle these fine gentlemen with displays of dexterity, I would much rather be delighting you with my dancing digits . . ."

Elm ignored them. He stared at a man sitting at the far table. The man had a face like a granite crag, and his intense gaze was like staring into the eyes of a hungry wolf.

He recognized those eyes. The family resemblance was unmistakable.

"... as I was telling my companion here—" The Judge elbowed Elm sharply, and Elm broke off his staring contest with the O'Halloran patriarch. "Pay attention; the lady has eyes you can drown in."

Elm looked at Mrs. Peabody and noted that—yes, indeed— her eyes were quite welcoming. "Charmed," he said, recovering his composure. "Elmore Stonebrook."

"My," Mrs. Peabody inhaled, her breasts expanding against the fine fabric of her dress. "And whatever will you be doing, Mr. Stonebrook, while Mr. Wallace—"

"Judge Wallace."

"—*Judge* Wallace lets his fingers dance across the cards and chips?"

Elm's eyes flicked toward the far table once more. "I suppose I will be sitting on one of those divans over there, sipping juleps and reading poetry," he said. "As one does to pass the time."

"And what a wonderful way to pass the time," Mrs. Peabody said. She tore her gaze away from Elm, and lightly pressed her hand against the base of her throat, which only made both men look at her flushed skin. "Did Mr. Baxter explain the rules?" she asked, drawing them back to the matter of the tournament.

"Mr. Baxter has grown tired of explaining the rules," the Judge said. "We were given but the briefest of orientations and then shoved up that iron staircase—like baby birds tipped out of their nest. We must throw ourselves upon your mercy."

"Oh, you poor dears," Mrs. Peabody said. She bustled between the Judge and Elm, lightly grasping both of them by an elbow. "Come and have a drink. I will set you right." Her hand squeezed Elm's arm. "I will show you how to fly, my little solitaires."

"You saw him? You saw Bart O'Halloran?"

Elm paused in the inventory of his jacket pockets. "He was playing cards in the salon," he said. "There is another salon, above the room on this deck, and it is where the tournament players are gathered. We didn't speak, but we made eye contact."

Isadora was standing near the narrow window of the stateroom, and she rubbed her arms as if struck by a sudden chill. "He is a hard man," she said. "There is no laughter in those eyes."

"No," Elm agreed. "I suspect he hasn't laughed in some time. Not in any way that you or I would understand, at least." Once again, he decided against telling her about the death of Tommy O'Halloran. Bart O'Halloran had reason to think ill of him and the Judge, even if he didn't know exactly why. *Or maybe he does*, Elm thought. Maybe he learned what they had done with Tommy's skull after they had burned the body.

That night, on the bluff overlooking the O'Halloran ranch, they had built their makeshift pyre for Tommy O'Halloran's body. Once the pyre was lit and the flames were devouring the dead man's skin, the Judge had sworn the two ranch hands to secrecy. *We killed the wolf*, he instructed them. *We need never speak again of what we saw after it died.* The Judge asked them to leave their heavy jackets before they went back to the ranch. The pair were puzzled by the Judge's request, but eager to be done with the night's foul work, they had shucked their jackets and hurried away, darting down the hill like frightened deer.

After telling Elm to wake him before he did anything rash, the Judge leaned against the rough rock where Tommy had been hiding and went to sleep. Elm stood and watched the flames devour the corpse of the wolf who walked—and died—like a man. When the bulk of the wood was gone and the corpse was nothing more than a twisted mass of blackened bone and gristle, he woke the Judge. They kicked sand over the fire until the remaining flames were out, and then they dragged the still-hot corpse free of the dying coals.

Must we defile the corpse? the Judge had asked when Elm explained what he meant to do.

It is nothing but poison, Elm told him, *and God will not forgive us if we bury it in the ground. It is better this way.*

Which was somewhat of a lie, but he had committed them to this course of action, and it was best to make sure neither of them had second thoughts.

Elm kicked at the head until it came free of the body. He undid his trousers and urinated on the skull, and when the Judge shouted at him to stop, he told him he was merely trying to cool the burn-blackened head down enough for them to touch it.

Which was the other lie he told that night.

He wrapped the skull in the jackets left by Purnell and Benjee.

They picked their way down the far side of the hill, down on to O'Halloran land, and as the eastern skyline was starting to bloom, they reached the large retaining pond which provided water for O'Halloran's herd. At the southernmost point of the lake, he unwrapped the skull and got to work. Using his knife he carved a circle and cross in the skull, and then—after carefully washing and cleaning his knife—he sliced his thumb and let several drops of his blood fall upon the skull. He offered his knife to the Judge. *We killed him,* he explained. *There is power in such deeds, and we must use that power to finish this work. Once we mark this skull—blood and spirit—then our desire will become real.*

The Judge cut his palm and squeezed his hand tight until blood dripped from his fist.

Elm knew there were words that needed to be spoken, but Orchilí had told him that his desire—his intent—was almost as important as the words, which, in most cases, were only meant to focus the speaker's mind.

As the morning sun creased the horizon, and a single spear of bright light lanced across the pond, Elm raised the burned skull and started to chant a wordless song. The water of the lake was smooth and dark, almost like polished glass, and it swallowed the first light of the sun. Most of the skull was still black, scarred by the fire, but the teeth were white. Still feral.

When Elm ran out of words he did not know he was speaking, he threw the head into the lake.

The light surrounded the skull for a moment, and its eyes gleamed with unholy fire, and then it struck the surface of the water and vanished without a ripple. It was almost as if the water parted, unwilling to touch the foul trophy, but once it was beneath the surface, the lake quickly hid away what it could no longer reject.

I gave him a chance, the Judge said, looking toward the farm house at the other end of the valley. *And he wasn't willing to talk.* He spoke as if he were convincing himself that O'Halloran had brought this on himself. That they had not chosen this path on their own volition. *Deus misereatur nobis*, he said, as he gathered up the jackets. *Our work here was just.*

Elm did not bother to contradict the Judge. They both knew what they had done had changed them too.

With a tiny shrug, he closed his eyes and buried the memory again—buried it much better than they had Tommy O'Halloran's burned corpse. When he was done, he opened his eyes and resumed his examination of his winnings. In addition to a bunch of coins and paper money, he had acquired a small Sharps Derringer, recognizable with its four stubby barrels, and a revolver with an octagonal barrel. He hadn't intended to pick up some armament, but during the confusing course of his physical bouts, there hadn't been time to wave off the fellows who had put up hardware for their bets.

He could easily hide the Derringer in his hand. It fired a .41 caliber rimfire cartridge, and from experience, he knew it was terribly inaccurate. It was the sort of weapon prostitutes and cardsharps carried—good for close-up work, and usually only against a single assailant. He slipped it into his pocket. Such a gun had proven useful in the past, when a card game had gotten out of hand . . .

"Did you win that during your fights?" Isadora asked as he picked up the revolver. She hadn't seen the Derringer, and he didn't mention it to her.

"I did." Elm squinted at the smooth cylinder of the revolver. The cartridges were exposed at the back, their tiny pins sticking up. "It's a LetMat," he said. He tapped the butt of the weapon where there was a metal ring for tying the weapon to a lanyard. "They were used by Confederate officers during the War."

"And did this officer survive the War?"

"I warrant he did not," Elm said. There were nine cartridges, and he saw no reason why they weren't still live. However, as there wasn't a ready supply of pinfire ammunition available, once these nine cartridges were fired, the gun wouldn't be of much use. But nine is better than none, he thought.

He offered the revolver to Isadora. "Just in case," he said.

She took the weapon, and he was happy to see she handled it with a promising familiarity. "And where should I hide this ugly thing?" she asked. "Down the front of my gown? Or should I strap it to my thigh, under my skirts?"

"Whichever is the most comfortable."

"Well, that is an important consideration."

"Let's hope you won't have to use it."

She offered him an enigmatic smile. "I fear such hope is a waste of effort."

Hope is never wasted, he thought.

21

Dinner was early the first night on the boat, and Isadora and the Judge left her stateroom for the dining room on the upper deck shortly before sundown. She was wearing a crimson dress with short sleeves and a high collar, and he was wearing a lavender-colored shirt with ruffles under his jacket. He had combed his hair, and hers was wound into a bundle held in place with a simple comb of pale hardwood. She had applied lipstick and rouge, and wore tiny earrings that looked like chips of frozen sunlight.

As expected, she turned a number of heads when they entered the dining room.

"Good evening. Good evening," Mr. Chester gushed as they stood near the entrance. "Mr. . . . ah . . ."

"Wallace," the Judge said. "Judge Wallace." He indicated Isadora. "And my niece, Isadora."

"Welcome, welcome," Mr. Chester said smoothly. "I trust your accommodations are satisfactory?"

They had two staterooms on the port side, and the Judge had graciously afforded Isadora the larger of the two, though both had a single large bed. She thought to ask how the sleeping arrangements were going to work between the Judge and Elm, and then realized she already knew the answer to that question. Elm was going to get the floor, and he wouldn't complain.

"The rooms are lovely," was all she said.

"Excellent," Mr. Chester said, clasping his hands together. "I understand you are sitting with Mr. Vance this evening," he continued, as he lead them toward a trio of long tables that ran the length of the dining room.

"Yes," Isadora said. "Mr. Vance has been very kind and generous with his hospitality." She knew the role she was supposed to play.

"Mr. Vance is a true Southern gentleman," Mr. Chester simpered. He nodded toward Mr. Vance, who was sitting on the right-hand side of the second table. Mr. Vance didn't see them at first, and as a result, she and the Judge were nearly at the writer's elbow before he realized they were there.

"Oh, gracious," Vance exclaimed. He shot out of his chair, nearly knocking it over. He had combed his hair and found a tie since they had seen him last, and he fawned over Isadora, leaping to grab her chair before the Judge could pull it out from the table. "You are a divine radiance, my dear," Vance said as she sat down. "Like a star who has climbed down from the heavens."

"You are as gracious as you are hospitable, Mr. Vance," she said.

"Oh, please, call me Merry," he said, eagerly falling into his own chair.

The Judge kept his amusement in check and arranged himself in the chair on the other side of Isadora. While Vance prattled on about her hair and her attire, he glanced about the dining room. Some of the faces were familiar from the private salon, and he nodded at a few of them. Like iron to a lodestone, his attention was drawn back to Mr. Chester as the foppish host greeted a new arrival.

Bart O'Halloran had no time for Mr. Chester's glad-handing, and he brushed past the smaller man as readily as a breeze blows through a field of spring flowers. His eyes were cold, like frozen chips of ice in his impassive and stony face. He wore a tailored suit—much too fine an outfit for Bitter—and the Judge could tell that such finery confined the broad-shouldered man in a way that made him irritable. He moved like an unstoppable avalanche until he was opposite Isadora. The seat was occupied by a younger man with curly hair, and O'Halloran cast a dark shadow over the man.

"This isn't your seat," O'Halloran said.

"Now, sir—" the young man started, but O'Halloran clapped a large hand on his shoulder, and his objections became a wordless squeak. He flew out of his chair, trying to get away from O'Halloran's grip.

Isadora was rigid next to the Judge, like she had been transformed into a marble statue.

"Don't you dare," she hissed.

"Good evening, Miss Van Horn," O'Halloran rumbled as he sat down in the now-vacant chair. "It's a pleasant surprise to see you on this boat."

"It is anything but pleasant," she said.

"Well, well," the Judge said. He put his hand on Isadora's arm. A light touch to remind her where she was. A touch that could turn firm in case she needed to be restrained. "If it isn't the villain himself."

O'Halloran turned his massive head toward the Judge. "Your tone is not to my liking," he said.

"Much of what is going to come out of my mouth these next few days will not be to your liking," the Judge said.

O'Halloran's jaw tensed, and the Judge could easily imagine those teeth crushing stone—or a finger, even, if one were to be so foolish as to let it slip between those rows of teeth.

"I say," Vance interjected. "What a fascinating development. You three are acquainted? My, my. What could possibly bring you all here?" The writer could smell a story.

"Money," the Judge said. "It's what brings everyone together. Friends. Enemies. Strangers, met but a few hours ago. Currency is the great unifier and divider, after all."

"Ah, yes, much of the world's ills stem from the filthy lucre. 'He that loveth silver shall not be satisfied with silver.'" Vance shook his head.

"Splendid," the Judge said. He removed his hand from Isadora's arm and slapped the table. "I do appreciate a man who knows his Bible. 'The sleep of a laboring man is sweet, whether he eat little or much; but the abundance of the rich will not suffer him to sleep.'" He grinned at O'Halloran. "How has your slumber been recently, sir? Not kept awake at night by ill humors or some other distemper of the bowels, perhaps?"

Isadora grabbed the Judge's wrist. "Stop this," she hissed at him.

"It's dinnertime conversation, my dear," the Judge said as he gently disengaged her fingers. "It is but polite words with the simplest of stings. It means little and leaves few marks."

"You are making this very awkward."

He raised an eyebrow. "Awkward? Wait until I insult the cook. Then it will get really awkward."

She growled at him, a sound that made Mr. Vance's eyebrows crawl up his forehead. The Judge gave her a stern glance as he plucked her napkin from the table and unfolded it with a snap.

There was a glint of cold amusement in O'Halloran's eyes. "Your choice of companions is telling, Miss Van Horn," he said.

"As is your lack thereof," the Judge replied. Isadora snatched the napkin from him before he could place it in her lap.

"I prefer to leave my wild dogs in their kennels."

The Judge returned his attention to O'Halloran. "Where you lay down is none—" he started.

"Well, well, well," Mr. Chester interjected suddenly. "We have a very lively assortment of guests aboard the *Sally* tonight." His hands worked themselves nervously. "As we will be enjoying one another's company for several days, may I suggest we elevate our talk to matters more fanciful." He waited a moment or two for someone to say something more in keeping with his suggestion, and when no one spoke, he made a suggestion. "How about the weather?"

O'Halloran's jaw worked for a few moments. "It might rain later this evening," he said.

"There," sighed Mr. Chester. "Talk of the weather is much more pleasant."

"You mistake rain for my piss, sir, streaming down from the deck above," the Judge said.

Mr. Chester let out an outraged squawk.

O'Halloran narrowed his eyes, and his lips firmed into a bloodless line. He toyed with the carving knife at his setting. "I do not know what game you think you are playing, but if you are here for the tournament, you will find yourself severely outmatched," he said matter-of-factly. "Your pockets will come up empty, and no amount of boot-licking obsequiousness will afford you any satisfaction. And when you go crawling back to your Dulcinea, I will break you with my bare hands."

The Judge inclined his head. "But for a lance and a trusty steed to carry me to battle against a giant such as yourself, sir." He shook a hand at Mr. Chester. "Pancho! Pancho! Fetch me my armor!"

Mr. Chester's face was rapidly changing colors. "There will be no fighting among guests," he said in a strained voice. "Any such actions will result in summary expulsion from the tournament and a forfeiture of your deposit."

"What of harsh language?" the Judge asked. "May we profane reputation and sully character with impunity?"

"Judge Wallace!" Mr. Chester shook with apoplexy.

"I'm not sure if I should take that as a 'yes' or a 'no,'" the Judge said, looking around for a second opinion.

"It is a difficult distinction to make," Vance noted airily. He leaned forward in his chair, a mischievous gleam in his eyes. "Not that I wish to be draw into this particular peccadillo, you understand, but if I were allowed to offer an outside opinion . . ."

"Please do, sir," the Judge implored.

"Well, yes, then what we are lacking is more empirical evidence. This is just my opinion, mind you, but such would allow us a more precise rendering of judgment in this regard . . ."

The Judge nodded at Vance, and returned his attention to O'Halloran. "Of course. Thank you, Mr. Vance, for your keen observation of what this conversation is lacking. Therefore, as we were speaking of shit-licking—"

"Champagne, Mr. Benson," Mr. Chester squeaked to one of the white-attired stewards. "Champagne for our guests." He pointed a shaking finger at the Judge. "But none for Judge Wallace."

Benson, well-trained in the art of defusing awkward conversational moments at the dinner table, leaped to Mr. Chester's bidding, and within moments, a flock of white-coated staff were crowding the table, pouring bubbling wine into crystal glasses.

O'Halloran watched all of the excitement without a single change of expression. *He's going to be nigh impossible to read*, the Judge thought, and when he leaned back in his chair, he caught sight of Vance's surreptitious signal.

"You can have some of mine," the writer said, offering the Judge his glass behind Isadora's back.

"That is most kind of you, sir," the Judge said as he leaned toward Isadora. "But my niece shouldn't be drinking tonight. She has a very delicate stomach and I'm afraid the motion of the boat might upset her." He disarmed her furious stare with a vulpine smile as he picked up her champagne glass.

"He said all of this before the first course?" Elm shook his head in disbelief.

Isadora nodded. She shivered beneath the heavy cloak Elm had brought up from her stateroom. She was a little unsteady from the two glasses of champagne she had managed to extricate from the Judge's grip, and she leaned against the hurricane deck railing. Below, the flat-nosed prow of the Sally glided through the dark waters of the Mississippi River.

Poles with oil lanterns were spread out at fixed intervals along the rail, and a fire burned in a stone-lined bowl near the center of the open-air platform at the front of the deck. The presence of fire like that on a wooden boat made Elm a little queasy, but he had to admit the heat radiating from the fire made standing on the exposed deck much more pleasant.

After dinner, the tournament players retired to the private salon at the back of the upper deck where they started the first night of serious play. Many guests—eager to watch the game—squeezed into the smaller salon, but for the remaining guests, there was little to do but enjoy the hospitality and ostentatious ambience of the boat. White-coated staff circulated among those who lingered on the hurricane deck, ensuring no glass went empty. Overhead, the the broad blanket of stars twinkled.

It was—the chill in the air notwithstanding—a fine night.

"I realize he was trying to get under the skin of the other players, but . . ." Isadora trailed off.

"He gets under everyone's skin," Elm said. "I'm not certain he can stop himself."

"I had to watch O'Halloran eat." She couldn't suppress another shiver, and Elm instinctively took a step closer. He leaned against the railing to disguise his action, but she acknowledged his presence by leaning toward him. "Right across the table from me. Gnawing on his steak like an animal during the main course," she said. "I could have stabbed Bart O'Halloran with a dinner knife."

"That would have been rather unladylike of you."

"I don't care. If he sits there again tomorrow night, God help him . . ." She shook her head. "I left the pistol in the stateroom," she said quietly. "And I'm glad I did. I would have used it."

"It would not have fixed things," Elm said.

"I know," she sighed. "Too many witnesses."

"I was going to say that it wouldn't solve your financial problem."

"Oh, that." She leaned more firmly against him and didn't speak for a time. When she did, he had to duck his head to hear her. "What?" he asked.

"Dulcinea," she said distantly. "He called me 'Dulcinea.' The Judge knew who he was talking about. Who is this woman?"

"O'Halloran said that?"

She nodded gently. Elm looked out at the dark water as he remembered the schoolroom at Silverglen where his mother taught the children. When they learned their letters, Miss Rebecca would sometimes loan them books from the main house, though as time went on and the other children grew bored and stopped coming, he was the only one who would beg for another book. Miss Rebecca delighted in telling him about all the great works of literature that he might read some day. She especially loved to talk about the great—and occasionally tragic—love stories: Romeo and Juliet; Lancelot and Guinevere; Tristan and Isolde; Orpheus and Eurydice; Elizabeth Bennet and Mr. Darcy. As well as those who yearned for love and even quested for it . . .

"She's a character in a novel," he said, remembering when Miss Rebecca had discovered Cervantes's story of the proud but befuddled knight. "The hero imagines her to be this great woman, and his dream inflames his passion and he does some . . . odd things."

"What sort of things?"

"He imagines windmills are giants, for one. And he gets beaten up more than once for his trouble."

"But does he rescue her?"

Elm shook his head. "He never meets her, as far as I know. She's as much a figment of the hero's imagination as she is real. He's crazy—the hero of the novel O'Halloran was talking about. Calling you 'Dulcinea' was his way of suggesting the Judge was a lunatic."

"He called for his armor."

"Who did? The Judge?"

She nodded. "He shouted for someone named 'Pancho.' Is he a character in this novel too?"

"He is. He's the hero's squire, and he was just as likely to get him into trouble as he was to help him escape."

Her hand crept across his chest. "Does that make you Pancho?"

Elm smiled. "The Judge isn't Don Quixote. He doesn't fight imaginary monsters." He regretted the words as soon as he said them. *No*, he corrected himself mentally. *The Judge fights very real monsters instead.* And did that make him more or less insane than the hero of Cervantes's novel?

But Isadora hadn't heard him. All the champagne was making her sleepy. "I could be your 'Dulcinea,'" she whispered.

Elm stroked her hair, and didn't correct her. Isadora was real and in his arms, which was more than Don Quixote ever got from his imagined paramour.

After taking Isadora back to her stateroom, Elm made a circuit of the boiler deck, wandering past the numbered doors of the staterooms. He ducked through the narrow corridor between the salon and the dining room, and emerged on the other side of the boat. He walked along the port side, nodding at the occasional passenger sitting in one of the many wooden deck chairs lined up along the inner wall. All of this walking about was helping him become accustomed to the motion of the boat. Steamboat captains did not, typically, float the river at night—the Mississippi was mercurial with its snags and sandbars—but the first stretch downriver from Keokuk was quite deep, and this early in the tour, Mr. Chester wanted the passengers to relax and enjoy the luxurious mirage of gambling aboard a floating palace.

When he reached the forward portion of the boat, he went down the broad stairs to the main deck. The forward portion of the main deck was where he had stumbled aboard earlier that day, and there were groups of men gathered there now, huddled around tiny games of cards and dice. Everyone gambled on the river. It was as much a part of life as eating, drinking, and tending to the boilers. He stood on the edge of several of the games, watching the roll of dice in the dancing light of storm lanterns.

Eventually, he drifted toward the back of the boat, weaving his way around the stacks of wood and bales of cargo. He assumed that the crew quarters were on this deck, along with storage and the chamber where the great boilers steamed and stank. He passed a trio of deck hands who were sharing a bottle of cheap spirits, and he heard rough talk that reminded him of the interminable hours waiting for orders to come down from the officer's tent.

Every man in the company might die in the morning as the generals sought to take or retake yet another town or fort which none of the company had ever heard of. The men on this boat didn't suffer from the same brevity of existence—none of them would die in the morning—but there was that same fatality in their talk. The days were all the same, and there was no end of them. Nothing ever changed. And so they drank and complained and spoke of pleasures they did not have.

Something splashed out on the river, and the men broke off from their talk. "Big'un," one of the men said.

"Nothing like that one we saw during the spring," another man said.

"Twern't no catfish you saw," the first man snorted.

The second man protested, and Elm moved on, all too familiar with the pointless arguments men got into while waiting for their lives to end.

He rarely fell prey to this same idle indolence. When he was on patrol with another sharpshooter, their success depended on remaining alert longer than the enemy. If the enemy thought they should wait an hour before moving out of cover, then Elm would wait two hours. If they thought they had to wait half the night, then Elm waited too.

Once, he had cornered a group of Confederate soldiers and an officer in an abandoned barn. The moon had been full on that cloudless night, and short of them inching on their bellies like slow worms, they could not leave the barn without being seen. And so they had waited. They had built a fire and made some revelry, hoping such activity would keep him awake as well, but he had figured out the merry makers were only a few of the men in the party. The rest had buried themselves in the stinking hay and slept.

In the morning, shortly before dawn, thinking their night-long noise would have rendered him dumb and senseless from lack of sleep, they crept out of the barn. The major had swapped coats with another soldier, attempting to hide among his men, but Elm recognized him from his bushy sideburns and he put a bullet through the man's head before the Confederates were more than halfway across the field.

He killed three more before the rest scattered—a few made it to the treeline and safety, but the rest had fled back to the barn, puckered with fear and the knowledge that it was where they were going to die.

After that, word spread among the Confederate troops: God's Finger never slept.

Two men were hanging around the periphery of the dice games when he returned from his stroll along the port side. They were pretending to watch the games, but they weren't dressed as deck hands nor did they seem to be itinerant travelers. They wore the heavy coats and rough pants of cattlemen, work gloves on their hands, and stiff-brimmed hats pulled low.

He had seen them earlier. They had been sitting in deck chairs on the boiler deck. They hadn't been sitting together, and Elm had nodded at the first man who had been slow to tip his hat in return. The second had kept his head lowered, as if to avoid notice. But both had been obvious to him then—just as they were now.

Elm could have crossed to the stairway on the starboard side, leaving both men on the main deck, but they would follow him back up, just as they had followed him down. It was better to resolve this where there was less risk of being seen by paying passengers. And so he turned right, where he ducked past the stairs and made his way past the bins of logs.

After several steps, he turned into a small niche between bins, where he waited. God's Finger, eternally patient. His hand brushed his pocket, feeling the hard outline of the tiny Derringer. Would it come to that? He would use the gun if he had to.

A few minutes later, he heard boots against the wooden deck, and he marked the step of two men, who were walking quickly. They knew—just as he did—there was no other way out from the side of the boat. He was boxed in, and the fact that they were coming after him, instead of waiting and watching, made their intentions clear. Elm calmed his breath.

The two men passed his hiding place, and neither glanced to their right or left. For a second, Elm considered letting them go undisturbed. He could dart back to the stairway and make it to the safety of his and the Judge's stateroom, but it wouldn't solve the problem. The men would still be on the boat. They'd still be watching him—waiting for another opportunity.

He crept out and grabbed the closest of the pair by the collar of his coat. He swung him to the left, shoving him toward the railing, and before the other man could turn around, Elm hit him twice in the lower back. The man grunted in pain, arching his back, and Elm grabbed him and shoved him against the nearest bin. The man hit the bin hard, and before he could recover, Elm hit him in the jaw, knocking him down.

The other man rushed Elm, and Elm ducked under his wild swing and shoved him with a shoulder. The man staggered a step, but it wasn't enough to stop him from swinging his heavy fists. Elm took a hit on the ear, which stung mightily, and blocked the second punch. The man kept at him, swinging his arms wildly, and Elm was forced on the defensive.

The man who Elm had bounced off the bin slammed into him, and Elm reeled off-balance. It was his turn to be thrown against the bins, and his assailant kept on him, landing punch after punch against his back and stomach. Elm squirmed and turned, flailing with his arms. He got a hand under the man's hat, yanked some hair, and managed to get a thumb into the man's eye. The man yelped and pulled back, and Elm lined up and hit him hard in the throat. He coughed and sputtered, falling to his knees as he struggled to breathe, and Elm kicked him in the balls, which put him down on the deck.

The other guy decided to change the rules and came at Elm with a knife. He was a ranch hand, used to skinning rabbits and cutting cows free of bramble. He hadn't used his knife against men before, and his attack was clumsy and slow. Elm trapped his arm easily, and as the man struggled to pull free, Elm hit him in the face until blood ran from his nose. Roaring with fury, the man tried to muscle him—he was taller and thicker across the chest than Elm—and Elm let the man lead their dance. They staggered across the deck until they slammed against the railing.

Elm banged the man's arm against the railing, which elicited a grunt of pain. The knife clattered to the deck, and Elm stumbled over the knife when he took a step back. His opponent swarmed him, and Elm ducked, his hands searching for the knife. The man swept Elm up, pinning one of his arms against his body. He hugged Elm, squeezing him against his chest. His breath was hot against the back of Elm's neck. "Got you," he wheezed, and he started to haul Elm toward the railing.

Elm raised his other hand, the one that was free to move, and the man's breath hissed at the sight of the knife.

He tried to shove Elm away before, but Elm was already pivoting, slashing low with the knife. The blade sliced through leather and something softer underneath.

Elm backed away, the knife held ready in case the man attacked him, but the man was leaning heavily against the railing. "You . . . you cut me," the man said. Black shadows slid down the man's pants, and there was inky darkness on his hand when he held it out.

He started to charge, but his legs twisted under him and he fell heavily. More shadows spread around him.

The other man lay on his side, his hands clutched around his groin. Elm grabbed the man's hair and yanked his head back. He made sure the man saw the knife. "Your friend is going to be dead in a minute," he whispered as he touched the knife blade to the man's throat. "And you're next."

"No, no, no no no no—" the man wailed.

"Who is your master?" Elm demanded.

"I can't—I don't know anything."

Elm tensed his hand. "Who set you on this task?"

The man whimpered for him to stop. Elm held his hand still, waiting. "Who?" he asked.

"O—O—O'Halloran," the man whimpered.

"Do you work for him?"

The man nodded carefully.

"Did he offer you extra pay for this brutish work?"

The man's breathing was rapid, and his body shook. Eventually, he shook his head in response to Elm's question.

Elm sighed. He moved the knife a scant distance away from the man's neck. "You are a blunt tool," he whispered to the man. "Ill suited for work given to you."

The man nodded quickly, eager to agree with Elm.

"What use do I have for a blunt tool like you?" Elm asked. "If I let you live, what is to stop you from trying again?"

"I won't. I won't!"

Elm lowered his lips until they were close to the other man's ear. "I don't believe you," he breathed. He moved the knife closer again and the man tensed beneath him.

"No, no, no," he blubbered.

Elm made the knife twitch and the man let out a tiny shriek, but the blade only creased the skin, drawing a little blood and no more.

"If I kill you, then I will have two bodies to dispose of," Elm said patiently. "And that is more work than I intend to do this evening." He held the knife out so the man could see the blade. "While you are getting rid of the corpse of your friend, you should imagine the story you are going to tell your master. Consider his response to your failure. Consider the other options available to you." Elm flung the knife over the railing, and the blade flashed in the moonlight. "Choose wisely," he finished.

He put both hands on the man's head and banged it against the deck. The man groaned and his body went slack, and Elm took advantage of his momentary befuddlement to slip away. He walked quickly to the front of the deck and danced up the stairs. As he reached the main deck, he heard a loud splash off the starboard side of the boat. He paused, a hand on the railing, and heard a second splash, nearly as loud as the first.

Catfish, he thought grimly. *Big ones*. Though he knew otherwise.

22

THE MORNING SUN TURNED THE RIVER INTO A SILVER STRAND running between fog-shrouded banks. The Judge rose early, and performed his morning ablutions with much pomp and ceremony. Once the Judge was done with the basin and mirror, Elm shaved and found clean clothes. There was a streak of dark blood on the sleeve of his coat, which he stared at ruefully as he and the Judge waited for Isadora to join them.

The Judge insisted they take breakfast on the hurricane deck, and they sat closely around a small table near the white-painted railing. A canvas umbrella was canted at an extreme angle to keep the morning sun off their faces, and Elm slumped in his seat as he waited for a steward to bring them coffee. Isadora had noted the dark circles under his eyes when she had first joined them, and he begged off her concern with a comment about the motion of the boat.

She wore a light grey dress under her cloak, and her hair was braided. Her cheeks were bright and rosy, and she exclaimed—at some length—about how well she had slept, all things considered. The bolsters were thick and all that champagne the previous evening had dampened her worry, providing her ample excuse to enjoy a deep and dreamless slumber.

Elm let his gaze wander about the hurricane deck, casually investigating the other passengers also taking breakfast on the upper deck. After the incident last night, he did not think there would be other ruffians who might mean them harm, but that did not stop him from keeping watch.

"I have determined who the career gamblers are," the Judge was saying. "There are only a handful, and of that grouping, one or two bear close consideration. The rest are but dilettantes and sheep to be fleeced."

A steward finally showed up to lay out cups and saucers on the table. He assured the gentlemen that coffee was on the way, and when he offered Isadora tea, he was taken aback by her dismissive wave. "I'll have what the gentlemen are having, thank you very much," she said. The flustered steward waved another man over, who he directed to pour coffee in all three cups. When they were done, both men hurried off.

Elm took a sip—tasting chicory with the bitter coffee—before curling both hands around the tiny cup and sinking back in his chair. He held the cup like he was sheltering a small bird from harsh weather.

"Now, Mr. Vance is an interesting player," the Judge said. "He is quite clever and bluffs well. If he had the temperament of the game, he might be quite dangerous. He claims he is more interested in watching people than he is in playing cards, but I do not trust such nonsense. Writers are nothing more than quacks who have memorized entire sections of the dictionary."

Elm stirred in his chair. "A writer?" he asked.

"Yes," the Judge said. "One of those fabricators of foolhardy nonsense and sensational slander."

Elm frowned. "What is his full name? Merry—Meriweather? Yes, that is it. Meriweather Vance."

"Dear God, save me from having to hear admiration spoken of this charlatan's work."

"No, no. I haven't read any of his books."

The Judge pressed his hands together and raised his eyes toward the sky.

"I heard his name recently," Elm said. He frowned, searching his memory. "Ah, yes. When I first met Benjee in Bitter. He and Purnell got into an argument about Vance's work."

"Not those two again," the Judge groaned. "Am I cursed to be haunted so continually?"

"Vance, at least, is not riddled—through and through—with guile and deceit," Isadora said.

"Oh ho!" The Judge chortled. "You protested mightily at first, but you have fallen prey to his spell."

"I have not," Isadora countered. "I am merely refreshed by his honesty."

"Is that what you think it is? The man is filled with flim-flam. Practically bursting with bull—"

"He bluffs better than you," Elm interjected. "Is that it?"

The Judge waggled a finger at Elm.

"You can't read him, can you?" Isadora said.

"That is not the case," the Judge said.

"You seem agitated by his character," Isadora noted.

"I am not agitated," the Judge said stiffly.

"No? Is it his apparent disinterest in the machinations of the game that bother you?"

"I am not bothered."

"Perplexed," Elm suggested.

"Nor am I perplexed," the Judge countered. "I was merely . . . cogitating out loud. Considering the permutations afforded by the competition."

"Is that what you are doing?" A smile played across Isadora's lips.

"It is difficult to play to a man's weaknesses when he has such a cavalier attitude about having them. Or not having them, as the case may be," the Judge grumbled. "Take Mr. Took, for instance, a fellow who sat at my table last night. It took less than an hour to realize Mr. Took displayed a remarkable involuntary quirk when he has court cards in his hand. One jack doesn't move him. But two? Or a pair of kings? Oh, my, he drums his fingers on the table. He tries to raise the bet without drawing attention to his hand, but long pauses between players try his patience mightily."

The Judge grinned at his recital. "And so," he continued, "when I see the fidget rising in his fingers, I linger quite some time when it is my turn to place my bet. It makes him furious, and the more angry he gets, the less he pays attention to the expressions and hints from the other players. In fact, I won nearly four hundred dollars from him in one hand because he was certain his flush would win the pot, but he was completely unprepared for my queens over sixes."

"This is why I like the wheel," Isadora said to Elm. "It's much less complicated."

"Hmmph," the Judge snorted. "Roulette is for children who yearn to have their lives governed by chance. And in a house like this, chance never favors the foolish."

"Speaking of foolish behavior, did you manage to keep that four hundred dollars you won from Mr. Took?" Elm asked.

The Judge eyed him for a moment, and then shrugged and reached for his coffee cup. "I'm cogitating," he said. "On the permutations."

"I had a run-in with two of O'Halloran's men on the lower deck last night," Elm said, shifting the conversation away from the Judge's shenanigans at the table.

"What?" Isadora whirled in her seat.

"Did you now?" There was an amused twinkle in the Judge's eye. "And what did they want?"

"We did not have a chance to get into the specifics," Elm said. "Though, I did get the gist of the message when one of them pulled out a knife."

"And?"

"I had to show him how to use it."

"An unfortunate and unexpected lesson to find oneself the recipient of," the Judge said. "And the other man?"

"I asked him to carry a message back to his master, though he may have elected to not bother."

"Fascinating," the Judge said. His gaze wandered over Elm's

shoulder. "And what have we here? Speak of the devil and he appears."

Standing at the top of the main stairs were Bart O'Halloran and a younger man who Elm judged to be Dickie Boy. The older son. The one who the Judge had tangled with outside of Bitter.

"This shall be interesting," the Judge said quietly. "Old Stone Face is having a little trouble keeping his temper in check. What could possibly be upsetting him? Did his thugs fail their simple task?" He waved to the O'Hallorans.

"I would warrant that is the case," Elm said.

The Judge stood up. "Ho, you craggy catastrophe of a man," he said loudly, now pointing at Bart O'Halloran so there was no mistaking who he was talking to. "If I am to stay in Mr. Chester's good graces, I should offer you some fine felicitations on this delightful morning, but I fear such an effort will bring up my gorge with great haste."

O'Halloran considered ignoring them, but there was nowhere else to go on the hurricane deck. The private salon for the tournament had closed shortly before dawn and would remain empty for a hour or two yet before play began. His son glared openly at the Judge, his fists clenched at his sides.

"How do you think you would fare in a bit of fisticuffs?" the Judge asked Elm.

Elm twisted around in his chair and examined Richard O'Halloran more closely. "What kind of odds are you going to ask for?" he asked.

The Judge made a noise in his throat. "Odds? Do you think he'll give me any quarter?"

Elm raised his cup and drank down the rest of his coffee. "No, he probably won't."

"What are you two doing?" Isadora asked.

"Your continued presence on this deck is going to ruin my appetite," the Judge continued, yelling loudly enough to be heard by the other passengers. "I don't suppose you would have the simple human decency to depart before I am forced to drop my trousers and piss on your boots?"

Richard started toward them, but he was stopped by his father's granite-like hand. Bart O'Halloran walked slowly across the deck, his eyes cold and his face colder. His coat was a thick traveling jacket—the sort worn by fine gentlemen who did not deign to travel on the back of a horse—and beneath it, he wore a dark wool suit. "I will rip your manhood off with my bare hands and feed it to Miss Van Horn there if you so much as touch your belt," he snarled at the Judge.

"All of it?" the Judge asked innocently. "Or just the shaft? Is your preference to keep some for yourself . . . "

O'Halloran stopped a few paces from their table, and he stared at the Judge without a flicker of emotion in his eyes. "What you do want, Wallace?" he asked finally.

"I want you to go away," the Judge said, putting aside the vulgar language. "I want you and your syphilitic son far, far away from here. From Missouri. From Miss Van Horn and from Thrush."

"And why would I do that?"

"Because I just asked you to," the Judge said. "Nicely."

A thin flicker of amusement ran across O'Halloran's face. "No," he said.

He and the Judge stared at each other, and as the moment stretched, Isadora began to fidget in her chair. Even Elm was starting to wonder how long these two were going to stare at each other, but then the Judge blinked and smiled. "Oh, well, there was no harm in asking, was there?" When O'Halloran didn't reply, the Judge looked over at Elm and gave him a quick wink. "What say we put aside all this peacock posturing and get down to the more serious business at hand?"

His response threw O'Halloran for a second. "What business is that?" he asked.

"Well, gambling, you damn fool," the Judge roared. "Why else are we here?"

Richard came up behind his father, and his gaze remained steady on Elm. O'Halloran tilted his head slightly and regarded the Judge. "Of course," he said eventually. "Why else?"

"Shall we have a wager then?" the Judge asked, his face breaking into a wide smile.

"What sort of wager?"

"To see who stays or goes," the Judge said. He held up a hand when O'Halloran started to speak. "From this deck," the Judge clarified. "Let us make a wager as to which of us gets to enjoy their breakfast up here. Shall we?"

O'Halloran let out a hard bark of laughter. "Is that all?"

The Judge continued to smile. "For now, yes."

O'Halloran looked at Elm and Isadora. "You are a noisy bag of wind, Wallace," he said, returning his gaze to the Judge. "And yes, I'll take your insipid wager. I will win. Just as I will win at the table. I will take everything you have." His gaze went back to Isadora. "If you hope to find salvation with this man, you are dreadfully mistaken. His arrogance will be your ruin."

"Well, let's not get in too much of a rush," the Judge said. He rubbed his hands together. "How about we start with . . . five hundred dollars."

O'Halloran shrugged. "Five hundred," he said. "And what is your wager?"

"My man can throw your man overboard."

Everyone froze for a second. Elm got as far as "Wha—" before Richard O'Halloran's hands descended on his coat.

Richard's strength surprised Elm, and before he could get his feet under him, Richard had dragged him out of his chair and over to the railing. He flailed with one arm, his hand sliding off the side of Richard's face. The railing caught Elm on the back of the legs, and he would have gone over right there if he hadn't managed to grab a handful of Richard's hair.

Keeping Elm pressed against the railing, Richard slowly peeled Elm's hand off his hair. Elm grimaced as Richard bent his hand back, and he managed a short jab under Richard's upraised arm. Richard shifted his weight to avoid the blow, and Elm was able to shove away from the railing.

They tussled for a bit, knocking aside a table and several chairs. Richard kept shifting his grip on Elm's coat as Elm threw wild punches—shoulders, belly, chest—which forced the other man to keep twisting and dodging. All in all, the fight seemed that it might be a draw when Elm's foot slipped on the deck and he lost his balance.

He saw Richard's fist coming, but the railing prevented him from getting out of the way. Reeling from the heavy blow against his cheek, Elm leaned back. He was in a precarious position, and he tried to scoot down on the railing, but Richard slipped under his arm and shoved.

Elm tilted back, and the sky wheeled overhead. A line of dark birds flew by, thin gashes cut out of the blue sky, and then he was falling. He tried to grab onto something, but his fingers clutched fruitlessly at the metal railing. He started to swear, but then thought better about it, and sucked in a lungful of air instead.

He heard someone scream, but then he hit the Mississippi with a loud splash, and the water closed over his head. After that, the only sound he heard was the throaty roar of his own panic.

The Judge looked down at the disturbed waters of the Mississippi. Shortly after Richard O'Halloran had thrown Elm off the boat, Isadora had fled the upper deck. She had shouted something about Elm's inability to swim, and within seconds after her departure, the bell atop the pilot house started to ring—alerting the crew about the desperate plight of the man in the water.

Bart O'Halloran joined the Judge at the railing, his eyes aflame with a perverse delight. "I do not pretend to understand your shenanigans, Wallace, but they will be of no avail," he said. "I will grind you to paste."

The Judge inclined his head slightly, his gaze still locked on the thrashing figure in the water. "Perhaps," he rumbled.

O'Halloran tapped his knuckles against the railing. "You owe me five hundred dollars," he said.

The Judge lightly tapped his coat. "I must have left my wallet in my stateroom," he confessed.

O'Halloran's expression hardened. "Your continued attempts to mock me are pitiful and—"

"You know I'm good for it," the Judge snapped.

"But for how long?"

"Long enough."

O'Halloran chuckled, and the sound was like listening to rocks banging together. "Your bravado will run out long before St. Louis," he said. "And then what will you have?"

There was another splash down below, and the Judge's face creased with a smile. "Them," he said. "I'll still have both of them."

There was a second person in the water—a dark-haired figure, dressed in white.

"She's a strong swimmer," the Judge noted. "Double or nothing says she rescues him."

O'Halloran glowered at the Judge, his chest swelling as he inhaled slowly. The Judge did not flinch from his gaze.

"Double or nothing," the Judge said. "Or is that too much of a wager for you?"

A muscle pulsed along O'Halloran's jaw. "Double or nothing," he said, his mouth chewing hard on the words.

The Judge nodded faintly. He leaned against the railing, peering at the figures in the water. "I think she's got him," he said. He smiled at O'Halloran. "Sounds like nothing for you."

He turned away from the river and looked over at O'Halloran's son, who was watching the pair in the water with a look of undisguised venom. "Unless you want to go two out of three," he said innocently. "Does Dickie Boy there know how to swim?"

23

"MR. CHESTER, I WISH TO LODGE A COMPLAINT WITH THE Commission in charge of this tour," the Judge exclaimed as the boat's host appeared in the door of their stateroom. "When we presented ourselves at the dock, you assured us we would be safe aboard this vessel. My niece, myself, and our man would not be in mortal peril. Not from the weather or natives or rapacious bands of marauders. We believed your fulsome claims and gave up the nominal trappings one might carry upon one's person in these dangerous lands. We put ourselves entirely in your hands."

The Judge indicated Elm, who was sitting on the edge of the bed, wrapped in several blankets. "And look what happened! My party has been attacked, sir! Our reputation has been sullied by sick malfeasance. I declare this enterprise is a sham, a fraud meant to steal currency from me and mine."

Mr. Chester's mouth kept opening and closing, like a fish, gasping for air. "Judge Wallace—" he started, but the Judge had only paused to draw breath.

"I will be filing claims of gross negligence, calumnious disregard for the people and property in your care, heinous thievery, and a wanton disregard for the unalienable rights of men to be without fear for their lives. There are prominent and highly-regarded barristers in St. Louis who have spent their entire careers protecting the rights of the good and righteous men and women of this country, and I will be securing their firms in this noble fight against the egregious aggression laid against my man here. You, sir, will be prominently named in my suit."

"Judge Wallace—"

"As will the captain of this accursed vessel. As will that loathsome degenerate who dared to lay his swinish hands upon—"

"Judge Wallace!"

The Judge blinked at Mr. Chester, who hurried into the stateroom and closed the door behind him. He licked his lips nervously as he held out his hands to forestall any further words from the Judge. "Let's not get too hasty, shall we?" Mr. Chester asked.

"Haste is the path taken by the impatient man," the Judge said, winking at Elm.

Elm glanced at Isadora, who was sitting on the low sofa, her hands in her lap. She was wearing a heavy robe provided by the stewards and she had a blanket draped around her shoulders and lap. Her unbound hair was wet, and he could tell by the firm line of her eyebrows that she was still angry with the Judge. Mr. Chester's arrival had interrupted a tense conversation between the two of them, and though she was biting her tongue now, he was confident she would pick up the discussion the moment the three of them were alone again.

"I am, of course, mortified by the events of this morning," Mr. Chester said. "I do not condone young Mr. O'Halloran's actions, and I assure you that you have the captain's full assurances that such behavior will not happen again. The Quincy Commerce Commission prides itself on—"

"It was without provocation," the Judge exclaimed. "That boy grabbed my man. Can you imagine what might have happened had my niece been sitting in that chair?"

Mr. Chester swallowed heavily, his face paling as he considered what the Judge was suggesting. "Judge Wallace, I ah-ah-assure you . . ."

The Judge waved a hand, silencing the nervous man. "Your assurances are like bird shit on the decking—a nuisance and easily washed off."

Mr. Chester recoiled as if he had been slapped. His face turned pink and his back stiffened. "Judge Wallace," he said, his tone sharpening. "Your language is unbecoming of your station and of this conversation."

"Is it now?" The Judge stalked over to Mr. Chester and towered over him. "Fuck your preconceived notions of what is becoming of this conversation. I'll have you know that this assault on my man was not the first offense against him by members of the party whom you are but a boot-licking toady."

"Wh-what?"

"Last night, on the main deck, two fellows in Mr. O'Halloran's employ attempted to murder my man."

"Murder?"

"Yes, the actions of young Mr. O'Halloran—in full sight of several unimpeachable witnesses—pale in comparison with the rough-handed efforts by foul rogues brought on board this boat by this imperious tyrant of a guest. A guest whose coin has clearly more value to you than my own." The Judge was getting into his imperious preacher guise. "Shall I speak with the other guests about the 'protection' afforded those who have greater privilege than themselves? We are second class citizens aboard your vessel, sir. I see that now, as plainly as I see the slick sheen of your greed on your brow."

"Wh-what are you t-t-t-talking about?"

The Judge levered a finger at Mr. Chester. "Bart O'Halloran is a dangerous lunatic," he said carefully. "He intends to do physical harm to my niece and my man in an effort to distract me from this game. He is a cheating cur and a coward, and you let him bring thugs and ruffians on this boat. There will be bloodshed on this boat—more than there already has been, sir—unless you take stronger action to protect your guests from villains such as this man."

Mr. Chester swallowed heavily, his eyes focusing on the tip of the Judge's finger. "Wh-what do you want?" he finally managed.

"I want justice," the Judge roared. "I want that man disbarred from any further gambling on this boat. I want him and his son bodily removed at the first opportunity."

Mr. Chester blanched at the Judge's words, and his hand gestures became more frantic. When the Judge paused to suck in a deep breath, Mr. Chester raised his hands and flapped them like they were birds struggling to take flight. "Judge Wallace. Judge Wallace, Judge Wallace," he squeaked.

The Judge paused and glared at the smaller man.

Mr. Chester calmed his hands. "Several other passengers have said that you were speaking ill of Mr. O'Halloran before this . . . unfortunate incident occurred."

"The devil I was," the Judge said.

Mr. Chester's face twitched. "Given your tone and language at dinner last night, I am forced into the undesirable position of having to consider the veracity of the numerous statements I have heard"—he sucked in a deep breath—"including yours."

The Judge chewed on his mustache for a moment. "Are you implying my testimony is less than pure, sir?"

Mr. Chester paled slightly, but he held his ground. "I . . . I am," he concluded, raising his chin.

The Judge nodded sagely. "Good for you," he said, and his response birthed a confused expression on Mr. Chester's face.

"I . . . what?" was all he could manage.

"I like a man with spine," the Judge said. He clapped Mr. Chester on the shoulder. "It suggests you'll do the right thing."

"The right thing?"

"Yes," the Judge nodded, like it was self-evident. "You'll escort Mr. O'Halloran and his party off the boat the next time we stop for wood and supplies."

"But I just said you were lying," Mr. Chester protested.

"Yes, you did, and I admire your fortitude at making such a declaration, but it makes no difference in regards to the vile intentions Mr. O'Halloran has toward myself and my niece."

Mr. Chester looked at Elm, pleading with his eyes for some assistance, and Elm could only shrug. "Judge Wallace . . ." Mr. Chester's hands started moving again, and when he caught sight of them, he gave up any pretense of continuing the conversation with the Judge. He turned and tried to flee as quickly as he could, but he caught himself on the door as he went, turning his exit into a graceless stumble.

"Marvelous," the Judge chortled after he was gone. "That went better than I hoped. Now he has no idea who to trust." He turned to Elm and Isadora and rubbed his hands together. "We never got any breakfast, and I am famished. Anyone else?"

Elm shook his head.

Isadora stared at the Judge. "You're, you're a monster," she burst out finally.

"Hmm? Now, look, dear. That's uncharitable of you—"

"He could have drowned!" She pointed at Elm.

"Nonsense," the Judge said. "I've swum through currents much swifter."

"Yes, but he can't swim."

"Don't be ridiculous, my dear. Of course he can."

"Actually, I can't," Elm said.

The Judge opened his mouth and then closed it. He looked at his hands for a moment. "Well, it was a good thing she could," he said, indicating Isadora, though he wouldn't look at her.

"You let him go into the river," she stormed. "The only one who has put Elm in danger on this trip is you!"

"Now, don't be so dramatic," the Judge said. "Was it my fault that Dickie Boy pushed Elm over the railing? Did I say, 'Oh, Dickie Boy, would you be a good lad and throw my man—who cannot swim, by the way—in the river?' No, I said no such thing."

"You dared him to!"

"I made a wager." The Judge looked hurt. "A wager I expected to win, I'll have you know. How is it my fault that Elm failed to best Dickie Boy in a wrestling match?" He looked at Elm. "And what happened there? He's not that much bigger than you."

"The deck was slippery," Elm said.

"You were irresponsible," Isadora argued. "You were reckless. You had no regard for the sanctity of the lives of others."

The Judge snorted. "Careful, girl. You're not too old for me to take you over my knee and—"

Isadora shot off the sofa and stalked over to the Judge. He backed up one step and then stopped when he realized what he was doing. She got in close and stared at him. "Try it, old man," she hissed.

The Judge returned her stare for a long moment, and then finally blinked. His face softened and he leaned back slightly, pitching his voice toward Elm without taking his eyes off Isadora.

"What did you learn?" he asked.

"Richard O'Halloran is fast and strong," Elm said. "He's prone to react first and check in with his father later. He's more of a wrestler than a boxer, and he doesn't close his fists tightly when he hits. You've planted an idea in Mr. Chester's head that O'Halloran is dangerous and might have men on this boat that are willing to rough up other passengers in order to increase his chances in the tournament, which—all of Mr. Chester's protesting aside—he can't entirely ignore. And you've taken Bart O'Halloran's measure, and I hope you've learned what you needed about how to get under his skin."

The Judge nodded. "That sounds like a rather productive morning, don't you think?" he asked Isadora.

She whirled on Elm. "This was all planned?"

Elm laughed. "He's not that clever."

The Judge put a hand on his chest. "My dear boy, you wound me with such lack of faith."

Elm rubbed his head with one of the blankets. "The next time you desire to go fishing like that, use some other bait."

"You're the only bait I have," the Judge said.

"Oh, you both deserve each other," Isadora said. She stormed out of the stateroom, slamming the door behind her.

The Judge rubbed his jaw. "You really can't swim?" he asked.

Elm shook his head.

"Well, I wish you would have told me."

"I wish you would have mentioned your plan."

"It was very spontaneous," the Judge said. "There was an opportunity, and—"

"We've talked about this," Elm said, interrupting him.

"I know," the Judge said. "But this was different."

"No, it wasn't. It was just like last time."

The Judge chewed on his mustache again. "Well, thank God she knew how to swim," he said softly.

Elm sighed and dropped his hands into his lap. "Just play cards," he said. "Don't make things more complicated than they need to be."

24

THE JUDGE LEFT THE STATEROOM SHORTLY AFTER ISADORA—
food, my dear boy, he said, *a man cannot think without food in
his belly*—and Elm finally had a few minutes to himself. His wet
clothes were draped over a wooden rack. He stared morosely at
the puddle of water forming beneath the rack. River water.

When Richard had tipped him overboard, he had the sense to
close his mouth before he hit the water. After the initial shock
of falling had passed, he thrashed his way back to the surface.
He needed more air, and as he frantically tried to keep his head
up, he inadvertently sucked in more water than air. Cold fingers
of panic were already clenching his lower back and belly, and
when water rushed down his throat, he nearly lost all hope. He
couldn't breathe. He couldn't stay afloat. The boat was already
out of reach, indifferent to his distress, and in a few moments,
he would be lost to the river entirely.

Sitting now in the stateroom—well away from the water—he
rubbed his head fiercely with the blanket, as if he could scrub
the memory of the last hour. He wasn't going to let that fear take
root. He wasn't going to panic again. He was warm and dry, and
the water dripping off his clothes was just water. He had been
wet before.

It had been during McClellan's assault on Richmond, when the
Army of the Potomac had nearly taken the Confederate capital.
The Confederate general, Johnston, made a desperate attempt
to cripple McClellan's forces by attacking a portion of the Army
of the Potomac which was south of the Chickahominy River.

The river was swollen with rain, and storms had turned all the ground to mud. The fighting had been fierce, and somewhere in the general melee, Elm had been struck in the leg with a bayonet. He couldn't walk; all he could do was crawl through the mud and fallen soldiers. Some were still alive, clinging desperately to life; others were dead, but still warm. Some tried to stop him—Confederate boys, using their hands and knives and bared teeth. He crawled away from those he could outdistance; the rest he dealt with—there, down in the mud, among the dead.

The panic had been with him then, too. He knew he was supposed to die. He knew his wound would go foul—all the muck and blood and whatnot that was getting into it as he crawled across the field—and that poison would claim his life. He knew a Confederate patrol, seeking to save those who could be saved, would find him, and they would not be inclined to let him live.

In fact, when he heard sound of a patrol passing by, he laboriously dragged several dead men atop himself and pretended to be yet another anonymous casualty of the awful fight between states. He fought to lay still, as the voices came closer. The stench of the dead filled his nostrils, making him want to vomit. The bodies grew heavier, as if they knew there was a scream hiding inside of him. As if they could force it out of him.

But it hadn't been a Confederate patrol. It had been a squad of Union men. And they found him. He didn't know how they did, but suddenly, one of the bodies was lifted off him, and he was being dragged free of the rest. He struggled, at first, not seeing the blue of their uniforms against the purple twilight suffocating the field. Then someone had said his name—a woman's voice, he was certain—and he stopped fighting. He stopping thrashing and went limp.

And that's when he saw her. Floating above the field of dead men. Her hair aglow with fairy light. Cloaked in peacock feathers, with eyes that winked at him.

Miss Rebecca.

When they put him on a stretcher and carried him off the battlefield, he had screamed and screamed at them. Pleading with them to take him back to her. Begging them to let him go to her . . .

There's nothing there, one of the men had said to him. Trying to calm him. *Nothing but ghosts . . .*

He didn't believe in ghosts. Not before that night, and not after, either, because such infelicity of spirit was the sort of weakness that made men falter in their duties.

Though, in the years since the War, he had learned otherwise about ghosts . . .

When he had swallowed yet another mouthful of river and had given up trying to stay afloat, he had seen her. Glowing in the water. Wrapped in a cloak of peacock feathers. He had not seen her for many years. Had not thought he would ever see her again, in fact, but there she was. He was sinking, falling into the darkness that lay beneath everything, and she reached out her hand, beckoning to him.

When he raised his arm, fighting the lassitude which was making his limbs so heavy, she smiled. And then the sky above him exploded with stars and light, and a different angel entirely caught him.

Isadora had been very angry when the sailors had hauled them back onboard the *Sally*. As he lay on the deck, coughing up water, she had struck him with her fists, shouting at him. Calling him a fool and an idiot—names he certainly deserved, given the situation—and when he finished clearing his lungs, he suffered her assault in silence. Eventually, she had thrown herself across his prostrate body, her cheeks hot against his, and hissed an inviolate commandment in his ear. "No, ma'am," he had croaked. "I have no plans to go swimming again."

He hugged her before she could get away, and she froze as his arms went around her, and then, with a sob, she had wrenched herself free and run off.

Elm threw off one of the two blankets and padded across the stateroom to the heavy luggage trunk. He dug around until he found a spare set of clothes. He dressed quickly, but he stopped at pulling on his wet boots. He carried them under his arm as he stepped out of the stateroom and made his way to Isadora's room.

He knocked lightly, and when he heard her voice, he tried the latch and found the door unlocked. He slipped inside and closed the door gently behind him. The room was dim—she had covered the single window with the heavy curtain—and it took him a moment to find her. She was sprawled on the bed. She was still wearing her robe, though its belt had been loosened and one of her legs was thrown loosely across the bed.

"It's been a very trying morning," she said quietly.

"It has," he agreed. He put his boots down by the door and stood there awkwardly, trying not to look at her naked leg.

"Judge Wallace vexes me considerably."

"He has that tendency."

"He didn't inform you of any of his idiocy prior to those words coming out of his mouth, did he?"

"He prefers to keep his plans to himself. There's less chance of me talking him out of what he's going to do if I don't know ahead of time."

"Why do you put up with that nonsense?"

"He means well," Elm said.

"Don't give me talk like that. He's not a child who needs a chaperone to keep him from setting fire to the world. You're just as mad as he—maybe more so—for allowing him to run loose like this."

"What would you have me do?" Elm asked. He wandered over to the plush chair next to the bed. "If I walked away, do you think he would act any differently?"

"Yes," she said. She fussed with the bolsters. "No," she admitted. "And he wouldn't have you to do his dirty work."

"He would not," Elm said.

"He would not be able to go a full week without insulting someone," she said. "And they would take offense. And there would be a gun fight. Or maybe he would get a knife in the belly while staggering out of a saloon. Or maybe three men would drag him out behind the livery and beat him to death with their bare hands."

"All of those are definite possibilities," Elm admitted. "And knowing that, how could I walk away?"

She shoved herself up on her elbows. "He's not your responsibility."

"No, but he feels responsible for the rest of the world."

Isadora shook her head. "Such a burden is impossible to bear."

"And so he shouldn't even try?"

She made a noise in her throat and threw herself back against the bed. "And now you are vexing me too."

Elm looked at the light sneaking around the curtain. "That is not my intention," he said.

He toyed with the edge of the blanket, thinking quietly for awhile. Isadora was watching him, and he knew she was waiting for him to give her a better explanation for why he tolerated the Judge's forceful character—his flaws, as she would undoubtedly correct him—and Elm would not entirely dismiss her clarification.

"After the War, I . . ."—he shook his head—"I was a young man when I joined the Union," he said. "Too young. I did not understand the true weight of the rifle I was given, but I wanted to prove myself. I wanted to belong to something bigger than myself." He eased out of the chair and sat on the edge of the bed. "And when it was all over, what was that thing I had bound myself to? What ideals had we fought for? What world had we made?"

"No one knew," she said softly.

He nodded. "No one knew," he repeated. "And with Lincoln gone, there was no one to guide us. Many of us wanted to go home—even if we did not know if we had any home left."

"Where did you go?" she asked.

"Ohio," he said. "But I didn't stay long."

She nodded as if she understood why he would not stay.

"I went to Europe," he said. He offered her a rueful grin. "I was still a boy in many ways. Prone to a boy's infatuations. Not yet mature enough to understand how the world really worked. And I was—well, I learned quickly how much I still had to learn." He fingered the hem of his shirt. "I stayed, and I fell in with a group of traveling entertainers."

"A circus?"

"Not entirely," he said. "But, for lack of a better word, yes, a circus. I have been to Spain and France and lands farther east. I have seen some of the great churches—Notre Dame in Paris and Hagia Sofia in Istanbul, for example. I have stood in the cold water of the North Sea and I have been on the warm beaches of the Mediterranean."

"You have seen so much of the world," she breathed.

He shook his head. "I have seen very little of it, because it is so much bigger than we can imagine."

"You have seen more of it than I ever will," she said.

Elm offered her a smile that said he did not believe her. She leaned back against the pillows on the bed, her eyes shining. He stood and stripped off his shirt. He tapped the tattoo on his chest. "This is a magic circle," he said. "It is from a tradition older than this country and older than many countries in the world. It comes from a time when people believed both more and less about the world."

He slid onto the bed and walked on his knees until he was next to her. She put up her hand and lightly brushed her fingers against his chest.

"What does it mean?" she asked.

"It is meant to protect one from harm. It gives you strength to ward off demons and evil."

"Does it work?"

"Do you recall when I said I had made a wager once upon a time with the Judge, and that I was waiting to collect?"

She nodded. The light in her eyes had grown brighter.

"He believes in monsters—in demons and dragons and strange creatures that belong in fairy tales and nightmares—and his belief is not entirely without cause. He has seen some of these things—monsters like what we saw in his bestiary—and he believes there are many more out there."

"I have seen them too," she whispered.

"Aye, as have I. But he also believes in God and that there is a balance in the world. If evil exists, then there must be an equivalent amount of that which is good and holy."

She started to laugh before she could help herself. She put her hand to her mouth. "I'm sorry," she whispered around her fingers. "But how can such goodness exist when . . ."

"When creatures like the wolf that killed your men exist?"

She nodded.

"I do not know. I have seen . . . I have seen too much ugliness and death. I don't . . . My faith is not as strong as Wallace's. He believes in the good. He truly does."

"And that is his wager?"

"It is."

"And that is why you stand beside him."

"It is, because, ultimately, I want him to be right. Because I need him to be."

"Even though he imperils your life?"

He ducked his head. "His companionship is not without peril," he admitted. "But what other recourse do I have?" He put his hand over hers, pressing her fingers against his chest. "This only works if I believe in it," he said. "It only aids me if I have faith. And so I must find reasons to believe. I have to trust someone."

"But I do not have the same faith you do," she said. "I do not trust him. Where does that leave me?"

"The same place you were before the Judge and I showed up at Thrush."

She frowned. "And where is that?"

"You've been running that ranch since your father died, and if it weren't for this nonsense with O'Halloran, you were successful, yes?"

"More or less."

"And when you jumped into the river to save me, did you stop and think about the danger you were putting yourself in?"

"No, I—you were going to drown!"

"And I didn't, due to your quick thinking and action." He held her gaze. "Thank you," he said softly.

She blushed lightly and looked away. "You shouldn't have—ah—you're welcome," she finished.

His gaze fell on her naked leg, tantalizingly close to his hands. He suspected she wouldn't mind if he put his hand on her ankle, and judging from the way her teeth were worrying her lower lip, he thought she might even hope that he would. "You have more faith than you know," he said. "And you believe in something stronger than this circle."

"What is that?" she asked.

He looked at her, letting her see the answer in his eyes. And her body relaxed against the bed as he leaned forward, letting his lips tell her what she already knew.

25

"MR. STONEBROOK!"

Elm was walking along the open deck toward the salon, and the sound of his name being called brought him up short. He paused and turned to spy the rotund writer and another man in a blue suit. Vance waved at him, delighted to have caught his attention, and he lifted his hand to acknowledge that he had heard them.

"Am I to understand that I missed an opportunity to win my money back from that scallywag?" Vance demanded when he reached Elm.

"Which scallywag?" Elm asked, delaying the conversation long enough for the man in the blue suit to catch up with Vance. Vance's sudden enthusiasm at having spotted Elm had caught him off-guard.

"Judge Wallace," Vance exclaimed. "What other scallywag is there?"

The man in the blue suit reached them, slightly out of breath, and Elm smiled at him. He was about Elm's age, and his beard and mustache were well-groomed. A gold watch chain hung from his waistcoat, and his boots had been recently polished.

"Afternoon, sir," Elm said, deferring to the gentleman's prosperous appearance.

Vance, realizing he was being a boor, quickly made introductions. "Elkabee, this is Elmore Stonebrook. Stonebrook, this is Charles Elkabee, out of Hannibal."

Elm shook the man's hand. "A pleasure," he said.

"You fought in the ridiculous conflict between the states, didn't you?" Vance asked, cutting Elkabee off. "Union man, I presume."

"Yes—" was all Elm managed to get out before Vance took over the conversation.

"His friend, Wallace—the *Judge*—you've met him at the tables. White hair, preposterous airs, gambles like a madman. Is he not like a character in one of my novels? Critics say that I exaggerate immensely, but how could I inflate the character of such a man as Wallace?" Vance laughed heartily. He nudged Elkabee rudely, and the other man bore the indignation with a polite smile.

"I have heard tales from the deck hands," Vance continued. "Stories that sound even more fantastic than the sort of tale I am known for. Naturally, I assume these boys are trying to have a bit of fun with me, but the more I press my inquiry, the more I understand that these lads do not understand the sublime truth offered by hyperbole." He nudged Elkabee again. "Wallace made a most unorthodox wager with Mr. O'Halloran, one that involved fisticuffs, wrestling, and the bodily disposal of one combatant into the mighty Mississippi." He turned to Elm. "Am I correct so far?"

"Catfish," Elm said, and as he anticipated, acknowledgment on his part was not required for Vance.

"You look surprisingly whole and hale, my friend," Vance continued. He looked Elm up and down as if he was examining a lady whose company he might be paying for. His face brightened when he spotted the damp end of Elm's trousers. "A little wet yet."

"My boots," Elm explained to Elkabee, knowing that Vance would not be troubled with such a detail.

The writer leaned toward Elm. "You can swim, can't you? It's okay. You can tell me. I won't ruin it when the Judge tells the story later—and mark my words, Elkabee, the Judge will tell this story. How many times do you think we'll hear it before we reach St. Louis? Five? Six? Oh, let's wager on this, shall we?"

Elkabee made a face like he had tasted something sour and he shook his head. Vance threw up his hands like he was performing for a theater audience. "We have four days to wager with wild abandon," he said. "And yet, I am surrounded by men with the constitutions of young girls. They are all afraid of their own shadows. It is most disappointing."

"I'll take that wager," Elm said, realizing it was the only way to get out of the conversation with Vance.

"You will?"

"Of course, but not for six."

"No? Less?"

"More," Elm said. "Ten times, before midday tomorrow."

Vance laughed. "You hear that, Elkabee? Ten times! Before lunch tomorrow. Marvelous. And how much would you like to wager, Mr. Stonebrook?"

"One hundred dollars."

Vance waggled a finger at Elm. "Aha! One hundred dollars it is. Elkabee: be our witness, would you? Now, who counts?"

"You can," Elm said. "I trust you."

Vance stuck out his belly and nudged Elkabee. "There it is, Elkabee. A wager, for one hundred dollars." He nodded toward the salon. "Should we repair to the salon and start counting?"

Elm stepped aside, indicating with his hands that he would graciously allow Vance to precede him. Vance preened briefly and strutted past Elm. Elm watched him go, and then the thought which he had meant to tell Isadora before and had forgotten came back to him.

Faith was important, but so was having a backup plan.

"Mr. Vance," he said. "A moment."

Vance stopped, and Elm motioned that the portly man should join him at the rail. "What is it?" he inquired, his eyes dancing with excitement.

"I have an idea," Elm said, ducking his head with a conspiratorial air.

"Yes?" Vance edged closer.

Elm frowned lightly as he looked over at Elkabee, and Vance, quickly catching on, made a shooing motion with his hands. "Elkabee: why don't you run along and order us some drinks. We'll be there in a moment." Elkabee blinked several times at being summarily dismissed, but when Vance turned away, he puffed up his chest in mock outrage and stomped off. Elm watched him go, and when he was well out of earshot, he spoke to Vance.

"The Judge and Mr. O'Halloran are—shall we say?—not very friendly to another."

"That is a monumental understatement, my boy," Vance said.

"I have not had the opportunity to participate in a tournament like this one before," Elm said. He tried to order his thoughts in a coherent fashion. "And there are some specific rules of play to consider, are there not? First, a man must buy a seat at the table and that seat is represented by a token he receives from the banker."

"Yes," Vance nodded. He patted the front pocket of his jacket. "I have one of those myself."

"And as long as you have chips—or money with which to buy chips—you can play."

"That is correct."

"And when you run out of money, must you surrender your token?"

"Ah," Vance shook his head. "No. Every player must sit at the tables during two of the three sessions during the day. If he fails to meet this minimum requirement, then he is eliminated. Though the only reason he would not sit is because he has run out of funds."

Or because he has misplaced his token, Elm thought, thinking back on the warning that the short man had given them.

"But I can go bust in one session—the morning play, for instance—and then return after lunch with more money and buy my way back into the game. Is that correct?"

"It is," Vance said. "That reminds me of a story. Oh, what was his name? Well, it doesn't matter. This gambler went broke on the last hand of the first night, and in the morning, when play resumed, he had managed to win enough money from the deck hands in dice to buy back in. It wasn't very much—not enough to last more than a few hands—but he had his token, and they had to let him play."

Vance broke off, his gaze wandering after a young man and woman who strolled by. When they were far enough away, he rubbed his chin and continued his story. "So, there he was, at a table with seven other players—some of whom had been party to his fleecing the night before. And they all knew his play was nothing more than desperation. A last effort to avoid calamitous ruin. How could they not play? They had all seen players like this before. Some of them might even have been in the gambler's position, once or twice upon a time. They knew the feeling. They knew the hunger. That desire to not lose. It's not that they wanted to break him. They would, of course. They were going to take his money and not feel the slightest inkling of regret about doing so. But they wanted to be there, just in case . . ."

"Just in case of what?" Elm asked.

Vance licked his lips. "In case he did something remarkable."

"And did he?"

Vance gave Elm a sly smile. "He did. In fact, over the next hour, he cleaned out two players."

"Fascinating," Elm said.

"And he kept on winning," Vance continued, his words tumbling together in his excitement. "In fact, he is the only one—that I know of, anyway—in the history of this tournament, who beat every player before the boat reached St. Louis."

He sighed suddenly and looked out at the river. "I do wish I could remember his name."

"So it is entirely possible that there will be a number of players left when the boat reaches St. Louis," Elm said.

Vance nodded. "Three or four, usually. And the game ends when the captain rings the bell. They all cash their chips in, and that is that. Well, the Commission takes its cut, of course."

"So, it is possible for a player to return to the table after going broke. But they have to bring more money to the table."

"That is correct, my boy."

"But it doesn't happen very often."

"It does not. Most play with everything they have. There is no reason to plan for failure."

"One shouldn't," Elm said, a tight smile on his lips.

Vance cocked his head and examined Elm's face. "You have some consideration in mind."

"I have an idea," Elm said.

"I would like to hear this idea," Vance said. "I would like to hear it very much."

Elm pretended to weigh an important decision, though he knew the writer was well and truly hooked. "Well . . ." he drawled. "The Judge and Mr. O'Halloran . . ."

"Yes? What of them?" Vance asked, his voice taking on a note of peevishness.

"I would wager—not literally, mind you—but I would wager that their play is going to be entirely focused on one another," Elm said. He paused, waiting for the idea to take root in Vance's brain. "To the exclusion of anyone else at the table," he said.

"That is an interesting observation," Vance noted.

"A crafty player—one who has managed to go unnoticed by either of them—might have an advantage at their table."

"Indeed," Vance mused, a thoughtful look coming into his eyes.

Elm smiled. Well hooked, indeed, he thought. He clapped the writer on the shoulder. "You have a medallion, Mr. Vance. You should be at the tables. Why on earth would you be chatting with me when there is money to be won?"

"Yes," the writer gushed. "Money to be won!"

Isadora heard Vance call after Elm, and a smile touched her lips at the mental image of Elm running away from the garrulous writer. If Vance wrote half as well as he talked about himself, he would be—well, he would be prolific. She hesitated to think of his work as having any lasting quality. She had found one of his books in the barn once, and she had read a bit of it while waiting for her mare—Smoke—to finish eating, and she had not been all that impressed. It was filled with all manner of specious nonsense: men fighting with one another; women constantly in the need of rescue; nefarious plots to rule entire countries. Though, she had to admit, the style was not altogether flaccid. The words did trip along with great relish, and she had found herself being drawn into the story in spite of her disdain.

The Judge was the sort of larger than life character that would easily fit into one of Vance's fanciful serials, and she could readily imagine a quite popular line of dime novels revolving around the Judge's quite considerable facility for trouble. Naturally, the Judge would require some manner of sidekick, and Vance would naturally attempt to sketch in a character like Elm for that role. But he would fail to truly capture the breadth of Elm's experience and would certainly ignore the man's complexity and depth.

She was more interested in the story of the quiet, quick-handed man with the haunted eyes.

The War Between the States had left the entire country haunted, and in the years since, as the South reeled under the oppressive Reconstruction effort imposed by the North, many struggled to find their place in a world they had not imagined. Many towns were decimated by the loss of their sons; others became defined by how many men died in their streets and fields. And now, with the railroads running all the way to California, settlers raced to find new lands that were not covered with blood. But these lands were not pristine. Native tribes who were there before the railroads resisted such expansion onto their lands.

Everyone was running from something, or running to somewhere else, she thought. Even Elm, though he tried to hide the emptiness in his heart. But she could see it in his eyes.

He had loved someone once—maybe even more than one woman. And these women still had a hold on him. He had told her about the tattoo on his chest, but he had not told her the whole story. And the scars on his body . . . Not all of them were from the War.

But when he put his hands on her, the few times they had lain together since he and the Judge had arrived at Thrush, he was present in his attention. He kissed her. He touched her. He held her tightly as their bodies moved together. He was not distant; he wasn't chasing some other phantom. In those moments, it was just the two of them: Elm and Isadora. She wasn't Miss Van Horn—the surviving daughter of Aloysius Gunter Van Horn and mistress of Thrush, a cow ranch three miles south of Bitter, Missouri; nor was she Mrs. Theodore Mulbridge, pale widow of the lamentable Mr. Mulbridge, who never learned to swim. When she was with Elm, she was merely Isadora, a woman worthy of love and able to love in return.

Did she love him?

She had put her own life in jeopardy when she dove into the river to save him, and yes, she had done so without thinking. What had caused her to act so rashly? She had done something not dissimilar earlier in the year when a young calf had been caught away from the herd during a sudden spring squall. It was easy to say her actions then had merely been because she was responsible for the herd, but she couldn't say the same about Elm. He didn't belong to her—she instinctively knew such an attitude would strike him as odd—and there had to be deck hands on the boat who could swim as readily as she.

Was it love, then?

Isadora sighed and buried her face in the pillows on the bed. When Elm had come into her room, she had let the belt of her robe slip, scandalously allowing her leg to show. He had noticed, and she had thrilled at his awareness of her naked skin. She had been fiercely annoyed with the Judge, and if it hadn't been for Elm's calm presence and the tingling fatigue in her arms and legs from the swim, she would have been much more vocal about her annoyance, but all of that had fallen away as Elm had moved closer and closer to her.

Her mother, Grace, had loved her father dearly, and Isadora had grown up in a house filled with attention and affection between both parents. When her father befriended Judge Wallace and brought him around for dinner, her mother was different. More luminous in some ways. More vibrant and alive. The following fall and winter had been a delightful time for young Isadora as she blossomed, in no small part due to the invigorating presence of the Judge in their house. When he left, it was as if the candles that had been so bright in her mother's heart were suddenly snuffed out. Isadora had suffered too. Withering, like a young sapling exposed to a long, hard winter.

She had survived, though, better than her mother, and she grew strong and resolute, having no illusions about men and their relations with women. She had not thought to feel anything remotely as strong as the feelings her mother had had for the Judge, and she had been surprised to discover that she could feel that intensely. Theodore had been surprised as well, and their marriage would be a singular joy in both their lives.

But it was not to last. Less than six months later, he drowned, and once again, she felt as if all her leaves had been torn from her branches. Her bark stripped from her trunk. A naked husk of a tree, exposed and dead.

And then the Judge had returned, and with him came a man with mercurial eyes that could be cold and icy one moment and then filled with incredible heat the next. When he looked at her, she felt like she could sprout new leaves, that she should straighten and raise her broken branches. She wanted to wrap her stiff arms around him and not let go until she was warmed to the pit of her stomach. She felt as if there was a bud of new growth hidden deep inside her, and if he looked at her long enough, she would show it to him.

26

VANCE TOOK THE LAST SEAT, BRINGING THE TABLE'S COMPLEMENT
to eight. He placed his wooden box on the table and, humming
to himself, proceeded to stack neat piles of chips beside the
box. Alexander Bracecourt—a lanky man with blond hair and
a peevish demeanor, due, somewhat, to a seemingly unending
string of bad cards—glared at Vance, who remained oblivious.
Samuel Took, one of three professional gamblers as far as the
Judge could tell, barely glanced at Vance. He plucked three
chips off his stack and tossed them into the pot, matching the
Judge's raise.

They were playing a fashionably new variant of poker, one
that dealt them several cards up and several down, with hands
of betting in between. It made play slower, but it increased the
betting and the chest-beating between the players, which the
Judge was clearly in favor of.

They were four cards into this hand, and each man had two
cards showing. The dealer was about to deal their final card,
and he began with a card to Douglas Leysinger, a ruddy-faced
young man who was breathlessly playing with funds his family
had somehow managed to not lose during the War. Next, cards
went to Bracecourt, Took, and then to the Judge, the last player
remaining in the hand. Since the final card was face-down, the
Judge's pair of eights was still the best hand showing, and so
betting fell to him again.

He waited a moment, watching as the other players peeked
at their final cards. He didn't bother looking at his. Not yet.

Bracecourt flicked the edge of his card a moment before letting it fall back to the table. He was showing a red ten and a black jack, and his betting had been strong. *He got what he wanted*, the Judge thought, watching the young man settle in his chair. *Two pair, at least. Maybe a straight.* He let a small grin tug at his lips. *His first good hand of the afternoon.*

Took folded, which didn't surprise the Judge. Took would be swift and merciless after nightfall—much as he had been last night—but in the afternoon, when the mood was quiet and tempers were at an ebb, he would bide his time. The Judge had already decided he was going to clean Took out before the dinner break. No point in giving the man another chance. Took was a distraction he didn't need. He just had to figure out how to draw the gambler into making a mistake.

Greed works, the Judge thought. *He that loveth silver shall not be satisfied with silver.*

"I grow tired of playing with toothless cubs," he growled. "The sun has already crested the canopy of heaven over us, and we shall be old and infirm when the sky grows dark. What are we waiting for?" He shoved out a stack of chips. "I'll open with six hundred dollars."

Vance stopped humming, and the air surrounding the table was suddenly still and thick—like the heavy sky before a thunderstorm. O'Halloran—who had folded after the third card—frowned lightly, as if frustrated to be left out of the windfall in the center of the table.

The Judge directed his gaze at Took. "Toothless," he repeated. "Like a suckling pig, blind and hungry," he said. Took's face darkened, but there was nothing he could do. He had already folded. He had to sit and watch the rest of the hand.

"What about you?" the Judge said to Bracecourt. "You think that jack will save you?" He smiled when Bracecourt flinched. *Two pair*, he thought, and then he wondered: *Was it a full house?*

"Too much for me," Leysinger said, shoving his cards away.

"Aye," the Judge said. "That's what your mother said too, the last time I visited her."

Leysinger's face went white, and he started to push his chair back.

"Oh, come now," Vance said. "He's playing you like a cheap fiddle, young man. Show some spine, or we're going to strip you naked in less than an hour."

Leysinger's eyes were wide and his hands were claws, gripping the edge of the table. For a long moment, everyone's attention was on the young man. Everyone, that is, except the Judge, who was watching Bart O'Halloran. O'Halloran fiddled with the cuffs of his jacket, and as the Judge watched, the stone-faced man twitched his left shoulder. As if he was adjusting something under his coat. He fiddled a moment with the edge of his jacket a moment longer, and then let his hands fall into his lap.

Ah, the Judge thought, *a harness.*

Cheating was as much of an art as rhetoric or seduction. The Judge himself knew a half-dozen ways to shuffle and deal from a deck so as to assure certain cards went to certain players, and he was certain many of the players in the tournament were equally skilled—which was undoubtedly why each table had a dealer provided by the Commission. Additionally, the Judge had, on occasion, used a variety of devices that would feed cards into the palm of his hand. The simplest was a spring-loaded brass rod attached to the forearm, and there were more complicated devices comprised of pulleys and straps that facilitated the delivery of multiple cards throughout a game. Based on what the Judge had just seen, O'Halloran's device went up his sleeve and across his back. When he moved his left shoulder in a certain way, it would release a card down his right sleeve.

A card the Judge was certain lay in O'Halloran's lap at this very moment.

O'Halloran was anticipating his move against Took, and he was going to attempt to blindside the Judge.

The Judge smiled at Bracecourt. "In or out," he said. He tapped his fingers near his cards, drawing Braceourt's gaze to the pair of eights that were showing.

Bracecourt squinted at the other cards in front of the Judge—the ones that were not turned upright. He had no idea what they were. All he had to go on was the Judge's bluster and confidence, and the Judge could read the man's confusion plainly on his face. Were the two eights all the Judge had? Did he have a third or fourth hiding? Bracecourt glanced around the table, vainly trying to remember what the other player had shown. Did the Judge have four eights?

"I might expire of thirst before this flower-headed fancy makes up his mind," he said. "Can I get another drink over here?" Behind him, a white-jacketed steward hurried away to the bar at the far side of the room. Vance called after the steward, ordering a drink too. "Anyone else?" the Judge asked the table. "It might be awhile before we see any action here." Most of the players demurred, but a few others indicated they were thirsty.

Bracecourt picked up his glass, and gulped what was left. When he put the glass down, his hand trembled slightly.

Two pair, the Judge decided. *He didn't get the full house.*

The Judge had a three, a seven, and a nine—all hearts. He had the eight of hearts and the eight of clubs showing. The black eight had given him a pair, but it had ruined his flush. He had been betting as if he had a flush—more so since the pair suggested he was sitting on a three of a kind or a full house—and there was no point in backing down now.

It was the only way he was going to win the hand, in fact.

"Come on, Bracecourt," he growled. "We haven't got all night. Six hundred to you. Do you want to see my pips or not?"

Six hundred dollars was more than half of what Bracecourt had left in front of him. The Judge suspected the young man didn't have that kind of spine, and when Bracecourt looked at him, he knew he was right.

"I'm . . . I'm out," Bracecourt said, deflating in his chair.

The Judge waited for Bracecourt to push his cards away, and only then did he let a smile crease his bearded face. Bracecourt paled at the Judge's smile and started to shake his head. "No, no, no," he moaned, his motion growing more frantic as the Judge leaned over and swept up the stack of chips. The Judge had a pair of eights showing, and an ugly realization was blooming in his head. "I had two—no, no." His two pair would have beaten the Judge's eights.

The Judge squared up his cards and handed them back to the dealer. "You did the right thing," he said, and while his tone was conciliatory, the gleam in his eyes was predatory. "Get out before you get cut too deeply. Once you start bleeding, we're going to drain you dry." He picked through the stack for a blue chip and tossed it back to the center of the table. "I'll cover the open," he said. "After that, I expect to see some action."

The blue chip was worth a hundred dollars. His dismissive gesture was the largest open played so far in the tournament.

He was getting bored, and he knew he wasn't the only one.

Besides, he was dying to see how heavy O'Halloran was going to go with that extra card hidden in his lap.

"I do believe you are trying to shove me out of this game," Took noted a few hands later. His pile had not decreased as much as the Judge had hoped, while the Judge's pile had taken a beating. "Too bad you don't have the chips to do it," he added, his eyes quickly tallying up the Judge's remaining funds. As the dealer dealt the next hand, Took smirked when he was given a red queen. "Where's your bite now, old man?" he asked as he threw a blue chip into the pot.

The Judge had a nine of hearts, and when he creased the corner of his down card, he saw the black club and the edge of a letter. He bent the card more, and saw the rounded crown of the Q. He had the queen of clubs. A face card, but mismatched color-wise with the nine, and so the best he could hope for was a straight—the very least he should take into the final showdown. The other players were paying attention to the play, like bloodhounds hot on the scent of a frightened fox. He made a production out of counting his remaining chips. Barely a thousand dollars was the tally. The only player with a smaller stack was a quiet and unremarkable man who was taking up space next to Leysinger. When the betting got to him, the Judge tossed in one of his two remaining blue chips. "Come closer," he cooed to Took. "I'll bite that bulbous monstrosity you call a nose clean off."

The rest of the players stayed in, and the dealer dealt the second face-up card to each man. The cards didn't help two of the players and they folded, while Leysinger took a long time to match Vance's opening bid. Took raised another twenty dollars and the Judge matched and raised when the bid came to him. He got a king, which kept his hope for a straight alive. He kept watching O'Halloran out of the corner of his eye, and the other man—who had also gotten an ace—seemed nonplussed and uninterested in the round. Damn these cards, the Judge swore silently. They were not cooperating. No one was getting a hand that would make them do something stupid.

When the dealer dealt the second round of face-down cards, O'Halloran and the quiet man folded. The Judge groaned inwardly and raised his eyes to the ceiling in a desperate plea to God. *Give them better cards*, he pleaded.

He got the ten of diamonds, which put a hitch in his breath, but Took had two jacks showing already, which meant the odds of him getting one were slim and none. And Vance and Leysinger were showing pairs as well—two and sevens, respectively. His nine/king pairing was a terrible place to be with the betting. His hand was worthless compared to the pairs that were showing, and even if he got one of the remaining jacks, the other players who were staying in had to bust completely.

The bet went around. Took didn't raise when it came to him, though he glared at Vance when the writer doubled down on his pair of twos. The Judge stayed in, though he knew he shouldn't. He was already on the hook for half of his remaining chips, and there was no sign that he was going to get the jack he needed. None of the other players were showing much enthusiasm either, but neither were they backing out. They were going to limp through to the end card. A sad, dismal death, the Judge thought.

The dealer slipped a card to the side, and then dealt the last card to each of the remaining players. Each man looked at his hand, and then Took—with queen high pair showing—led the betting. He gave the Judge a nasty grin as he tossed out a blue chip. "Come and bite me, old dog," he said.

The Judge peeked at his last card. He tried to bury his reaction when he saw the one-eyed visage. The jack of spades! His prayers had been heard. He had his straight. He wrinkled his nose and thrust his tongue against his lower lip. He let his gaze roam around the table. They all had pairs: Vance had twos, Leysinger had fours, and Took had queens. He had the straight, but . . .

"I'm in," he said, and it took him a minute to put together a hundred dollars from the meager pile of chips in front of him.

Vance and Leysinger stayed in, though Leysinger raised another hundred dollars.

The Judge rifled his meager pile of chips. Two-fifty, he reckoned. He could match the bet, but he had nowhere to go after that, and Vance still had to match Leysinger's raise. If Vance raised again, he would be done. If he folded, he could buy into the next hand, but he would quickly be at the mercy of the cards.

There was no point in trying to bluff. The others knew he didn't have much, and because none of them had folded, they probably all had threes of a kind. At least.

Vance raised, as expected, and the bet came to the Judge again.

"Shit," he said, pushing his chips into the pot. "Let's finish this."

He showed his straight, which made Took frown. One of Took's down cards was a jack, but three jacks was not enough to beat the Judge's straight. The Judge felt a momentary thrill run through his fingers. Had he won?

But then Leysinger turned over his cards. Eights. Three of them. Matched with his pair of sevens, and he had a full house.

"Son of a bitch," the Judge breathed. He was out.

27

"How can you be out?" Isadora demanded.

"The kid had a full house," the Judge slurred, as if that was all the explanation necessary. Or perhaps it was all the explanation he could muster. He had been drinking ferociously since leaving the table.

It wasn't just Leysinger's full house that had done the Judge in. Elm had watched the final showing of cards at the table. The Judge had been in a bind since the third card. Everyone else had a pair showing. He should have folded when O'Halloran had gone out, but he had stayed in. It had been a miracle that he had gotten the straight, but God touched the other players too.

They were in the lower salon, the Judge pinched between Isadora and Elm on one of the sofas. He had tried to get up and get another drink twice already, and they had taken turns pushing him back down. He had given Elm a lengthy re-creation of the game, and Elm had given up trying to point out that he had been standing behind the Judge during the whole debacle. When Isadora showed up, the Judge got sullen and Elm had to explain what had happened, but the Judge had disliked Elm's recitation and had taken over, painting the proceedings with a much better light cast on his actions.

"What are we going to do?" Isadora asked Elm, looking over the partially supine Judge.

"We have until morning," Elm said. "He can sit out one session—the one after dinner—but he has to be there in the morning or he forfeits his spot in the tournament."

"And what can we accomplish between now and morning?" she asked. "We're on a boat. We're not going to land anywhere, and even if we do, how are we going to get more money?"

"There is enough money on this boat," Elm said. "We just have to figure out how to get some of it."

"Bet it all on black," the Judge said, waving his arm toward the roulette wheel.

"All of what?" Elm asked.

"Whatever stash you have hidden away."

"I don't have a stash. I gave you all my money. I thought you were winning."

"That was yesterday," the Judge said. "Today?" He raised his arm and brought his hand down slowly, whistling as he let it fall.

"Unbelievable," Isadora said. "I'm going to lose the ranch."

"You're not—" Elm broke off and stared at the Judge. "What about your stash?"

"Me?"

"Yes. The double eagles."

The Judge shook his head. "We can't use that."

"We can."

"It's mine," the Judge whined. His face grew pinched.

Isadora sat upright, her face alight with a fierce anger. Elm motioned for her to hold her tongue, but she wasn't going to be silenced.

"That's it, then? 'It's mine'? What of my family? What of my mother? I knew you hadn't changed. You are still the same petulant child—the same coward you were—"

The Judge sat up, shoving his face close to Isadora. "Don't you dare presume to lecture me," he snarled.

Isadora didn't flinch. "O'Halloran was right. Your arrogance cost us everything!"

The Judge shook a finger in her face. "I didn't lose everything," he snapped.

Isadora wasn't having any of it. "No? You're out of the game. We have no money. We have no time left . . ."

"She's right," Elm said. "We're out of options."

The Judge whirled, his finger nearly striking Elm in the face. "We don't give up," he growled. "We are never out of options."

Elm shook his head. "We don't have time for your—"

"No," the Judge raged. "You, of all people, do not get to lecture me. You know better. I pay my debts. I will not suffer your sanctimonious attitude, boy. You are always thinking that you have to clean up after me. That I'm some bumbling old man who is going to shit the bed and spill the booze at the dinner table."

"God help us," Isadora moaned as she threw herself back against the sofa. "Please don't let him do this now."

The Judge lunged at Elm. "Paying off the debt isn't going to save her. O'Halloran wants her farm. It doesn't matter if we pay off the bank. If he can't buy it, he'll burn it down. We know that is his plan. We agreed that was his plan. Just as we agreed that we would take steps to stop him. And we did, didn't we?"

"We did," Elm said quietly. He did not like the way the Judge was ranting.

The Judge took no notice of Elm's sudden stillness. "What kind of man lets his own son be cursed? What kind of man lets such poison taint his own flesh and blood?"

"Wait, what?" Isadora sat up. She reached for the Judge's shoulder, trying to get his attention.

"He won't stop." The Judge let himself be pulled back by Isadora, and he collapsed on the couch. His body went slack. "There was no other way," he moaned. "We did what was necessary—what had to be done—and God have mercy on our souls."

Isadora stared at Elm, a horrified realization blooming in her eyes. "What is he talking about?" Her voice was barely a whisper.

The Judge's head lolled toward Elm. His body was loose and rubbery, but his gaze was not. His eyes were bright and fierce. *You tell her*, his gaze said. *It was your idea. You tell her.*

Elm shook his head. "We have to stop O'Halloran," was all he said, and the Judge's heated gaze didn't flicker. "The Judge is right. He wants the whole valley. He wants everything."

"Why?" Isadora asked. "What aren't you telling me?"

Elm felt a twinge of fear and disgust, deep in his gut. There were horrors lurking in the world. He had seen some of them, and such knowledge was a vicious weed in his belly that would burrow deep and poison him if he fed it. If he was afraid. If he let anger rule his emotions. That weed would grow and spread, like the kudzu that would overwhelm everything if it wasn't dealt with aggressively. You could pull it up. Hack off the vines. Burn it. But you could never kill it. A tiny sprout always escaped, hiding in the dark loam. Waiting to be nourished again.

Maybe Bart O'Halloran had cultivated that weed. Maybe he could not distinguish its hunger from his own. More cattle wouldn't appease him. All the women in Bitter wouldn't satisfy him.

"There will be no peace with him," Elm said. "You saw it in his eyes last night at dinner."

"I should have stabbed him," she snarled.

The Judge struggled to sit upright. "Don't—" he started. His limbs wouldn't work right, and he flailed about. "Pancho!" he wheezed. "My horse! My armor!" He fell back again, and his eyes fluttered in his head.

"Is he . . .?" Isadora asked.

She tentatively touched the Judge's shoulder, and when he didn't respond, she shook him. He snorted, stirred, and then slid over against Elm. His breath rattled in his throat.

Elm pushed the Judge upright. "He's asleep." He dug into the Judge's coat pocket for the wooden box. It was empty except for the silver tournament medallion. Elm reached into the Judge's other pocket and found a few bent cards. He showed them to Isadora: two aces and the one-eyed jack of spades.

"He was cheating?"

"Everyone cheats," Elm said. "Expecting the world to be fair is to be surprised and disappointed at every turn." He thumbed the edges of the cards, thoughts tumbling in his head.

"Look," she said, touching the cards. "They're not the same."

He turned them over. The backs of the aces contained a picture of a riverboat and the words "Salacious Sally" curled along a banner in opposite corners. The jack of spades was patterned with diamonds and triangles.

"It's from a different deck," Isadora said. "He couldn't use it. Everyone would notice."

The pattern struck Elm as familiar, but there were no other identifying marks. It was a cheap deck, the sort that came out at the end of any day's march, or that could be found in any easily forgotten saloon in an equally unmemorable town. He was sure he'd played cards with a deck like this, but where? When?

And then he remembered.

"Tishomongo," he muttered.

"Who?" Isadora said.

He shook his head. "Not who. Where."

"What are you talking about?"

Elm reached over to the Judge's supine form and felt around in the old man's waistcoat pockets. "He's a sentimental and superstitious bastard," he said. His finger felt something hard and metallic, and he pulled out a single double eagle.

One gold coin. Twenty dollars.

He clutched the coin in his hand and looked over at the roulette wheel. "We talked about faith, didn't we?"

Isadora rubbed her nose with the back of her hand. "Yes, I—I think. What are you talking about?"

"We have one coin." He nodded toward the wheel. "One bet. What color would he want us to play?"

She bit her lip. "I don't like having to make this choice," she said.

"I don't either, but regardless of whatever nonsense he'll start spouting the moment he wakes up, we really are out of options. So, we have to take a chance." He smiled at her. "Red or black?"

She traced a finger along the face of the jack of spades. "Black," she said matter-of-factly. "We go with black."

Roulette was a French invention, and unlike cards, there was no applicable skill to devote to the game. You placed your bets, and the croupier spun the wheel. If you spread your bets well—even, odd, red, black, a pattern of single numbers, either zero—you might win more than you put on the table. There were nearly as many theories as to how to beat the house as there were numbers on the wheel, but Elm had never seen a system that worked every time. Roulette was a game of chance, more or less depending on whether the house altered the wheel to change the odds.

It was a tricky proposition. Any shift in how often the white ball landed in a specific number or if red came up more often than black would be noticed by sharp-eyed players, and their bets would concentrate on those tiny differences in the odds. Since the house paid out heavily for single-number bets, they risked losing money if a wheel's predilections were realized by the players.

But betting across a wider spread of the wheel—all even numbers, red numbers, the first twelve—gave payouts that weren't much better than the initial wager. Elm knew they could spend all night at the roulette table, gradually building up a stake he could take back to the poker table, but it would take all night, and the stake wouldn't be that large.

They needed to take a risk.

He had a single double eagle, and he put it on one of the broad spreads. When it won, he split the winnings into two piles and bet them both. He lost one, but won with the other. It wasn't much, but it was more than he had a few minutes ago. He split and bet, again and again, and gradually his winnings grew to a hundred dollars. He split the piles into two again, and used one to take larger risks, while he let the other pile take the slow and safe route. He did not let his losses disturb his rhythm, and he kept money on the table.

The wooden wheel sat on the far end of the felt-covered table, and its golden handle flashed in the light as the wheel spun. The ball clattered and bounced noisily when it fell off the upper track, and the crowd around the roulette table would cheer and moan as the ball came to a stop in one of the numbered pockets. Elm didn't pay any attention to the crowd. He just watched the ball and listened to the wheel. Feeling its rhythm. Remembering the numbers that won. The room faded away.

Finally, he struggled out of a fog that had cloaked him, and he blinked as he tried to focus on the world beyond the spinning wheel. Isadora stood nearby, but all the other faces around him were not the same. He glanced around the room, and he sluggishly realized the Judge was gone from the sofa where they had left him. "Where . . . ?" he croaked.

"I had the stewards take him to his room a while ago," she said. "Just before dinner."

"Dinner?" His stomach grumbled.

"You've been here for several hours," she said. "I didn't want to disturb you." She nodded at the pile of chips in front of him. "You looked like you knew what you were doing."

He focused on the chips in front of him. Reds and white. Some blues. He ran his hand through them. "There's more than a thousand dollars here," he said thickly. His mind was still caught in the mesmerizing loop of the wheel. It had been different than when he had been waiting for a Confederate target to appear. Then, he was waiting for something to move. Now, there had been nothing but movement. He had adapted, learning how to wait for variations in the rhythmic blur of the wheel.

The croupier was looking at him expectantly, and Elm let his hands move his chips without thinking. A stack there. Another stack over there. And then, just before the croupier closed betting, he shoved the rest toward a single number.

The croupier nodded. "No more bets," he said. He reached for the wheel and gave it a spin.

Elm turned away from the table. He didn't need to watch. He could hear it well enough. The ball whirred as it raced around the wheel. When it slipped off the track, it clattered along the tops of the wooden trays. It was going to fall into one of the trays.

Elm closed his eyes, listening. He could see the spinning colors of the wheel, and the white dot of the dancing ball. *Very soon now*, he thought, and the ball fell into a slot.

A collective groan went up from the players gathered around the table as the wheel slowed enough for them to see where the ball had landed.

"Zero," Elm whispered, and the croupier echoed him a moment later.

All the losing chips were raked off the table, and the croupier called out for new bets. Players—still caught in the whirling frenzy of the game—jostled one another, urgently trying to place new bets. This time they were going to win. This time the ball would reward them.

As Elm turned back to the table, he realized Isadora was staring at him. She had heard him say the number before the croupier had spoken. He hadn't been looking at the table. His final bet had been on the zero. He hadn't been thinking about where he would play. He had just known.

"I'm getting hungry," he said absently as he picked up a stack of blue chips from his winnings and handed it to Isadora. He ignored her wide-eyed look and caught the croupier's eye. "I'd like to bet the rest of this"—he cocked his head and gnawed on his lip for a second, seeing the colors in his head—"on seven."

A hush swept through the crowd. The croupier smiled broadly and nodded. "Certainly, sir." He came around the table and swept the chips onto a wooden tray. His hands moved quickly, separating them into neat stacks, and when he was done, he announced a total of nine hundred and eighty dollars.

"Put it on the seven," Elm said.

As the croupier returned to the other side of the table, Elm plucked the blue chips from Isadora's hands and stacked them neatly on the double zero. The croupier marked Elm's bet with a brass disc and then called for all other bets to be placed. He smiled at the crowd as a few of the players stacked up bets on the seven as well—greedy gamblers getting sucked into Elm's orbit.

The croupier spun the wheel, and the crowd leaned toward him, their collective gaze locked to the wheel. When he released the white ball, the air went still.

When the ball started to clatter and bounce, Isadora stood on her tiptoes, trying to see where it was going to land.

Elm watched the croupier, and a tiny smile crooked the corner of his mouth when he saw the man reach under the table. He didn't know how the machinery worked, but the croupier could exert an influence on the ball. It wasn't much, but it was enough to pull the ball one direction or another.

There was a jagged line in the colors in his head. A fault that had not made any sense.

The ball fell into a slot, and Isadora gasped.

"No," someone cried out, and many of the crowd turned away, unable to look at the disaster that had just happened.

The wheel slowed, and everyone could see that the slot labeled with the '7' was empty.

"Double zero," the croupier announced when the wheel stopped. "Bank wins—" He stopped, his eyes wide as he spotted Elm's stack of blue chips, resting on that same number.

"We should eat," Elm said to Isadora, as easily as if he was commenting on the weather. "There may not be time later."

He had been patient.

28

"My apologies for being so delinquent," Elm said as he pulled out the empty chair. He flipped the silver tournament medallion onto the table, and then dropped the cloth napkin he was carrying next to it. The contents of the cloth napkin rattled, and blue chips spilled out when he let got of the ends. "I'll be sitting in for the Judge this evening."

"What?" Leysinger looked at the other players, his eyes wide. "He can't do this. The Judge went broke. I beat him. He's out of the tournament."

Vance clicked his tongue and shook his head. "No, he had to leave the table because he was out of chips, but he had until morning to buy back in."

Leysinger crossed his arms and sat back in a huff.

Elm picked up one of his blue chips and tossed it onto the large pot. "The Judge is resting. He might have had too much to drink after being ejected from the game this afternoon." He glanced at the other players, setting faces to the names Isadora had given him a little while ago. Leysinger. Took. Vance. Norman. Bracecourt. LeMan. And, of course, the stony-faced criminal himself, Bart O'Halloran. "A hundred dollars says you don't mind me watching this hand and being dealt into the next one."

Leysinger's mouth moved, but no words came out. Took stroked his chin. "I don't mind an extra hundred dollars," he said. He nodded at the sprawling mess of Elm's chips. "I don't mind those either. The rest of you have been terribly tight with your betting."

O'Halloran tossed a handful of chips into the pot. "Let's get this hand over with so we can take his money," he said.

"A marvelous idea," echoed Vance, and the rest of the players bet or folded—tacitly acknowledging Elm's contribution to the pot and his right to remain at the table.

Took won the hand, and as he was hauling the mess of chips toward his seat, a hand lightly fell on Elm's shoulder. It rested there a moment, and then wandered across his back. "What have we here?" a woman's voice asked. Mrs. Peabody's flared skirts brushed Elm's shoulder.

"A late arrival," Vance said. "But one who comes with a great many chips."

"Yes, I see that," Mrs. Peabody said. Her hand tightened on Elm's shoulder. "And he's got a token to play, so unless any of you gentlemen have an issue, the house is not concerned with letting him sit and participate."

The players nodded, and Mrs. Peabody smiled down at Elm. "Judge Wallace was boisterous and prone to unruly speech and behavior. I can't say I'm sorry to see him leave. You do realize he won't be coming back."

"Not tonight at least—"

"No, Mr. Stonebrook. He's done. He gave you his tournament piece. You can't give it back to him. Those are the rules."

Elm nodded. "I don't think that will be a problem."

"Good. Things are interesting enough without having to deal with that scoundrel calling me names."

"I'm shocked, Mrs. Peabody. Usually he reserves such inarticulate gibberish for knuckle-dragging apes like these fine gentlemen at this table."

She patted him lightly. "You're sweet and delicious. If it weren't for all these eyes watching us, I would eat you up right now."

"Yes," Elm said, noting the variety and intensity of the stares offered by the other players. "Well, perhaps when there are fewer of them, we can revisit this conversation."

"I look forward to that," Mrs. Peabody said. Her hand trailed down his shoulder. "Play nice, gentlemen," she admonished before departing in a swirl of fabric.

"Two hundred says she's all talk," LeMan said. He was a large man, with extra meat on his bones. He had a thick mustache that drooped over thick lips, and he had a tendency to let his tongue pick at his teeth when he was thinking. His eyes were on Mrs. Peabody's swaying skirts, and it was clear to everyone at the table where his thoughts were. Nor was he the only one.

"I'll see that wager," Took said. The professional, Elm thought, remembering what Isadora had told him. "But I want three hundred. She likes this fellow."

"You should go to five hundred," Elm offered. "At the very least."

LeMan's tongue fumbled against his cheek.

"You are wagering whether or not I get my hands up Mrs. Peabody's skirts, yes? Her interest in my hands exploring her hidden mysteries aside, is this wager not entirely dependent on my inclination to participate?" Elm wrinkled his nose. "Are you that stupid?"

"I'll bet two hundred dollars that he tells you two to go fuck each other," Vance piped up.

Without taking his eyes off LeMan and Took, Elm picked up two blue chips from his pile. "Now, are we going to play some cards, or do you two need some time to . . . ?" When neither Harcourt nor Took replied, Elm tossed the two blue chips to Vance.

Leysinger started to laugh, but hurriedly put his hand over his mouth when Took glared at him.

The dealer cleared his throat. "Shall we continue?" he asked.

"We should," Elm said. He looked at O'Halloran, who had remained silent during this exchange. The man was a formidable presence, even seated at the table with six other remarkable characters. O'Halloran's shoulders strained at his suit, and his cheeks and throat were so devoid of stubble that Elm wondered if whiskers were incapable of penetrating that stony skin. The Judge had lamented O'Halloran's lack of expressive range—comparing him to a granite statue with the inscrutable gaze of an alley cat—and Elm found himself agreeing with the Judge's evaluation. It was going to be very hard to read O'Halloran.

Elm let his gaze drop, and he did a quick calculation of the chips neatly stacked before O'Halloran. He doubted this was all of the money O'Halloran had with him, but at the moment, his pile was not as flush as Elm's. Maybe he wouldn't need to know whether the other man had good cards or not.

An idea started to germinate in the back of his mind. He glanced around, looking for Isadora. The dealer started laying out cards, and Elm pulled his attention back to the game.

His idea would have to wait.

First, he had to reduce the number of players at the table. His eyes flicked to each player's stash of chips, doing more calculations.

Bracecourt, he decided. *And then Leysinger or LeMan.*

Typically, the sharpshooters of Company C did not engage in the general melee. They were held in reserve for doing their deadly work when armies were not violently skirmishing, which meant the sound of a Sharps rifle firing was an incongruous noise. Confederate soldiers learned to dive for cover when they heard the distant thunder of a Sharps, and so a sharpshooter learned to pick several targets before he started firing. He would only have a few seconds before everyone scattered, and he had to hit as many targets as possible in that time. The breech mechanism of the rifle allowed for fast reloading, and Elm had heard stories of men managing to hit five targets in less than ten seconds.

He never tried for more than three. In his experience, he might get two, and the third would take several tries. During which, the enemy would be trying to ascertain his position and return fire. If they spotted him, he would have to retreat, and it would take hours for the enemy to let down their guard enough that he could try again.

Two players would be enough. The others would change their tactics after that, and he would have to try something different. But he could get two of them before the rest reacted.

The dealer finished the initial deal, and Elm lifted the corner of his down card. The five of hearts, and he had the ace of diamonds showing. He sighed inwardly, not letting his reaction show on his face.

It just might take longer than he thought . . .

LeMan went bust first, though it was Took who cleaned him out rather than Elm.

Took's fingers liked to dance on the table, and he had a habit of resting his palms flat on his hole cards. Elm was certain Took was doing something when his hands weren't on the table, but he hadn't been able to catch him at it. Took went from a pair of twos showing to a full house in the reveal, and it beat Elm's flush. He hadn't gone strong with the hand as he wasn't quite sure what else was on the table, and he was glad he had held back, but Took had managed to lure LeMan in with his twos. The quiet man had gotten flustered when Took raised the bet in the penultimate round and had bet everything.

In the next hand, Vance gouged Took for half of what LeMan had lost. He had been patient, and when the gambler overextended himself after dominating LeMan, Vance was ready. Elm saw Vance's play coming; it was, in fact, very in keeping with the conversation he and the writer had had earlier in the day about trapping players.

It took another hour to wipe out Bracecourt. Everyone got a piece of the man, though, as they slowly bled him hand after hand. Elm was starting to understand the Judge's frustration with the players. They were too cautious. His stack had not grown more than anyone else's during Bracecourt's demise, and he was still on too equal footing with the other players.

Leysinger had a couple of thousand left, and Norman wasn't much better off. Took's stack had toppled over twice in the last three hands, and he no longer tried to keep them ordered. Vance arranged his chips in a brick, which hid the true depth of his winnings. O'Halloran had ordered rows, and it looked like nearly ten thousand dollars worth of chips. Elm had been able to stay away from his stash of blue chips, but his loose piles of red and white chips were only about a thousand.

He was up several hundred dollars, and if he played as cautiously as the others were, he would continue to win. But that would extend the game all the way to St. Louis, and he didn't have that kind of time.

He needed a hand that would make someone charge blindly ahead.

And so the game went: Leysinger took a pot with a pair of aces. Elm tried to bluff his way to the end with a pair of threes, but was beaten by a low straight from Took. Vance fumbled what was most likely a full house—he bet too aggressively when the last card was dealt. No one was fooled by his meager pair of sixes showing.

There were straights that failed to get the missing card. Flushes busted by a single red face among a sea of black. Hands that would have swept the table if the fifth card matched the two pair.

The salon had emptied out but for the players at two of the tournament tables, and the room was thick with a grey pall of cigar smoke. Players were starting to nod, and betting had slowed to a crawl.

Elm tapped a finger against the three cards in front of him. He had a three and four showing, red and black, and his down card was a red seven. He was looking for the straight, and when the bet came to him, he stayed in. Leysinger's cards were red, but mismatched, and they were a six and another of the threes. Took was showing a pair of jacks, and he paused when Leysinger didn't fold. His eyes swept back and forth between the young man's hand and Elm's, and Elm cleared his throat at the man's hesitation.

"It's getting late," he groused. "Are you having trouble counting all our pips?"

Took glared at him, but wasn't drawn in. He met the raise, and the dealer gave them all another card. Leysinger looked at his card, his tongue worrying his bottom lip, and then he tossed in a meager twenty dollars worth of chips. Elm didn't even bother to look at his last card. He plucked two blue chips off his stack and threw them on the table. "Are those jacks all you have?" he asked Took, and when Took hesitated, he knew that was the case.

Took frowned, not liking Elm's insouciance with the garbage he was showing. He drummed his fingers on the table, and then shoved his cards away.

Leysinger wanted nothing to do with the two hundred dollars Elm had just bet.

The pot was his and they hadn't even gotten to the last card.

He raked over the chips as the dealer collected the cards and shuffled them. Not counting his contribution to the pot, it was a little over three hundred dollars.

God, the pace was aggravating.

Vance let out a loud sigh. "I am in penny-pincher hell," he grumbled. He played with a stack of red chips. "There are women yearning to be seduced and whisky bottles crying out to be drunk, and I am trapped at this table of geriatric grandmothers."

"We should raise the opening bid," Elm said.

Vance slapped the table. "Yes. We should raise the bid."

"We are not raising the bid," O'Halloran countered.

Vance looked at Elm, and there was a gleam in the writer's eyes that had not been present for several hours. Vance flipped a blue chip into the pot. "Yes, we are," he said. "I do not care who opens. I will see whatever the bet is and raise it to one hundred dollars. And I'll do so for every hand after this one until we are." He leaned forward and turned his attention to O'Halloran. "You can give up your seat any time, sir, if you do not have the stomach for more rarified play."

Took grunted at that, and he added a blue chip of his own. "Give us some cards," he said to the dealer. "I, too, am tired of this penny ante bullshit."

The dealer looked around the table, his tongue nervously wetting his lips, and one by one, the rest of the players threw in a blue chip. O'Halloran was the last, and his glare was full of malice as he anted in. The dealer nodded and announced that the opening bid would now be a hundred dollars, and he dealt the next hand of cards. Vance urged him to hurry it up, and the dealer acquiesced, giving them both of their up cards and one down card before he paused for betting.

The players were silent, considering the six hundred dollars in the pot and the terrible combinations showing. Elm had a king, Leysinger had a queen, Vance had a two/three combination, and O'Halloran wasn't much better off with a two and a five. Took and Norman had aces, but Took had the better hand showing with a ten for his second card.

The opening bid was his, and after some deliberation, he put in twenty. Vance snorted loudly. Elm doubled the bet to forty when it came to him, but it still wasn't enough when it reached Vance. "Yes, it is nothing but penny ante bullshit at this table," he echoed derisively as he raised the bet to a hundred. "I'm showing what could possibly be the worst hand in the history of this game, and you're only going to open with twenty?"

The dealer gave each man their second down card, and there was another long pause as the men considered the odds. Leysinger folded, which meant the opening bet passed to Elm. He glanced at his down cards. A second ten and one of the other aces.

"Five hundred," he said, throwing out five blue chips.

Vance raised an eyebrow. "Are you challenging my woefully inadequate pips?"

"I am," Elm said. "You had your wild luck with tiny cards already."

O'Halloran stayed in without saying a word, and Norman agonized over his hand for awhile before folding. The bet passed to Vance.

"I might still have some of that luck," Vance said, tapping his cards.

"You might." Elm stifled a yawn. "Can we find out before dawn?"

Vance laughed. "I had anticipated spending these late hours in the arms of a delightful companion versus sitting in this hard chair for hours, watching this group of pitiful pensioners count their pennies." He slung five blue chips into the pot. "Alas, my dream will remain but a dream."

Took shook his head and bowed out.

The dealer gave the three remaining players a final card, and Elm glanced at it briefly before making his bet. "One thousand dollars," he said, counting out ten blue chips.

O'Halloran grimaced and pushed his cards away. He had not stayed in to the end for over an hour. He still had a sizable stake, but his play had gone cold.

Elm stared at Vance. He had spotted a flutter in the writer's eye when he had looked at the final card. He knew Vance didn't have anything in his down cards. Vance frowned as he stared at the sea of blue chips on the table. He rubbed his cheeks for a moment, and when he realized what he was doing, he let out a large sigh and pushed his cards away. "It's yours," he grumbled.

The pot was generous, but Elm had contributed more than half of it. He was playing aggressively, and while it was working at the moment, all it would take was one good hand for another player to decimate his winnings.

As the dealer gathered the cards for the next deal, O'Halloran pushed his chair back from the table. He counted out a stack of chips and put them in the center of the table. "I'm going to piss," he said. "I'll be back for the next hand."

Harcourt nodded and struggled out of his chair. "I am going to attend to such matters as well," he said.

The dealer stopped shuffling and looked at the other players.

"I could use another drink," Took said.

"Let's take fifteen minutes," the dealer said. He put the cards aside and opened a new deck.

Elm eased himself out of his chair. His lower back complained, and he walked stiffly toward the bar. He spotted Isadora, and his face lit up. His expression changed when he saw the tension in her face. "What is it?" he asked.

"The Judge," she whispered, nervously looking over his shoulder. "He has a plan."

"Is it a good plan?"

"He wouldn't tell me. I fear it is going to cause mayhem."

"That sounds like one of the Judge's plans, all right."

29

HE WAS TRAPPED IN A BOURBON-FUELED NIGHTMARE. THERE were holes in the sky through which tongues of lightning licked, and the trees were all withered and leafless. He wasn't wearing any boots, and the ground was hot beneath his feet. There was a river nearby and he thought it might be the Mississippi, but the water bubbled as if it were boiling, and there were shapes moving beneath its surface.

His throat was dry and his tongue was stiff and swollen in his mouth. He was thirsty—that was the bourbon having its way with him—and, with a growing sense of alarm, he realized he was walking toward the river. With a groan, he stopped himself before he collapsed on the muddy bank and drank from the noisome river.

That water is poison, the Judge thought. The ground along the bank was barren of root and shrub. Nothing grew near the river. *And if the water doesn't kill me outright, then some monstrosity will leap out and drag me under.*

This was the way the terrible nightmares worked. He always found himself in a place like this one—a world he might have recognized once, but now burned and scarred. This was what was to come, he knew, a bleak future where men like him no longer stood against the creep of darkness. Hell on Earth. The damnation of all.

A long undulating howl spooked him, and he stumbled along the river bank. He was being hunted—that was what that cry meant—though he couldn't recall how long this hunt had been going on or where it had started. He was always running, as if all of these horrible dreams were but snatches of one continuous nightmare existence. He was running away, like a coward, but he had always been running away. Ever since Baton Rouge. Ever since . . .

Coward.

The word echoed in his head, and the reverberations made him shake violently.

The howl sounded again, and he twitched and nearly fell as he tried to look over his shoulder. It was closer. He needed to run. He had to get away before his past caught up with him. Before its claws caught his legs. Before its teeth tore his coat.

He patted his waistcoat and felt a reassuring weight in one of the pockets. He dug the object out and was reassured by the familiar sight and weight of a double eagle. A man is never lost as long as he has coin, he thought, and he thrilled at the momentary spark such a thought brought.

His foot caught on a white root jutting from the ground. Where had that come from? It was gnarled and twisted— whether from age or anger, he could not tell. As he tried to keep his footing, the coin slipped from his fingers, and he cursed his clumsiness. Or perhaps he cursed the root. It didn't matter, both were equally at fault.

The coin stayed on its edge when it hit the ground, and it rolled unerringly toward the water. He scrambled after it. His bare feet recoiled at the texture of the damp riverbank, and his gorge rose in his throat at the thought of the coin reaching the water.

A choking cry escaped from his mouth as he lunged for the coin. He smacked against the ground, knocking the air out of his lungs. He threw out his hands, stretching his fingers. Almost . . .

The coin bounced off a ridge in the ground, and he snatched it away from the river as it was airborne. Holding it tight, he scrambled back from the river's edge.

He wasn't fast enough. The water thrashed and parted, vomiting up something dark and scaly. Its head was long and dark, and it had a mouth full of crooked teeth. It had no eyes, and in the center of its blank face were two white marks: a cross and a circle.

The monster landed heavily on the bank, and its stubby legs clawed at the damp earth. The Judge tried to move faster, but the monster came at him. When it opened its mouth, its teeth lengthened, and with a snap, it bit down on the Judge's trailing leg and—

The Judge sat up in bed, propelled out of his dream by a throat-aching scream. He thrashed about, nearly falling out of the narrow bed, and he fought the confining embrace of the blankets. As he realized where he was, he calmed his limbs. Slowly, he came back to himself, and shivering now from the cold sweat which coated his face and chest, he curled up on the bed and hugged himself. Trying to make himself as small as possible. Just in case the dream still had teeth.

His right thigh ached. That was where the dream monster had bitten him. He could feel its gnarled teeth piercing his flesh. Grinding against his bone. So many teeth, like a field of crooked lances. And all that blood. His blood.

His head ached too, a parting gift from the bourbon, and it was that pounding in his head that eventually reminded him of who he was. Lying in bed, waiting for the nightmare to come back, wasn't for him. The first time he had touched the darkness, he had retreated into the bottle and the arms of any woman who would take his money, and both had kept the night terrors at bay. Eventually, though, the bottles emptied and the women became cold and distant, and he had no more money to fix either. He thought if he didn't sleep, the nightmare couldn't find him, but that was a foolish notions that lasted only a few days.

The Judge rubbed at his whiskers, and a low growl of frustration and annoyance rose out of his chest. He hadn't expected to lose at the table. Not like that. And the unexpected expulsion from the card game had knocked him out of true. He had gone to the bottle as a salve against his wounded pride, and the strong spirits served aboard the Salacious Sally had knocked him even farther from the path.

And now . . .

He swung his legs off the bed and slapped his stockinged feet on the wooden floor. He paused for a split second; a very tiny part of him screamed that there was a monster still lurking under the bed, but there was no monster. Not in this room, at least. When nothing grabbed him, the Judge stood, swaying slightly, and he closed one eye as the room went in and out of focus.

How much had he drunk? He waved the question away. The burning dryness in the back of his throat and the pressure against his forehead were answer enough.

He stumbled over to the table where there was a pitcher of water. He didn't even bother with the glass, and water splashed down his beard and chest as he guzzled greedily. He stopped when his belly ached, and when he put the pitcher down, he saw the double eagle on the table.

He stared at it, his blood buzzing in his ears. Was it the same coin? Had he woken from a dream within a dream?

Fingers trembling, he explored the pockets of his waistcoat. He found nothing, which only increased the agitation in his fingers. He cast about for his coat and spotted it draped across the back of a nearby chair. He searched its pockets, finding his illicit stash of cards—the two aces he had palmed earlier and the jack from the game in Tishomongo. His good luck card.

He didn't find the silver medallion.

He stalked around the stateroom, peering at the shadows. He found the wooden box he had gotten from the accountant, but the medallion was not there either. Nor were there any chips, which came as no surprise. His head hurt, but there was nothing wrong with his memory.

Finally, he returned to the table with the pitcher and the twenty-dollar coin.

It was cold to the touch, and when he wrapped his fingers around it, the gold started to warm. *Elm left it*, he thought, *as a message.* The Judge's headache started to ease. Elm was still playing, he realized. That was why the medallion was gone.

"Good man," the Judge muttered as he slipped the double eagle into his waistcoat. He cast about for his boots as he put on his coat. Once he found them and was fully dressed, he stared at the heavy trunk in the corner of the room. His tongued roamed around his mouth as he thought about the pistol buried beneath an extra pair of long underwear. Had it come to that?

Guns make people predictable, he thought, which was all the justification he needed, really.

After locking the stateroom door behind him, he walked to the railing and let the night air wash over him. He felt the rhythmic churn of the paddle wheel through the boards beneath his feet. It churned against the river, slowing the boat's downstream pace to that of an infant's crawl. The sky was falling to black, and a cascade of stars wheeled and turned like fireflies. The moon, waning toward a lopsided smile, was off to his right.

He stood awhile, letting the thrum of the boat tune him. His thoughts became less jumbled, and the outline of a plan started to form in his head. He smiled, pleased that his mind was still sharp, and he turned away from the railing. He set off toward the front of the boat, letting the idea continue to form, and as he walked, he listened for gossip. The tournament was still going, though players were starting to drop out. Men, like him, who had been stripped of all their coin. He heard talk of the food and the accommodations. Some wondered if it was going to rain tomorrow.

When he reached the forward deck and turned toward the port side of the boat, he looked toward the eastern shore. It was difficult to make out any distinct shapes, but he imagined there were trees close to the river bank. In the distance, there was a yellow glow, as if there was a small village not too far ahead. The Judge wondered if the riverboat's captain intended to tie up at a dock for the remainder of the night. Navigating the river was a never-ending challenge, as sandbars and snags constantly shifted.

And what of his plans? He had lost his place at the table, which would have thrown a lesser man into utter despair. But he was not as easily deterred—nor was Elm, for that matter. While he had been temporary distracted by the bottle and the ensuing nightmare, Elm had taken his place at the table. For a moment, he worried that the lad had dipped into the money he had already won and set aside. *He wouldn't*, the Judge thought, *even if he knew of it.* He had hidden the money well. Which meant Elm had found some other source of funds. That was what the double eagle had meant. He was sure of the message: Elm didn't need his money.

But O'Halloran was a crafty and cautious player. All the Judge's efforts to draw him out had failed. If he had to admit any failing in his play, it was his eagerness to break O'Halloran that had left him vulnerable to the other players. *And it hadn't been Took*, he thought, *it had been that damned writer.*

Grudgingly, the Judge had to admit the writer might not be as much a dandy and a jackass as he appeared. That wasn't the same as being awash with admiration for the man. No, let's not go that far. The writer was a ponce, but that didn't mean he wasn't crafty.

And speaking of crafty, how had O'Halloran come to be on the boat? He had been too caught up in the game to give much thought to the other man's presence. At first, he had thought O'Halloran's plan was the same as theirs: get money, and stop the other from doing the same. But that was too convenient. *Sometimes the simplest answer was too simple*, the Judge realized. No, there was too much deference to the stony landowner.

Mrs. Peabody was a delight, and she made everyone feel as if they were old friends, but she made little effort toward O'Halloran. Not because he was a brute—it wouldn't take long for anyone to realize that about the man—but because she knew what he was like. And it wasn't just him. The Judge cast back and tried to remember the way the other staff were with O'Halloran. *Yes,* he thought, recalling the way the dealer spoke and the bartender's uneasy manner, *they know him.*

O'Halloran had been on the boat before. He had played in this tournament.

Which posed an interesting question: if O'Halloran had played, had he not won? It was hard to imagine the rancher not coming away with full pockets. The Judge considered possible scenarios, and found more questions. Why wasn't O'Halloran's herd larger? Why wasn't his influence in Bitter stronger?

He was not entirely comfortable with what they had done with Tommy's skull. They put a curse on it, Elm had told him. A bit of Romani magic he had learned overseas. The Judge hadn't wanted to know, but Elm said it wouldn't work if they didn't believe in its efficacy. *Magic is faith,* he said, *and faith upholds magic.* It was dark work that undoubtedly put a stain on his soul—a mark that would never come off—but countering Elm's argument by claiming their mission required purity of intent and action had been met with derision. *And rightly so, damn the man,* the Judge thought. But he was not in a rush to become like those unholy monsters they pursued.

Regardless, the curse would poison the water, and when O'Halloran's herd drank from the pond, they would sicken and die. O'Halloran would be forced to move his herd. He would have to find a new source of water. The curse wouldn't ruin the rancher completely, but it would cost him men and resources. It would put a strain on his finances.

But the curse couldn't have worked that quickly. It had only been a week since they had hunted Tommy down and killed him.

If O'Halloran had figured out what they had done already—and if he had, then what did that say about O'Halloran's esoteric knowledge?—then he could mitigate much of the financial distress the curse would levy on his ranch.

And yet, all of O'Halloran's intimidation and posturing felt hollow, as if it was masking something else. Something desperate and—*was that the secret then?*—something feral.

The Judge popped his lips as he came to the conclusion that answered all of his questions. O'Halloran was broke. He couldn't afford to buy Isadora's ranch from the bank. He needed to get it some other way because he had debts he had to pay. Debts that her land and her herd could pay off.

The Judge kept popping his lips as his gaze roamed up to the hurricane deck. Mimicking the sensation of bubbles rising. An idea, floating up in his head.

On the hurricane deck, there was a row of rooms forward of the private salon at the back of the boat. Atop that long structure was the square block of the pilot house. Those rooms were where the crew and captain bunked, along with storage and other ancillary quarters—for members of the Commission, for instance.

Where was all the money the tournament players had paid to buy their way into the game? he wondered. *In a safe—without a doubt—and that safe was probably up in those rooms.* Guarded night and day by a number of well-paid guards.

The idea bobbed in his head. They didn't need to beat O'Halloran at the table. They just had to keep him from getting the money.

The Judge smiled wolfishly. *Fraught with danger,* he thought, recalling a conversation he had had with Elm. This idea certainly qualified.

But he couldn't waltz up to the hurricane deck and into the room with the safe. *Don't mind me, gentle sirs, I'm just here for all that coin and paper in that box there. Would you mind loading it into these satchels for me?* Such action, while the daring sort of nonsense that Vance would employ in one of his dreadful dime novels, wasn't practical. The guards were not going to be easily charmed, and besides, they would remember the Judge's face. They would report who had taken the money, and he wasn't interested in being the target of a manhunt by U.S. Marshals.

The Judge had employed the Marshals on one or two occasions, and he preferred to remain on the same side of the law as them. Not to mention every starry-eyed and scabrous bounty hunter from Raleigh to San Francisco who would be eager to claim the hefty reward posted for his capture.

The idea had merit, but it lacked practicality and a method of successful implementation. He needed a plan with a little more subtlety.

The Judge popped his lips one more time as his gaze wandered down from on high. Down to the boiler deck, where the state-rooms were located.

It was too bad he didn't have any dynamite . . .

30

"Time, gentlemen," Mrs. Peabody called. She clapped her hands, getting the attention of the room, whereupon she repeated her summons. The players drifted back to the table.

"What mischief is the Judge up to?" Elm asked Isadora. He looked for O'Halloran, but couldn't spot him in the crowd.

"He came to my room, looking for twine or silk—whatever he could find. And he took one of my dresses."

"Did he tell you why?"

She shook her head. "He said you had an hour, maybe two."

Elm spotted O'Halloran. The rancher had returned to the salon. He was standing near the door, talking urgently with a pair of hard-looking men. Elm frowned as he watched the conversation. What had he missed?

"I have to get back to the table," Elm whispered to Isadora, his gaze still on O'Halloran and the men. "We need to be ready for something to happen." He edged closer, his body nearly touching hers. "The money I gave you earlier," he said. "Make sure it is safe."

She nodded. "It is."

"And the gun. Get the gun too." He caught her chin with his hand and lifted her face. Her lips parted slightly as he kissed her, and then, without lingering any longer, he strode back to the table.

Elm was the last player to return, and as he sat down, the dealer started to deal, laying out the first of the two cards for each of the six remaining players. Elm rubbed his hands on his trousers, trying to put aside his apprehension. The Judge was up to something, and there was no time to find out what. The Judge's message was clear, though: stay and play. Win.

He could do that much. And hope the rest wasn't going to be too spectacularly messy.

The dealer finished, and the players examined the cards that were showing. Elm had a queen. O'Halloran had a four. Elm didn't care what the others had. His was the high card, and he opened with a hundred dollars. Norman and Leysinger folded immediately; the others stayed in, and after the second down card, no one was in a rush to increase the pot. Vance got a king with his second show card, which gave him the high card, but he bet small. Elm bumped it up to a hundred dollars again, but Vance wouldn't bite. The writer folded, leaving Took and O'Halloran. When the last card was dealt, Elm opened bidding with two blue chips. O'Halloran frowned and folded. Took, at least, thought about it for a few seconds before capitulating.

Elm had won the hand.

He got back what he bet, and three times over that. A day ago, it would have been a good pot, but right now—with the time pressure of the Judge's mysterious plan—it was a sluggish hand. Elm needed something bigger. He didn't have much time. He had to get the other players to do something rash.

Three hands later, his prayers were answered.

I need something that will make a lot of noise and something that will make a lot of smoke, the Judge decided. In a mining town, any of a half-dozen drunkards in the nearest saloon could improvise a smoke bomb without thinking (or being sober), but on a steamboat, the options were . . . rather lacking—truth be told— and so he improvised. The first bomb was nothing more than a bag filled with black powder from a handful of rifle cartridges, one of Isadora's cotton undergarments soaked in lamp oil, and a deck of playing cards—there was an abundance of those around the boat. The fuse was several inches of soaked twine, and it would start nicely when he applied the hot end of a cigarette to it.

He found a seat on the port side of the boiler deck—the same side of the boat where O'Halloran's stateroom was located. He knew which one it was: the young steward, Benson, had been happy to show the Judge when offered a double eagle for his trouble. The Judge sat and smoked a few cigarettes, passing the time. The boat continued to drift down river, and when the yellow glow of the village moved from being on his right to his left, he figured the captain wasn't going to stop after all.

He waited for a few more minutes, wanting to be sure he wouldn't be seen by late-night strollers, and then he stood up and hurried over to O'Halloran's stateroom. Each stateroom had a small window beside the door, and he knocked the glass out of the window with his fist wrapped in the end of his coat. Sucking heavily on his cigarette, he took out the first of the improvised devices. He applied the bright tip of his cigarette to the fuse, and when it started to burn, he brushed aside the thin curtain hanging inside the room and threw the smoking satchel inside.

And then he walked away, as if nothing untoward had happened.

Soon, smoke was leaking out of the shattered window, and he got out of the way as men came clattering up the stairs from the lower deck. A crowd gathered around the smoking stateroom, and the Judge spotted Richard O'Halloran. There was a scuffle as the deck hands tried to keep Richard from opening the door, but the young man was surprisingly strong. The Judge winced slightly as the fire burst out of the room with a loud roar, scattering men across the deck. Richard O'Halloran was not going to be deterred, and the Judge watched with some amazement as the young man rushed into the fire's wicked embrace.

Men with buckets of water followed, and that was his cue to wander up to the hurricane deck.

The betting had been spirited after the first pair, and when the second hole card had been given to each player, no one folded. Now, with the second show card dealt, the tension was almost palpable among the players. Elm had started off with a pair of fours—one up and one down—and his third card had been an ace. His second show card was another four, giving him a three of a kind.

Leysinger had a pair of threes showing, but judging from the way he kept staring at his hands, Elm guessed his down cards weren't helping. O'Halloran had started with a red jack, and he had pushed the betting hard the first round, but his second show card was a five, which had slowed him down. Elm wasn't sure if he was bluffing or if he had missed a chance at a good hand. *Probably can't beat my three of a kind*, he thought.

Vance had one of the other fives and an ace, and his face showed nothing about what his down cards might be. Norman had a seven and an eight, and Took had two clubs—the start of a flush. Nothing certain, but if their hands came together, they'd beat Elm's fours.

Took matched the last raise, and the dealer gave them their final down card. Leysinger peeked, and exhaled audibly. He led with two hundred dollars, and after Norman matched it, Elm did so as well, but he didn't raise. He could be patient.

He hadn't looked at his last card yet. It almost didn't matter. Not yet, at least. He had *that* feeling. That *itch* . . .

Playing to the crowd that had gathered around their table, Vance rained a handful of chips on the pot. "A thousand dollars," he announced. "Which of you lackluster lick-spittles has the balls to stick with me?"

Took frowned—it was hard to say if he was reacting to the writer's challenge or the sorry state of his cards—and after a long and intense conversation with himself, he finally matched the bet. As he played his chips, his eyes flicked toward O'Halloran's hand. *He's worried about a flush*, Elm thought. O'Halloran had a jack showing. If they both had five cards of the same suit, O'Halloran's hand would win because he had the higher card.

Leysinger fiddled with his chips, and Elm quickly appraised the young man's pile. He could match Vance's raise, but if anyone else raised, he would be in trouble. Leysinger reached that same conclusion, and he knocked over his stack and pushed it all into the center of the table. "That's all I got," he said. "Let's just get this over with."

Vance smiled. "You sure you don't have a little something hiding in your jacket pocket? Maybe down the front of your trousers?"

Leysinger glared at him. "That's it," he said. "You gonna see it or not?"

"Oh, I definitely want to see it," Vance said, and Leysinger flushed. A titter of laughter ran through the onlookers.

Norman stayed in, but that only left him a couple hundred dollars worth of chips. If he didn't win this hand, he'd be in the same sad shape as Leysinger on the next one.

The bet passed to Elm, and he touched the back of his last down card. Took was watching him carefully, and Elm smiled as he let his fingers slide across the back of the card. He didn't feel any bumps or marks—the deck was new and none of the players had dared try to surreptitiously mark the cards—but he wasn't going to look at the card with Took staring at him like that. He leaned forward and gathered up a handful of chips. "I'm in," he said.

Vance and Took matched, and then it was O'Halloran's turn. The rancher shook his head slightly before matching the bet. He didn't fold, but Elm suspected he hadn't gotten the card he had been hoping for. *If he didn't have the flush, what did he have?* Elm wondered.

Leysinger's hangdog expression changed as he picked up his cards. "Full house," he said. "Five and threes." He cackled at Vance's reaction. "I got your balls right here, old man."

Norman flipped over his cards. He had two pair, eights and nines. Staying in had been an expensive gamble for him. Took made a face and revealed that he had gotten his flush, but it wasn't enough to beat Leysinger's full house. O'Halloran showed his cards, and he hadn't gotten his flush—one of the five cards was a spade.

Vance groaned when he saw the rancher's cards. "Almost a straight flush," he sighed, pointing at the four hearts in O'Halloran's hand. "Wouldn't that have been a sight to see?" He leaned back in his chair and waited for Leysinger to look at him. And when the young man did, Vance made a production out of showing his cards. One at a time. The players watched the blood drain out of Leysinger's face as Vance kept revealing twos.

Four of them, in fact.

"I believe your balls are mine," Vance said, showing Leysinger his teeth.

Leysinger fell back in his chair, a stunned expression on his face.

Vance inclined his head toward Elm. "You haven't turned over your cards," he said. "Are you going to snatch my delicious victory away?"

"I might," Elm said. He turned over his first two cards.

Vance pursed his lips. "A three of a kind. In fours," he said. "And an ace. Hardly the stuff of legends."

"Hardly." Elm tapped the back of his last card. "But it is early yet." He flipped the card over.

He didn't look. He watched Vance's reaction instead, and when the writer's eyes got big, he knew what the card must be. Only then did he look down.

It was another four.

31

THE JUDGE'S SECOND SATCHEL CONTAINED A TIN MUG, WHICH he had stuffed with strips of cloth torn from Isadora's dress and a dozen pistol cartridges. He had bent the top of the mug closed, so that when he casually dropped it in one of the fire pits on the hurricane deck, the heat would bake the cartridges awhile before any flame managed to sneak into the mug. When it did, the brass of the cartridges would heat up, and eventually, the black powder inside the cartridges would explode.

It would sound like gunfire—a perfect distraction for what he needed to accomplish.

After dropping the satchel in the fire, he had strolled on toward the back of the boat, passing the crew quarters on the top deck. Near the back, he passed a sturdy door. If his assessment was correct, somewhere beyond that door was a room with a safe. It wouldn't take him long to find it.

Past the crew quarters was a narrow passage between the rooms and the private salon at the back of the boat where the tournament was being played. He ducked into the passage, disappearing into the deep shadows of the night.

He wouldn't have to wait long. The coals in the fire pit were still hot . . .

The crowd around the table erupted with shouts and cheers at the sight of Elm's four of a kind. *Now*, he thought as the dealer gathered the cards. *Now is the time to make the big play.* He could feel the energy in the room. Like knowing how the wind was blowing and how that breath would shift his bullet. *I need to do it now.*

Elm leaned over the table and gathered the chips into one large pile. He set his hand down on edge and separated the pot into two portions. "That's my opening bet," he said, nodding at the half he left as he scooped the remaining chips back to his end of the table.

The crowd fell silent. There was some jostling at the back as people tried to get a better glimpse of the table and the players. Elm ignored the crowd as he carefully stacked chips. He was in no hurry.

"I—I haven't dealt the cards yet," the dealer said. His eyes danced from player to player.

Elm shrugged. "So deal them. We'll ante and then we'll bet, and that's what I'm going to start with."

"You can't—" Norman started.

"You're done," O'Halloran snapped. "Shut your mouth and give us your chips."

"What?"

Vance chuckled as he started to count out enough chips to match Elm's opening bet. "He's right, you sorry lad. You haven't got enough." He nodded at the dealer. "Don't even bother giving him any cards, sir. He's going to make a meager contribution and sit the rest of the game out."

"I will not!" Norman protested.

Vance finished his count. "Two thousand and eight hundred dollars," he said, sliding his chips to the center of the table. "You don't have it."

"You can't just force me out."

"Of course not. We're buying you out."

"This is—where is Mrs. Peabody?" Norman pounded his fist on the table, making the chips rattle.

Elm felt the crowd move behind him, and he heard the rustle of the hostess's dress. "I'm right here, dear," Mrs. Peabody said.

She rested a hand lightly on Vance's shoulder. The writer smiled as he reached over and put his hand on hers. "Is something the matter?"

"They're—it's—I—" Norman sputtered. He couldn't decide where to start.

"Have you lost your enthusiasm?" she asked innocently. "Is your performance lacking?"

The crowd, reading all sorts of salacious innuendo into her questions, hooted with laughter. Several derisive comments floated up from the back.

Norman's face got red, and his hands balled into fists. He started to rise from his chair, but Mrs. Peabody stopped him with a cluck of her tongue. He froze, his right hand in the process of sweeping back his jacket, and she shook her head. "These good folk don't want to see you do something foolish," she said, and all the levity was gone from her voice. "Retire gracefully, Mr. Norman. There will be another game for you. On another day."

Norman shrugged, as if to brush off the threat beneath her words. He tugged at the bottom of his waistcoat, and with a final withering glance at Vance, he turned and shoved his way through the crowd.

Mrs. Peabody smiled, and all the hard angles of her face disappeared. "Now then," she sighed, "shall we get back to cards?"

"Indeed," Vance said. He plucked her hand off his shoulder and raised it to his lips. "Bless me, lady, for I intend to savagely strip the other gentlemen at this table of their money."

She pulled her hand free before he could kiss her fingers. "I am not your muse, Vance. Nor your good luck charm." She turned slightly, letting her gaze linger on O'Halloran. "It wouldn't be fair to the others if I were to show favorites."

Elm had been watching O'Halloran during the exchange with Norman. The rancher, who was normally very stiff in his chair, had been twitching. Jerking his left shoulder up and down.

"Speaking of fair play," he said as Mrs. Peabody turned away from the table. "Why don't we take off our coats and roll up our sleeves?" He shoved the sleeves of his coat up to show his bare forearms. With a raised eyebrow, he looked at the other players.

"Just deal the cards," O'Halloran snapped at the dealer. "We've had enough nonsense for the evening."

"Oh, well, we can never have too much nonsense," Vance said. He pushed back his chair. Smiling at Mrs. Peabody as he turned, he struggled out of his tight-fitting jacket. He arranged it on the back of his chair and then rolled up the sleeves of his white shirt. "Here are my arms, gentlemen. Nothing hiding here." He showed them to the crowd, who nodded and murmured.

"Sit down," O'Halloran ground out. "This isn't a theater performance."

"No!" Vance whirled and slapped the table with his hand. "It's much more entertaining than that. So play along."

"I will not," O'Halloran said. "Deal," he snarled at the man holding the cards.

Elm shook his head. "You will take off your coat," he said. He raised his hand from his lap. He was holding the small Derringer he had gotten from his barroom swindle before getting on the boat. He had slipped it out of his coat while everyone had been watching Vance. "Show us your arms," he said to O'Halloran. "All the way to the elbow."

No one spoke. No one dared to breathe. All eyes were on O'Halloran, who stared at Elm with such incandescent fire that Elm expected the air between them to ignite.

"You will not pull the trigger on that toy gun," O'Halloran said, slowly and distinctly.

"Not only will I pull the trigger, but this toy gun has enough of a pop that it will put a bullet right through the front of that thick skull of yours and make a spectacular mess of your brains."

The crowd behind O'Halloran started to edge away, trying to get clear of Elm's gun.

Elm smiled grimly. "Don't worry," he said, trying to alleviate their fears. "I won't miss."

O'Halloran stood up, and it was like watching a mountain thrust itself toward the sky. He undid the buttons on his coat and carefully peeled it back from his shoulders. He tossed it over the back of Leysinger's chair, and proceeded to unbutton his cuffs—first the left, and then the right. When he rolled up his sleeve, people in the crowd gasped at the sight of a brass contraption strapped around his right forearm. There were two cards held in place by leather bands. More brass tubing ran up his shirt.

"Mr. O'Halloran!" Mrs. Peabody stamped her foot against the wooden floor. "Whatever are you wearing?"

"I am shocked," Vance said in a loud voice. "That device is—that is very ungentlemanly of you, sir."

"We do not allow such—such—egregious behavior in this salon," Mrs. Peabody stormed. "This is a clear violation of—"

"It's all right," Elm said, lowering the gun. "Let him play." He put the weapon down on the table.

"Mr. Stonebrook, your opinion is kindly offered, but it is not up to you. The Commission has very explicit conditions for play on this boat. The use of such devices is not condoned by any stretch of the imagination," Mrs. Peabody said.

"It doesn't matter," Elm said. "We have plucked the teeth from that serpent, so to speak. It will not harm any of us." He tapped the table with a finger. "Besides, he's only going to play one more hand, anyway. We might as well let him lose with a tiny modicum of his dignity intact."

Vance chortled. "A final showdown!" He rubbed his hands together. "Your shenanigans continue to impress me, Mr. Stonebrook." He sat down in his chair and pulled it closer to Elm. "Can I play too?"

"Certainly," Elm said. He looked at Took. "You in?"

Took let out a forced laugh. "I'll sit this one out, if you don't mind. My desire to participate in shenanigans isn't as inflamed as Mr. Vance's." He indicated his modest pile of chips. "May I keep what I have?"

Elm shrugged as if it made no difference to him. Took nodded appreciatively and moved his chair back from the table. He left his chips alone. Like everyone else, his interest lay in what came next.

Vance plucked at his lip with a finger. "I do have a question, though, Mr. Stonebrook. What if Mr. O'Halloran wins this next hand?"

"He won't," Elm said.

Vance's finger kept plucking. "Your bravado is assured, young man, but it lacks a truly earnest ring of authenticity to it. Not quite the timbre of sweet victory I was hoping to hear."

"Well, he won't be cheating, so if he plays fair, what recourse do I have to complain?"

"Yes, but that device on his arm!"

"He hasn't used it yet," Elm said. "Not that I can tell, anyway."

Vance frowned. "Your logic is faulty, sir. What of those hours when we have sat at this table without you?"

"That's not a fault of my logic," Elm pointed out. "That was your own rather unfortunate lack of insight and awareness."

"Are we going to play cards or not?" O'Halloran wanted to know.

Vance clapped his hands together. "Fine, fine, fine," he chanted. "Let us play cards. One hand. Five cards." He raised an eyebrow. "Shall we play what we are dealt or have one draw?" he asked.

"One draw," Elm said. He held O'Halloran's gaze. "We might as well make this interesting, don't you think?"

"Very well," Vance said when O'Halloran didn't object. "Five cards. One draw. For all the money." He raised his hands overhead as he finished, and the crowd, swept up in his euphoria, cheered.

Elm looked up at Mrs. Peabody. She returned his gaze, a tight smile on her lips and a delirious light in her eyes. She was caught up in the fever too. She wasn't going to stand in their way.

"Let them play," she said to the dealer, and the man shuffled the deck once more. His hands moved quickly, tossing five cards in turn to each of them.

"You have performed a mighty service this evening," Vance said to the dealer when he was finished. The writer gathered his cards together and picked them up. "We appreciate your deft handiwork and—"

"Shut up and play," O'Halloran growled. He glanced at his cards, frowned, and then slid three of them toward the dealer.

Elm glanced at his hand. King and jack of hearts. The rest were worthless, and he, too, asked for three.

Vance played to the crowd, slowly peeking at each card in his hand in turn. If Elm hadn't been getting the hard stare from O'Halloran, he might have enjoyed Vance's theatrics. As it was, he fought to keep his breath calm. The game wasn't over yet.

"I will take four," Vance said finally. He kept one card, and he smiled beatifically at O'Halloran as the dealer dealt the replacement cards.

Elm plucked up the corners of his new cards. A nine and a ten. Had he gotten the straight? His heart beat faster as he slipped a thumb under the last card and looked at it.

No. His last card was a four.

"Show 'em," O'Halloran growled. His face was a storm waiting to break. He hadn't gotten what he needed either, Elm realized, and a sudden elation gripped him. O'Halloran flipped over his cards, scattering them across the felt table. Elm stared, trying to suss out what the rancher had. *A black queen*, he thought. *And a nine and a ten too!*

Elm's pulse started to race. *Did he get the straight?* he wondered. But then he spotted a red seven, and the breath he had been holding came out in a whoosh.

His relief was short-lived, however.

O'Halloran's other card was the king of spades.

"Turn over your cards," O'Halloran demanded.

Elm picked up his five cards and spread them out so everyone could see what he had. Like O'Halloran, he had nothing of value, and while his highest card was a king—matching O'Halloran's king—his next highest card was the jack.

Vance licked his lips and carefully squared up his five cards. As O'Halloran's face darkened with fury at his delay, the writer quickly put the neat stack down on the table. "Okay, okay," he said. His hands shook as he spread them out, and the crowd as a whole leaned forward, eager to count the pips on Vance's cards.

There was an eight, a four, a seven, and a five. *His hand is worse than mine*, Elm thought. He felt like he had swallowed a stone. He had bet everything, thinking that the four of a kind had been a sign. He had put his faith in . . . what? Luck? How had he been so gullible? How had he been so—

"Vance doesn't have anything." O'Halloran's voice cut through his frantic thoughts. "But we have kings." The rancher dragged one of his cards closer. "But I have a queen too. And she beats your jack."

The stone was heavy in Elm's gut, holding him in place. Pulling him down. O'Halloran was right. His second highest card was the jack of hearts. It wasn't enough to beat the rancher's queen.

He had lost.

"I win," O'Halloran said. He slammed his fist against the table, and the chips shivered and danced. "I win," he shouted, his voice like a thunderclap. "This is all mine." He leaned forward, his face stretched into a terrible grin.

"Actually—" Vance caught his attention with a single finger. Tap-tap-tapping on his cards.

There were only four showing.

O'Halloran paused, staring at Vance's finger. Everyone, in fact, was staring at the cards in front of Vance.

Except Vance, who winked at Elm.

The writer put his finger on the last card and slid it to the side, revealing the fifth card.

It was an ace.

"It's a good thing I kept it," Vance said. His face broke into a wild grin. "Because it means that I win. All of this money is mine."

32

THE FIRST CARTRIDGE WENT OFF WITH A DISTINCT POP, AND the Judge smiled in the shadows. He pushed away from the wall where he had been waiting. The second and successive cartridges exploded quickly, and soon thereafter, the Judge heard shouts and the sound of booted feet against the wooden deck.

He peeked out from the passageway, and watched as a trio of black-coated men ran toward the prow of the boat. They had come out of the nearby door, and the Judge darted quickly to catch the door before it closed. He slipped inside, and found himself in a broad room with racks of supplies and equipment along the walls. There was a table and four chairs in the room, and on the table was a hastily abandoned card game, a bottle of whisky, and three glasses. There was a second door, and it led to a narrow hall that ran the length of the crew quarters. At the end, it ended in an open area with a metal staircase that undoubtedly led up the pilot house. There were five doors all together, and he ignored the first four, walking swiftly to the last door before the staircase.

The door had a simple latch and it turned easily under his hand. He went into the room, closing the door behind him. He stood and listened for a moment, wondering if anyone had seen or heard him, but all he heard was the muted sound of voices. They were out on the deck, worrying about the gunfire. He tensed suddenly as he heard more boots, but they weren't in the hall. They were out on the deck. Had his incendiary device started a fire? For a second, his breath caught in his chest as he listened. One fire was enough. He didn't need two.

No, he decided, it wasn't a fire. Something else was going on. *It doesn't matter,* he thought. They weren't looking for him. Besides, all that confusion would cover any noise he might be making. Satisfied that he could operate with impunity, he turned to survey the room.

A small pane of milky glass set in the ceiling allowed some moonlight into the room, and the Judge peered about in the gloom. It was—as he had hoped—a private room. On his right was a rough mattress in a box frame atop a pair of cabinets. On his left was a wooden desk, and crouching between the head of the bed and the desk was a large iron safe.

The Judge smiled. He had guessed right. This was the place. He was about to examine the chest when a tiny flame guttered to light. The Judge stopped, surprised to see a match being lit, and he stared as a hand lowered the match to a fat candle sitting on the desk. The wick caught, and the room filled with a yellow glow. The Judge frowned as the candlelight illuminated the narrow figure of Mr. Chester, sitting in the chair behind the desk.

"Ah, Judge Wallace, why am I not surprised to see you here?"

Mr. Chester grinned as he pointed a large pistol at the Judge's belly.

The crowd surrounding the poker table roared their approval at Vance's win, and the writer basked in their adoration. He waved at them with one hand and pounded the table with the other. "I win. I win," he chanted, urging them to take up his cry, and they were eager to please.

O'Halloran's face grew darker and darker. Muscles pulsed in his jaw as he ground his teeth. His fury was growing, and even his massive frame was not going to be strong enough to contain it. He opened his mouth, but whatever he intended to say was lost in a furious roar that raged out of his belly. He grabbed the edge of the table, and as he shot to his feet, he yanked the table with him.

Elm grabbed for his Derringer as he kicked his chair back. The table heaved upward, scattering the chips in a storm of red, white, and blue. Vance was knocked aside, and the crowd surged back. The noise of the crowd changed from celebration to terror as the table flipped over. The dealer, who had been paralyzed with fear when O'Halloran had erupted, could only stare in horror as the heavy piece of furniture fell on him.

Elm's chair hit someone behind him, and his fall was slowed. He was jarred and bumped as the spectators tried to get away, but he kept his hand as steady as he could. His eyes never left O'Halloran.

In the distance, there was a sound like gunfire, a series of staccato reports that heightened the panic in the room. O'Halloran paused, his head cocked to the side. Elm's chair hit the floor, and he grunted softly from the impact, but he didn't lose track of his target.

He was on his back, his butt and legs raised by the seat of the chair. He was in a terrible position, but his gun remained steady. Aimed right at the middle of O'Halloran's chest.

The panic crested, and as it receded, it took the crowd with it. People ran indiscriminately, ignoring Mrs. Peabody's efforts to calm the room. Vance was on his knees, clutching his elbow which had been struck by the table. O'Halloran was a granite statute in the midst of the chaos, and his gaze slowly fell on Elm. His lips peeled back in a horrible parody of a smile when he saw Elm's gun. Elm wasn't fooled. There was nothing but an unholy fury in the rancher's eyes.

O'Halloran shook his head slightly, his grin becoming more feral. More dangerous. He took a step back, as if daring Elm to shoot him, and when Elm didn't, he took another.

A woman in a blue dress ran in front of him, and Elm grimaced for the brief second that his aim was spoiled. O'Halloran took more steps, putting more distance between them, and when Elm threw his legs off the chair, he turned and shoved his way into the crowd.

Cursing, Elm struggled to his feet and tried to chase after O'Halloran. He caught sight of the rancher as he bulled his way toward the iron staircase that led down to the lower salon. Tucking the gun into his coat pocket, Elm used both hands to clear a path toward the staircase. O'Halloran paused at the top of the staircase. He met Elm's gaze briefly, unmoved by the press of bodies around him, and then, like water draining out of a basin, he disappeared from view. Others followed him, and by the time Elm reached the staircase, the room was nearly empty.

Vance was still on his knees, vainly trying to collect his scattered chips with one hand. His other arm hung useless at his side. Mrs. Peabody leaned heavily against the wooden bar. There was blood on her forehead, and her skirt was torn. The crowd had gone right over her in their panic.

Elm's breath caught in his throat. Where was Isadora?

There were few things in the world that bored Isadora more than watching men play cards. At Thrush, the men would sit in the bunkhouse common room and play after the day's work was done, but she never joined them. Occasionally, Mrs. Walphin would talk her into a few hands of Put while enjoying a glass of sherry in the kitchen, but she played more to please the older woman than to entertain herself. Her preference was to take her sherry in the sitting room with a book, but as there was no sitting room and not much in the way of books on the riverboat, she made do with watching people lose money at the roulette wheel and playing billiards.

It was noisy in the lower salon—what with the balls clacking, the roulette wheel whirring, and the faro players talking loudly to one another. No one realized anything was amiss on the boat until bodies started tumbling down the iron staircase. And then, it only got louder as people started shouting. Someone had won. There was a gun. There were lots of guns. Someone had died. There were too many voices, too many different stories. The only thing they had in common was panic—that wide-eyed shudder, that frenetic darting back and forth. She saw it in the herd when a storm loosed lightning over the valley. There was no sense behind those eyes. There was only fear.

And it spread quickly.

Isadora looked for Elm as she tried to push her way toward the staircase. Where was Elm? Had he been shot? She tried to pick out more details from the stories whirling around her. A table had fallen on someone. Lots of gunfire. And a fire.

She stopped, trying to find the source of the story about the fire, and as she listened, she realized the source of all this chaos.

The Judge.

He had started a fire on the boiler deck. Her heart leaped into her throat. Was he insane? They were on a boat! Who started a fire on a wooden boat?

The press of bodies flowed around her, buffeting her back and forth. She stumbled, her thoughts as chaotic as the room, and suddenly there was no one between her and the base of the staircase. She caught her breath and looked up as a man in a grey suit came storming down the stairs.

O'Halloran.

He recognized her and lunged at her as she tried to turn and flee. His hand caught her hair and she cried out as he nearly yanked her off her feet. He hauled her close. "Where are you going, bitch?" he snarled. His breath was hot on her neck, and his grip was so tight it felt like he was pulling her hair out by the roots.

"Let go of me," she hissed. She tried to claw his face, but he slapped the side of her head roughly, and she cried out from the jarring stroke of pain that rocked her skull.

Her vision blurred and her knees wobbled. She tried to collect herself, gasping and squirming in O'Halloran's grip. She spotted a group of men approaching—no, just a trio; her vision finally settled down and half the men disappeared. She reached out to them, trying to get their attention, but her efforts were ignored.

"There's been a fire," the roughest of the three said to O'Halloran.

"What?" O'Halloran's hand tightened, and she stood on her toes to alleviate the tension in her hair.

"In your stateroom," the man said, clearly uncomfortable with his role as messenger.

"Where is my son?" O'Halloran snarled.

"Out there," the man said, nodding toward the salon doors.

O'Halloran shoved Isadora toward the three men. "Let's find out what is going on," he said.

She stumbled into the arms of a man whose scraggly beard was like a season's worth of moss on a young sapling. She yanked her arm out of his grip, and slapped him when he tried to grab her again. His eyes got wide, and she felt a brief flutter of elation in her breast. It didn't last. Something heavy struck her in the head again, and this time her knees gave way. She collapsed to the floor, gripping it tightly to keep it from spinning beneath her.

"Bring her," O'Halloran said as he stormed toward the salon doors. "Drag her if you have to."

The moss-faced man grabbed her arm again, and she didn't pull away this time. Leaning against him, she got to her feet. Her head spun, but when she focused on the back of O'Halloran's head, her vertigo passed.

Never again, she thought as the man nudged her toward the door. She acquiesced, and she could almost see his relief in his eyes. He wasn't the woman-dragging type.

That flutter of hope came back. *He'll hesitate*, she thought, *and when he does . . .*

She wouldn't make the same mistake.

"I must have gotten turned around somewhere," the Judge said. He offered Mr. Chester a congenial smile, hiding the frustration rising in his chest.

"Near Hannibal, perhaps?" Mr. Chester offered.

"Perhaps," the Judge said. "Have we passed that delightful town yet?"

"Earlier today. Shortly before lunch."

"Ah, yes, I was preoccupied before lunch."

"You are not the first man who has thought to steal from the Quincy Commerce Commission," Mr. Chester said. "I was not duped by your pathetic attempts to sow discord among our guests. Really, Wallace, such dull-witted nonsense—the sort of cheap chicanery I would expect from bedraggled orphans in the street." Mr. Chester screwed up his face and mimicked the voice of a young child. "'Oh, good sir, would you look the other way while I attempt to filch one of the biscuits from the tray?'"

"Well, it worked for Oliver, didn't it?"

"Who?"

"A character in a Dickens novel. A young—oh, never mind. I see that such an allusion is wasted on you, Mr. Chester." The Judge sighed. "Ah, it is like tilting at windmills."

"What are you talking about?"

The Judge waved his hand at Mr. Chester's gun. "Are you going to shoot me or not?"

"I . . . I haven't made up my mind yet!"

"Such theatrical suspense." The Judge shook his head as he wandered toward the bed. "I suppose I deserve it, in light of my dreadful *chicanery*." Mr. Chester hissed a warning, and the Judge raised a quizzical eyebrow as he sat down on the hard mattress. "Have you ever shot someone before, Mr. Chester?"

"Now look here, Wallace. I've got you dead to rights. I could shoot you, right where you stand—uh, sit, I mean—and no one would fault me. You are trespassing. You have no business here. Why, you aren't even in the tournament anymore."

The Judge raised a finger. "That may be specifically true to my physical presence at the table, but spiritually, I am very much in the tournament."

"Spiritually? What sort of idiotic claptrap is that?"

"My man, Elm. He's playing, and I suspect he's winning, too." The Judge nodded at Mr. Chester's expression. "You can go look, if you like. I'd be happy to wait right here while you—"

"I'm not leaving you here!"

"No, of course not. Pardon my oversight. You've got me—what was it?—dead to rights. Yes. You wouldn't want to give up that advantage." The Judge pursed his lips. "Pity, though . . ."

Mr. Chester grimaced, knowing the Judge was trying to draw him into further conversation. "Oh, for the love of God, what is it?" he ground out.

"Well, I am concerned about Mr. O'Halloran. He's cheating, you see. He's wearing one of those fancy harnesses. Very fine craftsmanship, if I do say so myself. I've seen a number like it over the years. It's a complicated contraption made from brass and twine; it runs up your arm and across your shoulders. Some even go down your legs and wrap around your thigh. They feed cards into your hands. Really very clever, when you get right down to it."

"I am familiar with this sort of rig," Mr. Chester sneered.

"You are? Well, excellent. I don't need to explain it to you then. You know what to look for, and frankly, I'm surprised your people haven't been watching more closely. Though, perhaps I've misread how the Commission operates. Maybe they don't mind if certain personages cheat a little, now and again. These men do, after all, contribute quite extensively to the Commission, do they not?"

Mr. Chester kept his mouth shut, and it was hard to tell in the flickering candlelight, but the Judge was fairly certain he had gone at the Judge's words. The Judge picked at something invisible on the knee of his trousers. "Now I'm disappointed, Mr. Chester. Your sudden loss of words suggests that you are also familiar with corruption and mismanagement of funds. Ah, such a pity." He shook his head.

"I've heard enough, Wallace," Mr. Chester said. He pulled back the hammer on his pistol.

"Now, wait a second there, Mr. Chester," the Judge said. He jumped to his feet, his hands fluffing his coat.

"I've been wanting to do this since—"

There was a loud clap of thunder in the small room, and Mr. Chester's mouth suddenly went to the shape of an 'O.' He blinked several times, his mouth struggling to shape a complete word, and his gaze slowly went down to his belly where a dark shadow was spreading across his waistcoat.

"Damnation," the Judge sighed. His gun was in his hand, and a tiny wisp of smoke drifted from the barrel. "Why did you have to force my hand like that?"

Spittle frothed on Mr. Chester's lips as he tried to speak. His face contorted as he struggled to lift his gun, which had grown extremely heavy.

The Judge stepped over to the desk and carefully pushed the barrel of his gun against Mr. Chester's hand, forcing it down on the table. "Shh," he whispered. "Close your eyes, Mr. Chester." He licked two fingers and reached out for the flickering fire. "Out, out brief candle," he said. "Fret and strut no more, poor player. It is time for you to leave the stage."

The candle hissed as he snuffed out the flame, and darkness swallowed the room.

33

RICHARD O'HALLORAN'S FACE AND JACKET WERE STREAKED with ash, and his eyes were bright with a feral gleam. He showed his teeth when he pointed at Isadora and the three men trailing behind his father. "It's her doing," he snapped.

She had heard stories about Bart O'Halloran's anger, and no small part of the Judge's plan involved pulling the rancher until he lost his temper. *A man consumed with rage is a man easily mocked and even more easily manipulated*, he had said. She couldn't help but wonder at the violence attendant with such a rage as she watched Richard tell his father about the fire that had been set in their stateroom. She couldn't believe the Judge would do something so idiotic as start a fire on a boat, but the crew of the *Salacious Sally*—clearly well-versed in responding to incidents involving flame—had managed to contain the fire before it had escaped the stateroom.

"Our luggage?" O'Halloran fumed. "What of the money?"

Richard took a step back as he shook his head. He didn't want to be standing next to his father when he answered, and even then, he didn't dare speak the words.

O'Halloran clenched his fists, and Isadora feared he was going to strike his son, but he managed to keep his temper in check.

"It doesn't matter," Richard assured him. "You're still in the game. We'll just win—"

Now O'Halloran lashed out, his hand clouting Richard, and Isadora winced, her head ringing in sympathy. O'Halloran grabbed his stunned son by the throat and hustled him against the deck railing. Richard struggled in his father's grip as O'Halloran bent him back.

The three men with Isadora shuffled nervously, unsure how to react to this family disagreement.

"I lost," O'Halloran growled. "There is no more game."

Richard gasped and spluttered, and when his father didn't let go, he stopped flailing. Isadora thought he had given up, but she was stunned when he brought his body back from the railing. His face was slick with sweat and his mouth was stretched in a toothy grimace. He pushed back against his father's grip until his face was close to O'Halloran's.

"Fuck the tournament," he gasped. "Let me take what we need."

Father and son remained immobile for an instant, and as Isadora watched, Richard seemed to loom over his father. And then, with a grunt of disgust, O'Halloran released his grip on Richard. He turned and stalked away from the railing, and Isadora tensed, fearing his hand was going to seek her throat next. He stared at her, his chest heaving. "Yes," he rumbled. "We shall take what we need."

Behind him, Richard let out a tiny howl of delight. Isadora shivered. The cry was unlike anything she had ever heard come from a human throat.

"What . . . what do you want us to do with her?" the moss-faced boy asked.

A cruel smile twisted O'Halloran's lips. "They'll come for her," he said. "The Judge and his lapdog. After you kill them, do what you want with her."

She launched herself at him then, her hands clawing at his face. Hitting him was like running into a wall, and he tilted his head back to avoid her hands. His smile didn't change as the three rough riders pulled her off him.

"I will outlive you," she shrieked. "I will kill you myself."

He laughed at her spirit. "Hurt her," he said to the leader of the threesome. "Make her beg for mercy before you kill her."

Elm had seen O'Halloran and several other men leaving the salon, and he was nearly certain they had Isadora between them, but he had gotten caught in the crowd when he tried to follow them. By the time he reached the deck, there was no sign of them. Cursing at the delay, he headed for the port side of the boat where O'Halloran's stateroom was located.

When he came around the corner, his heart danced in his chest. There she was, nearly halfway along the length of the boat. She was standing near a soot-darkened patch of the wall with three other men. Beyond them, he spotted O'Halloran and his son, and before he could figure what father and son were doing, one of the trio spotted him.

The man said something to his companions, gesturing in Elm's direction. One of the other men fumbled for his gun, and Elm brought up the Derringer. He frowned as he gauged the distance between the three men and himself. Too far, he thought, and then it was too late as the other man got his gun out of his holster.

Elm fired the Derringer anyway, more to spook the man than to actually score a hit, and he threw himself against the wall. His hand found the handle of the nearest stateroom door, and as he tried it, he heard the heavy buzz of a bullet zipping past his head.

The door was locked. As was the next one.

The other men had their guns out now, and Elm's tiny gun only had one bullet left. He scrambled back toward the salon, trying to get to the hallway that cut across to the starboard side of the boat.

He didn't have a chance against the trio, but if he could get to his stateroom before they did, he could even the odds . . .

"Look at him rabbit," the man in the middle of the trio said. He aimed and fired his gun again, and all he managed to accomplish was to put a bullet into the wood of the boat. "Little coward."

"He's not running away," the first guy snapped. "He's heading for the other side of the boat."

"What's on the other side of the boat?"

"His room, you idiot. He's gonna get his guns." The leader waved his weapon down the length of the boat. "You go after him, Chaz. Me and Earl will circle around."

Earl—the guy with the mossy beard—spoke up. "What about her, Rosco?" he said. He was still holding Isadora's arm.

"Bring her," Rosco said. "We'll have some fun after we kill the cowboy." He fumbled with his gun as he walked, checking how many cartridges he had left in the cylinder. Earl dragged Isadora along as he hurried to keep up, and she dragged her feet as much as she thought she could get away with. Her eyes flickered down to Earl's belt. He hadn't drawn his gun yet.

Chaz, meanwhile, headed in the other direction, intent on flushing Elm toward the front of the boat.

When the Judge heard voices again, he knew his time was up. Holding his gun ready, he backed into the corner of the room near the door. The first person who came into the room would get a gun barrel stuck in their ear.

There wasn't going to be enough time to come up with a clever explanation for his presence in the room. Any explanation was going to be complicated when the others noticed Mr. Chester's corpse, anyway. He only had a brief moment to upbraid himself for being caught in a room without a second exit when the door clicked open.

The Judge blinked in the light that spilled in from the hallway, and when it was eclipsed by a figure, he leaned forward with his arm outstretched. He missed the man's ear, but pushed the barrel of his gun into the man's cheek instead. The hot touch of steel—the barrel was still warm from the two shots he had fired—brought the man up short.

"Can you open the safe?" the Judge asked.

"Wha—what?" the man's voice quavered.

"The safe in this room. Can you open it?"

"N-n-no."

Keeping up the pressure of his gun, the Judge shoved the man back out of the room. He looked left and right as he pressed the man against the wall opposite the captain's room. There was no one else in the hall, and the staircase was empty. "Who are you?" the Judge demanded, returning his attention to the man.

"Nat-Nathaniel," the man whined. He was young—early twenties at the most—and he wore a heavy coat over rough wool trousers. His hair was shaggy and his sideburns extended past his jaw. "I . . . I work on the boat. Navigator's assistant."

"How many up in the pilot house?"

"F-four of us. Me, the captain, the mate, and the navigator."

The Judge listened, trying to track the voices. *Up in the pilot's house*, he thought. The captain had sent the boy to check on Mr. Chester. Distantly, he heard more gunfire. Nathaniel whimpered, and screwed his eyes shut, as if the pop-pop of other guns was going to be the last sound he heard.

"I'm not going to shoot you, son," the Judge said. "I just need someone to open that safe for me."

"I don't know how," Nathaniel reiterated.

"Who does?"

"Mr. Chester. The captain. Someone in the salon, I think. A woman."

"Mrs. Peabody."

"Yes. Yes, Mrs. Peabody."

"Can you get the captain to come down here?"

Nathaniel shook his head. "Cap'n can't leave the wheel when the boat is moving, sir. It's against regulations."

"What if I put my gun into his cheek like I am doing now with you?"

"Please don't," Nathaniel whimpered.

The Judge sighed. He glanced down the hall toward the storeroom. *Where are the guards?* he thought. *They should have come back already,* he realized. *This is turning into a mess,* was his next thought.

"Come along," he snapped. He shoved Nathaniel toward the staircase, and followed closely behind, his gun now pressed into the young man's back. "Let's go talk to the captain."

Nathaniel stumbled along the hall, and when he reached the base of the staircase that went up to the pilot's house, he paused. "Come on—" the Judge started, digging the barrel of his gun into the boy's back.

The door at the end of the hall opened. The Judge glanced over his shoulder, expecting to see one of the guards, but it was someone else.

"You," O'Halloran snarled.

But it wasn't the sight of the rancher that made the Judge's eyes widen. There was something behind him. Something that seemed to be more shadow than flesh and bone . . .

A trio of passengers pressed themselves against the inner wall of the boat as Chaz came around to the starboard side of the boat. They were alarmed at the sight of the rough rider with a gun, and Chaz was momentarily distracted by their frightened faces. Distracted enough that he forgot about the section of the deck to his right. The staterooms were on his left—that was where the cowboy was headed—and Chaz had been focused on catching up with his quarry.

Chaz was not the brightest of the bunch, and so he didn't see Elm waiting for him, with one of the wooden deck chairs in his hands.

One of the passengers cried out in alarm, and Chaz had a split second to wonder what the woman was wailing about before the heavy chair crashed into him. He stumbled, falling to one knee. His vision was all blurry, and there was something wrong with his tongue, but then Elm hit him again and Chaz went down.

His gun slipped out of his senseless fingers, and Elm scooped it up. He checked it quickly as he walked, nodding distantly to the three passengers as he walked by. *Remington,* he thought, recognizing the shorted loading lever and the elongated gap between the cylinder and the frame.

A commotion ahead pulled his attention away from the gun. Passengers were scrambling toward him from the front of the boat, and Elm realized they were fleeing the other gunmen. He raised Chaz's gun, looking down the pinched sight. He wrinkled his nose as he realized the front sight was bent out of true. Why would anyone carry a gun with a bent sight? he wondered.

And then the two men and Isadora came around the corner, and there was no more time to malign Chaz for his poor attention to his weapon. Elm brought his hand up and fired the gun without thinking. Trusting his aim.

Rosco cleared the way by waving his gun around, trusting the sight of the firearm would inspire the passengers to get out of the way. They did, but the trouble was they fled in the direction he wanted to go—around to the starboard side of the boat. "No," Rosco shouted at them. "Get out of the—" He gave up with a grunt of disgust and hurried past the broad stairs that led up to hurricane deck.

Earl struggled to keep up, his grip tight on Isadora's arm.

She wasn't paying him any attention. She was looking past both men, trying to spot Elm before they did. She had to warn him before—

Rosco skipped a step and spun around. She heard the sound of a gun, but didn't connect the sound with Rosco's sudden movement until she spotted the ugly hole in his face. Rosco's eyes rolled up toward the bloody hole in his forehead as he tangled in his legs and fell down.

Earl came to a sudden halt. He stared at Rosco's bloody face, not quite comprehending what had happened.

Isadora yanked her arm free, and she backed up against the inner wall of the steamboat, looking ahead to where Elm stood—legs apart, arm raised. She nodded, letting him know she was out of the way.

Earl realized she was gone, and he looked around, a wild look on his face. She saw him realize what was happening, a sudden dread blooming in his eyes. "No—" he started, but his plea was cut short by the bark of Elm's revolver.

Earl jerked forward. He staggered drunkenly, his head dropping toward his chest. He tried to get to his gun, but his hand kept slipping. He turned halfway, raising his head as he realized he shouldn't be staring at the ground when he met his end, and he tried one last time to pull his gun.

Elm's revolver boomed again and Earl's head shot back, his hair lifting with the sudden motion. He fell on his back, his mouth open, his eyes staring blindly at the roof overhead.

"Are you all right?" Elm asked as he reached Isadora. She nodded, unable to look away from Earl's empty gaze, and it wasn't until Elm crossed in front of her—blocking her sight of the dead man—that she was able to breathe again.

"Y-yes," she managed.

Elm knelt and picked up Rosco's gun. He barely glanced at either man. "Where are O'Halloran and Richard?" he asked.

"They—they must have gone up to the hurricane deck," she said. She swallowed heavily and ran her hands through her hair, trying to get them to stop trembling. "They said—they're going to take it all."

Elm nodded, his mouth set to a grim line. "They're going to find the safe."

"What about the Judge?" she asked.

"I'm sure he's got the same idea," Elm said. He touched her arm, and her heart beat faster at the contact. "Come with me," he said. "We're going to need more guns."

34

THE CAPTAIN OF THE *SALACIOUS SALLY* LOOKED THE PART: a heavy coat buttoned all the way up to his chin, a tri-corner hat pulled down low on his head, and a face full of bristling whiskers. "Who the devil do you think you are?" he demanded when he spotted the Judge behind the embarrassed navigator's assistant.

The Judge shoved Nathaniel out of the way and stepped out of the stairwell. A heavy hatch leaned against the wall behind him, with hasps connecting it to the floor. He slammed the hatch down, and spotting the heavy bolt at the front, he kicked it into the metal slot. "I'm not the Devil," he said. "But he's coming."

"Nathaniel, what is this?" the captain sputtered. "This man has no authority here. He should not be in my pilot house."

"Captain—" Nathaniel began weakly, but the Judge cut the young man's explanation short with a wave of his gun.

As the captain and the two other members of the crew who were in the pilot house eyed him nervously, the Judge took a moment to examine the tiny pilot house. *The view must be marvelous during the day,* he thought. Windows afforded an uninterrupted view of the river. Stools were bolted to the floor near a heavy table, and there was an annotated map of the river held in place with metal clasps. Lanterns hung from heavy hooks on the wall next to the table, providing a halo of light around the map.

"This is my ship," the captain said, his beard bristling with outrage. "Get out of this room before—"

"Before what?" the Judge interrupted. "Are you going to yell for those guards who were playing cards back there?" He waved his gun toward the stern of the boat. "How are they going to get up here since I've locked the hatch?"

One of the other men spoke up. "You put something in the fire pit, didn't you?" He had a narrow face and sad eyes.

The Judge nodded. "I did."

"I saw it. I saw it when it made all that noise."

The captain's beard bristled even further. "Saboteur!" he spat.

But before he could accuse the Judge of anything else, something banged against the hatch in the floor. The wood jumped in its frame, and the metal bolt rattled.

"What in Heaven . . . ?" the other man said. His hands went to the front of his shirt, clutching something under his clothing.

"Not in Heaven," the Judge said under his breath. While the other men were staring at the hatch, he went to the front of the pilot house where he could get a better look at the forward deck.

Black gouts of smoke drifted from the fire pit where he had dropped the satchel. He spotted a few passengers, running through the smoke, and his brows creased across his forehead. They were running to and fro, he noticed. Like they didn't know where to go. As if there was danger no matter which direction they turned. As he watched, a man grabbed the starboard railing and leaped overboard. The Judge felt an icy touch at the base of his spine.

"What's going on?" the captain demanded.

"What did you see after the gunfire?" the Judge asked, still peering through the drifting smoke. "The guards from the back. Did you see them? Did you see anyone else? Before—" He waved his hand to indicate the fleeing passengers.

"I saw them," the sad-eyed man said. The Judge figured he had to be the navigator. "One of them went down to the boiler deck. The other two—" He started to gesture toward the back of the boat, but his hand flinched when the hatch rattled again.

This time they heard something else. The scratching sound of an animal clawing at the wood. And then whatever it was growled, a guttural sound curling up from a throat that was not human.

"Well, shit," the Judge sighed. "I guess there was more than one of them."

Elm threw clothing and undergarments out of the trunk, searching for his revolver. He found it, along with a leather-wrapped object. He strapped his gunbelt on before he unwrapped the small package. Inside was the old bestiary and a silver cross hung on a rawhide loop. "Here," he said, offering the cross to Isadora.

"I'm—what is this?" He had already given her Rosco's gun, and she didn't want to put it down.

"Take it," he said. "If things go badly, it may be the only thing that can save us."

"God won't save us," she said.

He grabbed her hand and wrapped her fingers around the center of the cross. It was nothing more than two silver pegs fixed together with wire. "It's silver," he said. "Trust it before anything else."

He knew why the Judge had brought it along, and he hoped that the Judge was wrong, but it was better to plan for the worst. *Because it is always worse,* he thought grimly as he slammed the trunk shut.

"Ready?" he asked.

Isadora slipped the rawhide loop around her head and let the cross dangle down the front of her dress. She grabbed the front of his coat, and pulled him to her. She kissed him, her tongue pushing into his mouth, and once he recovered from her aggressive amour, he returned her kiss with equal passion. When he let go, gasping for breath, she smiled savagely at him.

"Now, I'm ready," she said.

One of the hasps at the back of the hatch tore out of the decking and the edge of the hatch canted up.

The men fell back. The chief mate clutched the cross around his neck, and his lips started moving in soundless prayer.

"What is that?" the captain demanded. The outrage in his voice had been replaced with something closer to fear.

"Let's hope that hatch holds and you never have to find out," the Judge said. He gestured at the river. "We need to put this boat ashore."

"What?" The captain stiffened with indignation.

"Beach it. Run into the shallows. Drop an anchor. I don't know what you need to do, but do it. Get this boat out off the water."

"I will do no such thing!"

The hatch bounced again, and this time, a finger's width of space showed. Something moved, blocking the light from below, and a rank smell crept into the room.

"Land this boat," the Judge said. "You need to do it now."

"Mr. Foster," the captain ordered. "Remove this man immediately."

"Aye, Captain," the chief mate replied. He came around the pilot wheel, his large hands held in front of him.

The Judge raised his weapon and pointed it at Foster. There wasn't much distance between the barrel and the center of the chief mate's forehead. "Put the boat ashore," he said.

"Mr. Foster!"

The Judge cocked the hammer back as Foster started to take another step. "I will shoot," he said, his voice patient and resolute. "I will shoot Mr. Foster first, and then I will shoot his quick-eyed friend over there who knows better than do something as stupid as this, and then I will shoot young Nathaniel next—God knows he does not deserve a fate as dim as this." His eyes flicked toward the captain. "And then, I will shoot you merely for being such an colossal failure of a leader to these men. After which, I will lean on that wheel myself and beach this boat with all the fury I can muster."

Claws ripped at the bottom of the hatch, and the noise was too much for Nathaniel. The young man shrieked and darted for the far corner of the pilot house. "Oh God, oh God, oh God," he moaned.

"Get this boat ashore!" the Judge shouted.

"Mr. Foster!" The captain tried to shout over the Judge.

Mr. Foster hesitated. His breathing was shallow and quick, and his eyes were focused on the barrel of the Judge's weapon.

"Sound the fucking alarm," the Judge ground out. He was speaking to the navigator now, no longer trying to get through to the captain. "Get everyone off this boat. I don't care how you do it, but do it now."

"This boat is my responsibility," the captain shouted. "I will not risk putting a hole in the hull."

Nathaniel continued to wail from the corner. "Oh godohgodohgod—"

"Captain . . ." the navigator tried.

"The boilers will overheat," the captain continued, running through the multiple reasons why the Judge's demand was utter nonsense. "The entire boat will be destroyed. I am not going to—"

"Listen!"

The urgency of the navigator's voice surprised everyone, and for a second, they all stopped talking. And in that second, they realized just how silent it was in the pilot house.

The navigator pointed at the bent hatch. "Look," he whispered. The men stared, holding a collective breath, and finally, Nathaniel broke the spell. "Oooohhhh," he moaned.

"What am I looking at?" the captain demanded.

"It's gone—" the navigator started, but the rest of his statement was cut off by a wild shriek from the deck outside the pilot house. The cry raised the hair on the Judge's neck, and he whirled toward the windows. The scream cut off mid-shriek, and the Judge gasped at the abrupt cessation of the sound.

Mr. Foster wandered toward the forward window, no longer concerned about the Judge's revolver. "There's something down there," he said thickly. His words summoned all of them to the window and they stared down at the smoke-obscured deck.

They saw its front paw first, with claws longer than a man's finger. It swiped at the edge of the roof with a blood-streaked claw that shredded the wooden shingle. A second paw grabbed the roof, and then something darker than the night hauled itself onto the roof of the crew quarters. It crept toward them, covered in darkness. They could see its eyes, though, bright and burning.

"God save us," Mr. Foster croaked. "What is that thing?"

"Dickie Boy," the Judge said, his voice cracking with alarm.

In a flash, the man who walked like a wolf leaped across the distance between the edge of the roof and the pilot house itself. He launched himself at the glass window, and Mr. Foster, who had been transfixed by the unholy sight of the monster, started to scream as the glass shattered. The beast came through the window, and Mr. Foster's cry of terror became something worse.

The Judge was on his knees already, reaching for the bolt on the hatch. He didn't need to see what happened next. Mr. Foster's screams were bad enough.

Elm and Isadora came to a sudden stop at the top of the stairs. The hurricane deck was hazy with smoke from one of the fire pits, and while they couldn't see very far, they could see the black shape clawing onto the roof of the crew quarters.

"The wolf that walks like a man," Isadora hissed. She grabbed Elm's arm. "I thought you killed it."

"We did," Elm said. "This is—"

"There are two of them?"

Elm's reply was cut short by grisly sounds from the pilot house. Men screaming. A beast, snarling and growling. A gun, firing—but only once.

Suddenly, the boat shifted. The prow turned to the left, and Elm and Isadora stumbled away from the stairway before they fell down the steps.

Someone was still screaming, and Isadora covered her ears and screwed up her face to block out the sound, but there was no escaping it. It was a cry of a man attempting to hurl himself to Heaven with the strength of his scream—and when it stopped with a horrible gurgle, Isadora gasped, her eyes filling with tears.

Elm staggered across the deck of the boat as it continued to turn against the current. He grabbed one of the deck tables, and tried to extricate one of the umbrellas from the hole in the center of the table. "What are you doing?" Isadora shouted at him.

"A lance," he shouted back. "Something to keep that beast at bay."

The smoke shifted, and she got a better view of the shattered window of the pilot house. Her breath caught in her throat as she spotted dark spatters on the wall inside. A man slumped against the pilot wheel, his face frozen in a terrible grimace. She looked away, her stomach tightening in horror.

At the table, Elm wrestled the pole out of the brace holding it in place, which was only half the battle. The umbrella kept trying to open and he fought to collapse it.

"What ever are you doing?" someone asked. The question was curious enough, but beneath the words there was a slurry of violence and pain.

Isadora glanced over her shoulder. Standing next to the crew quarters was a naked figure. His pale body was streaked with gore and soot. His hair was wild atop his head, and his eyes were lit with a baleful glee.

It was Richard O'Halloran.

The Judge ran down the stairs from the pilot house as fast as he could without tripping over his own feet, and he felt someone tumbling close behind him. The hatch banged shut overhead, mercifully muting the screams and terrible snapping noises coming from the pilot house. The Judge wheeled around the staircase, noting in passing that the person who had managed to escape with him was Nathaniel, the young man who had been blubbering in the corner.

The Judge hurried down the hall, and when the boat suddenly turned, he steadied himself against the wall. He noticed the door to the captain's room was ajar, and he paused. The safe was in there. Surely he could— He shook his head. There was no time.

As he stepped past the door, it was pulled open. He turned, shocked at the sudden movement, and a pair of large hands reached out and grabbed him. He tried to resist, but the hards were strong and he was yanked into the tiny room.

He fetched up against the desk, and before he could recover his balance and dignity, Nathaniel was hauled into the room too and thrown into his arms. He shoved the young man aside, trying to bring his gun to bear, but before he could find a target, something seized his arm. He struggled, but his assailant was stronger—it was like being caught in a fur trader's bear trap. He grunted in pain as his wrist was slammed against the edge of the desk. His revolver slipped from his senseless fingers and clattered to the floor.

He wrestled free of the iron grip, and he backed up against the bed, trying to figure out which one of the dim shapes was Bart O'Halloran. He had only had a brief glimpse of the rancher before he had been hauled into the room, but the man's strong grip was identification enough. He tried to quiet his breathing, listening intently for some sound that would distinguish the two men.

Nathaniel cried out as he was slammed into the wall next to the door. The Judge darted toward the center of the room, but he didn't get very far before a heavy hand caught the front of his shirt. He gasped as he was wrenched around and driven back against the deck a second time.

"You are a tick, Wallace," O'Halloran rumbled. He passed through the dim light from the skylight, and his face was a crag of shadows. "A trifling nuisance, clinging to my trousers. I will crush you between my fingers and toss you aside."

"You are overlooking the great bond between us," the Judge started. O'Halloran shook him much like a master does a recalcitrant hound. The Judge's teeth clicked together in his mouth.

"There is no bond between us," O'Halloran said. "You are a speck of shit. Nothing more." He shook the Judge again, and the Judge saw dancing spots in his field of vision. "I do not know where she found you two. Nor do I care. You have been a pest long enough."

"Surely—" the Judge choked on his words as O'Halloran shoved an arm against his throat.

"When you speak again, be useful or I will crush your throat."

The Judge choked and sputtered, waving his arms futilely. O'Halloran eased up his pressure, and the Judge drew in great lungfuls of air. His brain whirled in panic, trying to think of some way out of the situation.

"Given—given the choices, I would prefer to be useful," the Judge finally managed to gasp.

"Where is the money?" O'Halloran demanded.

The Judge raised his arm to point at the safe, but O'Halloran shook him. "Not you," he snapped. "Boy. Where is the money?"

"In—in the safe," Nathaniel whimpered.

O'Halloran turned toward the corner where the Judge had tried to point.

"I was trying—" the Judge began, but his words got all jumbled when the rancher shook him. *God damn you! Enough*, he thought, clenching his jaw to stop his teeth from rattling.

"Are you done?" he snapped when he could speak again, and when O'Halloran's hand tensed, the Judge slapped at his wrist. "Stop it," he barked. "I'm not one of your dogs."

He was genuinely astounded when O'Halloran did not thrash him again. There was a rough sound in the room, and it took him a second to realize O'Halloran was chuckling.

"The only ones who know the combination to the safe are the captain and Mr. Chester. And maybe the chief mate. All three of them are dead." He paused to inhale, enjoying the lack of violent side-to-side motion. "I only killed one of them, so this isn't my fault."

"Is this true?" O'Halloran demanded of Nathaniel. "Only the three of them?"

The Judge silently prayed that the boy would not name Mrs. Peabody.

"No," Nathaniel said, his voice quavering in the dark. "I—in the—I, I can open it."

The Judge's jaw dropped. "You little shit," he squeaked.

Nathaniel's voice rose. "I didn't know," he whined. "I didn't know what to do. You were pointing a gun at me. I just wanted you to stop."

"We'd be in a lot less trouble right if you had been more honest with me," the Judge snapped. "Did I not ask you nicely?"

"You put a gun against my face!"

"Did I shoot you?"

"You shot Mr. Chester."

"Allegedly," the Judge corrected. "You weren't here. Your testimony is hearsay, and won't be permitted in a court of law."

"You just said you did!" Nathaniel squeaked.

O'Halloran shoved his forearm against the Judge's throat. "This is not one of your garish courts."

"It doesn't have to be one of mine," the Judge said breathlessly. "I'm sure we could find a perfectly suitable court of law in St. Louis. We can let them sort this—"

"Open the safe," O'Halloran said to Nathaniel. "Or I break his neck."

"Boy, don't—" O'Halloran shook the rest of the Judge's words into a jumble.

Nathaniel edged closer, trying to stay as far away from O'Halloran as he could. "It's too dark," he said in a small voice. "I can't see what I'm doing."

"There's a candle—" The Judge beat at O'Halloran's fist when it tensed again. "No, damnit!" he shouted. "I'm trying to be useful." O'Halloran didn't move, and the Judge reached up and tried to pry the other man's hand off his shirt. He huffed and pulled. "This isn't—" O'Halloran let go of him suddenly, and he fell back against the desk. "There," he said, smoothing his wrinkled shirt. "That's better. We can be civilized about this thievery, can't we?"

When O'Halloran didn't say anything, he rapped his knuckles on the table behind him. "There's a candle here somewhere," he said. "If one of us were to have a flint or a match, we could make enough light for the young man here to open the safe." The Judge patted his coat pocket. "In fact, I have some matches myself, which I'd be happy to provide."

It was hard to be sure in the dim light, but the Judge was confident that O'Halloran's attention was still on him. Nathaniel, on the other hand, was—hopefully—looking at the desk. He might spot the candle, but the Judge was hoping that the young man would see Mr. Chester's hand first.

There hadn't been time to grab Mr. Chester's gun earlier, and he desperately hoped O'Halloran hadn't seen it yet.

"Have you found the candle, Nathaniel?" he asked. "It should be right there on the desk."

Dear God, let this kid be bright enough to know I'm not talking about the blasted candle . . .

35

RICHARD O'HALLORAN'S FEET LEFT BLOODY PRINTS ON THE deck as he strolled toward Elm and Isadora. "What are you doing?" he repeated.

Elm gave up trying to corral the umbrella. "Tilting at windmills," he said as he swept the half-folded canvas through the fire pit.

The canvas knocked out a spray of ash and sparks, and Richard flinched as hot coals pelted his naked body. Elm raked the umbrella back again, letting it linger long enough for the canvas to catch fire, and then he charged Richard, the makeshift lance thrust out before him.

The tip of the umbrella caught Richard in the mid-section. Elm kept moving, shoving with all of his strength. Fire crawled along the canvas, and Richard batted at the hot flames as they brightened. Elm slammed him against the wall, trying to pin him like a bug. Richard snarled and writhed under the flaming point of the umbrella.

"Shoot him," Elm shouted, and Isadora snapped out of the daze which had kept her rooted to the deck. She remembered Rosco's gun and brought it up. She squeezed the trigger, and the gun boomed in her hand.

Richard howled in pain. The canvas umbrella was smoking and burning, and she couldn't see Richard well enough, but it sounded like she had hit him. She fired again, and this time, the sound that came from Richard was more of a ferocious growl than a cry of pain. The sound squeezed her heart. It beat faster and faster, and she could barely breathe as she kept pulling the trigger until the hammer fell on an expended cartridge.

The boat struck an obstacle in the river, and the impact sent everyone tumbling. Elm lost his hold on the umbrella and Isadora staggered and fell as a table struck her on the thighs. She shoved it away before it pinned her against the railing.

The umbrella—not much more than a flaming stick at this point—rolled across the deck and vanished through the gap at the bottom of the railing.

Elm was on one knee, and he spared a glance over at Isadora. "Are you all right?" he called, and she nodded. She had dropped Rosco's pistol—not that it had any more bullets in it—and her hands went to the silver cross hanging around her neck. She stared past Elm, her attention rapt on the body slumped against the wall.

Was he still breathing? Was he still alive?

The paddle wheel kept churning, and the boat groaned as it tried to drag itself over the obstruction in the water. Distantly, she heard screams and splashing as passengers leaped into the water, trying to escape the mindless boat that was intent on destroying itself.

She climbed to her feet, adjusting her stance to account for the tilt in the deck. Had they run aground? She looked past the railing, but she couldn't see anything distinct in the darkness. There was no way to tell if they had run ashore or were caught on a sandbar.

The river foamed around the boat, the current raging against the large wooden structure at odds with its desire to flow toward St. Louis.

"We have to get off the boat," she shouted at Elm.

He nodded, indicating he had heard her, but he wasn't going to leave without making sure Richard was dead. He approached the naked man cautiously, his legs stiff against the tilted deck. His gun was out, and when he got within a few yards, he raised his revolver.

The boat shifted again, and the deck spun beneath them.

"Look out," Isadora screamed.

She had seen Richard move, and as Elm struggled to keep his balance, the naked man scrambled to his feet and charged at Elm. Elm's pistol barked rapidly, and Richard jerked and danced like a gibbering madman, but he didn't stop. He crashed into Elm, and both men tumbled to the deck, where they flailed at one another with their fists.

The small room lurched as the boat struck something in the river. Nathaniel was thrown against the table. Mr. Chester's corpse slid out of the chair, and the Judge spun away from O'Halloran. He heard the metallic rasp of his pistol as it slid across the floor, but he didn't know where it had gone.

O'Halloran grabbed Nathaniel before the young man could recover. "The candle," he growled, and Nathaniel whimpered. The Judge heard something clunk against the desk, and he guessed that the boy had found the candle. He quietly cursed that the lad hadn't found the pistol, but he didn't dwell on the lost opportunity. As Nathaniel tried to light the candle, the Judge listened intently to the vibrations shuddering through the deck beneath his feet.

The paddle wheel was still turning, and the boat was inching forward, as if were caught on a sandbar. They hadn't run aground, he figured, and the boat was going to slowly grind its way across whatever had snared it. The crew hadn't been told to shut the wheel down because there was no one at the helm to tell them otherwise. The captain and the chief mate were dead. Eventually someone on the main deck would take some initiative and tell the crew to shunt the boilers, but for the time being, they were still driving the wheel.

Nathaniel got the candle lit, and he paused as the yellow glow revealed Mr. Chester's pistol. He started to reach for it, but

O'Halloran cuffed him on the ear and hauled him away from the desk. "Open the safe," he snarled.

The young man stumbled, and the candle flame flickered precariously. Nathaniel managed to keep the light from going out, and he put the candle on top of the safe. With a nervous glance toward the Judge, he knelt in front of the iron box and started to fiddle with the lock.

O'Halloran picked up Mr. Chester's gun. He held it loosely in his hand as he turned toward Nathaniel and the safe. "Open it," he repeated.

Without moving his eyes, the Judge tried to locate his gun on the floor. *It had to be somewhere under the desk . . .*

The safe had a three-pronged handle on the front, along with a small brass dial. The dial was ridged with tiny numerals stamped in increments of five. Nathaniel spun the dial until he found the first number of the combination, and then he spun the dial in the other direction.

The Judge spotted his pistol. It was next to the leg on the far side of the table. To get to it, he'd either have to go under the desk or around it entirely, and he couldn't do either without O'Halloran noticing.

Nathaniel found the second number, and spun the dial clockwise again, coming around to the third and final number of the combination.

The boat groaned, and the Judge braced himself as the floor tilted. O'Halloran glanced away from Nathaniel, and the Judge was struck by the furtive motion.

He doesn't know why the boat is off course, the Judge thought. He took a step toward the desk, as if the slope of the deck was making him stumble. O'Halloran's eyes flicked toward him, but Nathaniel's soft exclamation drew his full attention back to the safe.

The navigator's assistant was sweating. He looked up at O'Halloran, his face tight with apprehension. "I must have—I, I, I got it wrong," he stuttered.

"Then you are no use to me," O'Halloran snapped. He raised the gun and pointed it at the young man.

"Wait!" Nathaniel cried. "I can—I can try it again."

"Quickly," O'Halloran urged him.

The walls creaked—adding urgency to the rancher's words—as the boat flexed in a way its builders never planned.

Elm managed to get on top, and he pinned Richard's arms down with his knees. He kept punching until his body was shaking and he was out of breath. He stopped, his hands aching, and he stared down at what he had done.

Richard—his face covered in blood, his nose mashed against his face, his lips torn—laughed, and when Elm drew back in shock, he bucked Elm off. Elm flailed and tried to roll away, but Richard caught his ankle and dragged him back. Elm kicked with his other foot, catching Richard on the chin, and when Richard's grip loosened, he wrenched free and scooted backward on his rump.

Elm took his eyes off Richard for a second, vainly looking around for his gun, which he had lost during their wrestling match. He spotted it, and as the deck tilted again, he rolled with the incline, reaching for the gun before it slid even farther out of reach.

Richard was faster, though, and his hand slapped the gun away.

It spun across the deck, and Isadora darted after it, but it flew past her outstretched hand and disappeared over the railing. Gone into the dark waters of the Mississippi. She dashed her hand against the deck in frustration.

Elm shouted at her, and she didn't understand what he was saying. His words were cut off as Richard tripped him, and he had to turn all of his attention to fighting off the bloody man.

Isadora grabbed one of the wooden chairs and rushed toward the pair. She hit Richard across the back with it, and when he stopped hitting Elm, she hit him again. He looked up, his face a crimson ruin, and when she tried to hit him a third time, he intercepted the chair and yanked it from her hands.

"The cross!" Elm shouted.

Richard threw the chair at her, and she barely got her hands up in time. She fell back, her forearms stinging with pain. The deck kept moving beneath her feet. She was having trouble keeping her balance.

"Use the—" Richard backhanded Elm, cutting him off. Elm lay stunned, and before Isadora could stop Richard, he put his hands around Elm's throat and started to squeeze. Elm kicked and bucked, but he wasn't strong enough to dislodge Richard.

The cross? Elm's words dimly registered in her mind. Why was the cross so important? It was just a simple piece of jewelry that some cowboy had put together on the trail—two silver nails, held together by looped rawhide.

Silver . . .

Elm's tongue was sticking out of his mouth, and his face was getting mottled. His motions were getting more frantic. Unless she did something soon, Richard was going to choke the life out of him.

Isadora yanked the rawhide thong from around her neck. Gripping the cross awkwardly with the top digging into her palm, she staggered over to the struggling pair. She didn't think. There was no time. She brought her hand down with all of her strength, and she hit Richard on the back, just below his left shoulder. The silver post of the cross sank into his flesh.

He jerked upright, his eyes wide and an inhuman shriek rising from his shredded lips.

She lost her grip on the cross as she fell back on her rump. She stared at Richard, who was no longer choking Elm. He was writhing and twisting about, like a mongrel dog trying to bite itself. He twisted his head around, trying to see what was causing him so much pain, and she recoiled from the animalistic fury in his eyes. Blood spattered from his misshapen mouth as he raged.

His teeth! She couldn't believe what she was seeing. She wanted to look away, even as she continued to stare. His teeth were too big for his mouth. Her terror mounted as his face continued to change. His jaw shifted and his forehead peeled back. When he slammed a hand against the deck, his fingers were long and his nails were longer.

He was transforming, turning into the wolf that walked like a man.

Nathaniel got the safe open on the second try. With a shaking hand, he picked up the candle and lowered it to reveal a pair of strong boxes and a heavy sack. The sack clinked with coins as Nathaniel hauled it out of the safe.

O'Halloran grabbed the sack and waved his gun toward the two strong boxes. "Get those," he said.

While O'Halloran's attention was on the safe and its contents, the Judge stumbled again, and he bounced off the table like he was auditioning for the town drunk at a community playhouse. He went to one knee, his body and arm hidden from O'Halloran's sight. "I'm sorry," he apologized when O'Halloran swung around toward him. "This boat is very unstable. We shouldn't tarry."

O'Halloran's face was unreadable, but after a long moment, he nodded in agreement. "Pick up one of those boxes," he said. He pointed his gun at the Judge. "And we'll be going."

The Judge's questing hand touched a metal cylinder. His gun! He carefully crooked his finger through the trigger guard. As he stood, he swept his arm under his coat and stuffed the revolver in the front pocket of his trousers. It wasn't the best place to hide the gun, but it would do in a pinch. Especially if he kept his arms at his sides as he carried the strong box.

O'Halloran backed up to the door, watching as the Judge and Nathaniel picked up the two strong boxes. He opened the door and motioned for them to go out first. The Judge let Nathaniel lead: partially to put himself between O'Halloran and the young man, but also with the fleeting hope that the young man would drop the box as soon as he left the room and run.

Which he didn't, unfortunately.

O'Halloran followed them into the hall, where he indicated they should head for the storeroom, and tottering under the weight of their booty, the three men walked and slid down the hall to the storeroom and the hurricane deck.

Outside, the thrashing noise of the paddle wheel was loud and frantic. The Judge heard a plaintive cry as a passenger fled the boat, and he wondered how deep the water was. He looked for the shore, but the night was dark and there was too much smoke in the air.

O'Halloran shoved him roughly. "Lifeboat," he shouted.

The Judge was surprised to see one of the lifeboats in its sling on the hurricane deck. Nathaniel staggered over to the narrow boat and lifted his strong box over the side. He dropped it noisily, and then stood there, a dejected frown on his face. The Judge elbowed him aside. "Run, you damn fool," he hissed at the young man. Nathaniel shook himself as if the idea had just occurred to him, and he stumbled away. But he only moved a few feet off from the boat and stopped. He had a dumb and docile look in his eye, as if he knew what his fate was. He was going to wait for it.

The Judge dumped his box over the side of the boat, and he smiled grimly when he heard the contents spill out. Coins rattled all over the bottom of the boat.

"You damned idiot," O'Halloran snarled. He surged toward the Judge, who danced out of the rancher's reach. O'Halloran wasn't fooled, and he stopped himself before he took another step away from the lifeboat. O'Halloran shook his head and walked backward until he ran into the lifeboat. Without taking his eyes off the Judge and Nathaniel, he slung the heavy bag into the boat. "I'm going to get in," he said, waving the gun at them. "And then you two are going to—"

Beneath them, a boiler exploded in the engine room on the main deck. The boat shivered and then shook itself, like a dog shaking off water. There was a noise like the ground opening up, and the private salon at the back of the boat came apart like a load of twigs thrown in the air by a petulant child.

The lifeboat pitched off the deck, and O'Halloran tumbled after it, his arms wheeling. The Judge had a split second in which to act, and as the back of the Salacious Sally fragmented from the explosive rupture of the boilers, the Judge ran forward and launched himself into the void . . .

Richard's flesh split and tore. He hunched his shoulders together and his back popped noisily. Something was coming out of his skin. Something dark, covered in fur.

Isadora's chest hurt, as if an icy hand was gripping her heart. She wanted to run. She wanted to close her eyes and leap over the railing of the boat. Her breath was caught in her throat. If only she could become a bird . . .

The thing that had been Richard O'Halloran rolled onto its side, and she was repulsed by the shaggy fur covering its legs and thighs. Its arm bent at an odd angle, and its long-nailed fingers could almost reach the silver spike in its back. The monster shivered and retched. Its joints made awful sounds that she wanted to blot out. She wanted to be free of the memory of those sounds.

Elm suddenly appeared behind the beast, and he grabbed the monster's arm, pulling it away from the silver spike. The beast thrashed and tried to reach Elm, but Elm darted away from its other arm as it flailed for him. "It hurts him," he shouted. "The silver is deadly."

His voice broke the nightmare holding her, and Isadora scrambled forward as the beast spun around after Elm. She got a glimpse of its back, and while its spine was knotted in a way that no human spine should be, the flesh was still pink. The silver spike seemed to glow in the moonlight.

The beast surged after Elm, and Elm tripped. With a frenzied howl, the beast leaped at him, and Elm put up his hands in a desperate attempt to keep the monster off him.

He was doing it on purpose, she realized. Giving her a chance. As the beast fell on Elm, she ran up to it and got her hands on the slippery shaft of the cross. She pulled it free, and the monster reared back, his disfigured face raised in a triumphant howl. She howled in return, her voice equally inchoate, as she stabbed the monster again.

This time, she aimed higher, and she drove the silver into the base of its neck.

The monster shot to its feet, and she fell back, awed by its sheer size as it stood upright. Dimly, she recognized Richard O'Halloran in its shape, but there was more wolf than man in its form now. Where Richard's face had been round and smooth, the creature's face was long and lean. Its ears were not flush with its head, and its mouth was filled with—*God save her!*—so many teeth. When it snapped its jaws, an involuntary cry slipped from her lips, a mewling whimper of animal panic.

The beast tried to reach the spike in its back, but its joints weren't as broken as they had been. It twisted around, snapping its jaws, and its claws dug bloody furrows across its flesh. But it couldn't reach the cross. It couldn't bend that way anymore.

He can't change, she thought. *He can't become the wolf with the silver in his flesh.* She didn't know how this magic worked—Elm had, evidently—but she felt a spark leap in her chest at the realization. Until he got the silver out, he was caught between man and wolf. Neither one nor the other.

With an agonized growl, the monster gave up trying to pull out the silver spike. It fell forward, landing in a stance more familiar to wolf than man. And, spying the man lying on the deck in front of it, it lowered its head, huffing and coughing. It took Isadora a second to realize the sound was laughter—voiced by a creature still human enough to remember the sound.

Elm had no weapons. He was on his back. Unprotected.

As the beast turned toward him, Elm scrambled backward. Isadora shouted at him, yelling at him to stop moving. Elm was like a frightened rabbit, and the monster was reacting to his fear. Stalking him. Savoring the futile efforts of the small creature. There was no escape from the claws and teeth of the wolf.

With a gasp, she remembered the other gun Elm had given her, and she frantically pawed at her skirts. The gun was strapped to her leg, held tight against her thigh by leather straps she had rigged earlier. A sob slipped out of her mouth as she pulled the gun free. She scrambled across the deck, chasing after the monster and the man she—

Elm threw up his arm as the monster lunged at him. Its jaw closed around Elm's forearm, and he screamed as its teeth bore down, piercing his flesh. Grinding against his bone. The monster shook its head savagely, yanking Elm back and forth across the deck.

"Stop! Stop!" she screamed. She fired the pistol, and the monster jerked as the bullet struck it in the back. Tears streamed down her face as she slid to a stop. She held the pistol out in front of her, both hands wrapped around its handle.

Slowly, the monster let go of Elm's arms and turned its distorted face toward her. Blood dripped from its mouth, and when it smiled, its teeth were red. It made noises, and it took her a moment to realize it was trying to speak. "You can't kill me," it growled. "You can't—"

Elm lunged forward, wrapping his arms around the monster's torso. "Isadora," he cried. "Shoot it!" He buried his head against the monster's chest and shoved, driving the beast upright.

The silver cross glinted, and she knew what Elm was doing.

"I am invinc—" the monster growled.

"Oh, shut up," she said, and she lunged forward, thrusting the barrel of the gun toward the silver cross. Making sure she wouldn't miss.

Elm held the monster tight, even as its claws raked his back and shoulders. Holding it steady for her . . .

She pulled the trigger.

The gun bucked in her hand, twisting and biting her like it was a living thing. She had a moment to watch the monster's skull split, like a bloody flower thrusting itself open, and then there was more thunder beneath her, as if the world was coming to an end around them . . .

36

DAWN STRETCHED PINK FINGERS ACROSS THE EASTERN HORIZON. Trees lined up along the bank, like silent watchers with upraised arms and hidden faces. They whispered among themselves as the narrow boat bobbed down the river. There was other wreckage in the water, all matter of floating debris through the night, but the lifeboat was the largest so far. There were two men in the boat, one at either end, and both were slumped against the wooden sides.

O'Halloran's face was pale and waxy, and sat with his left arm cradled against his belly. He was in the front of the boat, though given the mercurial glee of the Mississippi, the front could easily be the back in another mile or so.

The Judge looked like a wizened and waterlogged gnome. His coat was a misshapen plaster about his bony frame, and his beard was bedraggled and damp. His boots were wet from the standing water in the boat, and he shivered uncontrollably. His grip, though, remained firm about the revolver in his lap.

Bills floated in the boat, like pretty petals scattered across a bowl of water.

They had been floating all night, ever since the lifeboat had been thrown from the *Salacious Sally*. The Judge's recollection of that time was fragmented, made of bits and pieces that didn't quite fit together. The boilers had exploded, knocking the lifeboat overboard. He had leapt after it, though for awhile he was not certain why he had done such an idiotic thing. The Mississippi had struck him hard, knocking his breath and sense away. He imagined himself as a cork, bobbing in a basin of water, and he had been shoved against the lifeboat by the current.

The sides of the boat were too high. He could get a hand on the edge, but he couldn't muster the strength to pull himself up, and so he had held on, bobbing and banging against the hull of the lifeboat. Eventually, a strong hand had gripped his wrist and hauled him aboard.

He didn't understand why O'Halloran had saved him, and the rancher hadn't offered any explanation. They had crawled as far away from each other as they could get in the small craft, huddling in their respective corners. Shivering and spent. Waiting for dawn.

The Judge lifted his head as he heard a lilting bird song. The boat had drifted close to the eastern shore, and he peered at the trees along the riverbank. The sky was still too dark to spot a tiny bird among the leaves, but its voice was strong and sure. A smile creased his face as he thought about the solitary bird. "Warble your song, o shy and hidden bird," he whispered. His throat was dry, even though he floated in a wide expanse of moving water. "'Song of the bleeding throat / Death's outlet song of life . . .'"

O'Halloran shifted, like a mass of shale sliding down the side of a mountain in the wake of an earth tremor. His eyes fluttered, and his mouth twisted as he inadvertently moved his arm. "Are you still alive or are you a phantom that haunts me still?" he said.

"I live yet, and it is still my voice you hear," the Judge said. "'For well dear brother I know / If thou wast not granted to sing thou wouldst surely die.'"

"What are you talking about?"

"Life. Death. Lilacs." The Judge looked up at the fading violet sky. "A great star drooping early in the western sky."

O'Halloran groaned as he levered himself upright. "I should have let you drown."

"You are not the first—nor the last, I suspect—to harbor such regret."

O'Halloran ran his tongue along his lower lip as he looked at the tree-lined riverbank. "How far have we come?"

The Judge shrugged. "I am not conversant in the speed of the current, though I dare say we shall reach St. Louis before the bulk of the boat."

A grim smile tugged at O'Halloran's face. "Your optimism is wasted on me." He moved his feet, splashing in the standing water in the lifeboat. There was more of it than the Judge remembered from the night. "This vessel will be swamped before the sun crests those trees yonder."

"We still have some time yet," the Judge said.

"Time for what?"

"Confession. Absolution."

O'Halloran started to laugh, but the motion agitated his chest and arm, and his sense of humor drained away. "I have nothing to confess to you," he said, his voice strained. "And I need no absolution."

"Not even for your sons?"

"They chose to become what they became."

"Freely?"

"Aye."

"And how did it happen? How did they come into their . . . curse?"

"It wasn't a curse," O'Halloran said. "It was a choice, and I paid for it."

"Yes, you did. Losing both your sons to such bestial natures."

O'Halloran coughed, choking back a laugh. "I didn't lose my sons. You saw them. They were more than you or I could ever hope to be."

"They were monsters."

O'Halloran grimaced. "And we aren't?" He shook his head. "You know so little about the true nature of the world, Wallace."

"Enlighten me."

O'Halloran's face turned to stone. He leaned forward and spat into the standing water, though he had little spittle to make. "Die in darkness, Wallace," he said.

The Judge glanced toward the east where the sun was burning the horizon. "Not today, I think."

O'Halloran shifted in his seat, and a tremor of pain ran through his frame. *It was more than his arm,* the Judge thought. The rancher was suffering from at least one broken rib as well. "You killed my son," O'Halloran said. "Tommy."

"I did," the Judge said.

"My men found a burned corpse less than a mile from my land. They said the ground where it lay was black and ruined. They also said there was no head."

"The earth does not embrace such rough beasts. It rejects such poisons. They are—"

"What did you do with his head?" O'Halloran shouted. "Where is it?"

The Judge eyed him. "You can't bring him back."

"He was my son. He deserves better."

"No, he doesn't. He slaughtered innocent men. He killed for pleasure. He was a monster, through and through. The same as your other son. It was no choice that you gave them. You damned them. You cursed them. You just don't want to take responsibility for what you did."

O'Halloran shook his head. "What I did? I did nothing. I did what any father would do. I let my sons chose their own paths. When Milton showed them how to tame—"

"Who? Milton? What are you talking about?"

O'Halloran stared at the Judge for a long time, and finally a cold smile creased his face. "You don't know, do you?" he said.

The Judge made a blustering noise in his throat, though he knew O'Halloran was not taken in by it.

"You are blind," O'Halloran said. "You pontificate about being able to see better than the rest of us, but you don't know anything. You are an ignorant fool. You think there is good and evil, but both are a lie. There is no God, Wallace. There is nothing left up there but darkness, and when the heavens finally crack open and let it all spill down, it will be men like my sons who will be ready to rule."

"You have no sons left," the Judge said.

O'Halloran's face pinched, and a shadow clouded his eyes. "Richard," he said softly. "I still have Richard."

The Judge laughed. "Where was he when we were stealing all this cash? When he couldn't get through the hatch, you sent him around to the front of the boat. You told him to climb up to the pilot house, and he did. That was why Nathaniel and I were in the hallway when you found us. I saw him up there. Oh God help me, I saw him." The Judge cocked his head to one side. "But why didn't he join us on deck?"

"He's a good son. He follows directions."

"Did you abandon him?"

"He was protecting me." O'Halloran's tone sharpened.

The Judge shook his head. "Do you remember our wager the other morning? Between your son and my man, Elm? I asked if you wanted to bet again. Best two out of three. You refused. Why? Because Dickie Boy can't swim. Even if he got off the boat when we did—"

"He got off the boat."

"It doesn't matter if he got off or not. He still can't swim." The Judge gestured toward the moving water around them. "Watch for his corpse, if you don't trust my judgment. I'm sure it will float past eventually."

O'Halloran didn't look at the water. He kept his gaze on the Judge. His nostrils flared as he narrowed his eyes. "Is your powder dry?" he asked.

The Judge looked down at the gun in his lap. "Only one way to find out, I suppose," he said with a sigh.

O'Halloran leaned forward. "Only one way," he said.

"Is this how it is going to end, then?"

O'Halloran nodded.

"A pity," the Judge said. "It looks like it will be a lovely day."

O'Halloran heaved himself upright, and with a shout that was filled with more pain than rage, he stumbled toward the Judge. The Judge snapped his hand up and threw the revolver. It bounced off O'Halloran's forehead, and the rancher staggered. His foot slipped in the bottom of the boat, and the Judge leaned heavily to one side, rocking the boat. Grunting in pain, O'Halloran threw up his arms, trying to keep his balance. The Judge threw himself against the other side of the boat, and when the boat rocked in that direction, O'Halloran went over the side. More water splashed into the boat.

O'Halloran surfaced nearby, his face wild with panic. He thrashed in the water with one arm. "Wallace—" When he opened his mouth, water eagerly rushed in, drowning his words.

The Judge sat still, his hands in his lap. As he watched O'Halloran struggle, he recalled more of the poem he had recited earlier—Whitman's elegy for Abraham Lincoln, written after the president's death and the end of the War between the States. *Prais'd be the fathomless universe,* he thought, *for life and love, and for objects and knowledge curious, and for love, sweet love.*

O'Halloran gulped water, spit it out, gulped some more. His thrashing grew less frantic, even as his expression grew more desperate. He slapped at the water, as if he could beat the entire river away from him, but the river was not to be moved thus.

"'But Praise! Praise! Praise! / For the sure-enwinding arms of cool-enfolding death,'" the Judge said, passing sentence and bearing witness.

The Mississippi River flowed over O'Halloran, covering him with cold water, and the Judge didn't see him again.

37

Sheriff Taggert was sitting on the porch of his office when the pair rode down Bitter's main street. He had been carving a piece of hickory, without any clear idea of what shape he would ultimately coax from the stick. His hand paused, knife blade lightly touching his thumb, and he examined the pair of riders. After a moment, he recognized the woman, even with the wide hat and the brace holding her arm against her side. The man sat stiffly in his saddle, his torso awkwardly upright, and his face was shadowed with bruises and still-healing cuts.

The sheriff watched them as they rode down to the bank, where the woman got down from her horse and took out a sack from one of her saddlebags. As she went into the bank, he slipped his knife into its sheath and heaved himself out of his chair. He ambled down the street to where the man and the two horses were waiting outside the bank.

Up close, the sheriff finally recognized the man. "Sheeit," he said, adjusting his hat. "You look like you've been kicked by a horse. A couple of times."

Elm tried not to turn his body as he looked down at the sheriff. "More than a couple," he said. "Good afternoon, Sheriff Taggert."

"Been a while since I've seen you in town," the sheriff said. He nodded at the bank. "That was Miss Van Horn, wasn't it?" He nodded, knowing the answer to his question. "End of the month, innit?"

"It is," Elm said.

The sheriff gnawed on the inside of his cheek for a moment. "Where's your friend? The rude one."

Elm shook his head, and didn't answer.

"Well, last time I saw him, I said that I hoped to never see him again. He disagreed with me." The sheriff shrugged. "Though, I might be right."

"You might," Elm said.

"You staying long?"

"I'll let you know if I am."

"We don't want any trouble. Bitter's not like it sounds. It's a nice town. It's going to get nicer too. No reason to spoil that for the rest of us."

Elm cocked his head as if he had heard a whisper of a song, and a tiny smile carved its way across his bruised face.

The front door of the bank swung open and Isadora wandered out. She was carrying the same sack as she had when she had gone in, but she was also clutching a small white envelope between two of her fingers. She paused on the edge of the porch, a distant look in her eye—almost as if she was looking all the way to the edge of Bitter and beyond—and then she looked down and finally noticed the sheriff. She stared at the lawman for a moment, and the sheriff was struck by something he had never noticed about her before. Or maybe it was more evident now. Either way, he realized he had been a fool to dismiss her so arrogantly as he had in the past.

She stepped off the porch and walked over to Elm's horse. Balancing the sack in the corner of her injured arm, she offered him the white envelope. He leaned down stiffly and took it from her. There was a perplexed look on his face, and she gave him a knowing shrug in response as she crammed the sack into one of his saddlebags. The sheriff heard the familiar sound of coins sliding against one another.

She swung up onto the saddle of her horse with little diffi- culty, and the sheriff got a better look at the hand bound across her belly. It was wrapped in layers of white linen. "Sheriff," she said, touching the brim of her hat.

"Miss Van Horn," he replied automatically.

Without another word, she pulled her horse around and rode west. Elm followed, and when they had passed the barber's shop, the sheriff let out the breath he had been holding. He took off his hat and wiped at his forehead. He couldn't explain the sensation in his belly, but he felt like he had been spared a terrible fate.

The dog came out to greet them, and circling them thrice, he took off for the ranch house to tell everyone that the master of the ranch was back. Isadora let her horse find its own pace, and she leaned against the pommel of her saddle. She looked over at Elm and smiled. For a moment, the haunted look in her eyes went away, and he wished he could make her smile all the time.

"Is it from him?" she asked, referring to the letter she had passed Elm in Bitter. He had read it during the ride and then tucked it away without a word.

"It is. He's in St. Louis."

"He paid my loan," she said. "Mr. Phineas said a wire had come from St. Louis. Paid what was owed, and then some." She shook her head. "That's why I gave you the money you won for me. I don't need it. There is over thirty thousand dollars in my account now. I can rebuild the barn. I can replace the cows I lost." A shadow passed across her face. "I can honor those who we have lost."

"You can expand," Elm said, obliquely referencing something else the Judge had said in his note.

Isadora plucked at her bandaged hand. One of the other cartridges in the gun had gone off when she had pulled the trigger. The doctor said she had been incredibly lucky that she hadn't lost a few fingers. As it was, her hand had been badly burned. "Yes," she said softly. "I suppose I could."

She smiled again, banishing the shadows, and he caught himself grinning back at her. She looked away, as if embarrassed to be sharing the same thought with him. Her gaze settled on the front of the ranch house, where people were starting to gather. "How long will you stay?"

"A little while," he said. "Until this face doesn't scare anyone any more."

The dog, having done its job and alerted everyone, came running back. Isadora's horse snorted at the dog's approach, and Isadora tapped her heels gently against the flank of her mount. It ambled down the gentle slope toward Thrush. "I've seen worse," she said, and the smile that tugged at the corner of her lips was colder than the previous ones.

"I'll stay as long as you will have me," he said.

Her eyes lit up. "Oh, and I do intend to have you, Elmore Stonebrook."

He tapped his chest, where, under his clothes, bandages were wrapped tightly around his bruised body. "Gently, please," he said.

She laughed, and the sun broke from behind a cloud, dazzling him with its light. "'I will make this world less dreadful and mean,'" she called back to him as her horse broke into a run. "'And this time less like being dead.'"

And as he watched her ride down the hill to greet the cheering and shouting assembly of her ranch hands, he thought there could not be any sweeter poetry than that.

Acknowledgments

Richard Choate, Nancy Ekse, Ken Apple, Evelyn Nicholas, Kenneth Nicholas, and Melanie Hart provided daily encouragement during the drafting of this book to ensure that I stayed on task. Melanie was also kind enough to strike through a whole lot of adverbs without too much commentary. Thank you all for being supportive.

Exclusive material

One of the best parts of writing a story is knowing that someone is reading it, and not only that they read it, but that they'd like to read more. Reviews of this book (and other books of mine, or books by other authors, really) are very valuable as they help goose the all-mighty algorithm so that it finds me more readers. Please leave a review on your favorite online site.

Additionally, I have a low-traffic newsletter where I offer up advance information about new projects, exclusive material, and other premier access to content. If you enjoyed this story, and would like to keep up-to-date, please sign up for the newsletter at the following URL.

http://www.markteppo.com/mailinglist

About the Author

Mark Teppo lives in the Pacific Northwest, where he writes, reads, and sells books. Every once in a while, he goes out into the woods. His favorite tarot card is the Moon.

You may find him on the web at www.markteppo.com, as well as on Instagram (@mark.teppo) and Twitter (@markteppo).

In addition to frontier stories with monsters, he also writes stories about conspiracy theories and esoteric mysteries, dark fantasy stories, the occasional bit of science fiction, and books about writing. He also writes sun-soaked Southern California noir under the name Harry Bryant.

Elm and the Judge will return.

LONGSPUR